I0640309

Also by Donald J. McGill

Talk Radio Mysteries
Featuring Jerry Jeremy

Novels
Tune in to Danger

Talked to Death

But Wait—There's Murder

Short Mysteries
Deadly Vision

Disappearing Act

Watson and the Reality Crowd
*A Watson's Ghost Mystery Featuring
Sherwood 'Woody' Holmes*

Talked to Death

Donald J. McGill

A Talk Radio Mystery

The Dangerous Press
San Francisco MMXV

Copyright © 2015 Donald J. McGill

All rights reserved.

ISBN 978-0-9909527-4-9

Manufactured in the United States of America

No part of this book may be stored, reproduced, or transmitted in any form or by any means except for your personal use without the express written permission the author.

This book is a work of fiction. Names, characters, businesses, organizations, places, events and incidents either are the product of the author's imagination or are used fictitiously. Any resemblance to actual persons, living or dead, events, or locales is entirely coincidental.

Be sure to visit **www.Donald J. McGill.com** for the latest on Jerry Jeremy and his pals.

While you're there, if you can take a moment to let me know how you liked this book, I'd greatly appreciate the feedback.

Leaving a review on Amazon or Goodreads is deeply appreciated too!

To Doris,

For all your love and support.

Chapter 1.

Yessir, there's something special about chasing that little white ball around ye olde and ancient on a sunny Saturday morning. We were playing at the Canyon Country Club just north of Tucson and that "something special" I mentioned could just be a case of heatstroke. Summertime in this line of country is so hot the cowpokes out on the back nine are wearing tank tops and baggy shorts. If Mother Nature had her way, this place would be one large pile of sand with a few grass traps just to make it interesting. But here at Canyon you'd never think you were in the middle of a desert. As far as that goes, you're not actually in a canyon either.

You might say they've made the desert bloom. That is, the developers and the money-men behind the club have. Acres of manicured lawns, palm trees and tropical flowers are carefully tended to distract the membership as they slice one off the tee. In the rough? You should have it so rough.

A gorgeous, tile-roofed clubhouse overlooks not just one, but two championship courses. The upscale shack is Mediterranean in style, so they say, though it looks a lot like the local adobe. But hey, at these prices it can be the south of France if they want. And just so you don't forget where you really are, a couple of vultures ride the thermals high above the parking lot in case some geezer kicks it on his way to the Bentley.

At any rate, they haven't air-conditioned the fairways yet, so in the good ol' summertime you need to tee off before the sun comes up. With luck you'll finish your game before the heat finishes you. With red hair and fair skin I go from freckle to burn in one easy lesson, so coming straight from work is my style. It's the one advantage of getting off at six a.m.

I work when most people are sleeping, which is a bit of a problem for a radio talk show host. You probably knew that was my gig already—at least you would if you lived in Tucson and had insomnia. My driver's license says I'm Jeremy Jeremy—try explaining that at the local DMV—and from midnight to six in the morning, I'm KICK's top talk show guy. I have the same name front and back because Mom and Dad couldn't afford two different ones when I was born. Talk about the lasting effects of an economic downturn. Meanwhile, with five bucks a hole on the line, I was slowly golfing myself into the poorhouse.

"CHRIST a'mighty, Jeremy. We oughta be in the lounge by now, downing a couple o' cold ones."

That's Bronco Billy Wooten doing the talking. His voice made a fellow on the next hole shank his tee shot. He's the king of Tucson's used car trade, and a major sponsor of mine, so he can talk as loud as he wants as far as I'm concerned. Billy added, "Horsin' around waitin' for you, we didn't tee-off until goddamn' near six-fuckin'-thirty."

Guilty as charged.

"Don't I know it," I said hoping Bronco Billy would mellow a bit if I played along. Billy and the rest of our foursome had beaten the sun up that morning to get that early tee time. But me—I was already up; I had spent the night working at KICK radio which bills itself as the Talk of the West. "It's already so hot I need an oven mitt to hold these metal shafts," I said, playing along. "Next time maybe I'll skip your last three commercial spots and cut out early. The station has that great Boxcar Willie CD I can put on for the last half hour or so."

Billy groaned while Dale Andersen, KICK's program director, tripped on his five iron trying to smooth things over. "Jerry's only joking. You know what kidders these air personalities are." What a kidder Dale is. He's born-again, doesn't smoke, drink or lie, but still pretty much runs things at the Talk of the West. And he's pretty much the talk of the Talk of the West, as we kidders like to say.

When I started at KICK, Dale pretty much said to keep my slick, big city background as far in the background as possible, so on the night owl shift I try my best to be a down-home, right-wing, all-American buckaroo for all those night watchmen, long-haul truckers and other graveyard workers who make up my audience.

Did I mention Dale was born-again?

Since we were playing for five bucks a hole—gambling with

sponsors apparently not being a sin in Dale's book—I had been taking my time lining up a tricky seven-footer on sixteen when Dale spoke again. I could swear he said something about moving my show from night time to prime time. For a second I thought I might be hallucinating from the heat, but when Bronco Billy back-slapped me and shouted, "Holy shit, Jerry, ain't you the man now. Or more to the point, you're *my* man now. You're gonna be Tucson radio's goddamn' voice of the pre-owned vehicle. At least from seven to ten ever' evenin'."

Since Billy was pounding my back, I figured I must have heard Dale right the first time. And if Billy said I was the goddamn' voice of the pre-owned vehicle, that made it official. After all, he's the goddamn' sponsor. I was now the evening man. A big step up. After all, real people might still tune in at that hour.

"Gee, thanks, Bronco Billy," I said. "You too, Dale. For once I'm speechless."

"Bit of a drawback in a talk show host, ain't it, Jerry?" This from Henry Sequero, my golfing partner. Everybody's a critic nowadays. Where was he when Billy was moaning about the heat being my fault? On the other hand, as the Canyon golf pro, he was keeping our score within sight of the big guys'.

Let him talk. Dale—and more likely, Bronco Billy—had made my day. Until now, I'd been consigned to matching wits with nutballs at three a.m. Not just nutballs, but the kind of nutballs who make phone calls to radio stations in the middle of the night. It was either call me or the suicide hot line.

I had wound up in the all-night penalty box after being blackballed out of San Francisco radio, but that's another story. You may have seen it on CNN, all about murder and romance. Besides it had a happy ending when I followed the girl of my dreams out here. And now I was on the comeback trail as the trailhands say.

"Nice try, Jerry," Henry said as my putt rolled past the cup. He'd barely winced as he watched it slide by. "Maybe Dale's just trying to put you off your game."

"Sure," I said. "He's liable to do anything at these stakes. After all, he is a program director." I gave Dale a nice smile since he was still *my* program director and I didn't want to go back on nights before I had gotten off them.

"I ever tell you fellas, about how I heard Dale got to be the PD?" Billy asked. "It was on the championship course down to Silver Hills. He was playing with Joe Galoosa and they were all tied up after eighteen, so's they went into sudden death."

Bronco Billy was piling it on at Dale's expense.

"That's right, Billy," Dale conceded. "If I hadn't won that round, I would have had to take the General Manager position and Joe would be having all the fun as PD." Everybody chuckled, Dale being the boss and all, and Joe G. being Dale's boss. Everybody chuckled but Billy, that is. Being the sponsor he didn't have to chuckle. Dale added, "It was a darned close call if I do say so myself."

"You don't say," Bronco Billy said. "But wait just a damn' minute, you *did* say, didn't you? Right in the middle of my fuckin' story." Dale tapped in a twelve-footer bringing a smile back to Billy's face.

Bronco Billy was Tucson's largest used car dealer and one of KICK's biggest clients. His nephew Charlie Wooten, my sponsor back in the City by the Bay, had told me to look him up when I came out here and I did. I wouldn't have thought it possible for anybody to be as rough around the edges as Charlie, but as it turned out Billy was, only more so. On the other hand, his partner in today's foursome was a squeaky-clean, Young Republican, all tanned and blonde, blue-eyed, and just about no fun at all. His idea of a big weekend was a morning spent mowing the lawn and then taking the kids out to the waterpark in the p.m.

Henry Sequero, Canyon's golf pro extraordinaire, on whose sixteenth green I had four-putted, was one of the really good guys I had gotten to know during the short time I'd been living in Tucson. He even introduced me to a few of the regulars who hung out at Canyon. I wasn't a member, so having a few pals who were got me the occasional round of golf and more than a few rounds at the bar.

As it was, by the time we finished seventeen, Henry and I were down about forty bucks. Not too bad, but enough to let them know we knew who was boss. I'd figured having the club pro as my partner I'd be on the winning side, but now I was pretty sure my partner was holding back a little. He must have figured Bronco Billy would be good for a lot more in future tips than losing a few holes would cost. As for me, the only tip I ever got from Billy was not to buy a used car off his lot.

I was teeing up on eighteen, a par-four dogleg to the left, when Dale mentioned that the guy I was replacing on the evening show had taken a job pushing Bronco Billy's jalopies out at the lot on North Sixth Avenue. Dale was saying, "...he spent too darned much time talking about the old days. Not that we don't revere the memory of Barry Goldwater, but let's face it, that kind of thing really doesn't spark ratings any longer."

"Sure, of course not," I said. "Remember, I'm new in town, I hardly know a thing about the old days with Barry. The '64 landslide and all that. I thought he still ran the department store. I hardly know anything about back then."

"And you know even less about selling cars," Bronco Billy chimed in.

"Yes, but I liked the Indian costume."

Bronco Billy's was the elephants' graveyard for broadcast talent coming and going in Tucson. I had spent a little time out on the lot thanks to my pal Charlie Wooten, but it didn't take long for Billy to realize I'd probably sell more cars reading his commercials in the middle of the night.

"You won't be sorry, Dale," I promised. "Back in San Francisco I had one of the top shows on KPMT. I do have one question though—if I was losing ten bucks a hole to you instead of five would I have a shot at the morning drive slot?"

"HEY, Ben! Great morning, ain't it? You too, Ollie! How's business in TV land? What'd you guys shoot today?" I was giving the big hello to a couple of local boys holding down the bar in the clubhouse lounge. Henry had introduced me to Ben and Ollie when I was new in town and they were always good for a round of drinks and a few laughs, though I don't recall ever having seen them actually hit a golf ball. The boys sold advertising for KOW-TV, a local Tucson station. They must have been good at their work because they always seemed to have time to hang out at the Canyon clubhouse.

"We didn't get the chance to ruin our handicaps today—too hot for us," Ollie said, waving the bartender over. "What are you drinking?"

"That's okay; today I'm drinking on the station. You guys need to get an earlier start. Tee off about four a.m. and you can catch the last part of my show, not to mention the cool of the night."

"If you made the jump to TV, we could DVR you and sleep late too."

"Sure, but your game would go to hell. Not that I wouldn't be interested, if you get my drift, in case that's where you were drifting."

"Well, one never knows. Who's that over there with

Bronco Billy anyway?"

"Gee, I think your drift just turned into an undercurrent."

Billy had dragged Dale over to a booth with a clear view of the pool. I knew Billy was hoping to study this year's crop of college girls home for the summer. Unfortunately for Billy, the heat had sent the girls indoors, the pool being too hot even in a bikini. The college babes had all headed for the spa, instead of the sauna outside.

I gave Ben and Ollie an *au revoir* and went to join my golfing partners, trying to put any thought about jumping to TV out of my mind. I figured Ben and Ollie's only chance to ink a deal with Bronco Billy would be if they were buying one of his pre-owned jalopies. Still you never can tell and they were always good for a few laughs.

THE evening show was a pretty nice career boost. Even better, I had high hopes it would also give a boost to my love life. The way I figured it, there would be more time to spend with the delectable Christy Marshall, my girlfriend and partner in crime-busting. Not that we didn't have time together now— I slept days while she went to graduate school and then we linked up in the evening.

Once she finished her homework, there had been a good two hour window for us before my midnight show—just me, her and her mom. Since Mrs. Marshall's husband had been killed the year before, it was only natural that Christy would feel guilty about leaving her alone while heading for parts unknown with me. At this rate, our best parts were going to stay unknown.

With my new hours though, I could get off at ten and be at *casa* Marshall in time to tell the old girl goodnight and drop an Ambien or two in her cocoa. Maybe I'd get a chance to explore some of those unknown parts I'd been missing. Christy might lose a little sleep, but how many zzz's do you need when you can catch a few in class?

"JERRY, that's wonderful, honey." My dream girl had caught on without any help from me. "Did you hear that, Mom? Jerry's show is going to be on from seven to ten now. No more overnights."

"That's good, dear," Mrs. M said. "Now he'll have something to do in the evening instead of hanging around here."

Ah yes. Sassie Marshall, mother of my one and only love. If she was my mom I'd have volunteered for the orphanage. Probably she was clinging to Christy because of Mr. Marshall's violent death. Murdered to cover up a little skullduggery at KPMT. Who says radio isn't a tough racket. Solving Marshall's murder not only got me the girl, it got me blacklisted from San Francisco's airwaves.

"These are for you." I handed the supermarket bouquet to Mrs. Marshall. An upfront peace offering in case war broke out later.

"Oh, how nice," Christy said. "Mom, isn't it nice that Jerry brought these for you?"

Of course, they had been for Christy but under the circumstances, Mom probably needed them more. I had hoped that some of her daughter's feelings might have rubbed off on Sassie by now. After all, I'd hit a home run with Christy when I'd solved her dad's murder. Truth be told though, Christy actually knew who the perp was before I did. But then she had had a big advantage—she was kidnapped by the killer which in my book was a dead giveaway.

"Listen, babe," I said to Christy, "the way everything is coming together, I'll be the toast of Arizona talk radio before long. Why if things go right for me, I might even get the call that all is forgiven and I'm needed back in the Bay Area."

"Bay Area? Jerry, what are you talking about?" Christy said. My girl didn't seem to be sharing the joy. "I thought your future was here with Mom and me."

"Gee, Christy, I didn't really mean it that way. But on the other hand, you've got to admit San Francisco is a great town and a great radio town at that. And you don't even need air conditioning there. That'll help offset the cost of housing."

"Well, I for one like the warm weather," her mom chimed in, although I knew for a fact that Sassie Marshall spent her days hopping from her air conditioned Lexus to the air conditioned Tucson Mall and from there back to her air conditioned house. Even the garage was air conditioned.

"I don't get it," I said. "You actually lived in the Bay Area up until Mr. Marshall's death." Mrs. Marshall grimaced and covered her eyes when I said her husband's name. The good news was she didn't faint dead away. I guessed things were looking up.

"*Jeremy Jeremy!* Look what you've done to Mother. Sometimes you can be so insensitive." When Christy goes to the trouble of using my full legal name, it's a pretty bad sign. I've heard "Jerry, Jerry, Jerry..." repeated at times, but that only happens in the dark.

Anyway, the romance was rapidly leaking out of my evening. I thought about taking back the flowers and giving them to Christy after all. They were practically wilting before my eyes. And they weren't all that was wilting.

"Come on, ladies, let's kick this up a notch. I'll call over to the Highlander and get a table for three. Surf and turf—nothing like a lobster in the middle of a desert." My intimate, candle-lit table for two at the elegant Sylvester's was out and a table for three at the expensive, overdone Highlander Steakhouse was in. Sun-baked potatoes with adobe dressing, hold the romance.

A HUNDRED and eighty smackers later, our little group was gathered back at Mrs. Marshall's front door. Mrs. M had her keys out but wasn't making a move to unlock anything. I took the opportunity to pull Christy a little off to the side and whisper a few nothings into her shell-like.

"What say we put Mom to bed," I suggested, "and once we hear snoring, I'll tuck you in."

"Well, Jerry dear, I think Mom's still a little upset about you using the Bay-word."

"Actually I think that's two words. But forget I said it. After all I'm just starting a new gig and I love the weather here anyway; think of the money I'm saving on saunas."

"Okay, Jerry," she gave me a small smile and turned her high beams on me. "Maybe it was just a slip of the lip, but really—that's not a good thing in a big-time talk show host." Just what I needed, another critic.

But there *was* something I needed more. "So-o-o..."

"Not tonight, Jeremy. I better get Mom settled down with a nice DVD, maybe *Terms of Endearment.*"

I was behind the wheel almost before I knew it.

If I ever got Christy alone again I was pretty sure I could come up with some endearments myself. I just wasn't sure I'd ever get her alone again. I was doing sixty down North First Avenue before I caught myself and slowed to the limit. Bronco Billy had put me in a nice, bright yellow Grand Cherokee loaner for the past few months. Maybe he thought it would grow on me so I'd want to actually pay for it someday. More likely, he just thought the big sign on the door advertising his lot would be worth the wear and tear I'd put on the rig. The steer horns fastened to the grill would get folks looking too.

At least I could park it pretty much anywhere and not worry about it being stolen.

The wheels aside, Bronco Billy Wooten seemed to be playing a large part in my life, pretty much like Charlie had in San Francisco. Maybe the Wootens were some kind of guardian angels. Cigar-smoking, roughneck angels, but hey, whatever works. Hadn't I started out here beating a tom-tom on a used car lot and now wasn't I Billy's go-to guy on KICK Radio, the Talk of the West? And I definitely planned to *be* the talk of the west.

I was beginning to get that old feeling again. You know the one. It's the one that says that the light at the end of the tunnel is reflecting off a vein of pure gold. Anyway, I was pretty sure it wasn't the Orange Blossom Special hurtling my way.

Little did I know.

Chapter 2.

As you head west from San Francisco's more celebrated hills, out past Golden Gate Park, the streets all become avenues, their numbers counting ever higher through the rows of two and three story homes packed cheek-by jowl 'til you get to the Great Highway stretching along the Pacific. San Franciscans pretty much all refer to this as "out in the Avenues". Not quite the put-down that living in near-suburban Daly City is, but close. Anyway the Avenues hold some of the City's last real neighborhoods including what's called the Sunset District. Not that you get much chance to see any sunsets out there.

A cold, steady onshore breeze creates a thermal inversion–I used to do the weather–anyway, it somehow condenses into the high fog that blankets that part of the City. Something to do with the Japanese current maybe. Anyway, young mothers of all nationalities wisely bundle their kids in ski parkas just to visit the park and the streetlights come on by mid-afternoon. That's when the weather is still nice. You know, like in July and August.

When I lived in San Fran, I made myself at home in a downtown high-rise close to the station. I could get several minutes of sunshine on most days. Still I put in my share of time out in the Avenues, mostly at a little cabaret holding up a seedy diner on the one side and a used clothing store on the other. And if one day you should find your way out there, you'd also have a good chance of finding The Great Rondini at work there. He's an old school chum. Of course, back at Passaic High, he was just plain old Ronnie Green.

Tucson was quite a ways away from the City by the Bay, but when I got back to my place, Ronnie was there waiting for me. He was winking at me from the answering machine on the kitchen counter. After all, the kitchenette had to be good for something since I didn't really own any pots and pans.

My place was a rented condo just off north La Cholla. It managed to be small but drab at the same time. The dishwasher never worked, but the air conditioning was first-rate. I probably wouldn't have tumbled to the dishwasher problem if the super hadn't come by with a promise to fix it. I had already turned up the aforementioned AC, poured myself a glass of lemonade with plenty of ice and stripped down to my boxers, before I noticed Ronnie had called. I don't check the machine much since it's mainly there to field messages from phony charities or the local politicos, which I guess pretty much amounts to the same thing.

I replayed Rondini's message a few of times and then gave up trying to make heads or tails of it. Instead I scrolled through the contacts on my mobile until I found the backstage number for the Blue Sphinx. Not being a mentalist myself, I could only hope to catch The Great One between shows. I wouldn't want to disturb Ronnie while he was sawing somebody in two.

"Hey there, is that you, Junior?" he asked when I finally got him on the phone. A silly question for a mind reader with caller ID. His ESP must have been on the blink. He said, "You must have been surprised when you listened to the message I left."

"Yeah, I was. I never knew you spoke in tongues. Try English the next time, the machine's Japanese, not me. It sounded like you said something about my gas range. Not having taken the Home Ec course back in school, I didn't understand the gag."

"Slow down, Red, I wasn't talking about *a* range, I said *the* range. Like in all those cowboy tunes about tumbling tumbleweeds and home on the you know what."

"You're giving up magic to be a singing cowboy? I'll take Satyra if you're done with her." Satyra being Rondini's gorgeous stage assistant. "I need someone to help around the house, all one-bedroom of it. You know, rattle some pots and pans. If I had...well, you know."

"Calm down, slim, you're getting overwrought. You've already got a girl unless she already caught you playing in the tall grass with somebody else."

"The only grass they've got around here is what the Indians smoke. This is the desert—Christy would have to catch me out in the tall sand. Not that there has been anything to catch. I'm a one-woman man now, brother. I'm just having a little difficulty with the other woman."

"I knew it."

"Oh no, Ronnie, don't be all jumping to confusions. I'm not fooling around with anyone and I'm not fooling either. It may be your fantasy to hook up with a mother-daughter combo, but in the real world it doesn't happen that way. My problem is I can't pry Christy loose from Mommy Dearest."

"Ouch, wire hangers. And here I thought you were a mama's boy."

"If I was, this has been the cure. Mom's apron strings are tied so tight it'll take a kitchen full of Boy Scouts just to undo the knots."

"Well then, Junior, listen up. You are talking to a man who can untie any knot known to mankind—or womankind for that matter—all the while hanging upside-down inside a gunny sack in a shark tank full of water in front of an stadium crowd of fifty-thousand people."

"Paying customers?"

"That's beside the point. Hasn't your old pal always been looking out for you? Haven't I always helped you out of any jam?"

"Sure thing, pal. You're still in San Francisco while I wound up doing the rain dance at a used car lot."

"Hey now, that wasn't entirely my fault. You wanted to get the girl and you did."

"Sure, and I got her mom, too. Talk about happy endings."

"Well, it's a good thing I called you then," Ronnie said, a smile distorting his voice. "I've got just the answer to this little problem of yours."

Chapter 3.

"*...So this is Jerry Jeremy signing off on KICK, the Talk of the West. And just to prove we are really the Talk of the West, next week my show will be coming to you from the Circle-K Ranch and Spa near beautiful downtown Kirby, the liveliest ghost town in the big A-Z.*

"*We'll be staying compliments of the Circle-K management and we'll be getting there in one of Bronco Billy Wooten's fine pre-owned Jeep Cherokees. Stop by and let Bronco Billy put you in one of your own; they come in sizes for all shapes and in a variety of boudoir pastels—oops, that's the Lydia's Lingerie copy—but not to worry, Bronc Billy will be glad to put you in something sexy too.*

"*And if you happen to drive that brand new—to you, anyway—jalopy down Kirby-way, make sure you drop on by and watch us do the show live from—did I mention this before—the Circle-K Ranch and Spa. Even better, Jerry's old saddle-pal, The Great Rondini, will be pulling ten-gallon rabbits out of a five-gallon hat down at the Silver Birdcage Saloon, the west's only certified haunted beer joint.*"

I⊤ had been a week since I got the magician's call and I was settling quite nicely into my new seven to ten time slot. It fit me like a custom-built golf cart. I'd pop out of the sheets around noon, maybe hit an air-conditioned driving range, check-in with Christy to see where to meet after the show, then detour past the line next door at Tacos-2-Go and be on my way to the station. At last it was all falling into place.

Except for one unforeseen cloud on the horizon. My new hours.

I know, I know—a guy who only works three hours a day shouldn't go around bellyaching, but who knew they started those post-grad classes so early in the day? Nine or maybe nine-thirty? When do the professors find time to flirt with the coeds? Don't they have a life of some kind? Not one that goes past ten at night apparently.

"Jerry dearest, I already told you I'll listen to you on the air every evening, just as soon as I finish with my homework."

So much for my number one fan. I'd call during the seven-thirty news break to get a fire started for after the show. But higher education was getting in the way. Christy went to class during the day and between her homework and my evening show, there wasn't much time left before she headed to bed. To sleep. Alone.

We spent so much time calling each other, my cell phone needed a cell phone. I was telling her, "...baby, I need to be able to reach out and touch you, smell your perfume, nuzzle your neck...we're spending so much time apart, I may have to matriculate. I think that's the word."

"Better stop there, Jerry my dear, or I'll be up late finishing this paper. I know you wouldn't want me to drift off during the Sexual Ecology lecture tomorrow morning, would you?"

"Hey, some of my best shut-eye was during class. I'd still be in school today if they hadn't asked me to wake up and leave."

"I don't believe that."

"That they woke me up? I couldn't believe it either. But really, babe, when you're not at the library or on a shopping run with Mom, you're rehearsing for the school play or getting your nails done. How many times a week do you need to do your nails anyway?"

"Now don't get sore, darling, blah, blah, blah...." I won't go into the mushy stuff, but I decided having Christy over the phone was better than not having Christy at all. Still I did wonder how fast the average woman's nails grew. I'll have to remember to Google it. As it was, I had to get back on the air. The show, as they say, must go on. Otherwise you don't get paid.

Later that evening I hit number one on my speed dial again, "Hey babe, I didn't get a chance to tell you before, but I'm on to something that I—er, I mean you—will really like. But you'll need to play hooky for a few days."

"Is this the one where I dress up like a school girl and you play the truant officer?"

"Sure, I'll even bring the handcuffs. But that'll have to wait until you're back here in school again."

"But if I'm in school, you won't be able to arrest me."

"Don't worry. I'll think of something—but hey, that's not why I called. If your mom had let you stay up to catch my show tonight, you'd already know me and a guest of my choice are being comped for a week out at the Circle-K dude ranch. I'll be doing my show from there while The Great Rondini—you remember him—headlines in the local ghost town. Have mic, will travel."

I gave Christy the backstory the way Ronnie had explained it to me. The Great One's road show had been making the rounds and wound up being booked into the Silver Cage Saloon, a renovated dance hall that the Circle-K used as a tourist   attraction-slash-nightclub   for   the   visiting dudes. Ronnie said they'd renovated and fixed it up so even the ghosts had new sheets. The ranch even brought in clean dirt for Main Street.

What with Rondini and me being pals and all, and this bump in the trail being a part of KICK's broadcast area, Ronnie had somehow managed to soft-soap the head dude into letting me come over and give him a million bucks worth of free publicity.   In   return   I   got   a   week's   free   room   and board. Ronnie also figured that in return for setting it up, his old pal might throw a little plugola his way too. Well, that wasn't exactly how he put it. For one thing, he didn't say little.

So I'd be plugging Rondini and plugging the dude ranch, plugging their spa and plugging the ghost town, and hoping the FCC didn't unplug me. With a little luck I might be able to squeeze in a paying sponsor like Bronco Billy. I didn't mind bending the rules a little to get a week alone with Christy. I was sure Mrs. Marshall would enjoy some alone time too. So what if there were a few strings and maybe a government investigation attached?

Chapter 4.

"SHEE-IT, boy," Bronco Billy said. All-in-all I thought it sounded like he gave it a positive reading, basically a good "shee-it" as it were.

We were on the sixth green at Canyon, Dale and me against Billy and Dakota Holiday, KICK's top female air talent. Dakota was the competition in more ways than one, on top of which she had a follow-through that would knock your eyes out. Since it was turning into a beautiful morning and Bronco Billy was already ahead by forty bucks, I figured the timing was right to pitch the Circle-K remote to him. After all, if he sponsored it, I could charge a few of the incidentals to the station on his tab. I was saying, "...why I'd be the Talk of the West, actually broadcasting from someplace in the West. You know all the local color, saloons, hitching posts, horses, more saloons..."

"Shee-it, boy! Ain't it amazin' y'all can just broadcast over the radio from way out there?" Billy let loose with a cloud of cigar smoke, obscuring the cup as I missed my three-putt. So what's another five-spot when he was lining up behind me on this dude ranch thing? I breathed in some second-hand just to see what burning money tastes like.

"Why, Bronco Billy," said Dakota. "I can't quite believe you don't remember those many times when I broadcast live from your little old dealership. Remember my changing into that little Indian princess costume in your private office?"

"Let's not go into that right now, darlin'," Billy smiled, probably remembering the changing if not the costume. Honey-toned and honey-tanned, she had worked her way into a steady afternoon slot with those remotes from the dealership. She'd also landed Billy's sponsorship like he was a trout taking the hook on a leggy nymph fly. Not that I should talk, but at least I didn't take my clothes off in his private office.

"Billy, sweetie, I'm sure I heard you declare I was the best thing to happen out on North Sixth Avenue since...since when was that?"

"Kinda slips my mind right now, Dakota. I'll remember later, maybe after dinner, but right now I got a shot to make." He took his eyes off the ball and Dakota long enough to say, "Jerry, I think you may just have treed a bobcat with this thing. KICK Radio bein' the Talk of the West n' all and there ain't nothing more west-like than a fuckin' cattle ranch, even if this one only rounds up tourists. And a ghost town to boot? No goddamn' ghost town in New York City or L.A., eh?"

Billy's ball found the hole and another smoke cloud from Havana wrapped itself around the green. What with all the smoke I'd lost track of my ball but didn't say anything, not wanting to upset any apple carts since Bronco Billy and his advertising bucks seemed to be backing my pitch. Those stogies probably cost as much as I'd pay for a new set of tires. Not that I actually planned to buy tires since I had the loaner from Billy's car lot.

I looked around in a casual kind of way while Dale was lining up his putt. Dale gave the pill a light tap and it looked like it was on rails. Except the engine stopped six inches short of the station. He smiled anyway, showing off some well-groomed choppers, and said to Billy, "You know KICK radio has what amounts to a radio station in a box. It comes in handy for these remotes. All we need is a cell phone or a wi-fi connection and we can broadcast from anywhere in the world. Even do video."

"Cable news does that," Dakota said bending over to spot her ball. Even clean-living Dale stopped to watch that. She was saying, "They even use their mobiles to broadcast from way out in Iraq and Afghanistan. You know, internationally."

"So you're sayin' Jerry here could be doin' his show from fuckin' Baghdad? I sell a lot of vehicles to our brave boys and girls in uniform. Mostly the boys, I guess. Hell, I even give 'em ten percent off."

"Maybe we ought to start off closer to home," I said wishing Dakota would stick to stroking Billy's putter and stop trying to float ideas that put my life in jeopardy.

"Just kidding, Jerry," Dale said. "We were just kidding, weren't we, Billy? Billy?"

By then Bronco Billy was helping his partner adjust her form. Her golfing form, that is; otherwise I don't think he'd find anything wrong with her form. Not that she could hold a candle to Christy. Well, maybe a small candle, one not too bright. Even Dale, young, married and church-going, lost his train of thought for a moment which was fine with me. I had figured that making the Circle-K boondoggle into a broadcast event and pitching it in the right social milieu might slip it past Dale's better judgment.

Not that I thought Dale would actually tear my head off or anything what with him being born-again. He wouldn't yell. He wouldn't curse or throw things. Dale would just give me a disappointed look and tell me to clean out my locker. And I didn't even have a locker.

"*Bill-eee!*" Dakota squealed. So I was pretty sure Bronco Billy wouldn't have any more questions. With Billy and his pre-owned jalopies lined up to cover gas money, Dale would be on board too. _

Best of all I didn't actually have to ask for the time off. As far as KICK was concerned, it was all work, work, work. Maybe I hadn't been quite up front about how the room and board had come about, describing it more like a deal I had set up for the station's benefit. Who knows, maybe next time that might be true.

I POPPED out of bed bright and early Saturday morning—not so early as for golf, but well before noon—and by the early p.m. was pulling up in front of Mrs. Marshall's white picket fence ready to whisk her little girl away for a week of cowboy love. Ridin', ropin' and yippee-ki-yea! And that's just in the bedroom.

Judging by the pile of luggage set out on the porch, Christy must have packed a month's worth of negligees, not to mention her other unmentionables. But I figured she knew what she was packing for, because after all she had spent her formative college years out here, ridin', ropin' and—well, let's hope not too much of that other stuff.

Anyway, there must have been eight or nine bags there, not counting Mrs. Marshall who was keeping her eye on everything including her daughter.

"So I guess when you couldn't decide what to pack, you decided to take it all," I said, giving Christy a peck on the cheek. I figured I'd save the heavy artillery until we'd left Mom behind. I looked over the stack of luggage and asked, "Where'd you put the the spurs and the lariat? The rest isn't essential."

"Well gee, honey," she oozed, "you know they're not really

all mine. Only two are really mine. The rest are actually my mother's."

"Oh, I get it. She's hitching a ride with us to the airport and since it's only around twenty miles out of our way, we can drop her off. Or is her taxi already on its way?"

"*A taxi!*" Mom gave me a look. My guess was we were dropping her off.

"Well listen, sweetie," Christy said giving me a different kind of look, one that pleaded and promised at the same time. "Mom thought maybe it would be better if she came along with us, rather than being left all alone at home. After all, she really never gets a chance to travel much anymore."

"Never gets a chance to go anywhere? Why didn't you say so? One of my sponsor's is a travel agent. I could give him a call right now and get something arranged. I think they even have a Club Med for boomers." I had a few other thoughts about where she could go, but Christy leaned softly into me, wrapped her arms around my neck and pressed a lingering kiss over my protests.

Okay, Mom could go, but Christy had better make good on the promise of that kiss. I was able to hide my look of hopeful longing by lugging about a half ton of Samsonite over to the Cherokee. Maybe Billy should have loaned me a truck.

"Jeremy, we have a problem." Mrs. M said as though it was my fault. "I get carsick if I sit in the back on long drives."

I wasn't sure if I was being blamed or not.

"Sure Mrs. M. Why don't you sit right up front next to me," I heard myself saying. "It should only be about a two hour drive. I'd let you steer but the car's not really mine."

"Well, I'd rather navigate anyway, but Lord knows, your driving is bad enough."

"Care for some music? I've got a few CDs I borrowed from the station. Roy Acuff? Charlie Pride? Ludacris? Funk-Master Robbie? Or how about this one, Rod Stewart's 'Back in the Saddle Again'? He's doing covers of all the old cowboy songs."

"Jerry honey, maybe we should hold off on the tunes for now," said Christy. "Let's just get on the road."

"Sho'nuff, boss lady. But first I have to stop at the station to pick up some equipment. If I'm going to do the show from the Circle-K, I'll need some mics and a board. They've got a whole station's worth of electronics stuffed into an overnighter."

"It must be complicated," Christy said.

"I hope not. They said even an idiot can hook it up and I took them at their word. With this set-up I can literally call in my show."

"They said 'even an idiot', huh?" Christy's mom echoed.

AT the station I found Dale huddled in his office with Dakota Holiday. I had expected Dale to be there to check me out on the studio equipment I was borrowing, but I was surprised to find Dakota keeping him company on her day off. Maybe another golf outing was in the works and they were just waiting for Bronco Billy to show, although by now heatstroke would have pretty well cleared the fairways. I doubted that born-again Dale was trying to beat Bronco Billy's time with Dakota, but you never know. Maybe he was a Mormon.

"Jerry—come on in," he said like he was glad I showed up. "Glad you're here," he confirmed it.

Maybe Dakota was chasing him around the desk. At any rate, neither one looked like I had caught them with any of their hands in any cookie jars. Or anywhere else they shouldn't be.

"You two must be working on that strategy to kick up Bronco Billy's ad rates," I said. "Planning to break the news out at Canyon? You know, do it while Dakota's giving the old boy a few strokes, er—on his handicap, that is."

I didn't get an answer, but I figured it was probably better not to press it in case I was too close to the truth. Dale gave me a quick rundown on the board and mic setup, where to plug in the phone connection and so on, while Dakota looked on with feigned interest, hanging on our boss's every word. Maybe I wasn't too far off thinking Dale might be trying to beat the auto czar's time.

"Are the instructions for this contraption written down somewhere?" I asked. "It's simple enough when you do it, but I usually have a board op to figure out the flashing lights and stuff."

"Don't worry, Jerry. Dakota's used this plenty of times out at Bronco Billy's dealership. She can help you if you have a problem setting up."

"Sure," she said, "there's nothing to it, Jerry. Since you're driving, it's the least I can do to help out."

"Sure," I said. "Wait a minute—what do you mean, 'Since I'm driving'?"

"Ah...well, Jerry, listen," Dale hemmed just before he

hawed, "I did forget to mention it, but Bronco Billy thinks we should go all out on this dude ranch thing. He'll not only be sponsoring your remotes, but he wanted Dakota to do her show from there also. Like you said, the Talk of the West goes west.

"The line-up will be Dakota from the ghost town, a break for news, weather, traffic from five to seven, then you round out the evening and we're back here for Jack's show."

For a second I couldn't tell if the room was spinning or if it was just my career swirling around the toilet bowl. My getaway with the girl I'm crazy in lust for was turning into a convention of vipers. Not to mention my little coup with the remote from the ranch. First, Christy's mom, and now a female snake in the grass in...well, in snakeskin cowboy boots anyway.

"Great, Dale, great," I said looking around to see how much more luggage I'd have to haul. "Did you have time to pack, Dakota, or was this just a spur of the moment thing?"

"Did I get a chance to pack? Does a cactus have a prick? A girl can't go anywhere without packing a few necessities."

Dakota's mountain of luggage was still in the back of her pick-up. By the time I had loaded it into the Jeep and we were ready to hit the road, I had to tie my suitcase and the broadcast setup on the roof. Inside every available space was crammed with carry-ons, makeup cases, overnight bags, duffel bags and a matched set of suitcases that had to Mrs. M's. Lucky I was the driver or they might have voted me off the island.

"WE'RE only about twenty miles east of the ranch." I was trying to give the ladies an update in answer to Mrs. M's anguished howl.

"East! How can we be east, sweetie?" Christy asked. "We started out west of the ranch."

"You must have overshot the turnoff, Jerry," Dakota chimed in.

"Maybe there's a bug in the GPS," I said. "But the ranch should be coming up anytime soon, no matter which direction we're going."

"Jeremy, that defies all logic."

"Thanks, Mrs. M." Christy and I must be fated for each other. Why else would Mrs. Marshall sound so much like a mother-in-law?

Anyway the women batted my navigation back and forth

while I tried to watch the GPS with one eye and the road with the other.   Just about the time the ladies' critiques were winding down, a sign advertising the ranch and ghost town tipped us off that it was just ahead.

The Circle-K Ranch and Spa seemed to overshadow the town of Kirby, a one-time ghost town, but now a full time tourist trap.   Kirby had rivaled Tombstone during the silver rush, but like many other boom towns, it had gone bust when the mines did.   The old Kirby Hotel's front desk mostly served the Circle-K now although the hotel had a few old-timey rooms overlooking the dirt street out front.   The guest ranch itself was set back a hundred yards or so from Kirby's main drag.   It was an expanded and modernized version of an adobe hacienda— the kind with an Olympic swimming pool and thermal baths just like the ones down Mexico way.   Well, Acapulco maybe.   I was pretty sure though that most of the water in this part of the desert was trucked in.

The clerk at the desk was dressed like an old time railroad conductor wearing a starched collar, a vest with a watch chain and fob, and had garters on his sleeves.   In other words he blended right in.   All he needed was three other guys and a handle-bar mustache to start a barbershop quartet.   A brass plate on the counter said his name was Sherman Huntley, and old-timey conductor or not, Sherm was saying they were all booked up.

"I never realized how many people it takes to do a radio show," he was saying.   Apparently the ever efficient Dale had forgotten to book a room for Dakota although I was all set with a double for Christy and me thanks to The Great Rondini.

"...so we have Mr. Jeremy in the Screaming Buffalo bungalow and Miss Holiday has Lonesome Beaver--" even Mrs. Marshall did a double take at that "--but that leaves the ladies without lodgings."

"If you can find one more room, it'll solve the problem since Mrs. Marshall and Ms. Holiday can double up," I suggested.   "You don't mind do you, Dakota?"

Point, match, set.   I was impersonating the cat who swallowed the canary.

"I need my own room, Jerry," said Dakota, eying a muscular cowboy across the lobby.   "I think that I may be having company."

"Maybe you should wait to invite him over until you actually meet him."

At that point another guy in a muscle shirt came up and

put his arm around the cowboy. It looked like Sassie Marshall would be sharing Dakota's bungalow after all. I was up to a two canary smile now.

"Jerry, darling," Christy turned her big, shiny blues in my direction, "I know you had everything all planned out and all, but remember we brought Mom along so she could be with me and not be lonely."

"Don't worry, I hear Dakota can be great fun. Bronco Billy says she's a ton of laughs."

Dakota chimed in again, "I still plan on having company."

"I don't want to be a burden," said Mrs. Marshall. "But Christy needs a place to sleep—"

"Mother won't feel comfortable imposing on Dakota," Christy said.

"But...but...."

"Mother and I can take your bungalow—"

"My...our...bungalow?"

"That's the Screaming Buffalo," Sherm said, eying the muscular cowpokes, "one of our best bungalows."

"—although that leaves you without a room, darling."

Great.

My plans for a week of romance—not to mention debauchery—having gone down the drain, I was just hoping I wouldn't wind up sleeping in the Jeep. With Dakota. As it turned out, I bunked in with Ronnie while the mother and daughter act took my bungalow and Dakota wound up rooming with Satyra in the Lonesome Beaver bungalow. With everybody doubling up, I figured that name would be prophetic. As long as Ronnie didn't get lucky, at least I'd have a roof to sleep under. Of course, since the Circle-K was footing just my personal tab, I'd have to wind up paying for Christy and her mom's room.

My only hope was if Mama hit the rack early and Rondini got stuck doing a few encores at the late show. If everything fell into place, Christy and I might be able to get fifteen or twenty minutes alone sometime around midnight.

Chapter 5.

"...AND now, The Great Rondini will blah, blah, blah...."
Satyra was running through the patter. I had heard the spiel at
least a thousand times, having seen Ronnie's act that often
back in San Francisco. They do all kinds of gags like mind-
reading, fantastic illusions, sleight of hand, foot and mouth,
hypnosis and anything else they can cram into an hour show
and not get arrested for.

"...The Great Rondini, blindfolded and locked in a
hermetically-sealed chamber will now identify through his
amazing mental powers alone, blah, blah, blah...."

I never get tired of watching them. Well, I never get tired
of watching Satyra in an amazingly revealing costume. I'd
never tell Ronnie, but she's the mainstay of the act. Of course,
I tell her that all the time.

Before I wound up on the Talk of the West, I was San
Francisco's seventh highest-rated talk show host. In my time
slot anyway. Not counting the Spanish-language stations. The
great old days, hopping out of bed in time for the four o'clock
afternoon drive show, Starbucks just eighteen floors below my
apartment. In those days, just a few months ago actually, I
spent many evenings after my shift hanging out at the Blue
Sphinx watching Satyra hanging out as it were. Of course,
Rondini's magic was almost as spellbinding too.

Then Christy Marshall walked into my life and now I only
have eyes for her. Well, I can still look though, can't I?
Anyway, with a little help from Ronnie, I managed to track
down the guy who murdered Christy's dad. I was a hero,
Christy's hero. But as things worked out, it didn't go down so
good with the station owner and first thing you know I was on
the bus to East Podunk. Not that Tucson's not a great town in
some respects, after all the love of my life lives there. Even if
it's with her mom. But like they say, that's show biz. At least

the part we call talk radio is.

Without a show to tie me down, I was able to follow Christy out here. Christy and her widowed mom settled in near the university so she could work on that graduate degree. And I settled in in my low-rent apartment not too far away. This way we could both be closer to Mom. Lucky me.

Meanwhile, back at the Silver Cage Saloon, Satyra was waist deep in the audience collecting odds and ends for Rondini's mental telepathy trick. She got a scarf off Dakota at our table and Mrs. M's watch. One by one, Satyra held up the scarf, the watch, a cowboy hat, a purse from somebody wearing a scarf and cowboy hat.

"...what am I holding in my hand, Oh Great One? Can you see blah, blah, blah...."

"I see...yes...this is just off the top of my head, but I see a hat."

And so it went. Ronnie always got it right and the crowd applauded every time. I had a feeling these folks didn't get out much.

One by one, Ronnie, after some phony false starts, would write the name of the item—while blindfolded—on a chalk board in his glassed-in booth. Every so often, he'd start writing the wrong thing, suddenly erasing it and putting it right. Meanwhile Satyra kept up a line of patter that wasn't too bad considering she'd had a few tequila shooters to calm her pre-show jitters.

"The Great Rondini laddies and gentiles...." When Satyra finally ran out of things to hold up from the audience, Ronnie capped the trick by flipping over the chalk board revealing he had already written the name of each item on the back. Pure magic, I guess. Anyway the cowboys and cowgirls ate it up.

"Oh, Christy, isn't he just marvelous?" Christy's mom was eating it up too. "Does he still help Jerry with his show?"

We'd managed to grab a near-ringside table, me being a big radio dude and knowing the magician and all. In a few minutes I'd get to play the big man for Mrs. M by having Rondini and Satyra join us for a drink. Who knows maybe Ronnie could take Mom off my hands for a while. She's a little older than he is, but it couldn't be much worse than back in the sixth grade when Mrs. Gridley made Ronnie stay after school to clap her erasers. He was so good at cleaning Gridley's erasers, she held him back two years running.

For his big finale, Rondini wrapped Satyra up like a mummy, locked her in a sarcophagus, doused kerosene over it and set the whole shebang on fire. It flashed up, the mummy case disintegrated, clouds of colored smoke blew off the stage, and just like magic Ronnie's beautiful assistant re-materialized, slinking through the wreckage wearing a diaphanous gown and looking like an angel. Charley Sheen's idea of an angel anyway.

Giving credit where credit's due, Ronnie Green—once voted the student most likely to be convicted of a major felony—did have a flair for picking assistants. And, like I say, the magic's not bad either. Even Mrs. Marshall was impressed. When I introduced her to The Great One she practically swooned. While the swooning was going on, Christy got some kind of girl talk thing going with Dakota and Satyra.

"It seems like ages...."

"Yes, with Jerry on KICK radio..."

"Don't you miss...."

"...be graduating next year...."

"...San Francisco...."

Meanwhile, Mrs. M was moving in on Ronnie like a chicken hawk on...well, a chicken I guess. "Please call me Sassie, Mister Rondini, or should I call you Ronnie?" she cooed. "I was just amazed watching you at work. I won't ask how you do it, because I know a magician never reveals his tricks."

"I thought it was your age you never revealed." I figured Ronnie couldn't be more than three or four years my senior, the two of us having been in the twelfth-grade together.

"If you ask me, I'd say you're in your prime right now," Dakota jumped in.

"Well, thanks. I think you look pretty prime too. Of course—"

"I don't think age means all that much any more, dear," Mrs. Marshall said, looking a few daggers in Dakota's direction. "Except for those of us whose only attraction is their fading youth."

For once she didn't mean me. I could have been wrong, but Ronnie was looking more and more like a rump roast caught in a tug of war between a lioness and a wildcat. They'd probably tear him to pieces rather than to lose to each other. This trip might be more fun than I thought.

"Anyway, you were fabulous," they both said. I wondered which one would still feel that way in the morning. Maybe the one he didn't hook up with.

"Well, Mom, it's been a long day," Christy said, throwing in a fake yawn. She seemed a little bit thrown by Sassie Marshall's interest in the world of legerdemain and Kirby's hottest new practitioner thereof.

"Another round," Satyra circled her finger in the air for the dance hall gal serving drinks to see.

"There you are, dear, we're having another round," Mrs. M said. "I can sleep in tomorrow. Do you sleep in, Mr. Rondini? I mean, Ronnie?"

"No, I make it a rule to be up by noon. One, two o'clock at the latest."

According to my plan, Mrs. M should have been cutting zzz's by now and I should be on the honeymoon Christy and I never had. Not that marriage was in the offing. But it looked like I had to come up with a Plan B. I needed to cut Christy out of the herd while Mom was focused on the magician; this time *we'd* do the disappearing act.

I made eyes at Christy and she made eyes back. So close and yet so blue...er, far. Most times like this, Mom kept her eyes on us too. But not tonight. Right now, she only had eyes for Rondini. I quietly said to Christy, "You look pretty tuckered out, though you still look pretty. Maybe it's time to head for the Screaming Buffalo bungalow. I'll walk you there and maybe tuck you in."

We said our good-nights, not that anyone seemed to care, Mrs. Marshall and Dakota being busy giving Ronnie the old one-two. Satyra had done her vanishing act also, materializing with a bunch of urban cowboys at the bar.

THE desert night closed in on us as we headed down the moonlit trail to the bungalows. Moonlight shining through a stand of pepper trees cast nighttime shadows across the path giving it a sinister feel while behind us the moon bathed the ghost town in, well, a ghostly light. Christy nestled under my arm and we stopped for a long embrace underneath an acacia. All the emotions, all the ups and downs of the past year, came back as we held each other and our lips met. What a kiss, what a—

"Who's that?"

The voice had all the charm of fingernails on a chalkboard.

"That's not you is it?"

"No, no, it's not me," I answered. "Nobody here, just us kids playing in the dark."

"Oh, I'm very sorry. For just a second, in the dark I mean,

I thought you were Bruce." A woman, short and round, stepped out of the shadows. I could just make out a large purse one hand clutched to her ample bosom. In her other hand was a gun. I was hoping that this wasn't going to turn into a shoot-'em-up. I was hoping in spite of the dark, she'd know I wasn't Bruce. And that Christy wasn't either.

"I'm trying to find Bruce. You haven't seen him have you?"

"No, no Bruce here. I haven't seen him. Ever."

She looked at the pistol and just said, "Rattlesnakes." Then she hurried down the path like she had someplace to go.

"What the fuck," Christy said. "Who was that?"

"Bruce's mom?" I grabbed her hand and pulled her toward the bungalow. "Speaking of mom's, while yours is being charmed by The Great Rondini, we may finally get the chance to sample each other's charms."

"I know Ronnie is your pal and all, but with my mother! I couldn't look him in the face again if anything happened."

"Don't worry, he may have a few small tricks up his sleeve, but when it comes to the real magic, it's just an illusion. C'mon, let's get our own abracadabra going before that illusion wears off."

"Well...."

MORNING dawned bright and sunny. A string of fluffy clouds perched on the horizon keeping watch on the cactus already baking in the sun. Of course I was actually sleeping when morning dawned, but when the alarm shook me awake a couple hours later, the sun was still shining, the clouds were still fluffy, and enough said about that. You get the picture.

Christy had set us up for a morning horseback ride through the high desert with a cowboy from the ranch to guide us. With any kind of luck Sassie Marshall would be scheduled for a spa appointment or be planning on taking the ghost town tour.

In the other bed Ronnie managed to sleep through the alarm. Must have had a late night. He hadn't turned up until after I had already tucked Christy in at her place and was sound asleep back at our bachelor digs. Deep inside my evil little heart, I was hoping Mrs. M had been his late night companion and maybe she wouldn't hear the alarm either. I can't say that she was really Ronnie's type, having a good twenty-five years on him, but it could be he was just tired of having sex alone; stranger things have happened.

My luck held. When I stopped by the Screaming Buffalo, Mrs. Marshall was still dead to the world, so Christy and I moseyed over to the pool where a chuck wagon was hitched up for an *al fresco* breakfast. My man Sherm, taking a break from the reception desk, was overseeing the buffet. More accurately, he was trying to stop a cornflakes fight the kids were having in the Jacuzzi. He'd also given up the desk clerk's green eyeshade and sleeve garters for a ten-gallon chef's hat and an apron with cowboy chaps printed on it.

"Morning, Sherm," I greeted him, "what looks good today?"

"Personally," he said, "I'd opt for the guy in the green Speedo."

"Thanks, for over-sharing, but I was hoping for something less raw."

Breakfast turned out to be a light repast of fried eggs, fried potatoes, fried ham and re-fried beans. Just what a trail hand wants before bouncing around on a horse all day.

"Maybe we should get a couple of those fried donuts to go," I said.

"I don't know, Jerry," Christy replied. "We've got a long ride ahead of us. How much of a beating can these ponies take?"

"I'm more worried about the beating we'll take. My job calls for me to work sitting down you know."

"Well I noticed a bottle of liniment in my room if you need somebody to rub it where it hurts later."

"You're hired. Maybe we should try it before the ride."

"Mom's the expert at rubbing it in, you know."

"You can say that again. Oh, you mean the liniment. Maybe I can wait." I washed down the last of the toast and jam with the last of the coffee—more perfect timing. But before we could make our getaway, a shadow crossed our table.

"Mr. Jeremy? May I speak with you?" Her voice, even throttled down to a whisper, still raised the hairs on the back of my neck. A natural chalkboard reflex. She was silhouetted against the sun, but I could still see her better than I could last night. That wasn't necessarily a good thing.

About thirty years too old for *Annie Get Your Gun*, the woman had nonetheless managed to squeeze most of her substantial girth into the kind of cowgirl outfit that they might use on Broadway. Brassy red curls were fighting their way out from under a pink Stetson. I have unruly red curls myself but they paled in comparison to hers. Either the hairdresser was colorblind or she was. Maybe both.

"Mr. Jeremy," she repeated, "do you have a moment?"

"Er, hi," I said as she plopped down next to Christy. "I mean sure. I mean I'm all ears." In spite of the squawk and dye job, I figured I'd better be nice in case she was a listener or maybe a distant relative of Bronco Billy's.

"Thank you. And pardon me for barging in on you young people—" this last to Christy "—but I have a favor to ask of you, Mr. Jeremy, though I believe it will be of mutual benefit."

"Like they say one hand washes the other, or maybe it's one hand clapping, Mrs., er Miss...."

"Edelbaum, Beverly Edelbaum, Missus." Once again to Christy, "And you are, my dear?"

Christy owned up to who she was and the ladies shook on it. Then Mrs. Beverly Edelbaum borrowed my napkin to wipe the guava jam off her hand, picking up some bacon grease in the process.

"About this mutual favor," I prodded.

"Certainly, that's why I barged in, isn't it?"

"So far only you would know."

"Well, when Sherman told me you were broadcasting your radio show from the ranch and might be looking for people to interview, I just thought how nice it would be for you to interview Rex. He's a very well-known western artist."

"Rex? Like Cher, only one name?"

"Heavens no. Bowman, Rex Bowman." The lady's jowls shook with sincerity. "He's a very famous western artist. His portrait of the Navajo Princess Heroleta is in the Phoenix Museum and he has a Barry Goldwater in the state building. Painted from an original photograph, of course."

"Do tell. Princess Heroleta? Any chance she can make the show too?"

"I hardly think so. She has been dead for a hundred years or more."

"Kind of like Goldwater, eh?"

"Please, Mr. Jeremy," Mrs. Edelbaum jiggled with suppressed laughter, "you really are a stitch. Rex is, of course, only thirty-five. The portrait, although based on extensive research, is a work of creative genius."

"Ah, gotcha. The girl next door in costume. Or maybe not in costume?"

"In authentic Native American dress."

"Sure. Well let's have him on tonight then. Maybe you can sit in also, being an expert on western art. You know, make

Rex feel right at home."

"Well, of course, if you like. Oh, and did I mention that Rex has a one-man show going on here at the Kirby Art Gallery?"

"You really didn't have to. Nobody comes on talk radio unless they have something to pitch. I plan to set up right over there in the lounge at seven o'clock. See you then."

"How nice, I'll bring Rex over at seven then," she said getting up.

"Tell him we'll want to cover the Barry Goldwater. Kind of a political tie-in." As she turned to leave I asked if she'd ever found Bruce, but she seemed not to hear me.

Chapter 6.

"...*OUR guests tonight include the lovely Christy Marshall who managed to lasso me into an afternoon of horseback riding here at the Circle-K Ranch and Spa—which reminds me, has anybody seen a big rubber doughnut? If I don't find it, I'll be doing the show standing up.*

"I don't want to say I'm saddle sore, but by the time we got back to the corral, even the horse was walking funny. I'm not kidding, folks, it literally turned out to be a pain in a word you can't say on the radio. Next time maybe I'll try riding side-saddle. It will hurt twice as much, but only on one side.

"Seems to me the last time I was on a pony I was trying to impress a girl named Sylvia Dunkerson. I was eleven at the time and as I recall that also turned out badly. By the time we trotted home, Sylvia had slapped me so hard my cheeks were as red as...well, as my other cheeks."

My guests for the show consisted of folks who were hanging out at the Circle-K so that my listeners would get a picture of life on the ranch. In other words, I was singing for my supper, not to mention my room, the Circle-K having decided to comp my bungalow after all—that is, Christy and her mom's room—as well as free board for us all. While I was at it, I threw in some free publicity for The Great Rondini too. After all, I was taking up half his bungalow.

We were set up with the studio in a box perched on the biggest table in the Palomino Lounge with my guests arrayed around it. We had a live audience too, consisting of a few of the folks that were hanging out at the Circle-K, a couple of families with kids, a few older couples, even a pair of newlyweds. I could tell they were newlyweds because of the way they stared in each other's eyes and held each other's hands and mainly because they went back to their room before the show was over.

Sharing the mic with me were Christy of course, and Beverly Edelbaum, dressed to the nines and looking every bit the rhinestone cowgirl. Next was her protégé, the famous Rex Bowman, who also dragged in the proprietor of Kirby's best—and only—art gallery, introduced as Bryan Forbes-Collier. In spite of the moniker he didn't look too artsy. I figured he was a couple of inches taller than me at about six-three, and going against local fashions, he had on an Armani blazer.

Filling out my dance card was Amanda Piccard, the ranch's executive chef, who Sherman Huntley had volunteered to sit in and pitch the hotel food. That only left The Great Rondini. He was looking forward to dropping by between shows at the Silver Cage for a little self-promotion. After all, since I'd moved to Tucson, his plugola quotient was way down.

Nonetheless, since I was getting free grub, I let Ms. Piccard pinch-hit for Ronnie during the intros. Bowman didn't have to pitch his pictures since both Forbes-Collier and Bev Edelbaum couldn't say enough good things about him and his one-man show up in ghost town. Meanwhile, her Bruce—Mr. Edelbaum as it turned out—was still MIA as far as I could tell. During one of the commercial breaks Bev claimed she hadn't really misplaced the old boy after all, he was just sticking close to their bungalow having been fed a batch of bad clams or something. Amanda Piccard looked a little green herself at that point and said he must have eaten something from that Mexican place in town.

When we came back on the air, I figured I'd change the subject, being a guest of the ranch and all. So I gave it a try. *"Tell us, Beverly, what brought you to the Circle-K? Was it the riding, the roping, the songs around the campfire, or maybe just the campfire? I hear the cowboys light up some funny weeds around it and sing to the cattle, er, the guests. How do you pass the time at the Circle-K anyhow?"*

"Well, Jerry dear, the main reason I came was because of their wonderful spa. I'm afraid I'm just not built for sports, you know, riding and all. I believe, as even you discovered today, horseback riding isn't quite what it's cracked up to be."

I had my finger on the dump button just in case anybody tried to slip in a crack about her crack. Or mine. But nobody spoke up and Bev just rattled on. It looked like she'd use the entire segment on the first question.

"No riding or tennis or swimming or hiking," she was saying. *"Just the massages, the facials, the manicures, and the waters--"*

"*Must be that special desert water? Dry enough to grow cactus. So you met Rex here then, maybe splashing around the hot tub? Or getting soaked at the bar?*"

"*I had actually met Mrs. Edelbaum before coming here,*" Bowman smarmed into the microphone. "*She's quite the friend of the arts and has also been kind enough to purchase a few of my works.*"

So we chatted about Bowman's being a famous western artist and his interest in painting Native Americans. As the guests got more relaxed and forgot about the mics, I could see that Bev and Forbes-Collier, the gallery owner, were trying to one-up each other in praising the artist. In the normal course of affairs, I would try to build a minor competition like that into a shouting match that the listeners could really enjoy, but I didn't want to cause a scene on my first sleep-away for the station.

Bev was saying, "*...he presents a view of the new West with the technique of the fabled old Western painters.*"

"*I agree,*" agreed Forbes-Collier. "*Rex can rival any of the greats, Frederick Remington, Charles Russell, even Max Leibergard...*"

"*You two are making me blush,*" Bowman said without blushing. "*That's mighty high praise for an old country boy like me. Of course, I have a lot of ties to the land and the Native American tribes, even having been in a ceremony to become blood brother to an Apache shaman.*"

"*Oh, Rex, I agree you are as good as those famous artists,*" Bev said. "*Just remember to paint in your own style; you don't want to be accused of aping some old school master. You know I love your modern interpretations of the West and what's more I can help you find some good representation. I mean real representation in real art centers, like Dallas or New York of course. After all, you've only got Bryan out here in Kirby.*"

"*And I have contacts in major galleries around the world,*" Forbes-Collier replied. "*As I think you know, I currently am engaged in representing one of Leibergard's best works, which is on display at my gallery. But I value Rex's talent even more.*"

"*Sure, he's still alive. Who knows if you will be able to find any more undiscovered old masters like the Leibergard.*"

Blah, blah, blah.

I HAD to cut the sweet talk short for a commercial, and when we came back, I worked in some chit-chat with Christy about how we all were having a great time at the Circle-K. Executive Chef Piccard tried out her audition for the Food Network. Too bad for her that cooking on radio is about as the same as listening to a ventriloquist—not much good if you can't see their chops.

All in all, we had a lot of happy talk masquerading as a radio show so everybody could get their plugs in. In my mind's eye I could see the listeners surfing the dial for something a little more exciting. Then as if by magic, Ronnie finally showed up. He claimed he was late because he had had to do three encores. I wondered if any of them were with Christy's mom, but kept my mouth shut.

"*So I've been keeping an ear to the ground,*" Ronnie started in after his intro and a pitch for his show, "*and what I've been hearing besides a lot of foot traffic is that the Native Sons here are reviving some ancient spiritual practices. They can actually talk to the nether world of ghosts and animal spirits.*"

"*I thought you were a skeptic when it comes to the supernatural,*"

"*Well, sure, unless a guy has a little help from his friends, if you catch my drift.*"

"*You're not drifting, you're running the rapids.*"

"*Ah, but these Native Americans use a little of that magic dust to help them reach a whole 'nother plane.*"

"*They're probably flying without a plane. Say, exactly how many encores did you have at the Silver Cage Saloon? And for our listeners here in the high desert, the Silver Cage is located in beautiful downtown Kirby, just five miles off route 80.*"

"*Hey, I'm not kidding, kid. I've decided this is my thing— I'm planning to hook up with a hookah. I'll be seeing the laughing coyote.*"

"*Sure, why not? Chances are you'll be the one he's laughing at.*"

So anyway my pal continued to drag the show along with Indian spook stories he'd picked up somewhere. I was about to go back to Bev Edelbaum and her art appreciation class when we ran out of time. I was also thinking that maybe it wasn't just Native American art she appreciated; maybe she appreciated Rex Bowman more than she should. Where was Bruce anyway?

Chapter 7.

"MAN-ALIVE, that was a tough one," I told Christy. "Politics is a cinch compared to this travel and leisure stuff. I wonder how Tony Bourdain does it. I could hardly stay awake and it's my show."

"It wasn't that bad," Christy said. "You were able to show a kinder, gentler Jeremy Jeremy tonight, honey."

"By the end of the week, I'll be the male Oprah. But that's not what brings in the radio audience. If they want Oprah, they'll turn on the TV. I don't know why I let Ronnie talk me into these things."

"Well, Ronnie did get us a free week here. That's not so bad."

"I'm grateful, but not enough to have to share the Paleface Suite with him. If all my plotting had worked out right, you and I would be sharing screams with the Screaming Buffalo about now."

"Come on, Jerry, perk up. I've got an idea I think you'll like." Christy took my hand in hers and pulled me toward the horse corral. And I was just beginning to walk without smarting.

THE desert by moonlight. Even though I was getting chapped around the chaps, I had to admit that a nighttime ride in the great wide open was pretty high on the scale romance-wise. Christy had pulled me over to the corral after the show since it looked like Mom was staying in tonight.

The nags knew the way, following the path down the dry creek bed we had come through on the guided tour earlier. And doing without the tour guides was just fine with me. Deke and Slim called it Dutchman's Creek. The two cowpokes struck me as the Laurel and Hardy of the west. Only without the comedy.

When Christy and I reached a cottonwood stand we had passed earlier in the day, Christy pulled up. A natural spring fed a pool of cool, dark water shadowed from too much moonlight by the trees.

"This is great," I said. "Let's have a picnic?"

"Sorry, Jerry, but I forgot to pack the food."

"I wasn't really talking about food?"

"Well, I'm talking about going for a swim," Christy said.

"But I forgot to pack my swim trunks."

"And I really wasn't talking about clothes."

"Now, that's more like it!"

Christy swung a leg over the saddle and slid off Buttermilk like she'd been riding all her life which I think she had. I couldn't quite match her style, having to get down more gingerly. The only ponies I had grown up around were out at the track on the days dad decided to skip taking me to little league. Looking back, I'm sure that knowing how to bet a trifecta has come in a lot handier than learning to swing at an outside curve ball.

Christy and I stripped off our duds scattering them over and around the boulders, playing a little hide and seek by the light of the moon. Ducking behind a big chunk of red granite, Christy spotted something sparkling in the moonlight. It was a silver arrowhead that practically glowed when the moon hit it. Probably left by some medicine man skinny-dipping here way back when, but it was our keepsake now.

We played a grown up version of tag splashing into water which was as cold against our sunburned bods as an Arctic breeze. We frolicked in the shallows for a while, stopping every now and then to share a little body heat. It didn't take long even with the warm-ups to start to chill a bit though—gooseflesh and shivering and all that kind of stuff.

"If we get deeper in, we'll be warmer," Christy said, wading in up to her chin.

"Seems like it should be the other way around," I said as she faded into the darkness of the water. The overhanging trees and a couple of transient clouds cast inky shadows over the deep end, but I could just make out Christy's white form floating ahead of me. She was just beyond my reach, waiting for me to catch up. I knew there would be some real body heat generated when I did.

"Jeez, babe, you really are cold," I said, moving in for the good stuff.

"Jerry, what are you talking about? I'm over here. Where

are you?"

Uh-oh.

"Christy? If you're over there, who am I holding over here?"

Seems like you can never find a match when you need one. Even though I was treading water I felt my pockets for one until I realized I didn't have any pockets either. I was hoping for a swarm of fireflies when old man moon found a hole in the clouds. And after the black of night, the moon now lit up the place like it was high noon. Light enough anyway to make me wish I hadn't wished for more light.

A wide, pale torso floated in front of my eyes, kind of roundish with her hair spreading gently out in the water. She was face down, but I didn't need to see her face. Even by moonlight I could recognize that brassy red hair. Not to mention that less than an hour ago she was sitting just across the table from me.

"You'd better get your clothes on, babe," I said not able to look away from Mrs. Edelbaum. "Turns out we're not alone here. We may be a million miles from San Francisco Bay, but nonetheless, I think we've found a floater."

"Oh God, Jerry. You mean...."

"Yes, I'm afraid so. We got to stop meeting dead bodies like this."

Just for drill, I figured we should whip a little CPR on the old girl in case there was a spark of life left in her. I took one of her cold arms for balance and tried to pull her up by the hair.

"Jeez, I think she's been scalped!" I froze, holding a tangles mass of bloody hair in my hand.

"It's her wig, Jerry." Christy bobbed up next to me. And believe me watching Christy bobbing usually would take my mind off anything, let alone Bev Edelbaum, but it didn't seem to be working now. Christy said, "You must have known that red hair couldn't have been real."

"Sure, sure," I said. I could see now that Bev had short silvery hair, except for a dark spot about the size of my palm— not very brassy, but definitely blood red. I looked at Christy standing nipple-deep near me and said, "Let's try to float her over to shore, near the horses. I think we can skip the CPR though."

With Christy pulling on one of her arms and me on the other, we steered and swam and pulled Bev to the far side of the pool. Floating in the water she moved easily, but getting her up the rocky bank was a bitch.

"My god, Jerry...she must weight three hundred pounds."

"She's certainly dead weight."

"Jerry!"

"Oh, sorry...I wasn't thinking."

Resting her on the high bank, Christy and I walked a few steps away before flopping down to catch our breaths. Two naked people sitting on some pretty uncomfortable rocks and sand. I thought I felt a cactus down there too, but I was too blown out to move.

God, Christy was beautiful. Too bad Mrs. Edelbaum had gotten to the ol' swimming' hole before us. Too bad for Mrs. Edelbaum, too.

After resting a minute, we started gathering up our clothes. They were still there anyway, so with some reluctance we got dressed. Sometimes it's just one damn' thing after another.

Things being what they were—a murder and all—I figured I'd better use my cell to call the Paleface Suite. Out in the middle of nowhere and I still had three bars of good reception. Native Americans must be big on iPhones. Anyway, I wanted to get Ronnie on the blower to see if he had any ideas on how we could make some hay before the sun did shine on this murder. As it turned out he might have, but all I got was his voice mail. And leaving a message wasn't the idea I wanted. It looked like I was all on my own this time. Well, actually me and Christy, but I wasn't sure she appreciated the media possibilities. After some mental wrangling, I came up with a plan of action.

While I was formulating the plan, Christy called her mom to check in and reassure her it was only a murder, not an elopement. Meanwhile I looked up Dale Andersen's home number.

"Hi, Mrs. Andersen? Betty? I hope I didn't wake you...I need to speak with Dale right away.... Me? I'm Jerry Jeremy, the seven to ten show? Must be a bad connection, you not recognizing my voice and all...." Seems I had woken up Betty and the kids—must be they don't stay up for Leno—but finally she got Dale to pick up.

"Hey, Dale, get ready to print up new rate cards, the Talk of the West is about to have the Scoop of the West."

"What? Jerry, have you been drinking?"

"No, I'm just high on death. I've stumbled across a murder out here in the high desert. And it's all mine, I'm right here with the body."

"Jerry, steady yourself, man. Are you okay?" Dale seemed

a little disturbed by the news. I hoped he was all right, but he asked me first.

"Sure, I'm fine. I admit I was a little nervous about the scalping, but there wasn't any reason to be as it turned out."

"Just stay calm, boy.... Is Dakota there with you? Is she all right?"

"Dakota? No need to worry about her. She's not going to let it out. As a matter of fact, I'm pretty sure she's probably all tied up right now. At least handcuffed by now."

"Listen, Jerry, the station will stand by you, but we don't want anybody else getting hurt. Where are you right now?"

"Down by the creek a mile or so from the hotel. The creek bed turns here making a deep pool. We pulled the body out of the pool though, so she's drying off now."

"She? But not Dakota? Jerry, listen...it's not that girl you brought up there?"

"Christy? Not on your life, I wouldn't be this calm if it was her. As a matter of fact, Christy's right here. She's in on this with me."

"Christy's in on it with you?"

"Don't worry, Dale. I'll make sure she doesn't let anything slip. After all, for a lot of people, murder is a once in a lifetime thing."

"Sure, Jerry. Uh...there wasn't anything sexual about the murder was there."

"Well, not since I got to her, but I doubt it anyway. She didn't look the type."

"Good. But you don't really know the victim, do you? You just got there yesterday."

"Yeah, but I'm a fast worker. She was a guest on tonight's show—Mrs. Beverly Edelbaum, the art patron."

"A guest! My god, Jerry."

"Well, you did hear the show didn't you?"

"Uh, sorry, Jerry. My wife's mother's birthday. But I'll listen to the sound checks first thing. You just stay calm. Believe me, help is on the way. Betty called on the other phone. Just don't put up any kind of a fuss when they get there."

So after one or two more pleasantries I finally got Dale off the phone. For a radio exec he seemed kind of namby-pamby, letting a murder throw him like that. I doubted Mrs. Edelbaum was even a steady listener.

Christy and I sat with our backs to Mrs. Edelbaum and looked out at the moonlit desert. Someplace out there was the

ranch, but all we could see was barren land spotted with the
occasional tumbleweed. The desert stretched as far as we
could see which in spite of old man moon wasn't very far. We
huddled together for warmth and security while on some
unseen ridge a coyote howled causing the horses to shuffle
nervously. Christy and I huddled closer.

Christy was snoring lightly in my arms and only the chill of
the desert at two a.m. kept me from drifting off. Even under
the circumstances, the smell of Christy's hair and the warmth
of her—

"Freeze, motherfucker!"

Blinding light exploded around us. Christy screamed,
waking up to the nightmare.

"Don't move, asshole!"

"Hands above your head!"

Shouting came from all directions, khaki arms and legs
pulled us apart. I was suddenly face down in the dirt, my
hands cuffed behind my back.

"Don't move...cocksucker!" He probably meant me, but
nonetheless I tried to see what was happening to Christy and
got my face jammed back in the dirt for my trouble. "I said
don't move!"

Who were these guys? Indians? Mexicans? Bev's killers?

"Speak English? ¿Habla ingles? You have the right to
remain silent—" It dawned on me that it probably wasn't
Indians. "You have right to have a lawyer present..."

"Okay, you guys, slow it on down now," a deep voice
rumbled through the havoc. "The gal says they're together.
Circle-K dude ranch. She says he's on the radio, some kind of
deejay."

"Talk show...talk show host," I spit the dirt out of my
mouth. "Jeremy Jeremy...law and order talk show...."

"Take his cuffs off and get him on his feet if you ain't broke
any bones on him."

Pulled to my feet, I found myself staring into the steely
gray eyes of the Marlboro man. Slightly older now, his long
hair and walrus mustache turning white, but he looked like he
could still step out of the west and onto a magazine cover. But
maybe lose the mustache first.

"I'm Sheriff Darrell Lee Redhawk," the Marlboro man said.
"You do any podcasting? Ya' know, streaming audio or
something? I can't pick up the Tucson stations for shit out
here."

"Podcast— Sure, I'm almost positive I do that. Computers

and all that stuff. Sure, the Internet. I'm sure I do."

Christy stepped over and slipped her arm around me. That made me feel a lot better. That and an idea that was starting to float around in my head. The Marlboro man had a voice made for the airwaves. He made Sam Elliott sound like a teenager. If I could talk him into coming on the show, and with Rondini to supply some brain-power, this story could go national. Shades of KPMT San Francisco, only this time I wouldn't get canned—though I might be moving up and moving out after the networks got a load of me.

By now, Dale probably had the entire news crew in the KICK van heading my way with board ops, engineers, producers and God knows what all. Not that the Talk of the West really had more than four or five staff they could send here and still stay on the air. But after all, Bronco Billy was sure to get more than his money's worth with his name right up there next to the killer's.

For now though, Darrell Lee seemed to be doing the talking, "...so this head man from the radio station had his wife call down here telling everyone that you might just be a homicidal maniac." He gave me a squinty look that made me wonder if he didn't still believe it. He added, "If she's really your boss's ol' lady though, you probably want to start working on your resume."

"Hey, I'm not afraid of that. The message probably just got lost in translation. I've got the inside track on this murder. He can't fire me until I solve it...er, until it's solved, that is."

Redhawk aimed a stream of tobacco juice just south of my shoes.

"That's right," he said, "remember 'until it's solved'. And the solving will be done by the Cochise County Sheriff's office, not some tenderfoot from Tucson."

"Don't worry, Chief. I'm not really from Tucson."

"The onlyest thing I'm worried about is that body over there—" Mrs. Edelbaum was lit up like a movie set and surrounded by people in paper clothes "—that and the county elections coming up."

"Of course, Sheriff Redhawk," Christy said. "Jerry and I will give you our complete cooperation."

"I know you will, ma'am." Darrell Lee gave me another look, but this time his face crinkled into what passed for a smile. "Tell me a little more about that show of yours, Jeremy. You ever do anything on politics?"

Chapter 8.

A BRIGHT light burned though the wet towel cooling my face as I surfaced from a drowsy nap in the sun. People were laughing, the pool was splashing, music played from somewhere and the ringing in my ears was slowly fading. I was lying out by the Circle-K pool, catching some rays and some much needed zzz's, Christy and I having been up all night, for the most part at the Cochise County Sheriff's office in downtown Bisbee. While we re-charged poolside, Satyra would wake us enough every now and then to turn over. That way we'd burn evenly on all sides.

The hot weather had pretty well filled up the pool and its surrounding patio with guests opting to skip more strenuous activities like prodding the saddle ponies across the desert. I wondered if our midnight swimming hole was now a big attraction on the horse tour or if they detour around it entirely.

Among the well-toned and well-tanned folks catching rays by the pool a middle-aged couple caught my eye, maybe because they stood out a bit. The gent was heavy-set, wore a large gold Rolex and had a farmer's tan (golfer's tan?) that left his chest and shoulders white while his arms and face were the color of toast. A lady fluttering around beside him had a sixties' bouffant of platinum blonde and looked to have spent a little too much time in the tanning bed, her bounteous chest and her shoulders having acquired a walnut sheen. I would have thought Little Italy or Las Vegas or both would have been more their speed.

To my left, a nicely bikini'd Christy was quietly snoring and to my right, Satyra, also showing miles of skin and deftly balancing an iPad on her perfect belly, surfed the web single handedly. That is, with just one hand, the other being used to hold a tall drink that looked as delicious as she did. My mouth felt like it had just hiked across the Mohave Desert, so I decided to order a cool one too. But before the thought could make it to my tongue, I was back in dreamland.

Christy and I had agreed to visit the county hoosegow last night to make our statements instead of waiting until morning. Strike while the corpse is hot, you might say. Sheriff Darrell Lee Redhawk led the questioning and a perky lady deputy they called Lou, apparently short for Louise, copied it all down and typed it up. When I got to the part about skinny dipping with Christy, a few of the male deputies looked at me with a new respect. Deputy Lou gave me a look too, but I wasn't too sure about the respect part. Probably some kind of an environmentalist, not wanting the pristine waters hereabouts to be fouled with anything more than the occasional dead body.

Anyway, they taped and typed what we said, we swore and signed the papers, and Darrell Lee witnessed and filed them away. Then we got down to brass tacks; Redhawk would be my main guest on this evening's show.

By the time we got back to the ranch it was already mid-morning and I was feeling like I was back to doing overnights. The sun was shining though and Satyra had already staked out a spot at the pool. Back at the Screaming Buffalo, Mrs. M was having a late breakfast, watching the shopping channel. Christy and I agreed to change and meet out by the pool. On the way back to my room, I bumped into Sherman raking the gravel. I asked whether anybody else from the station had shown up yet, but Sherm said he hadn't seen anyone. He did volunteer that Dakota had gone over to the ghost town though, setting up for her broadcast at the Silver Cage Saloon.

I figured I should call Dale Andersen and see what the game plan was, but I had to get some rest first. Also I needed to get Ronnie's take on the murder—when it comes to wringing every last drop of publicity out of something, he's my man. I was also thinking The Great One might be able to come up with a theory about the murder. He's good at that kind of thing, having the mind of a born criminal.

Anyway, by the time I got to the Paleface Suite, it was empty. A few of Ronnie's things were scattered around, but it didn't look like his bed was slept in. Anyway I was too tired to care since I hadn't got any use out of my bunk either. An early day for the housekeeper.

I found a pair of snappy swimming trunks—aqua with yellow fishies—and a Tommy Bahama aloha shirt into which I slipped. Flip-flops and a towel completed my ensemble. For some reason I felt more at home in my poolside gear than wearing cowboy boots and a ten-gallon hat. So far the best part of dude ranching had been the skinny dipping. Until Mrs. Edelbaum floated by, that is.

My old buddy Sherm was back on duty when I called the front desk. I asked if anyone there might know where Ronnie was, but Sherman reminded me it had only been twenty minutes since I asked him the last time. To cheer me up, he ran the old gag by me about the magician doing a disappearing act. With material like that, I hoped he wasn't working for tips. I gave him one anyway—not to give up his day job. So much for career advice, I still needed to find Ronnie if I was to do *my* career any good.

Christy and I bumped into each other on the path to the ranch's big pool. In her bikini, she was only a couple of polka-dots shy of skinny dipping again. When we reached the pool, I spotted the magician's assistant wowing the crowd just by lying in the sun. Ronnie probably figured this would build up the turnout for his show. If the wives didn't put a stop to it.

"Hey, Satyra, have you seen Rondini around here today?"

"Hey, Jerry, how are you guys doing? The boys here been holding a couple of lounge chairs for you." The boys being a couple of college drop-outs working as pool boy-cum-ranch hands. They were intently massaging suntan lotion over Satyra's back and shoulders. "I haven't seen Ronnie since his last bow yesterday evening. You know those magicians, Jerry, always pulling their famous disappearing act on you."

"Hey, guys," I said to the pool boys, "how 'bout taking a break while she still has some skin left. Don't worry, I'll take care of the rest myself." Christy landed an elbow in my ribs while I greased the kids for oiling up Satyra. More than likely they would have paid me to let them keep at it if I hadn't sent them off to round up some *venti*-sized iced lattes. I told them they could work on her later if they promised to stay below her knees.

With Satyra pretty well oiled, Christy turned up the heat by rubbing me down with sun screen and I returned the favor. Stretched out with a floppy hat covering her face, Christy was out almost at once.

"Poor girl, last night must have worn her out," I said.

"I noticed she didn't sleep in her own bed," Satyra said.

"No, she was with me. But it wasn't what you might think; we weren't having fun. How did you know she didn't sleep in her own bed anyway? Are you keeping tabs on us?"

"Down, boy, down," Satyra rolled onto her side causing a wonderful shifting of body parts. "I know that simply because I slept in her bed last night."

"What?"

"Yeah. Your radio colleague Dakota brought Ronnie back to our bungalow so I needed to find a new space. They said it was just for a nightcap, but I didn't want to see what that might lead to. After all, I have to work with the guy."

"Believe me, you didn't miss anything. Take it from me, Ronnie and I were in gym together back in school, so I should know. Not that I'm trying to run the boy down. I imagine Dakota has done that by now. Anyway, I thought it was Ronnie that had the power to cloud men's minds, not Dakota."

"Maybe she took a course online. 'Look deeply into my boob tube.'"

"You probably got the first half right," I said. "Not to change the subject, but how did you wind up in Christy's room?"

"I ran into Sassie up by the spa. She was with Rex Bowman. They were just coming back from his show at the gallery. I guess he was actually going to walk your future mother-in-law to her door, but he made some excuse to take off when I showed up. Up until then I thought they looked pretty damn' cozy."

"Bowman, huh? I thought he already had a patron here. Unless somehow he knew Mrs. Edelbaum wouldn't be around for any more portraits."

By now the pool was swimming past my eyes for lack of sleep. Satyra said she was going to go splash around with the pool boys and I arranged a couple of towels over my fair skin and went to greet the sandman.

I WAS half asleep, dreaming about skinny-dipping with Christy. And in my dream, Satyra was doing a backstroke around us. But then I realized it wasn't Satyra after all, it was a chubby woman in a red wig. The three of us were riding through the high plateau and Deke Rowen, the ranch's dude wrangler, was with us. We all had on big cowboy hats and shirts with so much piping and fringe they would shame Roy Rodgers. We were all riding ponies about the size of Delaware. Except for Rowen, he wore a black leather jacket and was riding a Harley.

I seemed pretty much at home on horseback, at least

compared to my waking state. I even felt I could brush up against Christy and put some moves on her like we were in an equestrian version of a Chevy backseat. I leaned toward her and she leaned toward me, I puckered up and she puckered back—

A pounding splash left me gasping for air, the ponies had vanished, my planned smooch disappeared, and water was all over the place. One of the urban cowboys had cannonballed off the high board, drenching us and a number of other sunbathers nearby. Satyra was shaking the water off her tablet and mumbling words under her breath that I dare not repeat. I rubbed my eyes and looked around blinded by the light. Kids of all ages were playing in the water, Christy was stretching herself awake after the deluge, Satyra had waived down a pool boy for more drinks while various and sundry guests were scattered about slowly broiling. Gene Autry or Tex Ritter music was spilling out of speakers hidden someplace in the sagebrush. All in all, things seemed to be shaping up okay—we had cowboys serenading us, beautiful women in bikinis, hot sun beating down and a pool close at hand. And we had a murder just to keep things interesting.

Finding Beverly Edelbaum's body already seemed a long way off. It was more like a dream than the sight of Deke Rowen on two wheels. If I was going to make the murder investigation the centerpiece of my show, and I was—

"—coming to you direct from the murder site at the Circle-K Guest Ranch here in our li'l ol' ghost town of Kirby, Arizona." Dakota's not so dulcet tones poured out of the speakers.

"What the—where's Tex Ritter! And what's all this stuff about murder sites? I'm the guy that got cavity searched last night." Unless she was teasing my show for this evening, Darrell Lee might need to haul me in for real after I got through with Dakota.

"Today my special guest is going to discuss the violent, sexually charged Dude Ranch Murder with us. He is a world-renowned mentalist and illusionist who solved San Francisco's famous Radio Murder case. Here is The Great Rondini!"

WTF?

I looked at Christy, she looked at me, we looked at Satyra, and she looked guilty for Ronnie's sake.

"Thank you, Dakota. You're too kind," the turncoat said. "I'm glad to be here. I hope folks who have a chance to come *on out to Kirby's ghost town—scene of this latest crime—will remember to stay for my evening show at the Silver Cage Saloon. If you mention you heard it on Dakota's radio program, you'll get twenty percent off the cover charge."*

What the fuck!

"I hate to bring this up, Ron honey, but my sources tell me that one of KICK's own minor air personalities may have played a role in this case while undertaking some bizarre sexual behavior. I understand you've actually had a few run-ins with this individual as well...."

"Minor? What's she mean 'minor'?" I fumed. "Come on, Ronnie, straighten her out."

Instead my XBFF was saying, *"...that guy Jeremy's always had a wild streak. Why back in school, I remember once at the homecoming dance..."*

"Jerry, you hardly ever take me dancing," Christy pouted.

"Probably 'cause nobody does 'the robot' anymore," Satyra said to smooth things over.

"So running around naked is a regular thing for him?" Dakota asked in front of the whole listening audience. I could only hope my listeners had more class than to tune in to her blathering.

"Well, I didn't really know the boy had kept it up. No pun intended."

"Whadda they mean? Skinny-dipping is as American as apple pie," I said. "Didn't Tom Sawyer take little Becky Thatcher skinny-dipping?"

"I think that was Huckleberry Finn," Satyra answered.

Meanwhile Christy was trying to get the conversation back on track. "Please, don't go around telling everyone that I was skinny-dipping with you last night."

"No, I won't mention it, but everyone seems to know already," I said and then to Satyra, "Huck Finn took Becky skinny-dipping?"

"No, Tom and Huck. Adolescent boys experimenting. You know, didn't you ever experiment at that age?"

"Sure, but I was all alone. Talk about being scared the first time."

From the speakers we could hear Ronnie describing the scene of the crime even though the phony had never laid eyes on it. *"...Jerry Dwayne Jeremy, talk show host rides down to a wide spot in the creek. He tells his companion that it's dark enough her modesty won't be offended. Knowing Jerry I would be surprised if that wasn't a flashlight in his pocket though. He lures this innocent, young thing into the deep end of the pool for some strange goings-on and.... Well, I just hope they didn't scare the fish!"*

"That was no worm he was fishing with," Dakota said.

"I can't believe Ronnie would drag you—us—into it," Christy said. "I can't even believe your middle name is Dwayne."

"It's not, but it makes for a better story. You'd be surprised how many people with Dwayne for a middle name turn out to be homicidal maniacs. It's on TV all the time."

"And what kind of strange goings-on is he talking about anyway?"

"Probably Dakota had the boy roped and tied to the bedpost last night."

"But The Great Rondini can escape from any knot known to mankind," Satyra said. "Or womankind for that matter."

"Only if he wants to."

The phony.

Chapter 9.

So Dakota Holiday managed to outflank me on my own murder. Even Ronnie hadn't known about it last night since I didn't leave him a message or have to call him for bail money. While it might have made the news someplace online, I didn't think it would have surfaced with my name attached yet. Anyway Dakota wouldn't have done that much research and I'm pretty sure Ronnie only surfs the web for porn.

Only one person could have tipped Dakota off about what happened. I hit the speed dial on my cell for Dale Andersen, KICK's misguided program director back in Tucson.

"I really have to apologize, Jerry," Dale said after I unloaded on him. "I didn't understand the situation when you called last night. I thought you had been arrested. I was planning to rustle up some old air checks to play in your time slot, you being in the slammer and all."

"I guess you didn't bother to try rustling up a lawyer for me, my being in the slammer and all."

"Oh, I promise the station would stand by you as far as possible. But if you were behind bars, it seemed like Dakota would be the logical choice, blah, blah, blah..."

How did this guy ever get to be a PD? He's gotta be one of Bronco Billy's illegitimate offspring.

"Listen, Dale, we all make mistakes, even program directors," who can't keep their traps shut, "but that's all water under the bridge. What I'm wondering is when you're gonna send in the troops? We could use a news team here and some engineering support, maybe the KICK mobile van to do some remotes from crime-side. We don't have a mobile four-wheel drive, do we?"

"Well, Jerry, you know we're not like those big city stations. No extra cash for OT or anything, probably not even gas money. I think this is going to be up to you and Dakota to cover. Maybe you can guest on her show. You know, she can interview you about finding the body."

You bet she will. *Not!*

Once I heard Dale missing the point I tuned out and wrapped up the call as fast as it's humanly possible to when talking to your boss. All in all, he was pretty nice on the phone, maybe still thinking I was the villain and that I might be wanting to up the body count.

REMEMBER those pals of mine that were always hanging around the nineteenth hole back at the Canyon Country Club?

Ben Hyland and Ollie Something-or-Other were hooked up at KOW-TV. I was pretty sure they did more than just push brooms over there since the country club was pretty pricey and they seemed to have nicely-sized expense accounts. A nicely-sized slice of the old KOW-pie one might say.

Anyway I had them in my contact list, so I gave them each a call. No answer since they were probably still out on the back nine, but I left each guy a nice voice mail in my sweetest radio baritone. With any kind of luck, KOW would have a network feed and want to work with me on the story. Maybe they'd pass it to CNN or Fox.

Either way, I was sure they'd get a camera crew out here to cover the murder. They could probably get some advertising tie-ins, like mortuaries or life insurance, to cover travel expenses. I could do the talking while Christy supplied the sex appeal. The main thing I needed now was a hook to hang my pitch on. And suddenly it hit me—this murder was in a ghost town or at least near one. And now, there was a new ghost in town.

The beginning of an idea began to rattle around in my head.

"LADIES and gentlemen, yesterday evening a wonderful woman was sitting across the microphone from me. Beverly Edelbaum. She was a patron of the arts, having brought her good friend, the artist Rex Bowman—"

Mr. Edelbaum coughed up a loogie at this point. *"Sorry, I haven't been feeling so good lately,"* he explained. *"I've been down with food poisoning or something."*

"No problem, Bruce. Ladies and gentlemen, that was the late Bev Edelbaum's husband, Bruce. As I was saying, if you're feeling up to it, Mr. Edelbaum, we have the famous

western artist Rex Bowman here. Rex was close to Mrs. Edelbaum. As a matter of fact, she brought Rex to my attention yesterday. He currently has a one-man show running here at the Kirby Gallery right near the wonderful Circle-K Ranch where we are broadcasting from—drop on by to see the show, no admission charge—and as I said before, Bev liked to patronize the arts...."

I was afraid Bruce Edelbaum would start gagging again so I moved on to Christy's intro and then had Sherman Huntley say a few words about what a great guest Beverly had been during the two days she had enjoyed the Circle-K's hospitality before getting herself bumped off. Trying to nail the employee-of-the-month vote, Sherm went on to say that her death of course had nothing to do with the ranch or its activities, probably just a passing serial killer, probably a one-in-a-million chance of ever happening to a guest again.

"You got more chance of dying from the food," Bruce muttered while I cut Sherm off before he launched into another commercial.

"Speaking of dying, we'll continue our tribute to the murdered woman in a moment, but first I want to take this chance to let our listeners know that our magician friend, The Great Rondini, is appearing here nightly at the Silver Cage Saloon in the Kirby ghost town. And speaking of ghosts, the star attraction in Rondini's act, The Astounding Satyra will be on my show later in the week, using her gift of spiritual unity to channel the spirit of Beverly Edelbaum. With luck, Bev's ghost will provide an eye-witness account of her very own murder. How, when, where and why. And, oh yeah, who."

This gag had almost worked back in San Francisco when Ronnie and I used a so-called clairvoyant named Madame Zoroaster to corner the killer of Christy's dad. If it almost worked then, it might almost work now. We just needed to get the usual suspects together and stir the pot until somebody breaks. I've seen it done in a million movies.

My guests and I were huddled around a corner table in the Circle-K's dimly lit cocktail lounge *cum* coffee shop with the portable KICK rig connected up to the wifi while a handful of dude ranchers hung around checking us out. One young couple in particular seemed to be fascinated by the show although they did manage to turn their attention back to one another every few minutes; their shy smiles and their lingering eye contact pretty much pegged them as newly hitched. The lucky stiffs, no mother-in-law to bust up their fun yet. Anyway, I couldn't wait to get Christy all to myself later.

After I teased the DIY séance, I broke the news that Christy and I were near-witnesses to the brutal murder and we burned some show time describing how we found the body.

"Just out for a midnight ride...."

"No thought of swimming...."

"...didn't even bring our suits."

"No indeed...."

Somehow we never got around to how we got naked, not wanting to pander to the lower instincts of our listeners. Not like Dakota and Rondini. I don't do that. Not when it's about me. Not if I hoped to get a repeat with Christy anyway.

Since Mr. Edelbaum and Rex Bowman were along for the ride, I hoped they could add a little color and help fill air time until Sheriff Redhawk showed up—with, I was also hoping, something new about the investigation. Redhawk was running late though and the minutes remaining before the show wrapped at ten o'clock were rapidly disappearing.

I hadn't heard back from my country club pals either. With any luck at all, the TV crew from KOW might actually show up before we solved the case. I didn't see how they could let a chance like this slide by.

*"S*ORRY *about bein' late, but we had to run a traffic break over to Sierra Vista. Farm truck spilled a load of horse manure."*

"Well, Sheriff Redhawk, it sounds like you've had your hands full. Mind if we don't shake?" Darrell Lee Redhawk, Cochise County Sheriff, up for re-election and up to his neck in murder and manure, had finally showed. Like Ronnie and Bowman and even Sherm Huntley, the good sheriff was here on a mission. He had a gig to plug.

"Sheriff Redhawk, Christy and I have just been telling our listeners about how we found Beverly Edelbaum floating in Dutchman's Creek last night. Bruce Edelbaum, her husband, has described to us what a wonderful wife she was—" More hacking from the bereaved interrupted my spiel. *"—and how she helped Mr. Bowman here with his career and all."*

Edelbaum gave Bowman the evil eye about then. Paint that, you scumbag!

"Yessir," said the lawman, *"she had a hubby and a hobby, looks like."*

This got Bowman going. He wanted everyone to know that he was a well-established artist long before meeting Bev, although she was a great friend and provided encouragement when he was blue, brought him up when he was down, probably picked out his clothes and well, you can guess the rest. He got in another plug for the one-man show and a mention that he and Bev helped Forbes-Collier, the gallery owner, obtain a precious Max Leibergard painting for the Gene Autry Museum in downtown Phoenix last year and that the gallery had another Leibergard ready for sale.

"He should be hanging someplace too. By the neck," Edelbaum muttered. I thought I might just try to stir this particular pot a little more. Listeners love a good knock-down, drag-out on the air, but Darrell Lee must have thought he was here to keep the peace.

"The only hanging going on around here will be after somebody gets hisself arrested and has a fair trial," the sheriff announced. "Then we'll hang the varmint. That's a promise Mr. Edelbaum. Direct from me to you."

Well, that killed that. Good time for a commercial. One that was actually paid for, for a change.

"You heard it here first, right on KICK, The Talk of the West. We'll be right back after these words...."

Back in Tucson, the board op switched in my pre-recorded "live" commercial for Bronco Billy's pre-owned jalopies, while I introduced the Sheriff to Edelbaum and Bowman. Off the air, the lawman expressed his sympathies at Bev's death, showing a warm and caring side I hadn't noticed in the interrogation room. When we came back, I planned on giving Darrell Lee my own version of the third-degree. We only had twenty minutes left and that included another break; I was a little sore about him putting a pile of manure ahead of my show.

"VAMPIRES...?"

"That ain't what I said," Darrell Lee said. Talk about dealing with a shit storm!

"I'm not trying to put words in your mouth," I said, "but...."

"I said 'twas like a vampire had swooped down and sucked the blood out of her—not that one actually did. The victim lost a great deal of blood per the M.E., that's all."

I didn't know much about the politics hereabouts, but I'd have bet that Darrell Lee wasn't doing himself all that much good vamping vampires on the campaign trail. Not unless he could wind the case up by pounding a stake through somebody's heart. I hoped it wouldn't be mine. Meanwhile he was trying to recover the fumble, *"All we know is what the autopsy shows, what the coroner found, that her jugular vein had been torn open and pretty much all the blood had been drained out of her."*

"Like a vampire, like you said."

Oh, mama! What an angle!

I could just see the headlines "Sheriff Claims Dead Woman Killed By Vampires". And that's not even the *Weekly World News*. This case would make me famous. San-FRAN-cis-co, open your Golden Gate!

Meanwhile, Redhawk was busy digging himself into a deeper hole, talking now about cults and visiting psychopaths. But until I discovered the real killer, this baby had vampire written all over it. Wait until Ronnie hears about this.

Oh, I forgot. We're not talking. The traitor.

Maybe Dakota was just a passing fancy. Do Dakota, do her show? Something like that probably. After all, Ronnie was always a gentleman when it came to his best interests. I'd see whose bed he'd sleep in tonight.

"Drained of blood, eh? The medical boys think it might be a vampire then?" I wasn't going to let this get away. *"And here I thought The Great Rondini was the only bloodsucker around here. Or words to that effect ...."*

Chapter 10.

THE Paleface Suite was staged for romance. The cozy, little bungalow wasn't a bad setup if you doused the lights and chilled the champagne by candlelight. Chill the champaign on ice, that is, and the candlelight for...ah, light. It was still a little warm for a fire, but maxing out the AC fixed that. I had showered and shaved after my show and was pacing around with anticipation, waiting for Christy.

Her plan was to put Mom to bed and then beat it over here for some red-hot lovin'. How long had it been since we'd been alone together? I don't know, but too damn' long anyway. Tonight would be the night.

About then I heard he door opening and was I ready—

"This all for me, Junior? I didn't know you cared."

"Ronnie? What the hell are you doing here?"

"Don't you remember? I bunk here," he said looking around at the bubbly, the candles, the fire. "Say isn't it a little cold in here? Let me turn down the air a little. Mechanics was never your strong suite."

"I thought you were 'bunking' over in the Turncoat Bungalow with the radio slut."

"Easy now, boy. I never made fun of your girlfriends. Take that one with the buck teeth back in Little Rock, I never said a thing."

"She told me it was from sucking, ah, her thumb, you know, as a child. But that's not the point. You sold me down the river."

"No, no, no, I would never do that," he gave me his best little boy smile. "I was just trying to work up some listeners for your big show—the one where you scoop everybody. You found the body, you called the cops, you claimed it was a vampire, right there on the air."

"What do you mean?"

"Well, I'm not too sure how many of your listeners believe in ghouls and goblins."

"It's a political talk show, so probably most of them," I said. "Anyway, how come you're not snuggling up with Dakota tonight? Or has she given me enough publicity?"

"Oh no, the little lady still needs some help from The Great One," Ronnie kicked off his shoes and spread out on one of the beds. "And she's crazy about The Big One too, if I do say so myself."

"You're the only one who would. Anyway, what are you doing lying down? How come you're not back there giving her the old sleight of hand? I got a hot date tonight and I don't want you to get hurt when things start flying."

"Slow down, Jerry," Ronnie began unbuttoning. "Just pretend I'm not here. Unfortunately, Dakota has an overnight guest. Sounded like maybe an old relative and unless Satyra can lure him into the hay loft, I'm here for the night."

"You can't be here tonight. This is the first chance I've had to get Christy alone in weeks."

"Not true, not true. You had the chance last night and what did you do with it? Tried to steal poor little Dakota's thunder by turning up a dead body—and vampires to boot."

"Steal Dakota's thunder? The only body I wanted to see last night was Christy's. Mrs. Edelbaum found us, we didn't find her."

"As I heard it," Ronnie folded the pillow around his fat head, "you two had your clothes off and let Mrs. Edelbaum distract you from the plan. You could have waited twenty minutes before calling the cops. Bev Edelbaum wasn't going anywhere."

"No, but I couldn't do it with her watching us."

WITH Rondini all settled in for the night, I killed the AC, turned up the fire and waited for Christy outside with the chilled wine bottle against my forehead. When she appeared she looked like a sexy angel as she tiptoed past the Manzanita bush edging the bungalow. Low-cut, diaphanous, split up to here, blonde curls tousling around her lovely neck....

"Guess what, Jerry, I just bumped into Satyra and apparently she got ousted again by Ms. Holiday." Luscious red lips, eyes like moonlit pools. "Only—get this—this time it wasn't The Great Rondini shacking up with her."

"Tell me about it."

"Oh, so that's why you're standing out here?"

I allowed as how it could be, but that it wouldn't be a problem as soon as I went in and killed Ronnie.

"Oh don't worry about that lovey-dovey stuff, babe. We're here to have a good time. Put down that silly champagne and let's go find Satyra. She said she'd be in the Palomino Lounge."

"Ronnie's mind-reading act must be rubbing off on her; somehow she knew I'd need a stiff drink about now."

Arm-in-arm—not the connection I had envisioned—we strolled up the pathway past the flood-lit swimming pool. Bruce Edelbaum was practicing his belly-flop off the low board to the amusement of a couple of college girls who seemed to be entertained by his bravado. He wasn't showing any sign of having *turista,* or for that matter any grief over Beverly Edelbaum. Maybe the cheering girls figured he'd come into money.

In the lobby of the hacienda, Sherm waved me down. Either that or he was trying to swat a flock of no-see-ums. At least we couldn't see 'em.

"Mister Jeremy! Mister Jerry Jeremy!" No luck, it wasn't the insects. "Oh paging, Jerry Jeremy!"

I thought at first he might have news of the KOW-TV crew which was still MIA. But no, he had a fistful of pink telephone slips.

"Don't you check your messages?" Sherm sputtered, as pink papers spilled out of his hand, floating onto the desk, some fluttering past to the floor. "Your Circle-K voice mailbox is full and everyone's been calling the desk."

"Calling for me? Who exactly has been calling?"

"The *Arizona Daily Star*, for one. Some TV people. Even cable news. Somebody claiming to be Megyn Kelly, but if that was her, she must have a cold since it sounded more like a man. Anyway I gave him or her a sound bite he or she could use about how the Circle-K does not allow the undead to murder our guests."

Christy said, "Jerry, I think you've turned loose another media monster."

"Not a monster, babe—a vampire. And it may be *desa vu* again, but I think I'm seeing my name back up in lights. TV lights, that is. I'm off and running."

"I'm not sure the owner wants this kind of publicity," Sherm said. "I need to call him at home. I hope it's not too late in New York. I wouldn't want to wake him up."

"New York? What kind of cowboy is he anyway?"

"The rich kind. And the kind that might not want vampires staking out the old corral."

"Well, the idea was to get a crowd out here, wasn't it? Make the Circle-K a household name and all. Kirby, Arizona will be the only ghost town that has a vampire too."

"Jerry, honey," Christy was saying, "don't you think you're taking this a little too far? After all, there really aren't any such things as vampires."

"Sure, people also say all those little green men Art Bell talks about aren't real either. And yet he's been in syndication for years!"

By now Sherm was on the phone and had gotten through to a butler or something. The way he was jabbering on about vampires on the radio I figured Jeeves would probably screen him out and bitch to the people running the Do Not Call list.

Meanwhile, Christy was pulling me away, saying, "...and what about Mr. Edelbaum's feelings, having his wife's memory all cluttered up with ghosts and vampires?"

"Actually, I'd say he was recovering fast from what I saw going on at the pool. And don't forget, someone actually did kill Bev and I'm going to find out who it was."

"But what about all the publicity? No one wants that."

"Hey, you're talking to Jerry 'Just Spell My Name Right' Jeremy. This story is gonna make me the morning lead on CNN. This is my ticket back to San Francisco."

"Jerry, what about mother and me? Are you just going to leave us in the dust? We live—I live—here in Tucson. I'm not moving to San Francisco."

"What about LA?"

THE lounge was seriously chilly. And I don't mean the AC kind either. We pulled Satyra away from a gang of tenderfoot cowboys at the bar to act as referee. Tenderfeet? Tenderfoots? Never mind. Anyway we needed someone to translate Christy's "Tell Jerry that I..." bits and my "Tell Christy that I..." bits.

"What are you guys doing," she asked. "Rehearsing a vaudeville act?"

"Not even. I'm afraid that playing the circuit would require leaving the desert for days at a time."

"Jerry, you're talking about leaving for good."

"There'll always be visits home, once, maybe even two

times a year. You'll be able to talk to Mom on the Internet, they even have video now."

"Oh, no. If I'm coming, so is Mom."

"Hey guys, let's not fight or I'm heading back to my free-spending dude ranchers. Besides, don't we need to make up a plan to catch the bloodsucker? Isn't that what Ronnie would do?"

"That traitor."

My radio equipment was still sitting on the corner table where I did my show and the thought crossed my mind that locking it up in the Jeep might take the wind out of Dakota's sails. She'd have to call her show in on a cell phone. On the other hand, the plan didn't really have deniability, but....

"...the plan," Satyra said, taking the words right out of my mind for the second time that night. Maybe there really is something to that mind-reading stuff.

"Well, sure," Christy was saying, "it would really be easier if we could get Ronnie to help us."

"Ronnie! Why that guy's so two-faced he shaves with his back to the mirror. He's so two-faced he parts his hair on both sides. Why I remember once back in Tampa—well, never mind Tampa. All I know is that Ronnie would be making plans with Dakota right now if her favorite aunt or whoever hadn't dropped in."

"More like her favorite uncle, I'd say," Satyra said.

"What do you mean?"

"I'm not stuck sleeping up at the Kirby Hotel tonight because she's having a pajama party. Dakota's sleepover guest is some old cowpoke...I remember she said something about bucking broncos."

"Broncos? She didn't say Bronco Billy, did she?"

"Oh, yes. Now that I hear it, that was what she said— Bronco Billy. Kind of a silly name." This from somebody named Satyra.

"It may be silly," I said, "but at least he's got a last name— Bronco Billy Wooten, my sponsor. That's his Grand Cherokee I'm driving."

"It sounds like he may be sponsoring somebody else tonight," Christy said. "But maybe that means that Ronnie will be coming back to our side."

"Sure, only if he crawls."

But Ronnie didn't come crawling back. I got to share the bungalow with him, but the relationship the next morning was decidedly on the cool side, neither of us speaking unless spoken to. Which pretty much makes talking impossible. We jockeyed for the shower and the shaving mirror, and both dressed and left at the same time.

I kept up a fast pace walking to beat The Ungrateful One to the breakfast chuck wagon, but I couldn't open any distance between us without running. We arrived poolside in a dead heat, the chuck wagon buffet spread out before us.

"Well, look at that won't you? Who says these boys are feuding? Good to see ya, Jerry!"

There at the big main table was all two-hundred and sixty pounds of cigar-chewing, whiskey-swilling, Dakota-humping Bronco Billy Wooten.

He was flanked by Dakota and Satyra on one side and Christy and her mother on the other. Brunettes on the left and blonds on the right. Sherman Huntley, Amanda Piccard and a swarm of busboys were buzzing around the group, pouring the o.j., serving up the eggs, handing out espressos and whipped creamed lattes.

Billy must be some tipper.

"Sit your skinny behind down here, Red, and get a real cowboy feed. Brunch is the most important meal of the day, next to dinner."

Ronnie sat next to the brunettes and I sided with the blonds, so we faced each other from opposite sides of the table. I had managed to squeeze in between Billy and Christy so that if he put his hand on anybody's knee, it would be mine.

"So I guess you heard me break the big vampire story, Bronco Billy," I said. After all, he pays my salary. I figured I'd better cozy up to him. Not as cozy as Dakota, but I was sure Billy could tell our talents lay in different directions. I was sure he'd already scoped that out last night.

"Hell, yes. I happened to be gabbin' on the blower to my nephew Charlie, back in Frisco." Bronco Billy paused to wipe away a chuckle with his napkin. "He told me I'd better get my ass down here to make sure things didn't get out of hand."

"Honestly, Bronco Billy, I'm sure Jerry's glad to have somebody keep an eye on things," Christy butted in. "For both Jerry and Dakota."

Nice save. No wonder I'm crazy about the girl.

"Harrumph..." Rondini said.

"To tell the truth, Billy, I think this could be great for all of us," I said. "You know between Dakota and me there's six hours of air time—a lot for just one measly vampire attack."

"There was no—" Ronnie started to say, but I kept plowing

ahead.

"Dakota could do the women's angle. You know, the lonely widower, the victim's support of the artist, er, the arts. Maybe some Amanda Piccard recipes, heavy on the garlic."

"I use plenty of garlic," the chef said, running by with a tray of fresh-baked pastries. "Just wait until you taste my garlicky *Frites de Vaqueros*."

"Sure, Jeremy, you're full of ideas for everyone else," Dakota chirped up, taking her tongue out of our sponsor's ear. "But I don't need any help from you. You may have found the body, but I'm going to solve the murder. And I'm not going to be KICK's vampire hunter."

"That's right," Sherman Huntley dropped off a basket of fruit for Billy. "It was some drifter or maybe a passing rock group. You can tell your listeners that, Dakota. That vampire thing is going to scare off our guests. We've already had a cancellation or two, but not enough to sue you over yet."

Sherm gave me his impression of a dirty look, sort of a cross between a smirk and a romantic come-on. At least I hoped it was a dirty look.

Rondini tried out another "harrumph" to ward off any of the undead that might be hanging around the pool. Meanwhile, Bronco Billy was saying, "...this might just be the thing to get us all a little good publicity. Dakota, Jeremy here, the magic show and the dude ranch, not to mention Bronco Billy's Pre-owned Vehicles."

"But, but, but murder and vampires..." Sherm stutter-butted.

"The only bad publicity, they say, is your obituary," Satyra said.

"So is it only bad for Mrs. Edelbaum?" Christy asked.

"Like I said," I said, "this could be great for all of us."

"Here's my idea," Billy said, "I'm thinking of making this the first TV reality show to solve a murder."

"But, Daddy, we're on the radio." This from Dakota. And she didn't really say "Daddy", I just remember it that way somehow.

Chapter 11.

"...Brought to you by Bronco Billy's used trucks and cars. They're pre-owned, pre-washed and pre-dented for you.

"I know all you listeners have been following the tragic and compelling story of Beverly Edelbaum, whose dead body I discovered at great personal risk. Well, risk aside, yours truly, Jerry Jeremy, plans to find the vampire who did this and have a little stakeout of my own. And you'll be right there listening to it on KICK radio and watching it on KOW-TV. Maybe I'll need your help or maybe I won't, but one thing is certain—you'll be right there as it happens."

So it turned out that Bronco Billy was a pretty big spender with KOW-TV too. Big enough to keep those two KOW-boys hanging around him back at the Canyon CC. Enough to get a camera crew, with a producer and director, and a mobile TV van to materialized as if out of thin air right here in downtown Kirby. Definitely one better than Rondini pulling a live boa constrictor out of Satyra's cleavage. Lucky snake.

"Sure, you say, 'Jerry, that's cool and more than interesting,' but who wouldn't want to see a bloodsucking refugee from Night of the Living Dead? But let's kick it up a notch: Dakota Holiday on our afternoon show will be competing with me to see who will be first to—you should pardon the expression—nail the monster. That's right, this is the first radio-TV reality show competition actually trying to solve a murder. What more could you want?

"Well of course, the answer to that is you're probably looking for a high-quality used car, truck or van..."

The way Bronco Billy's idea worked out, Dakota and I would compete to solve the murder. She'd have The Great Rondini on her team while I'd have Christy and Satyra on my team, and what a team that makes. Both Dakota and I would compete for Sheriff Redhawk's help, eye-witnesses accounts and anything else we could jam in. And the main idea was to get a ton of publicity for Bronco Billy's beaters, as well as for the radio and TV stations and just about everybody else. Even the Circle-K signed on when Billy started spreading the moolah around.

Aside from the publicity, there wasn't much of a reward for winning, but that didn't bother me. My plan was to make my name with this gig and maybe get back to the City by the Bay. Maybe there'd be syndication or even a TV show. With luck I could spend my time on a better class of crook, focusing on murderers and gunmen. A big step up from politics.

"About here, wasn't it," Christy asked.

We were riding back down Arroyo Verde the next morning heading for the desert oasis that had proved to be so unhappy for Bev Edelbaum. The only difference now being the klieg lights, the camera equipment, assorted engineers, a director, a producer and Sheriff Redhawk who was keeping to himself off to one side. Christy, Redhawk and I were on horseback while the TV crew was carefully threading around the rocks in a mobile TV van.

We were returning to the scene of the crime, or more precisely the scene of the discovery of the crime, so we could reenact that very scene for the KOW-TV cameras. Minus the nudity, of course. We had kept that to ourselves.

"Sure, this is about right," I said. "Here's the mesquite we tied the horses to."

"Just act natural...do what you did that night...pretend we're not even here," the director, an artsy young guy named Martin Something, said. "You're just two sweethearts out for a moonlight ride."

"I wonder what Marty thinks two sweethearts do alone in the bushes after dark," I whispered in Christy's direction.

"Whatever he thinks, I'm not doing it on camera."

"It didn't hurt Paris Hilton."

"Well, maybe you need to go riding with her."

"I don't think I could take the wear and tear."

"The camera loves ya, Christy," a guy named Joey said, swinging his camera in close while we hopped off the ponies. "Could ya stand back a little, chief. I want a good shot of Christy here."

"Stick with her as she first sees the body," Martin Something directed the cameraman.

"Hold on. Hold...cut...cut..." I was beginning to hyperventilate. "I spotted the body first, me. Sure, Christy helped pull her out, but I found her."

"But it'll play better with Christy discovering the body, Jerry," Marty said. "Here—right on the shore."

"But the body was in the water."

"In the water? What are we doing here, vampires or sharks?"

That being his attitude, I wondered over next to Darrell Lee Redhawk to wait for my close-up. I asked if he had anything new on the case and he complained they'd taken down the yellow police tape roping off the old swimming hole for the shoot, but it didn't matter much as they had pretty much gotten all the evidence here.

In addition to vacuuming the sand and rocks for trace evidence, they had dragged the creek in case something might have been hidden or dropped in the water. At the time I didn't think to mention the silver arrowhead Christy had found.

"Not that we found much," Redhawk said. "We got people down from Phoenix to help out with the crime scene so if anything was left here we shoulda got it."

"Was she killed here? It was dark the other night, but I didn't see that much blood."

"She was probably killed someplace else, lost a lot of blood and then was carried here. I don't think we got any vampires and that's what I'm gonna say here on the television if they ever get done shooting your gal there."

They had Christy lying on a boulder, a couple of buttons undone. At this rate, Darrell Lee and I would come off looking like chopped liver. I wondered how many buttons Dakota would be unbuttoning for her fifteen minutes of fame.

"Okay," Marty said, motioning to Redhawk and me, "let's get you boys in the shot before we wrap it."

THE sheriff and I barely got enough camera time for Redhawk to get in his pitch for re-election. Traffic tickets and all having the priority, he never did go back on the vampire statement, so I made a mental note to get a sound bite from the previous night's broadcast. Not that I wanted to make Redhawk look bad. I didn't want to give him grounds to lock me up and throw away the key. Not when I had Dakota and Ronnie to contend with in solving this murder.

Chapter 12.

"COLONEL Winston with Indian Scout, Fort Apache, N.M." held the place of honor at the Kirby Art Gallery. Upon entering the place you'd either see it or trip over it. In spite of Rex Bowman's one-man show, Bryan Forbes-Collier had managed to showcase Max Leibergard's painting of the old cavalryman and his trusty scout. According to the small sign next to it, it was painted from life back in 1874. The trusty scout didn't get any billing, so it just shows how far things have come since then. My trusty scout, The Great Rondini, always manages to get in a plug.

I did kind of miss Rondini. Too bad he decided to scout up Dakota. With the father fixation she has on Bronco Billy, I think Ronnie's liable to wind up as the Lone Ranger, not to carry the analogy too far. I snapped a picture of the picture and emailed to Ronnie from my phone. The only message was "You're the Indian." Maybe it would remind him that we're a team even if he didn't believe in vampires.

Or at least believe in the power of vampires to get a guy on a cable news channel.

"Pretty different on the inside," Christy was saying, meaning the gallery of course. From the outside on Kirby's main drag, the place looked like an attempt to replicate an old time emporium that might be the cow town stop for dry goods and sundries. Once we stepped inside however, we fast forwarded into the twenty-first century. Smooth, white walls bathed in soft, reflected light. Soft country rock absorbed by the soft gray carpeting and silver drapes completed the setup. All the excitement was hanging on the walls.

A few of the Circle-K's guests were milling about drinking in the art as well as the free champaign. The Soprano look-alike I had noticed at the pool and his good lady were eying the

Leibergard. Maybe the Colonel was a long lost relative. Or maybe the Indian was. The newlyweds that had watched my show the other night were there too. The young lovers spent as much time looking into each other's starry eyes as at the pictures. I noticed they must have been working on a honeymoon album too, using their iPhones to video the festivities. I wonder what they videoed back in the honeymoon suite.

"JERRY, look at this beautiful sunset," Christy pulled me over to see one of Bowman's western vistas.

While Christy and I moved in for a closer look, Bryan Forbes-Collier moved in on us. "I think it's one of his best, definitely a mature Bowman."

"What's a mature Bowman cost as compared to an adolescent one?" I asked, hoping he might take it the wrong way.

"Hah, very good, Mr. Jeremy. You have a droll sense of humor." Forbes-Collier looked at a number stuck on the wall next to the painting and said, "Twenty-five thousand dollars."

Mature indeed.

"That's not too bad," Christy said.

"Maybe not, but still it's a little rich for my blood," I said.

"Let's think about that," Forbes-Collier said. "This painting will be something to hand down to your children, and they to theirs. Someday it will be worth as much as that Leibergard over there."

"As a matter of fact," I said, "I like that one better anyway. And maybe my grandkids will too. What's the damage for the colonel and his trusty scout?"

"A true masterpiece by a fabulous Western painter. Two hundred and fifty thousand is our asking price." It took me a while to catch my breath. So the play was that if I bought Rex Bowman's sunset, in a hundred years it would be worth ten times as much as it cost. A good selling point if I was planning on still being around then. I was hoping I would be, but you can never tell.

About then Forbes-Collier rushed off to cozy up with a couple in matching plaid Bermuda shorts. Even at this distance I could see the old guy had a gold pinky ring shaped like an oil derrick. So Christy and I wandered around the gallery until we bumped into the artist himself. The twenty-five G artist, not the two-fifty guy. That one had been dead since the twenties if there was any truth to the card pinned next to his painting. Bowman was staring at a painting of wild mustangs that had his signature in the lower right-hand corner. His name was big enough to tilt the canvas from the weight, but maybe that was just an optical illusion.

"I'd bet wild horses couldn't drag you away from that picture," I said about the wild horses. He didn't seem to get it though.

"I remember painting it," he replied between sips from a plastic cup. "I had done an oil sketch for this one on a beautiful spring day, early enough in the year that the wild mustangs still had their winter coats. All my work is based on sketches made directly from nature."

"So you know the territory."

"Yes, I'm one thirty-second Apash—ah, I mean Apache. I spend as much time as I can with my distant relatives in the high desert here although I actually reside in Scottsdale. I think they help me see nature in a different light. They'ff, uh, guided me in the sweat lodge puri...uh, purification. I've gone out in no man's land with them for a week at a time. We take no food or water into the desert with us. We lived off what we can find in the wilderness. You know, in nature."

I was thinking Jenny Craig ought to hear about this diet. But Christy was warming up to the subject though, saying she had "heard that it could be very spiritual."

She continued, "At UA we were given a number of seminars on the coyote way. I always wanted to see what the experience would be like."

"I'd like to introduce you to this Yaqui medicine man I know. Maybe it can be arranged..." he emptied the plastic wine cup. "Of course, you too, Mister Jeremy. I would love to get you out in the desert."

Rex looked across the room at Forbes-Collier and said, "There's a special thing my ancestors did to rid themselves of evil spirits. I wonder if that included gallery owners. Hah, just the wine talking, of course. But I appear to be out. Let me see if there is any more of this fine Syrah left. You two look around."

"What's up with him and Bryan Forbes-Collier? I thought they were pals," Christy said.

"I think he's had a little too much of that Arizona red. Hey, there's Satyra over by that painting of the cows."

This time I dragged Christy across the gallery. Satyra had been sampling the local wines as well, so I figured I'd see if it brought out the Indian sign on her too. Besides I wanted to see if Ronnie had said anything about coming back to the side of the angels. Well, maybe we're not angels, but we're not the dark side either. Dakota had that one wrapped up. Anyway, Satyra said she hadn't seen The Great One since their show last night so she hadn't had a chance to take his temperature.

"SAY, ain't you the guy we saw on the radio?"

The guy not only looked like a Mafia *capo*, he sounded like one too. I had seen him and his lady at the pool yesterday and he didn't look much different with his clothes on. He gave Christy a toothy smile, but his eyes were all over Satyra. I don't want think about what they were doing all over her.

"Gloria Palucci," the blond lady chirped, handing me a smile while eying Satyra too. Needless to say, she was viewing her a little differently than the Godfather was, maybe sizing her up as a potential competitor. At any rate, she blinked away any destructive impulses she might have had and asked, "You folks interested in Western art too? A lot of our associates back east seem to be going crazy for it, although I'm not sure how many Italian cowboys there were."

I allowed as how we were just amateurs when it came to the west, to art in general and to western art specifically. Personally, I couldn't recall ever going to a museum unless it was to impress a date. Christy and I introduced ourselves and the *Soprano* doppelgänger told us his name was Sal. He didn't bother with a last name. Probably too many syllables to remember anyway. Just plain Sal took his time looking over the ladies before saying, "I'd be glad to show you around the gallery if you like. I have an eye for the finer things in life, if you get my meaning."

I think Gloria got his meaning if nobody else did as she stepped between Sal and his view of Satyra's assets, if you get my meaning. In spite of Sal's gravelly voice and Gloria's nervous giggling, they seemed to be happy to be in the halls of culture. After all, they had to keep up with those 'associates' back east, didn't they. I wondered if I could get a monologue for the show out of leg-breakers laundering their dough by embracing art. With the price Forbes-Collier had stuck on the Leibergard, let's just say it's a lot of laundry. I wondered if I could get a framed copy of Sal's arrest record to hang on my wall.

So we all wandered around, sometimes together and

sometimes apart, until I realized I needed to put in a call to Redhawk for an update. I was short of guests and didn't want to get stuck having the same crowd on this evening as I did last night, so I herded Christy out the door into the oven that Kirby used as a main street. I was just pulling out my phone when Christy elbowed me in the ribs.

"Ouch!" I said, never being at a loss for words.

"I was trying to get your attention in there without being obvious," Christy said.

"Why? Do I have something stuck in my teeth?"

"No, Jerry. One of the paintings—it was the scene of the crime!"

"You mean Bowman painted the murder?"

"Of course not, Jerry, it was from sometime before. Just a landscape of the trees and pool and all, a couple of ponies drinking the water...but don't you see what that means?"

"Of course I do. Beverly getting herself killed there will add a zero or two to the picture's price tag, right?"

"Well, sure, there is that. But what I mean is it proves Rex Bowman was familiar with the spot. He had been there before."

"So he returned to the scene of the crime. No wait, it wasn't a crime scene until he returned. If it was even his crime. I'm going back in to take a picture of the picture. You can do me a favor, too. Round up a ranch hand or two who's familiar with the area and can describe the murder venue."

"To all of you out there in my listening audience, this evening we go one step further in our three-sixty coverage of the unsolved Edelbaum dude ranch murder.

"KICK radio, the Talk of the West, has joined with Tucson's KOW-TV to investigate and solve this grisly killing. There may be a madman on the loose, there may even be some vampires batting it around, but I'm here to bring the perp to justice in our brand new reality contest.

"The KICK evening team lead by myself with the aid of Christy Marshall of the University of Arizona criminology department and the well-endow—er, I mean well-known—parapsychologist, The Great Satyra are up against a team from Dakota Holiday's afternoon call-in show. Whoever snags the killer first will be number one in the heart of our sponsor Bronco Billy's rootin' tootin' square-shootin' pre-owned vehicles, right out there on North Sixth Avenue in

Tucson. Come on down, after all, Bronco Billy's footing the tab for this murder."

I introduced my panel for the evening which consisted of Christy, Slim and Deke, our tour guides from the previous afternoon's horseback ride, and last but certainly least, my pal Sherman Huntley, taking a break from running the front desk. I think Sherm had pushed his way in to make sure we didn't say anything that might scare away any potential dudes or dudesses. Satyra had promised to drop in between shows so I could plug Friday night's big show exposing the murderer, that being the limit of Bronco Billy's willingness to foot the bill. I couldn't really explain to Billy that a murder investigation takes whatever time it takes, him being the sponsor and all. And me not wanting to go back on nights and all.

"So Christy tells me you boys know your way around the territory hereabouts."

No response. Slim and Deke just sat there looking moon-eyed at Christy.

"So fellas, let me put this another way—didn't you guide Christy and me down by that desert oasis yesterday, the one where Beverly Edelbaum was found?" Christy smiled and nodded a little to encourage the boys to answer, but they just nodded back. *"Look, guys, this is radio. You know, where we need to talk so people will know we're here. That's why we call them listeners."*

"Maybe I can help," Sherm jumped in. *"Okay, fellas, listen up. You all know down by the rattle smake pool on Dutchman's Creek, don'cha? Down where the body was found. Mister Jeremy needs some answers to his questions or we might be looking for some new wranglers come morning, right?"*

"Oh yeah, we know that place pretty darn well," Slim finally confessed.

"Oh yeah, the rattler pool by the spring," Deke echoed.

Rattlers? Was this guy putting me on? Christy and I had been hanging out there with no clothes on. That's really hanging out. Anyway, once we got the boys going, they carried on like a couple of magpies. Heckle and Jeckle, I think. I somehow managed to get the lay of the land out of them, not to mention some home-on-the-range philosophy, various thoughts on vampires, and several offers to take us riding. Christy was up for the ride, but I was afraid I'd wind up walking home. I didn't want to do that with rattlesnakes around, though I was pretty sure the only snakes hereabouts wore cowboy hats.

About then, the radio gods took mercy on me and brought in some, you should pardon the expression, fresh blood.

"I'm glad to announce that the well-known mind reader, Satyra the Great, has joined us now. Satyra is the main attraction in the fabulous magic show currently at Kirby's Silver Cage Saloon. Tell us, Satyra, how much longer will you be there?"

"Hi Jerry, glad to be on your program and 'hello' to all your listeners. This is the last week for the show..."

Satyra carried on about how everybody should head on down to see the show until I cut off her mic. Then I let Sherm put in a pitch for the Circle-K so he wouldn't change the lock on my bungalow. Like a good little boy he told us that the only spirits within a hundred miles of Kirby were those served at the Silver Cage Saloon. I didn't really mind the plug because it gave me time to queue up the sound bite about vampires from Sheriff Redhawk.

"As our KICK radio listening audience knows, Satyra, I am in a race to solve the murder of a prominent patron of the arts. So far the police have been stumped—" play the Redhawk sound bite *"— There have been rumors of paranormal sightings that might be tied into the crime, and Satyra, this is where you come in."*

"Yes, Jerry. Your fans may not realize it, but before the killer can be caught the Circle-K must be rid of evil spirits. And I think I'm just the babe to do it."

"Well, you are a babe alright—" the toe of Christy's boot tried my shin on for size *"—and so maybe you think Sheriff Redhawk was on the right trail, paranormal-wise."*

"You bet, Jerry. Your listeners may not realize that in addition to being a certified medium, I am a licensed exorcist. On Friday night's show, I will run the ghosts right out of ghost town!"

Satyra was holding up her end okay, and believe me I'd like to hold her end up too, but I doubted my shins could take it. All that aside though, I was beginning to miss Ronnie. He had the magic when it came to promoting himself on the air, but his assistant was going a little overboard. Still I wish I had thought up that exorcist line. Particularly since the KOW crew was filming. The TV guys seemed to love Satyra's flimsy magic show costume; it would be great for sweeps week or perhaps the occasional bachelor party.

Christy gave the audience a recap of how we found the

body, glossing over why we were out in no man's land in the middle of the night with no clothes on. After all, it's a family show. Not like some afternoon shows I could mention. The kind of afternoon shows that lure your trained magician away with the promises of...well, let's keep it on a family show level.

That reminded me that Christy and I still hadn't gotten a chance to snuggle. I planned remedy that as soon as we were off the air.

Anyway, the tech crew that Bronco Billy had brought out with him had somehow managed to hook up a couple of laptops to a couple of phone lines or something, but anyway we were able to take calls while we were on the air. I would have used Sherm for our screener but he'd have wound up selling timeshares to the callers on hold, so Christy put Mrs. M to work answering the phones and pecking out the caller's name and topic on one of the computers. Christy and I would read it off the other laptop and press a button to connect the caller. Since Mrs. Marshall was only about two feet away from us and since she only used two fingers to peck with, passing it over on a bar napkin might have been faster. On the other hand, making her part of the team might soften her up where I was concerned. Christy and I might even get the chance to spend some time alone. That is, not alone, but together. Together alone, I guess.

"Benjamin calling from Phoenix—you're on the air!"

"Hi Jerry, I have a question for Christy. I saw you on TV and you're gorgeous! When are you going to get your own show?"

"Well, Benny, thank you very much. I'll bet you're a looker too. Have you ever gone to UA?"

"I hate to break up the mutual admiration society," I jumped in, *"but do you have a question about the murder?"*

"Jeez, buddy, I just wanted to tell her my problems."

"They have psychiatrists for that sort of thing and they have to listen to you." I tapped the magic button and Ann from Phoenix replaced Benjamin.

"Thanks for taking my call. I just was wondering if this Beverly Edelbaum person might have been up to something, like meeting some kind of drug shipment at night out in the desert."

"Thanks, Ann. We saw the movie too."

Travis was next and he wanted to know more about the vampires. We gave him the run around for a while to see if the v-word would take off, but the callers following him were more

Conan Doyle than Bram Stoker.

So I said, *"Richie from Tucson, you're on with Jerry and Christy, radio crime busters. Whatcha got for us?"*

Like the man says—the (radio) show must go on. And so we went on and on and on with another round of callers, who all said how sorry they were, how we should butt out and let the cops handle it, and how they would go about solving it without any cops if it was them. There were also a couple of heavy breathers looking to breathe on Satyra.

By ten o'clock we had covered every aspect of the case from motive to opportunity to—well, we drew the line at what Christy and I were doing out in the desert.

I had hoped Sheriff Redhawk might stop by, but I think he was still sore about the vampire thing. I would have bet though that his name recognition among the local voters was way up.

Chapter 13.

EVEN without Sheriff Redhawk coming on the show to embarrass himself again, it had been a pretty good day. The TV crew had got plenty of footage of Christy and me out on the Pecos, Bronco Billy had set up a neat reality stunt, and Christy had discovered that Rexford Bowman had taken his paint set to the scene of the crime at some point in the past. We even got to see a picture worth a cool quarter of a mil. Worth it to somebody anyhow.

The one thing that was still bothering me was that I hadn't had a chance to snuggle with Christy without finding a dead body, or even worse, her mom hanging around.

The way I figured it, Rondini's second show started at ten o'clock, just when my show wrapped. Depending on the number of encores he took, Christy and I would have the Paleface Suite all to ourselves for an hour or more. I was hoping the audience really liked Ronnie tonight. The plan would be perfect if Christy was willing to give it a try.

And she was.

The great thing about radio is I didn't have any make-up to remove or clothes to change. The show ended at ten and I was smooching Christy in my bungalow by five after. The smell of her hair, her soft, peachy skin, her sweet, ripe lips—well, all that was great, but I was ready for sex. And so was she.

I was sure we could have gone all night if we'd had more than an hour, but I didn't think the crowd at the Silver Cage would give Ronnie that many bows. So we were reluctantly catching our respective breaths when the afterglow was suddenly interrupted.

A tomahawk hurdled through the sitting room window sounding for all the world like a Native American SWAT team paying a call on General Custer. At first I thought maybe Darrell Lee wanted to fingerprint us again, so we threw on a couple of hotel robes. But when I crept into the front room behind Christy, she said, "Look, Jerry. Somebody tossed a ball peen hammer through your window."

Well, it could have been a tomahawk.

"It must be one of Ronnie's fans," I said.

"I wonder...." Christy peered through the broken glass. "I don't see anyone out there now."

I peered too. The dim lights marking the pathway didn't help much, but the full moon was enough to show that nobody was standing in the small garden outside. Of course, anyone making the least effort to hide behind some cactus or other would have escaped detection.

"Jerry, there's a note tied to the hammer. We'd better not touch it though."

"You're right. It could be a federal offense to open Ronnie's mail."

"I meant the police will want to check for fingerprints. I had a law professor in college who...hmmm," Christy drifted off thinking of the long ago prof. I was hoping she got her passing grade through hard work and study.

It didn't take too long to find out what was in the note though. My new BFF, Darrell Lee Redhawk must have been in the neighborhood because he practically beat the locals in responding. Maybe because I had Christy make the call, a damsel in distress and all.

"So this note says 'Jeremy, you S.O.B., you got in over your head and you will regret it. Stop sticking your nose in other people's business or you'll get it chopped off. Get out of Kirby while you still can.'" Sheriff Redhawk was reading from the note, now separated from the hammer and safely tucked away in a transparent plastic envelope. The hammer itself had been bagged carried off somewhere too.

The sheriff adjusted his Stetson and asked, "Any idea who might have written that?"

"My first guess would be Dakota Holiday, trying to scare me off so she can win the contest."

"Oh, Jerry," Christy protested, "you can't actually believe she would do something like this with a killer on the loose."

"Oh yes I can. That killer had better hope I find him before she does. She'll tear him from limb to limb."

"Okay, let's settle down now," Redhawk said. "I was on Miss Holiday's radio program and she is a perfect little lady.

Who else has it in for you?"

"I know it's not Rondini. He can't spell that well. Let's see, how about the guy we're doing all this coverage on—the killer himself. Let's get that thing dusted for prints."

Looking around the bungalow, you couldn't blame a guy for thinking they must have bagged the hammer and the note to keep all that fingerprint powder being dusted around from getting all over them. Everything else was covered in it. Meanwhile, my pal Sherm had rustled up some guys with their own hammers to nail plywood sheeting over the broken picture window. I hoped the room comp extended to any incidental damage. Turns out we were harder on a hotel room than Axl Rose.

"So you really think you're getting close to the killer?" Redhawk said straight-faced while the CSI team let out a few good ol' boy guffaws. Luckily, Christy answered for me or I'd have wound up in the Cochise County clink again. She said, "At least Jerry has a plan to catch the guy, even if it kills him. Oh! I didn't mean it like that, babe."

Nothing like total support from your loved ones.

While the crime scene guys packed up, by now on a first name basis with us, Darrell Lee gave us the once over once again. "So you two were in the altogether when you found Beverly Edelbaum. Now you were wearing birthday suits again when somebody goes an' tosses a threatening message with a hammer tied to it through your window. Seems to me things would be a lot more quiet if you two kept your pants on."

"I dunno, Sheriff, you may be right" I said, "but like I said before, we're out to catch Bev Edelbaum's killer, and we plan to do just that, no matter how much sex it takes."

THE camera crew was already set-up at the poolside chuck wagon when Christy and I showed for breakfast the next day. I'd like to say we had spent the night together, woke up together, got dressed together and headed to breakfast together, but the only thing we did after the cops left was walk over to her place, say goodnight and promise to meet in the morning. On the way we passed the newlyweds who were heading for their bungalow to do what newlyweds do.

Rats.

Speaking of which, The Great Rat-ini had found his way home by the time I got back to the bungalow and was snoring up a storm. I would have thought a smashed-out picture window might have piqued some curiosity, but I guess that's what killed a cat, not a snake in the grass.

I would have also thought he might have thought traveling magician might have thought it was some local farmer's daughter's old man seeking him out. That alone should have kept him awake until I got back anyway. But maybe I'm over-thinking this...let's get back to breakfast.

Bronco Billy and Dakota had already snagged a table by the pool and had Sherm dishing up the grub for them. Dakota looked to be having a sliver of grapefruit and black coffee, while Billy was going big on the bacon, sausage, eggs and flapjacks. He seemed to have worked up quite an appetite somehow. Christy and I negotiated the buffet line and joined the happy couple.

"Christy, you look as pretty as a dewy rose in the morning if you don't mind my saying so," Billy so said while Dakota stared a few daggers Christy's way. "I'm glad you two actually made it down here for breakfast."

I didn't want to break it to Billy that we had hardly gotten warmed up last night and before that we hadn't had a much of a chance to do anything that didn't involve horses or TV cameras. And I don't mean in a good way.

"Yo'all know when it comes to representing the West, I'll stake my credentials against almost any living bein'. Somebody dead like Sam Houston or John Wayne may beat me out, but I'm shootin' to catch up before I go. And they's ain't nothin' symbolizes the new West like Bronco Billy's Pre-owned Vehicles and Used Trucks LLC."

"You tell 'em, Daddy," Dakota said, though again the "Daddy" bit might just have been my imagination.

"Word up, big fella," I just imagined me saying.

"So...I've done gone ahead and jus' bought that pitcher up to the Kirby Gallery."

"One of the Bowman paintings?" Christy asked, but I already knew the answer. I had that same queasy feeling I get passing a Porsche dealership—some real money was changing hands.

"No, sweetie, though I got nothin' against Bowman. But my vehicle and truck business just bought that cavalryman and his trusty scout. Just between us kids, I got the price down to a cool quarter million by throwin' in a good deal on a trade-in. Heh, heh."

"Daddy! That's an awful lot of money."

Hmmm...*down* to a quarter million. Plus a car. I gotta

hand it to Forbes-Collier, he certainly knows his marks—er, market. I wouldn't have thought Billy would be so extravagant considering how much he hates to lose a dime on the golf course. All those dimes must add up.

"So, Billy, will you be donating or loaning it to a museum?" Christy wanted to know.

"Well, maybe someday I might do that, all dependin' on the tax man of course. But right now that cavalryman is gonna be standing tall right at the front entrance to Bronco Billy's used car lot. With the publicity I'm gonna get, it'll pull folks in to see it from all over."

"You'll need to keep it under archival conditions though," Christy said, Art Appreciation 101 coming in handy.

"Sure, but out here in the desert, why it's a snap, low humidity and all. The damn' picture still looks like it was painted just yesterday. But looky-here, sweetheart, maybe you can help me work out how to set up them arc-curv-all conditions...ah, ouch!"

"Oh, was that your toe, Bronco Billy?" Dakota explained.

The B-man recovered enough to get back on track, "Jerry, why don't you and Christy here take the TV crew over to get some good footage of the paintin' while it's still on display in that gallery. Talk it up on camera with that hyphen-named guy, ya know, like what a patron of the arts ol' Billy is and the usual good stuff about the used cars."

"Sure, we'll get on it right after brunch."

"Well, I got a Brinks truck due here afore noon, so it mightn't be there if you wait too long. Maybe wrap up them vittles and see if you can scoot over there now." Billy turned to Christy summoning up as much charm as desert coyote and said, "If that's okay with you, little lady."

Of course the TV crew, chowing down within earshot, made a last pass at the buffet. Meanwhile, Christy for her part allowed as how she stood ready to help Bronco Billy commercialize an historic piece of western art, only not in quite those words.

About that time Ronnie the Rat showed up and shoved in at our table, this time next to Christy and me. He gulped some coffee to get his heart started and asked what happened to the lovely view from our bungalow. When I explained that ball peen hammers had replaced Western Union hereabouts, Bronco Billy chimed in after some elbowing from Dakota. He wondered if my tell-all could really wait until the evening show since it would certainly spice up the reality contest. After a bit of whose story is it anyway, Billy ruled that Christy and I would be special guests on Dakota's afternoon show, thereby scooping myself on my own story.

Chapter 14.

THE bright gold lettering on the display window said the gallery opened at ten ayem. But the discrete sign on the door was still flipped to 'Closed'. We all kind of stood there trying to peer into the shaded interior. No one was moving about as far as we could tell. And no one came to the door when we knocked. I knew from our San Francisco adventure that Christy had had an apprenticeship in lock picking, but wasn't too sure she'd want the TV camera to catch her breaking and entering. My guess was that Sheriff Redhawk would take a dim view of those kinds of shenanigans. Particularly if the vampire gag cost him the upcoming election.

Of course, we've all seen it in a hundred bad movies. That scene where the hero tries the knob on a supposedly locked door and—surprise—it's not locked. And rule nine, sub-paragraph 'b' of the screenwriter's code of ethics requires there to be a dead body on the other side of the door. In the movies the killers never lock up after themselves.

Things like that can't be expected to happen in real life though, so why even try turning the doorknob. After all, doesn't the little sign say 'Closed'? That means keep out.

So I turned the knob and it opened.

And true to form, a body was sprawled out in the middle of the floor. Regardless of what they do in the movies, I made up my mind not to pick up the murder weapon if it was lying there. I wouldn't want to get my fingerprints all over it and have our video show me standing, gun in hand, over the dead man.

As the shock wore off and the cameraman started moving in for the shot, the body on the floor moaned and tried to roll over. "Look, Jerry," Christy said. "He's alive. It's Mister Forbes-Collier!"

And so it was. Christy and I rushed to help him up, thinking maybe he'd passed out from sampling too much desert Cabernet at the opening. But no, there was a spongy spot on the side of his head that still had blood seeping from it. I volunteered my clean handkerchief to stop the flow while we eased him on to a chair. Christy dialed 911 on her cell and got the ambulance started. The audio guy suggested one of us get Forbes-Collier some water and Christy put the glass to his lips so he could take a sip while I finger-splattered a little over the rest of his face.. The water, sipped and splattered, seemed to revive him a bit.

"What the hell happened?" he said. "I was just opening the shop when..."

He kind of tailed off at that point so Christy poured a little more water in his mouth and I said, "We were hoping you could tell us what happened. We found you on the floor just now and called for an ambulance. Do you remember how you got the bump on your head?"

"I'm not sure. I had just unlocked the front door and something hit me from behind. The next thing I remember was waking up just now." Forbes-Collier suddenly noticed the camera crew. "How did the news get here so quickly, did you call them?"

"Not a bad idea," I admitted, "but they're with us. We came over to shoot a piece on Bronco Billy's buying the painting. Where is it anyway? Not packed up already, is it?"

"The painting? My god, the Leibergard—it's gone." Forbes-Collier pointed at the empty easel sitting in the middle of the floor.

"Hey, you just got your bell rung. You probably don't remember moving it," I said.

Christy started for the back room saying, "I'll check around, Jerry, but I hope you don't have to break this to Bronco Billy on the air."

She was right about that.

I tried to think of a way to get Dakota to do it. Too bad Ronnie and I weren't pals anymore; he was great at getting people to do things against their better instincts. At least I hoped it worked on somebody besides me. At any rate, with us not being pals right now, that option was as dead as Missus Edelbaum.

"It's nowhere to be found," Christy said, coming back to the huddle around our victim. "It's definitely not on the premises." She bent down to look Forbes-Collier in the eye and added, "It's only a guess, but I'd bet whoever knocked you out, took the painting."

What with the vampire killing, hammers smashing through windows, and now this, little ol' Kirby was having quite a crime wave. We needed an appearance by the sheriff about now and this time at least we had our clothes on. With luck I could get Christy to lay on enough charm Darrell Lee would sign on for Dakota's afternoon show. That way he could break the news and Billy would run *him* out of town. After all, a cool quarter mil pays for a lot of greens fees.

A few minutes more and the EMT guys showed up with a couple of uniformed cops in tow. The paramedics pushed and prodded and determined the gallery boss had been hit on the head. The cops asked some questions and mugged for the camera hoping to be on the evening news. After questioning everyone on our team, they figured Forbes-Collier had been hit on the head and that a valuable painting had been stolen. Our TV crew got to shoot a little more footage as the EMTs packed Forbes-Collier up and drove him away, their sirens breaking the stillness of the desert. Even the vultures stopped circling so they could watch the goings-on.

No sooner had Forbes-Collier been carted off, than Darrell Lee Redhawk showed up with a gang of CSI lookalikes. I thought they might be getting tired of being called out to the ghost town all the time, so I volunteered to buy a round of lattes to heal any bad feelings. After all, I might just be a suspect again. I figured Sheriff Redhawk could clear that up for me. I managed to corner Darrell Lee since he didn't have all that much to do what with the victim having already left the building.

"So I'm slated to guest on Dakota's show this afternoon and the plan was to tell the world about a certain ball peen hammer, but now it looks like the hammer has hit home. You might want to show up too. After all, you don't want the electorate to think you've let this law and order thing get out of hand."

"Before anybody," Redhawk said, "even thinks about going and getting on the airwaves, you folks are going to make your written statements about what's happened here. I haven't figured out why yet, but you and Miss Marshall—" he smiled in her direction "—always seem to be in the thick of it."

"Our statements? Of course. You interview us," I said, "and then we'll interview you. Just remember, statement or not, every word we say is copyrighted, so don't pass any of our eye-witness accounts on to those other networks."

We made a deal with the Sheriff that he could watch the video of us finding Forbes-Collier and discovering the painting was gone as long as he came on Dakota's show with me. He watched it play back on the video camera and the camera man promised to hand over a DVD the minute we were off the air. As for me, I promised that the vampires were as good as dead.

"THANKS, Dakota, it's great to be back on your show." Of course I had never actually been on her show before, but it sounded better to pretend it was a return engagement, like maybe she needed the ratings boost. *"What I'm about to reveal will have your ratings"*—and mine—*"jumping."*

"Well, Jerry—"

"As your listeners know, the Jerry Jeremy Show has been tracking down the murderer of Beverly Edelbaum. She was killed after her ground-breaking appearance on my show a brief four days ago."

"Well, Jer—"

"Christy Marshall and I have been working the case and are close to solving it. So close that the murderer has attempted to scare us off with a vicious ball peen hammer attack. Isn't that right Christy?"

"Jer—" Dakota tried to break in again, but my girl was right on cue.

"Yes, that's right, Jerry," Christy took the pass. *"And Cochise County Sheriff Darrell Lee Redhawk is here with us today to confirm multiple violent attacks by the killer."*

Redhawk opened his mouth to make a campaign speech, but didn't get the chance.

"Multiple attacks?" Dakota bellowed, having been thrown out at first. *"The only one I know of was some disgruntled listener tossing a hammer through your window."*

"We'll see when the culprit is caught," I said. *"I'm still a little concerned that somebody else might have had a motive, Dakota. Can you just write 'Jeremy—you SOB' here on this napkin. Sheriff, make her do it. You can check her handwriting and maybe any DNA that rubs off."*

So even if I wasn't getting closer to the killer, at least maybe I could nail Dakota. And I do mean 'nail' not in a good sense. Not the way I'd like to nail Christy when I finally get her alone. If that time ever comes again.

So Dakota and I burned a little more air time insulting

each other until Christy and Darrell Lee pulled us back on track.   Christy gave an eye-witness account of the Olympic hammer throw while Sheriff Redhawk provided the color commentary.   No fingerprints, no DNA, hammer probably bought with cash. The killer—or maybe Dakota—was playing it smart.

"*I wouldn't be surprised,*" Dakota said, "*if you smashed your own window to get attention.*"

"*Don't be jealous, just because the perp hates my show more than yours. But enough about me, I've got bigger fish to fry. Er, not that I'm a fish, er, small fry, er.... Anyway, as I was about to say, I have another scoop for our listeners—*"

"*Actually this is my scoop*" Dakota jumped in, "*and I have prepared a fitting introduction to this wonderful story, so zip it until I get to the Q&A.*"   Don'tcha just love watching somebody use their tongue to dig their own grave? So I zipped.

"*Arizona's path to statehood was written on horseback in the closing days of the old West,*" Dakota led off with. "*The railroads and the telegraph lines were charting a new course as the nineteenth century came to a close.   Soon the automobile and the used truck would replace the pony and the mustang.*" I think a certain sponsor must have helped her with that part. "*But before that new day dawned, it was the United States Calvary and their trusty Native American guides that tamed the Wild West.   Of course in the old days, digital cameras or even picture-taking cell phones were hard to come by, so it was up to pioneering artists to paint—*"

"*So anyway,*" Christy spoke over the history lesson, "*Dakota, your sponsor, so to speak, bought a classic Western scene painted by Max Leibergard in 1874. Painted in 1874, not bought then.*"

"*Bought just last night as a matter of fact,*" Dakota said, unable to contain herself. "*And I was there. Bronco Billy Wooten, CEO of Wooten's Fine Pre-owned Vehicles, purchased the painting for a cool quarter of a million dollars.*" Sure, pour it on, girl.

"*Let's hope his homeowner's will cover it,*" Christy added.

"*What's that supposed to mean?*" Dakota snapped.

I would have loved to see a real catfight, but Billy was my sponsor too. Plus, I began thinking maybe the cops hadn't had time to break the news to him yet, since we'd hustled Redhawk into the makeshift studio before the ink was dry on our statements.

Time to swing into action.

"*Ladies, let's not forget our guest today, Sheriff Darrell Lee Redhawk,*" I said. "*I think he has something important to say. But before that, let's take it from the top. Sheriff Redhawk, who—I want to make it absolutely clear—has my unconditional backing for re-election this fall, didn't just happen to stop by.*

"*He's got a grisly unsolved murder on his plate. Not to mention the vicious assault on my picture window last night. But he is here today, investigating the attempted murder of Kirby Gallery owner, Bryan Forbes-Collier, a frequent guest on my radio program which can be heard each weekday evening from seven to ten. Forbes-Collier, a man of great integrity for an art dealer, was found in a pool of his own blood on the floor of his gallery this morning by none other than your host, er, I mean yours truly, Jerry Jeremy.*

"*In the face of great personal danger, the fearless Christy Marshall and I took control of the situation. Calling in the Emergency Medical Team and the police, we searched the premises, hoping to catch the villain red-handed, knowing that if we did, we would have the Edelbaum murderer.*

"*It looked like the hammer-tossing crook had struck again and it wasn't a pretty picture, no pun intended.*"

"*You're telling me that someone tried to murder Bryan Forbes-Collier?*" Dakota piped up. Meanwhile Darrell Lee and I gave her pitying, sad-eyed looks, knowing, as Paul Harvey might say, the rest of the story. And this being her show and all. Poor girl.

"*Sheriff Redhawk,*" I said, "*will you do the honors? Where is that high-priced work of art now?*"

Chapter 15.

I HAD a couple of hours to kill between Dakota's flameout and my show, so I hoped maybe Christy and I could find an unused bungalow to make use of. But she hadn't been spending much time with Sassie and wanted to keep the home fires burning instead of mine.

For a second I wondered if the hammer toss could have been Mrs. Marshall acting out, but no—she wouldn't have let me off with just a warning.

So, much to the disappointment of the KOW-TV crew, Christy headed off with Mom to shop the Native American handicrafts while Dakota, Darrell Lee, the crew and I went to face Bronco Billy. We were all a little worried that he might not take to the loss of Colonel Winston's portrait too well, having just paid a quarter mil for it. I was a little extra nervous that my having been the one to break the news might give the camera crew a chance to film Billy killing the messenger. I hoped he hadn't already reached out to Dale Anderson, the all-American career killer.

"I JUST hung-up on a call with Dale Anderson," Bronco Billy said. "After puttin' our heads together, we figure the low-life polecat that stole my pitcher gotta be the same low-life what off'd the Edelbaum woman. From now on he's gonna be known as the Desert Oasis Killer we decided on ever' single show we do. As a matter of fact, my lawyers are working on copyrightin' that name right this moment. And that's not all..."

I could feel the lump in my throat become a knot in my stomach.

"Jerry," he said, "and Dakota sweetheart, you two won't be goin' back to Tucson. No, you gonna need to extend your stay here, and your shows here, until one of you two reveals the identity of the murderous bastard that took my quarter million dollar paintin'."

Dakota and I then made the obligatory squeals of delight at still having jobs. Bronco Billy being too cool to offer Darrell Lee a reward if he found the painting, made noises about a substantial contribution to his re-election campaign fund instead. Of course, like most campaign contributions, there were a few strings attached, including liberal TV and radio coverage of the police investigation. But what the hey, it's an election year.

"One question, Mr. Wooten," Darrell Lee said. "Did you happen to put the painting you bought on to your insurance last night?"

"She-et, no," Billy answered, "I'm self-insured. If I had to insure all o' them damn' cars being test driven into each other, it'd break me. And don't worry about my quarter million. Having it come out of my pocket makes me real motivated. And if I'm motivated, pretty much ever'body 'round me gets motivated too."

Well, that was enough to motivate Sheriff Redhawk to mosey on out to his county-insured SUV and me to hitch a ride with him just to see where he and the investigation were going. Dakota had opted for some bikini time at the pool, so Billy and the TV crew opted to stick close to her.

As things turned out, Darrell Lee was planning a hospital visit to check on Bryan Forbes-Collier. The sheriff had gotten an update that Forbes-Collier was alive, if not well. He was taking solid food and ready to talk about the robbery. Since the crew wasn't tagging along, I figured I could always use my iPhone as a recorder in case there was something worth recording.

On the drive to Bisbee, Darrell Lee and I compared notes to see who knew more about art in general and collecting the good stuff in particular. The way I figured it, if we pooled all our knowledge, it still wouldn't be enough to tell a Picasso from a pitchfork. Too bad Ronnie wasn't along—he took a life drawing class a few years back because he was crazy about the teacher's curriculum. Yeah, you know what I mean.

Redhawk was the strong, silent type so I figured I'd better keep the ball rolling.

"So what's the word from forensics on today's excitement?" I asked. "They find any DNA lying around the art gallery?"

"Whoa there, fella. Don't start heading down that trail.

Truth be told, I should be questioning you. You're a material witness to a felony, you know."

"Hey, you already got *my* statement, now I need one from you. Any evidence who might have broken in?"

"That's one of the reasons I want to question Mister Forbes-Collier. There doesn't appear to actually have been a break-in. No busted windows, no forced locks, you figure it out."

"I'm no pro, but that head wound didn't look self-inflicted. Maybe he thought the perp was a customer and let him in."

"Forensics? Perp? You seem to know the territory. You ever wear a badge?"

"No, but I've spent some time in jail. Er, as a journalist, you know. Not as a...um, you know. Probably picked it up there. I watch a lot of TV, too. Maybe too much."

"Well, the *numeró uno* rule in police investigation is to find three things—the means, the motive and the opportunity to commit the act. You should focus your radio program on them things. Who knows, maybe somebody will call in, having seen something."

Was I using him or was he using me? Without a spotlight and a rubber hose my third degree technique didn't seem to be making much of a dent. Of course, it could be that he was as stumped as I was. Anyway I booked him for my evening show to see if my callers could pry anything loose. After all, they paid his salary.

I'd have to think about the means, motive and, er...oh yeah, a good time to make it happen. About that time we bumped across the last of the potholes in the driveway leading up to the emergency room and made a safe landing in an "Emergency Vehicles Only" parking space. The sheriff knew his way around the place, so before very long we were facing a bed-ridden Bryan Forbes-Collier with two black eyes and a turban-sized bandage wrapped around his head. Not that it mattered since I'd seen the "before" pictures in person. In between bites of hospital jello, Forbes-Collier recognized us and said hello. He thanked the sheriff profusely for saving his life, and Darrell Lee played the modesty card, saying it was all in the line of duty.

And to think I was the guy who ruined his good hankie on Bryan's bleeding noggin. "Lucky for you the Sheriff remembered the number for 9-1-1," I said angling for some acknowledgment. Anyway, in my pocket the iPhone was recording just in case the art dealer said anything that might mean a break in the case. Or anything at all for that matter.

"*...So for all you folks out there in radioland, that was Cochise County Sheriff Darrell Lee Redhawk with an report on what I call the Ghost Town Gallery Rip-off. And don't forget yours truly, Jerry 'Rambo' Jeremy, was first on the scene along with my charming co-host tonight, Christy Marshall. A few minutes earlier and we'd have caught the perpetrators in the act.*

"*Immediately after he regained consciousness, I had the chance to speak with gallery owner Bryan Forbes-Collier while he recuperated in the beautiful downtown Bisbee hospital. Here's how he described what happened...*"

Lucky for me when Bronco Billy opened his wallet, a couple of sound engineers had fallen out. They managed to make the audio from my phone as good as, well, let's just say it wasn't embarrassing bad. It had been edited for content (wink, wink) and on cue Forbes-Collier's voice boomed out.

"*I don't know what happened. I was just preparing to open the gallery for the day and the next thing I remember I awoke here with a splitting headache.*"

"*I'm sure Sheriff Redhawk will ask you to take inventory when you're feeling better, but it looked to me like the only thing missing was the painting of Colonel Winston with an Indian Scout by Max Leibergard.*"

"*Really? The Leibergard? How strange.*"

"*How strange? How so?*"

"*Well, what I meant was, of course, it is valuable, but would be impossible to sell anywhere. For what it's worth, I mean. It would be tricky to cover up the theft.*"

Sheriff Redhawk then asked whether Forbes-Collier had a picture of the picture, "*...I'll put out an APB on it.*" But Bryan admitted he hadn't actually got around to photographing it before it was taken.

"*Don't worry,*" I said. "*I know your sign said no cameras allowed, but then my phone isn't really a camera. I have a good shot of the old cavalryman and his trusty scout right here. You can crop Christy out of the picture if you want, but it may bet more attention if you leave her in.*"

"*Thanks, Jerry, seems like you thought of everything,*" Redhawk said. "*A person might think you knew the painting might be stolen before anybody else. And you were right on the scene after it happened...*"

"Sure, well, ah..." I explained. Note to self: Remind the audio boys that their livelihood depends on mine; edit out the part where I get backed into a corner.

Meanwhile Darrell Lee was asking Forbes-Collier if there was any indication he might get assaulted and robbed. Like maybe a couple of guys in ski masks carrying a selection of blunt instruments? Even I knew the answer to that one, although the victim was non-committal, pleading amnesia. While the recording played, I tried to think means, motive and.... Just who would have had the opportunity? No sign of a break-in, so amnesia or not, Bryan Forbes-Collier must have known his assailant.

THE show bounced along pretty well with the call-in lines all lit up until we finally had to say our *adios's*. Between the recorded interview and the callers, I barely said a word all evening. When things got slow, I asked Christy to repeat how we found Bev Edelbaum floating around least anyone forget what started it all. Christy was getting pretty good at the story by now, putting in a lot of stuff we hadn't even told the cops. Stuff that maybe hadn't even happened yet.

After the show wrapped, Christy and I had a choice—find someplace to be alone, which didn't look too promising with all the extra crew Bronco Billy had brought on and me not being interested in popping up on some adult website, or else knuckle down and see if we could find a solution to the Circle-K's crime wave.

Chapter 16.

KIRBY didn't have much of a suburb, the main thing outside of town being tumbleweed and scrubby cactus. There appeared to be only one paved road not counting the interstate and that road took us to an updated, up-scale copy of an old-time ranch house about ten miles out of town. We were heading there in the dead of night, somewhere around one a.m. Even so, the moon was bright enough to count the grains of sand by if we had the time and inclination.

As we approached the ranch house we saw a low adobe wall fronting the street and pretty soon our headlights picked out a black iron gate. It looked like it could have been hammered together by some long-ago cow-town smithy in between horseshoes. The gate was open, but even if hadn't been, Christy assured me that it would have been no problem. "A guy I knew in college showed me how to pick 'em," she said.

"Yeah, it sounds like you know how to pick 'em, alright."

I started to turn in to the driveway, but had second thoughts. Some nosy night rider might mosey past and get to wondering why a bright yellow SUV was parked in the drive. Particularly if said rider happened to have caught my show where I practically announced that nobody would be at home tonight. I hoped none of the local cat burglars had been listening.

Anyway I doused my lights and drove over the desert scrub to park out of sight behind the house. We'd bounced over the terrain a bit and may hit a cactus or two when we landed on a couple of tire ruts leading to a small barn-like building behind the main slab. The barn door was unlocked and just big enough for the Cherokee to fit through. I parked and left the keys in the ignition in case we needed to make a quick getaway.

"Think Bryan keeps his herd in here at night?" I said.

"I haven't heard of a herd," Christy punned.

"Keep that up and you're off the show. Anyway, this place seems empty, but there's a light coming from the main *hacienda*." Before I could stop myself I whispered, "I hope nobody beat us here."

"Why are you whispering? The place is deserted. That's only a night light inside, the kind they use in case somebody needs to find their way to the bathroom in the middle of the night."

"Pretty thoughtful of somebody to turn it on for us."

"It's probably on a timer," she said as we crossed the large flagstone patio to the sliding door. It was locked which meant nobody had come through it before us tonight. Unless they locked up after themselves. I was thinking one of the pots full of wilting flowers might be just the thing to bust open a window when Christy called to me from the open door.

"Jerry, hon, hurry up, come on."

Okay, I take it all back. She really would have made a great burglar. Thank God she decided to use her talents for good instead of evil. That's assuming we were still on the side of good, having broken into *chez* Forbes-Collier.

A LITTLE earlier, after I had signed off for the night, Christy and I had snagged a table for two near the back of the Silver Cage Saloon. Fortunately it was too late for Rondini's early show and too early for his late show. None of the rest of our crowd—Dakota, Bronco Billy or even Sassie Marshall—seemed to be around either.

"What'd they do, call a meeting without us?" I wondered. Not that I minded being alone with Christy, I just had a slight fear that a conspiracy might be brewing. Just because you're paranoid doesn't mean that somebody's not out to get your evening radio slot.

"...means, motive, opportunity," Christy was saying. "We don't quite have all those pieces yet, but in my journalism class they also taught us who, what, when, why and how."

"We didn't even get the first three and now we have six more?"

"Well, I think it would be five more."

"You forgot number six—how much?" I said. "So far the only money involved has been Bronc Billy's quarter mil. I think we need to follow that trail."

"You think the art theft and Mrs. Edelbaum's death are connected?"

"Well, something seems to be going on here unless the crime rate in Kirby is higher than Detroit's. And tonight is perfect for checking out Bryan's digs. Are you up for it?"

"Don't worry, Jerry. I'm sure I can pick the lock to get in."

"Means, motive, opportunity. What are we waiting for?"

WE had been in such a hurry to check out the gallery owner's own home that we hadn't thought to bring a flashlight. And the little night light he'd left burning wasn't strong enough to illuminate too much in the way of clues that might have been left lying around. For that matter, it didn't even prevent us from tripping over the furniture on our way to the powder room.

Instead the light from our cell phones allowed us to find the windows where we closed the drapes. Having blocked the view from outside, we felt okay turning on a few table lamps. That handled, we could use the phones for what they were intended for—taking pictures.

The inside of the *hacienda* was as nice as the outside had promised. High-end cowboy furniture, even an easy chair made out of steer horns, though I wouldn't want to try sitting on it in the dark. Western paintings and photographs decorated the walls and a Navajo blanket was thrown over the back of a leather couch. Christy pointed out that a couple of the paintings were by Rex Bowman and looked pretty much like the ones in the gallery. One was a view of the old swimming hole that started all this.

Living room, dining room, a half-bath, kitchen....

"Look, Jerry, a walk-in closet..."

"...bigger than my whole apartment..."

"...a lot more house..."

"...a *bidet*?"

We weren't finding out much about the owner except he was neat and had impeccable taste in this line of furnishings.

"I DIDN'T realize that the art world paid so well," I said as we sized up the dining room. A leather-topped table that could seat ten comfortably or fourteen with crowding was the centerpiece surrounded by chairs upholstered in some kind of cow hide, the kind with the cow hair still on it.

In the pantry a wine cooler with a glass door was chock-full of bottles. And well, what's the use of breaking in if you don't take something?

"Not that one, Jerry," Christy advised. "He'd definitely miss that bottle. I saw it listed for over two hundred dollars at Tucson Liquors. That sauvignon blanc—the one with the yellow label—doesn't look too special. Let's try it. Maybe it'll quiet my nerves."

"It's your party," I said, popping the screw cap. I had to admit I was ready for a little nerve tonic myself.

As it turned out, the wine wasn't half bad, and after a few glasses, we were in the mood for more than just pawing through Forbes-Collier's underwear drawer (Egyptian cotton boxers). I admit we began to get a little sloppy, pulling pictures off the walls and books from their shelves. One bottle also led to another as we went through every drawer and cupboard in the house.

Along about two-thirty in the morning as we began to tire, we took our glasses and a fresh bottle—the one with the blue label this time—out on the patio for a break from housebreaking. The moon had dropped by then and a million stars looked down on us, all alone in a desert hideaway, just cool enough to inspire some inspired cuddling.

"This must be what home on the range means even if it isn't really our home," I said holding Christy tight.

"I know. We'd have had more time for this—being together, not searching the premises—if I hadn't brought Mom with me. But you know she's all alone now."

"Don't sweat it. And it wasn't her fault our midnight swim didn't work out."

"Too bad it didn't," Christy said, nuzzling my ear.

And I did some nuzzling of my own.

Chapter 17.

"JERRY, wake up," Christy shouted as loud as a whisper would allow. I was half off the bed from her nudging me awake. "Wake up! Somebody's in the house."

I had to shake myself a few time to realize where we were. Where we were was in Bryan Forbes-Collier's bedroom having fallen asleep after making you-know-what between his expensive sheets. I rolled out of bed stepping on a two hundred dollar empty that rolled under my foot sending me rolling too. The good thing was that Bryan had the foresight to choose deep plush wall-to-wall carpeting so I had a relatively soft landing. Too bad he didn't think about what red wine would look like on light beige though. When I came to a standstill, and got barely standing, I could hear somebody quietly moving around in the living room.

I also realized that Christy and I were in the altogether and must have done the stripping someplace out there. If we wanted to dress, we'd have to ask the intruder to toss our duds in to us. We decided we didn't want to get caught with our pants down, so to speak, and with a lot of hand signals and head bobs we decided that discretion was the better part of valor and we had better scram. With no better plan in sight, Christy and I wrapped ourselves in bed sheets and slipped out onto the patio.

What with dead bodies and ball peen hammers and now a stealthy visitor, I was beginning to think somebody other than Mrs. Marshall wanted to put a kink in my love life. Every time Christy and I got around to taking off our clothes, something came up. And I don't mean in a good way.

So we tippy-toed on bare feet out to the little barn where we'd stashed the Cherokee. Luckily it was still there with the key in the ignition, ready for a speedy getaway. We spent a few minutes adjusting bed sheets to cover our modesty as best we could though I was still half in the bag and half asleep. That didn't leave much room for clear thinking.

"Let me help drape you," Christy whispered. "Or you'll be quite drafty in back."

"How did you get so good at this anyway?"

"Well, I did attend a few toga parties back in school."

I had to ask.

With the barn door cracked an inch, Christy and I took turns peeking at the house. I couldn't see anyone looking back at us which I took to be a good thing, but a dust-caked pickup was parked near one side and I was pretty sure I would have noticed if it was there last night. Maybe it was just the cleaning lady or maybe it belonged to somebody who'd just stopped by to steal a few more paintings but either way, we hoped they wouldn't bother checking out our hiding place. In the meantime we were pretty much trapped.

But at least we weren't totally naked anymore and so far today we hadn't found any more bodies. When they found ours, at least we'd have togas on. Still no sign of life from the big house. I was thinking about how to make our getaway in case the dusty pickup didn't make its getaway in the near future. This is where Ronnie's magical thinking would come in handy. I was weighing the pros and cons of whether I would call him if I had a phone and was going to get Christy's opinion if—hey, where *was* Christy?

Like one of The Great Rondini's illusions, she had vanished into thin air. Stepping away from my guard post I checked the car in case Christy was catching a little shut-eye in the back seat. No Christy. I could see the front of a loft above the car and a little room jammed with every kind of gardening tool. I wondered if Forbes-Collier had plans on making the desert bloom? He should only see the Canyon Country Club.

No soap anyway. That is, no Christy.

"Jerry, look over here." Unless my ears were playing tricks on me, I could swear I heard her voice.

"Jerry!" There it was again.

Then I saw a section of the wall under the hayloft move and I could see it was some kind of hidden door. Christy leaned out, waving me on through to a dimly-lit room. As I stepped in, Christy hit the light switch and—

OMG!

There had to be a couple dozen paintings, some on easels, some in stacks along the walls. The room smelled of turpentine and varnish. Tubes of paint and jars of brushes sat on a table to one side. There were paintings of desert scenes and herds of wild horses running...well, running wild, I guess you'd say. Several portrayed Native Americans in Indian costumes and one picture was of the watering hole where Bev Edelbaum's corpse had been left. But what I couldn't stop looking at, what Christy and I both couldn't take our eyes off, were half a dozen versions of Colonel Winston and his Trusty Scout in various stages of completion.

If one of them wasn't Bronco Billy's painting, they were all certainly its brothers and sisters. What the heck, at a cool quarter million apiece the hidden room in the little barn must have held...well, an awful lot.

"This must be why Mrs. Edelbaum was murdered," Christy said.

"Because she knew about this room?"

"Because she knew about a big time art scam. That would be motive enough."

"Sure. Means, motive and opportunity..."

"I think we should take this with us," Christy was holding up a twin to the painting Bronco Billy had shelled out big bucks for.

"That would be stealing. Maybe we broke in, but we're not crooks," I said hoping it was true. "Not counting the wine, I mean. Anyway we need to leave these for the sheriff so he can catch Mister Forbes-Collier red-handed."

"That's true, but we need to preserve the evidence. What if he—or maybe the guy in the house—decides to burn these?"

"Well, yeah. We don't know who's in the house or if they even know about this room. We don't even know whose side they're on." That thought didn't make me feel any better. "I know it's not Redhawk. His truck's not that clean."

"Okay, Jerry. Then let's just take one with us. I wish we had our phones so we could video the rest."

"Yeah. I'm thinking reality TV. That would be a great segment."

"Take a look outside also. Maybe that truck will be gone."

"Or maybe I'll see somebody on his way back here. We gotta think about getting out of here before they or he or whoever it is thinks about checking this place out."

There were a bunch of fairly clean rags lying around, waiting, I'd guessed, to be used for wiping up the odd paint spill or for cleaning out brushes, so I corralled a few to protect our copy of Colonel Winston. It would have been sweet to have had some string to tie it all up with, but who's complaining.

This was a major breakthrough and we'd soon be tying up the case instead. I covered the canvas with a few clean paint rags and stuck the entire package under a flap that covered the cargo hold of the Bronco Billy's Cherokee.

"THE pickup is gone," Christy said from the doorway. I walked over and took a look for myself, not that I thought there was anything wrong with her eyesight. I just wanted to feel the joy of seeing an empty parking space. Kind of like when I lived in San Francisco. Anyway, I pushed the barn door wide open and looked around outside. The coast was blessedly clear.

"This is great," I said. "We have enough time to get back to the Circle-K and phone in an anonymous tip to Darrell Lee. With any luck I'll have him on this evening's show and beat Dakota to the finish line."

"Slow down, cowboy," Christy said as we climbed into the Cherokee. "First off, this doesn't prove that Forbes-Collier is the killer, only that he's doing something very shady with these paintings. Or at the very least Billy's painting."

"Yeah, I suppose you're right.... Should we even break the news about Bronco Billy buying a phony? He might be pissed if it makes him look bad." I eased the car slowly over the bumps and ruts taking it slow until we got back to the roadway. With each bump some part of Christy's toga came undone. While she tried to pull it back together, I tried to keep my eyes on my driving.

"Why don't you just tell Billy what we found off the air?"

"I don't know.... He still might be pissed *and* give the scoop to Dakota. I wish I knew what to do. If Ronnie wasn't so busy giving me the cold shoulder, he'd probably come up with a plan to handle Billy as well as the killer."

"As I recall, Jerry, his plan to find my dad's murderer almost got us killed."

"Yeah, but we got great press coverage."

"So either we get killed on our own or have Ronnie plan it for us."

I didn't have a comeback for that, so I just gunned the engine as we headed down the narrow ribbon of blacktop that led back to town.

Chapter 18.

WE were a bit giddy having dug up a huge break in our mystery, even if it turned out not to be the mystery we started out to solve. I had the pedal to the metal and we were flying down the highway. Even if the best Bronco Billy's jalopy could do was maybe seventy, it certainly felt like we were about to take flight.

"We gotta be close to closing this case out," I said as we ate up the miles. "But I just can't quite put all the pieces together."

"Listen, Jerry dear, as I see it, we may need to call for backup."

"Darrell Lee?"

"No, he's running for office so he would want all the credit. And not to put too fine a point on it, he may be a little sore about you sticking him with the v-word."

"Hey, he said it, not me. Or at least he said it first. Besides, after we aired, his popularity spiked, he even went national on some outlets. Let's see Joe Arpaio top that."

I backed off the gas a little remembering the road curved around some giant boulders and that might just be them up ahead. Nobody else was on the road except maybe a car that was barely visible in the rear view mirror.

"Still," Christy was saying, "Darrell Lee may not see a connection between a stolen counterfeit masterpiece and the death of Mrs. Edelbaum."

"C'mon, he's blind if he doesn't see it. Both crimes are connected to the art world right here in little, ol' downtown Kirby, Arizona. Forbes-Collier was running a scam and Bev found out."

"That makes sense to you and me, but what happens if the sheriff arrests Bryan Forbes-Collier for the art scam and then can't connect him to the murder? If he's locked up in the pokey, we won't have a chance to catch him making a mistake."

"So if Redhawk is out, who's got our back?" A glance at the rear view mirror told me that the car behind us was a pickup. I could tell because the truck had closed the distance and was practically on our tail.

"Don't look now, babe," I said, "but I think we're being followed!"

The truck caked with dust and dirt was right behind us and moving fast.

If I sped up those curves just ahead might... well, they might throw me a curve. Meanwhile, the pickup had moved awfully close. Bumper-car close.

The first jolt tossed us into the on-coming lane. With nobody else on the road, I managed to pull back enough to straddle the centerline. The truck banged us again, but I was ready—I twisted the wheel, got off the shoulder, back to the blacktop. Fishtailing, I pumped the gas with one foot and the brake with the other.

The maniac behind the other wheel kept pounding the back bumper—I only hoped my insurance would cover the bodywork. Not to mention our funerals.

I floored the petal and the car started flapping like it had wings. Christy held on to her toga for dear life, but mine was already south of the Mason-Dixon Line. The pickup pulled out to pass, but when I swerved trying to cover my modesty, the Cherokee's rear fender bounced the truck a little bit off the road and it dropped back. Take that, you mother...

We were moving way too fast to slalom through the boulders lining the curves ahead, but the demon truck was putting on even more speed. He was alongside of us now and a sideways glance told me our cowboy pal, Deke Rowen, was at the wheel. Maybe he was sore about the tip, but what's fair for a horseback ride?

I could see his face twisted into a grotesque sneer. Side-by-side, running flat-out, neither vehicle able to take the lead, Rowen started in on our door panels, side-swiping the Cherokee. We careened off the road through the rock-strewn desert at high speed, plowing up sand and sagebrush.

I was bouncing too much now to hold on to the wheel and Christy was just trying to hold on to me, toga be damned. Before we somersaulted, I figured I'd better do something and yelling for Christy to brace herself—"*How?*"—I slammed the brakes with both feet and threw it into reverse.

We spun and bounced even more, the Cherokee doing some kind of airborne rain dance. Dirt and rocks turned the

windshield into a web of cracks. Who knew how fast we were
going, except too damn' fast. The steering went wild, left,
right, left, up, down, up. It felt like being in the spin cycle at
the laundromat. Just as we saw a giant boulder speeding our
way, the car spun and tilted up on two wheels, skidding to a
halt on its side lodged against a mound of rocks. And for all I
knew, maybe a nest of rattlesnakes.

I was able to force open the driver-side door and boost
Christy out. Then she leaned back in, pulling on my toga while
I climbed up the dashboard. We finally landed on solid
ground, checked ourselves for missing parts and tried to
arrange our bed sheets so we could run if Deke Rowen came
back for another swipe at us.

"You okay?" I asked. And she allowed as how she was and
asked in turn about the state of my health. "Fine and dandy,
but I have the feeling Bronco Billy won't get bupkis for the
loaner now."

"Did you see where the guy in truck went?" Christy asked.
"Did he keep going?"

"I don't think so," I said looking around. "Not unless he
tossed a lit cigarette out over there." I pointed to wispy black
smoke rising above a giant boulder. Although a light breeze
was shredding it, the wisp seemed to be growing into a pretty
decent sized smoke signal. "You stay here. I'm going to check
it out."

"Oh, no, I'm not letting you die alone. I'm going too. But I
think we had better go armed just in case it's a trap of some
kind."

"Good idea, you don't have a concealed weapon under that
bed sheet do you?"

No such luck

We searched for any weapons that might have been left
lying around, Christy settling on a tire iron thrown from the
Cherokee, while I selected a good-sized branch from the
sagebrush. Just my luck, bringing a club to a gunfight.

We crept slowly around the big boulder until we spotted
the pickup. Like the Cherokee, it was on its side only the
engine compartment had turned to kindling, a fire blazing
where the carburetor should be, giving off puffs of smoke.
Deke Rowen, the meanest dude west of...well, west of
someplace, was hanging half way through the shattered
windshield, his bloody face only inches from the flames.

Christy quietly said, "He doesn't look so tough now," and I
replied, "No, but I still don't like him." However, I figured it

wouldn't look good to send Christy in for the rescue, so I buckled up my courage and said, "This time you stay here and I'll—"

No go after all.

Fire reached the gas tank and the explosion kicked us on our backsides. Fortunately the boulder shielded us from the blast to some degree and a cactus patch had cushioned our fall. Pin-cushioned, I should say. We were shook up but basically okay. For the second time in as many minutes we checked ourselves and each other for injuries and came up lucky. We should have bought a lottery ticket.

DEKE Rowen was a goner, and because Christy and I had been close to being gone ourselves, we were still in shock, although I had to admit the adrenaline rush had pretty much taken care of any hangovers. While Christy retrieved a water bottle from the Cherokee, I tried to scope out some way to get it back on all fours. Unfortunately it would take somebody a lot smarter than me to figure out how to right-side it without somebody a lot stronger than me to do the lifting. Going back to Forbes-Collier's place would be a very long walk in the sun and heading to Kirby would be even longer.

"Maybe there'll be a mail delivery or the paper boy will come by," I said, hoping the locals out here weren't all on the web yet. Not that we had seen many houses along the road either.

"Do you think they'll see the smoke from the truck as far away as town?"

"Sure," I lied. "The volunteer fire department's probably hitching their nags up to the hook and ladder right now."

Chapter 19.

A<small>N</small> hour later we were still there, sitting in the shade of the boulder. We had started rationing our water, and speaking for myself, I wasn't sure whether we would die from the heat, dehydration or starve to death. Peering through the spots in front of my eyes, I scanned the horizon for signs of life, but the only life I saw looked a lot like vultures. I think they were looking back at us. And licking their chops.

Christy shook me out of my funk, saying, "Jerry, listen! I think I hear a car." I strained my ears and began to think I heard a motor too. After all, the buzzing in my ears couldn't have been loud enough for Christy to hear too.

Yes, definitely. It sounded just like a car; my training at Bronco Billy's used car lot having not been for naught. What's more, I could swear it was getting louder.

Christy and I ran into the center of roadway; we could see a car heading toward us now. In spite of the heat waves rising off the blacktop, we began jumping up and down, arms waving, bed sheets and private parts flapping, while we shouted for it to stop. If this baby didn't pick us up, it would have to run us down.

As it drove closer, we could see it was a rag-top jeep painted up just like the ones they use at the Circle-K to haul the tourists around in. Of course, it must be a Circle-K desert tour. I hoped we wouldn't have to leave any of the tour group behind to make room for us.

"I hope it's not a friend of Deke's."

I immediately wished Christy hadn't said that. I was just beginning to feel like we might get out of this alive. I held my breath as the jeep slowed and finally came to a stop in front of us. Good news—we were rescued—and a little bad news too.

The bad news hopped out from behind the wheel and asked if we were okay. "I was worried," he claimed, "when you didn't show up at the bungalow last night, and then this morning Sassie said she hadn't seen Christy either. You guys stay too long at the toga party?"

"No, Ronnie, we're just fine, thank you. We called for a cab, so you can just mosey along. When you see Dakota, give her our best."

"Oh, Jerry, don't be like that," Christy chimed in. "We are really glad to see you, Ronnie. There's no cab coming and our car is wrecked."

"So it appears," Ronnie said squinting at the undercarriage of the Cherokee. "I was told that somebody saw you headed out of town late last night, so I figured I'd better see if you'd run out of gas or got a flat tire or something."

"Yeah, well the 'or something' is right. But you should see the other guy."

"That him over there?" Ronnie looked at the burning truck.

I wasn't sure if he saw any stray body parts lying around since Christy and I hadn't had the moxie to check out the damage post-explosion. We knew without looking there was nothing we could do for the mangled wrangler.

Ronnie said, "Come on, you two don't look so good. Hop in and let's head back to civilization."

"Maybe I'll wait for the bus."

"Aw come on, Red. Let's smoke the peace pipe, bury the hatchet, uh, hit the firewater, maybe. Even better, I'll buy you lunch back at the ranch."

That Ronnie. Some guys will go to any length to get a few free plugs.

"Go ahead, babe, get in the jeep," Christy said. "I just need to get that thing out of the car."

"That thing?" It took me a minute. "Oh sure, 'that thing.' We don't want to leave 'that thing' behind."

I HAD spent enough time girl watching with Ronnie to know he was checking out Christy as she wiggled her way through the back window of the Cherokee to get 'that thing.' Somehow she just managed to keep the bed sheet from slipping, but Ronnie still got his money's worth. I couldn't fault him though—he has great taste for such a low-down rat.

"What's she getting there? What's so important?"

"Listen, pal, it's just a souvenir we picked up in our travels, but I really don't want to have Dakota spilling the beans on her little afternoon show."

"No way. Dakota and me? That's ancient history. Days since I've even said a word to her."

"Or maybe you should say 'day'? I know Bronco Billy cut in on your time, but you're still trying to help her find the killer, right?"

"Well, not so much. Bronco Billy seems to be a big-time contributor to the Sheriff's election campaign, so she's teamed with Redhawk during the day and Billy during the off-hours. Not that it means anything to me. I was really trying make sure she didn't get too far out ahead of you."

"Just an albatross around her neck, eh? Double-crossing her while you double-cross me. What's that—a quadruple-cross?"

By now Christy was stuffing the artwork in the back of the Circle-K jeep, being careful to keep it concealed. As luck would have it, while Christy took the passenger seat up front and I clambered in back, my toga snagged on some bolt or strut or something. I grabbed for the sheet but got a handful of paint rag too. So there we were—Colonel Winston, his Trusty Scout and me—naked to the world.

"I don't believe it!" The Great Rondini said, sounding as astounded as I'd ever heard him. Since I knew he'd seen me in the locker room plenty of times, it had to be our detective magic that put the amazement in him. He said, "You guys actually found the stolen masterpiece. Jerry, I don't have to be a magician to see a big raise in your future. A very big raise."

Ronnie was spewing out questions so fast we didn't have time to squeeze in any answers. Somehow we got him driving and aimed him back toward the Forbes-Collier homestead so Christy and I could return the bed sheets. While we sped down the highway Ronnie was imagining a fantasy that had a killer smashed up in a burned-out pickup and Christy and me taking bows for saving a fabulous painting. He figured Bronco Billy would probably drop Dakota and start dating me, it being his quarter million that I rescued. We let him carry on as long as he didn't hurt himself or drive off the road. After all, he might be right.

After a while though I figured we'd better cool the boy down to keep him from spreading the word around back at the ranch. A day or two earlier I might have been happy to take the credit for solving Kirby's crime wave, but now I had my eyes on bigger fish. I needed to be a more responsible, more mature, big-time air personality if I was to break out of cowboy radio. Besides there was just a long shot that Sheriff Redhawk and his posse might find out that Rowen really wasn't the killer. Not to mention we had Bryan Forbes-Collier painted—no pun intended—into a corner and couldn't let that go to waste.

"Listen, Ronnie, I'm very glad to see you get so excited for us, even if it's just because Dakota dumped you and you want to get back at her, but since we're pals again, there's something I have to tell you."

"No effing way," The Great One said. "I still can't believe that painting's a copy."

"Sure as you're buying us lunch." We had made it back to Kirby and since Christy and I had missed the breakfast buffet, our minds were more on food than forgeries. We'd given Ronnie the lowdown on the forgeries as well as a quick tour of the Forbes-Collier spread. He helped pick up the empties while Christy and I dressed. I wasn't sure how much our search last night had messed the place up, but it looked like Deke may have contributed his share to the clutter. We gave the place a quick straightening up and tried to wipe away any prints we might have left. Of course this wiped away any of Deke's too, but maybe he was wearing gloves anyway.

Since we were in a little bit of a hurry, we didn't take the time to visit the little barn with the hidden studio, but I figured there would be a chance to visit with the authorities later on. Maybe video them scratching their heads when they see all of Colonel Winston's brothers.

We made it back to the Circle-K in good time and just as Ronnie turned into the drive, he hit the brakes hard enough to leave me and our package on the floor.

"We can't eat here," The Great One said.

At first I suspected it was the old disappearing luncheon invite trick. But then he added, "We need to go someplace where we can discuss everything without being overheard. No telling who else might be tied up in this."

"Guys," Christy said, "The first thing we need to do is report the smashup to the cops."

"Hey, the cops are on Dakota's team. And I'm not sure I'm ready to tell Bronco Billy that I lost one of his fine, pre-owned jalopies."

Ronnie sided with Christy about the cops so I was out-voted, but then he added, "...before getting the Sheriff involved, we should get our stories straight. I'm beginning to see a way we can stir the pot a little."

So we swung by our bungalow and stashed the painting in the back of our closet. Ronnie phoned Satyra to meet us and we drove over to Kirby's dusty downtown which was only about fifty yards from the Circle-K. Parking was a cinch anyway. We found a spot next to a couple of saddle ponies in front of the Dusty Burger Cafe. You've heard of the golden arches? This one had fallen arches. Apparently it was Ronnie's secret rendezvous spot with Dakota back in the old days. You know, like the day before yesterday.

The only person around to eavesdrop on us was a Mexican cook who doubled as the waiter and tripled as bartender. The burgers were cold and the beer was warm so everything evened out. Satyra arrived wearing a tee-shirt over her bikini holding a margarita in a paper cup. Our Tijuana triple-threat perked right up when he saw her, choosing a good spot to watch our table in case she needed a refill.

Anyhow, the old gang from the City by the Bay was together again.

We reprised our story for Satyra who didn't seem all that taken aback about Deke Rowen, but said she figured it must be something like that. I think she probably meant the part about us and the wine and sleeping in Papa Bear's bed, not Rowen's side job.

I turned to my old chum, Ronnie, and said, "I feel like I almost have all the pieces to the puzzle, but I just can't fit them together. Bev Edelbaum was killed because she knew about the forgery, sure. But that would have been Forbes-Collier's play. Who coshed him and stole the forgery? And why? You don't suppose the one Billy bought was real do you?"

"We don't even know if it's still missing," Christy said. "Maybe the one we took actually is the one that was stolen."

"When I saw your copy of the painting I thought it was the real deal, though I'm no expert," Ronnie added.

"Neither is Bronco Billy."

About then, the cafe became real crowded.

"I been looking for you, Mister Jeremy," Darrell Lee Redhawk said. "I think you're going to have to come along with me just as soon as I read you your rights." Darrell Lee had about half the county police trailing after him, which totaled maybe four or five, all trying to look tough. And, as far as I was concerned, succeeding.

"Whaddup, Sheriff," I tried to sound cool.

"I understand you drive a yellow two thousand-seven Jeep Cherokee?"

"Well, yeah, but if it's the registration or something, it really belongs to Bronco Billy. I think it's still got dealer's plates." What with getting back with Ronnie and all, I had almost forgotten our little fender bender out in the desert.

"Sorry, but I'm going to have to take you in for leaving the scene of an accident."

"An accident, eh?"

"So that's why it wasn't where you thought you parked it, Jerry," Christy jumped in. "Somebody must have stolen it."

"Sure," I said, "some kids joy-riding out in the desert."

"I didn't say the accident was out in the desert."

"Well, where would you go joy-riding, assuming you were ever a kid? They'd be spotted here in Kirby and with only a half-mile of road there's not much joy in riding right here. Oh sure, they would go out of town."

Christy said, "I can vouch for Jerry. We've been together all day."

"I might have known you'd have a story."

Ronnie and Satyra piled on to shore up the alibi.

"I have to get back out to the scene right now, but I want you two to come in and make a statement tomorrow. Also you'll need to fill out a stolen vehicle report."

"Was anybody hurt in the, uh, accident," Satyra asked.

"There was a second vehicle, but the driver was burned so bad we haven't identified him yet. We don't have the driver of the Cherokee yet, but we will. It could be a case of vehicular homicide, so don't any of you plan on leaving the county."

Redhawk turned and left without looking back.

It would have been a good exit if it hadn't been for all the deputies scurrying after him. Vampire flubs aside, the Sheriff was no fool and it probably wouldn't take long for him to trash my alibi if he put his mind to it.

Chapter 20.

I HAD the "who", the approximate "when" and "where" the body was found, and the "why" had to be connected to the forged masterpiece. Still there was a lot missing. Deke Rowen couldn't have been the brains of the operation; Bryan Forbes-Collier would be the head of that department. But then who stole the painting from Bryan? And was it the one we picked up back at his secret studio? Or, if copies were being ground out like sausage, why steal that particular one? Was the painting Bronco Billy bought really the original? Or not so much?

I wasn't getting very far with means, motive and opportunity either.

Ronnie and I and Christy and Satyra spent the afternoon trying figure all the angles. At least Ronnie did, that being his particular angle.

We finished our lunch at the cafe and then wandered back to the Circle-K, hanging out by the pool until we couldn't take the heat any longer. Our plan though was beginning to come together.

Step one required Christy to track down the TV crew and do some arm twisting. The way those guys had been drooling after her, I didn't think she'd have to twist too hard, although I usually prefer to do my own drooling. I spent the rest of the afternoon lining up my guests for the evening's show. Without a real producer, I was stuck tracking down people and making all the arrangements myself. Talk about being motivated I was more than ready to break the case and start looking for the big city and the bright lights.

Since the sheriff already knew about the accident, we didn't have to worry about reporting it to the local cops either, but I was a little worried about reporting it to Bronco Billy, the

Cherokee being a loaner and all. I hoped he'd understand it would all be good in the long run.

Anyway Mickey's big hand had almost reached the top of the clock and show time. Time that is to stir the pot a little bit more.

"Hello, folks. You're tuned to the Jerry Jeremy show on KICK radio, The Talk of the West, coming to you from the famous Palomino Lounge at the Circle-K Ranch and Spa. We have a live audience tonight and on our guest panel this evening we have Bronco Billy Wooten, a well-known collector of western art and memorabilia, as well as owner of Wooten's Fine Pre-owned Trucks and Autos right down there in nearby Tucson. Next we have Cochise County Sheriff Darrell Lee Redhawk and Arizona's own western artist, Rex Bowman. And rounding out the panel, the only guy I know—at least in Kirby, Arizona—who has the power to cloud men's minds, The Great Rondini. Too bad it doesn't work on women, huh?"

Bronco Billy being on the panel, I tried to hold down the number of free plugs since he had to pay for his, but I did throw in a few kind words about the Circle-K hosting us. I also said a few words about KOW-TV doing the video for their Facebook page or the eleven o'clock news or whatever. Little did I know I'd be eating those words before long.

"And thanks to the good people at KOW-TV, we have a special video feed from Bisbee General bringing us the owner of the Kirby Gallery, Bryan Forbes-Collier. Out there with Bryan is my own number one reporter and—well, let's just say she's divine—Christy Marshall.

"Hi Christy, Bryan, are we coming through okay?"

Christy allowed as how we were and I said we could see them fine too. Since Sassie Marshall had decided to accompany her daughter on the trip, in my mind's eye I pictured her stepping in to direct the shoot. Trying to focus on something else before my show went south, I jumped into my opening monologue giving the audience a rundown on the criminous goings-on over the past few days. I was winding up the story of the theft of Colonel Winston and his Trusty Scout with some emphasis on the good parts, like how I saved Forbes-Collier's life.

"...and just this morning, one of Bronco Billy's fine pre-owned automobiles was hijacked right out of the Circle-K's corral. For all you tenderfeet out there, a corral's a lot like a

Safeway parking lot only you gotta be careful where you step.

"Corrals and parking lots aside," I said, "the stolen vehicle was involved in a fatal accident on a lonely desert road around one o'clock this afternoon. Sheriff Redhawk, can you fill us in on what happened?"

"Yes, Jerry. A yellow Jeep Cherokee that left the Circle-K, time unknown, was found on its side by Apache Rocks about six miles south of Kirby. Although the Cherokee appeared to be abandoned..." Darrell Lee droned on about police efforts to find the driver and so on and so forth. Having convincingly buried the lead, he finally got back to the main story. "The other vehicle involved in the crash, a dark green 2010 Ford pickup truck, apparently burst into flames with its driver still inside. He was pronounced dead at the scene."

"What is known about the driver of the pickup, Sheriff?"

"He was burned so badly that we are trying to confirm his identity using dental records. We know who the vehicle was registered to, but are not releasing any details until the victim's identity is confirmed."

"There you have it, folks, at least as much as can be told for now. Earlier, I mentioned the theft of a two hundred and fifty thousand dollar painting from the Kirby art gallery and tonight we have the painting's owner Bronco Billy Wooten here, as well as on a remote feed from the Bisbee hospital, the owner of the gallery where it was purchased. Bryan Forbes-Collier is recovering from injuries sustained trying to prevent the theft."

Forbes-Collier seemed to puff up a little at the intro or maybe the bandage around his head just made him look that way. So, after giving the man his due, I turned it over to Christy for the interview. She had him describe how he thought he was all alone in his store when suddenly he was cracked over the head from behind and woke up in the hospital.

"So you didn't have an opportunity to see the person who attacked you? But did you even know someone was in the gallery with you?"

"Why no, I was totally surprised."

"When you woke up?"

"I don't understand."

"You were knocked out cold, so it was a surprise when you woke up here at the hospital, right?"

"Well, yes. I was surprised to wake up here, but also surprised when I got hit, I'm sure."

"Wow, that must have been some hit. But that aside, you must not have known the painting had even been stolen until the police told you, right?"

"I... uh, I guess not."

"How long had that painting been in the gallery, that is, when did you originally get it?" Gotta hand it to Christy, she was great at this interview stuff. I was really getting interested, so I bet the listeners were all ears too. A perfect time to slip in a commercial break.

"Christy, I know we're all dying— no pun intended—to hear more of Bryan's story, but right now...."

SINCE it was Bronco Billy's dime, I pulled him into the commercial to tell us how great his auto deals were. I took a run at how listeners could get a super deal on a certain yellow fixer-upper out on the highway south of town, but Billy didn't seem to think it was all that funny. I knew he'd be back on my side later though. After all, I had something he wanted.

After the break Christy continued working on Forbes-Collier. We had decided not to bring up the Leibergard copies we found until we had enough to bag him and to bag any accomplices he may have had. After all, somebody did slug him and steal the original so there had to be somebody else involved. Our theory is it was somebody who knew it was being copied. The only artistic talent hanging around was Rex Bowman, but Bev had been pretty high on him so I didn't think he would have slit her throat. A guy needs all the fans he can get; I oughta know.

With a little prodding I got Rex Bowman to give us the high points of Leibergard's career and then asked how he felt when he first laid eyes on the masterpiece. He said, *"It was an extraordinary experience. I could see right off it was created by a master. I only wish I had gotten a better opportunity to study it further. The first I knew of it was when it went on display at the gallery opening two days ago. I can only hope it turns up. For everyone's sake."*

"I'll need to run this by Mister Forbes-Collier," Bronco Billy said, *"but to my way of recknin', if I can get my hands back on it, with all this publicity it'll be worth twice what I paid for it. Darrell Lee, how's that investigation comin', son?"*

"It's the department's number one priority," the sheriff replied, *"because it follows so closely on the heels of the recent homicide. Our working theory is the crimes are connected*

since it would be too great a coincidence if an art patron's murder and an art theft just happened to occur right here just days apart."

Okay. That sounded like it could be my cue. I broke in, but not for a commercial.

"Well, I'm not a great believer in coincidence either, but I have a major one right here." I signaled Rondini who waved to Satyra who would have been just off-stage if we had had a stage. She walked past our small audience and stepped into the limelight with a package wrapped brown paper. *"As my regular listeners all know, Christy and I found Beverly Edelbaum's body and then found Bryan Forbes-Collier knocked unconscious in his gallery with a famous painting gone missing. Well, your truly is now going for the trifecta."*

"Not another body," Billy shouted.

"No, not tonight." I looked around to make sure the TV crew were focused on Satyra, not that they wouldn't have been anyway. *"Tonight what I found was this—"* Satyra and Ronnie tore at the wrapping, ripping open the package. There revealed for all to see, our guest panel, the live audience and especially for Bryan Forbes-Collier on the video remote, was the missing Leibergard. Everyone was dumb with shock. Not so great for a radio broadcast. Suddenly the room erupted, everyone talking at once. Billy jumped with joy, Redhawk demanded some answers and Bowman was just stuttering. From the audience both the newlywed Hastings and Sal No Last Name jumped up to get a closer look. I never realized we had such a bunch of art lovers here at the ranch.

"For those of you listening in, we have just unveiled the stolen masterpiece 'Colonel Winston with an Indian Scout, Fort Apache, New Mexico'. As you can probably tell, it has caused quite a stir here..." I continued with the play-by-play while everyone settled down. As the commotion died, I figured I had better try to get on Darrell Lee's good side since I'd sandbagged him on this. *"Sheriff Redhawk, I expect you have a few questions concerning the recovery of this painting. Fire away. With your questions, that is."*

"Your expectation is correct, except I have quite a few more than just a few questions. There may be some you'll want to have your lawyer present for, but I'll get to them when we're not on the radio."

"What a kidder you are, Sheriff. I know your number one question and that of our listeners is how I managed to find the stolen painting? And I don't want to keep everybody in

suspense any longer than necessary, but it is time for one of Bronco Billy's wonderfully informative messages—"

"Shee-<bleep>, Jeremy, <bleep> the commercial!" screamed Billy. *"Tell us about the pitcher!"*

"Well, you are the sponsor and it is your picture. But to tell the truth, I don't know how I recovered the painting." Redhawk looked like he was ready to go on the warpath, so I backpedaled as fast as I could. *"That is, I heard a knock on my bungalow door—and I really want to thank to the Circle-K and its staff for their great hospitality—when to my surprise I found someone had left a package on my doorstep. We opened it and* voìla, *Colonel Dub-ya!"*

"I do have a question or two for on the air after all," Redhawk said. *"First you just said 'we' opened it. Who is we? Was someone else there who witnessed your good fortune?"*

"I was with Jerry," Rondini said. *"We share the bungalow and I was there. I heard the knock on the door, saw the package, helped open it."*

"Besides," I added, *"the good fortune was really Bronco Billy's. It's his picture."*

"Okay, you were both there," the sheriff conceded. *"I am hoping the paper wrapping you just ripped to shreds wasn't on the object when it was delivered?"*

"Oh, no," Satyra answered. *"I wrapped it up for tonight. You know, so nothing would happen to it."*

Redhawk turned to me and asked, *"Just how many people have handled the evidence so far?"*

"Not many. I mean just Rondini and me and Rondini's assistant. Maybe Christy too." When I mentioned Christy, we all looked at the video feed from Bisbee General. Nobody at our end had been paying much attention to Forbes-Collier what with all the excitement. The hospital camera had been squeezed into the hallway and all we could see were a gang of medicos crowded around Bryan's bed with a bunch of machines and tubes and scary instruments.

I called out to Christy hoping she hadn't fainted or something.

"Jerry, I'm here."

"I can hear you, but I can't see you. What's happening?"

"I'm fine, but I think Mister Forbes-Collier has had a heart attack." Off-screen I could hear Sassie say, *"Of course, it could be a stroke."*

Chapter 21.

I SUPPOSE a really thoughtful person might have guessed that Forbes-Collier would go all cardiac on us when we brought out the famous painting or at least what looked like the famous painting. Assuming he really knew who had snatched it. I usually rely on Ronnie for that level of thoughtfulness, so it's pretty much his fault if you look at it that way.

At least all the commotion sidetracked Darrell Lee's attempted interrogation.

The medical drama took the spotlight away from Colonel Winston, the rest of the show being pretty much devoted to crash carts and IVs and Christy collaring doctors for a few sound bites. I was glad to see none of the MDs were under the age of fifty. While Christy and her mom were driving back from Bisbee, Billy ordered up champaign for the rest of us in celebration of his painting's return. Since he was buying, I didn't see any reason to tell him right now it was just a cheap copy.

"Goddamn' it, I jus' knew things would start to pop if we all jus' kep' after it," Bronco Billy was saying. And to Sherm who was personally caring for Billy's every need, "Keep the bubbly comin' we got a lot to celebrate."

"I'm so-o glad you got your painting back," Dakota cooed into Billy's good ear. "I bet in another day or two, it would have been left on my doorstep."

Even Bronco Billy had to wince at that one. But he still seemed pretty happy.

Less happy was Sheriff Redhawk. I won't say he was in a pout, but he barely touched his wine. I didn't really like the way he was looking at me either, as though maybe I had been holding out on him. Of course I was, but for his own good. I didn't want any of those vampires to get him.

"You must lead a clean life to get that kind of good fortune." Sal the Godfather smiled down on our little group and stuck out a paw to shake Billy's hand. "Whoever snatched that painting in the first place must have had a change of heart."

Sal accepted a glass of champaign while he and Billy chatted about how good life is. Meanwhile, Gloria, Sal's aging gun moll, engaged Satyra in a discussion about the lack of humidity in the desert, it being the desert and all. Sal seemed to be full of good cheer having recognized a fellow shyster. When he finished off the wine and pried his eyes loose from Dakota's cleavage, he paused to give me the once me over, but this time he wasn't smiling.

THE look did make me nervous, but when Gloria sidled up and let him pat her fanny, Sal switched from a frown to a full megawatt smile, maybe remembering I didn't owe him any money. I didn't have time to consider it any further though because the newlyweds burst in on us, saying how much they liked the show and wasn't it great the painting had turned up again.

The very clean-cut David Hastings was saying, "It's so seldom a person gets the chance to see a real masterpiece. Do you suppose Mr. Wooten would care if Jennifer and I took a real close look?"

"After the look-see the Italian took at Dakota," I replied, "I don't think Bronco Billy would mind a couple of my fans and potential car buyers checking out a picture. Are you big art *aficionados*?"

The very pert Jennifer said they never passed up seeing any of the shows blowing through the Phoenix Art Museum. I said that was swell and they moved off to see the Colonel and his Trusty Scout close up. I only hoped the paint had time to dry.

By now Rondini and Satyra had stepped over to the main room at the Silver Cage Saloon for their late show, so I slipped into a seat at the table between Bronco Billy and Darrell Lee. On Billy's other side, Dakota gave me a friendly smile and said it was right good work finding Billy's painting. It just shows what a half-dozen or so glasses of champers can do. Meanwhile Billy poured one for me and topped up the sheriff's cup as well. Maybe the wine was working on Darrell Lee too, because now he was smiling at me. With all these smiles I wondered if maybe I had something on my nose.

"Jerry, this here evenin' was real swell, what with you gettin' my pitcher back," Billy said. "I been sittin' here thinkin' of som'thin' that could be real great for the station an' all. An' needless to say, real good for Bronco Billy's auto business too."

"Sure, that's swell, Billy," I said. "I guess it would be back to Plan A, putting the Leibergard on display out at the lot. Better put it in one of those bulletproof glass cages, like you see in the movies."

"Well, yeah. There is that." Bronco Billy unwrapped a family-size Havana and rolled it between his fingers. Since it was illegal to smoke indoors even in a ghost town, he had to be content sticking it in the corner of his mouth and clamping down with his mail-order choppers. For Billy though, this was about as contemplative as I had ever seen him. "There is that," he repeated. "An' that's mighty fine. Mighty fine. But what I was thinkin' of was som'thin' else."

"Excuse me." David Hastings leaned in looking just the slightest bit inquisitive. Jennifer peered over his shoulder, kind of blank-faced. "Sorry to interrupt."

Although Christy and Ronnie and Satyra and I had looked the forgery over and compared it to the one we found on the web, I couldn't be sure it was an absolute match. If the Hastings really did know something about art, they might have found something bogus in our copy and couldn't wait to break the news.

"By the way, it's a great painting. Jen and I truly appreciate being allowed to look at it up close. But we wondered—and we're sure you're way ahead of us on this—but since it has already been stolen once, is there a secure place to keep it now?"

"Well, o' course, one of the big things any crook needs to know," Billy waived away any concern with the hand gripping his cigar, "is *where* to find it in the first place. An' that is top secret information." Billy topped this off with a chuckle and offered them a refill on the champaign, but they begged off, it being a little past their bedtime. Newlyweds, you know.

As I watched the Hastings head for the door, I saw Christy and Sassie coming in, having made it back from Bisbee in record time. Christy scooted in next to me and downed two glasses of the bubbly before she could say anything. Even Mrs. M was putting it down like she'd never saw reality TV before. Anyway, Christy gave an update on Forbes-Collier: heart attack, intensive care, positive prognosis, and nothing else we didn't already see and hear on the video. Sheriff Redhawk had a few questions about Forbes-Collier's reaction to seeing the recovered painting, but it seems that it was just a quick case of cardiac arrest. It didn't necessarily follow that the painting and the heart attack were connected, but then again some people still believe in the tooth fairy. Darrell Lee didn't seem to be one of them.

He was saying, "...it seems like a few too many things going on here. Jerry, you claim your vehicle was taken by party or parties unknown, but you never got around to reporting it stolen—"

"Well, I didn't realize it was stolen until you told me so," I protested.

"I'll let that go for the moment. But the vehicle eventually is discovered at the scene of an accident. An accident involving a fatality. Are the auto theft and the accident just a couple of random events? I admit it's possible. But then later the same day, someone leaves a valuable stolen painting on your doorstep. This seems awfully coincidental."

Bronco Billy dropped his cigar in the ice bucket and asked, "What exactly are you gettin' at, Sheriff?"

"Just trying to see how this all plays out. I was working on the theory that the painting was somehow tied to the Edelbaum death. But now some good Samaritan has maybe indicated that that ain't the case having dropped the painting off right on Jeremy's doorstep. Otherwise, I'd have bet my badge that the painting was already destroyed."

"Don't fret it, son," Billy said. "You may not be the world's greatest detective, but you ain't gonna lose that badge whilst I have som'thin' to say about it."

And I'd bet that Darrell Lee was a shoo-in with Bronco Billy in his corner. Of course, solving a big murder case would help too. Anyway, the sheriff bid us adieu, only not in those words, and headed out. I was about to suggest to Christy that we do the same when Bronco Billy signaled us to scoot in close like he had a secret to share.

"I got something I want to tell y'all, a secret for the time bein', but once we get back to Tucson, I'm gonna make it so."

Announcements like that in radio don't always signal glad tidings, so even Dakota looked a little put off. As for me, I only hoped he'd remember who got his expensive painting back. Apparently Dakota couldn't stand the suspense as Billy fiddled with his cigar. She said, "That sounds exciting, Bronco Billy. What can it be?"

"Don't nobody get a case of the heebie-jeebies, especially not you, darlin'. This will put the kick back in KICK Radio. Jerry here has been using Christy here as his guest host and I for one like the job she's doin'. So much so, I am goin' to give Christy her own slot on KICK."

"Why, Bronco Billy," Christy began, "I am very flattered by your offer and also, I must say, very surprised."

"Listen to that little sweetheart," Billy said. "Shy as the day is long. Until she gets that microphone in he hand, that is. Purfect, jes' purfect."

I was hoping Billy hadn't tired of Dakota and wasn't planning to upgrade.

"Well, Bronco Billy, I don't know what to say," she said. We all knew what was coming next.

"Jes' say yes and make this old man happy."

So Billy and Christy, with a little encouragement from her beaming mother, dickered back and forth and figured they could figure out how to work around her graduate studies and this and that. Meanwhile, Dakota and I were counting up the hours in the day and figuring the Talk of the West already had them all covered. I didn't want to hear that part of the plan, but Dakota rubbed up against our sponsor and asked, "I think this is an absolutely *great* idea, Billy, but which time slot would Christy take?"

"The way I got it figured, she'd be a natural from one to four."

At this point Dakota blanched, popped her eyes and squeaked, "But baby, that's my time slot, that's my show."

Bronco Billy had to laugh at that one. "Don't worry, honey-bunch. This here's the crux o' my idea, namely you an' Jeremy here will team up on the evening show."

It was my turn to blanch now

Chapter 22.

AFTER Bronco Billy dropped that bomb, minor things like murder and stolen masterpieces took a backseat to career planning. Dakota couldn't decide whether to stare daggers at me or Bronco Billy. At this rate, Billy might find himself bunking in with Rondini and me. As for me, I was trying to walk a three-way tightrope—give Christy all my love and support for starting a new career, avoid pissing off Bronco Billy with my sour grapes and pretend I wasn't going to elbow Dakota in the teeth if she put the moves on my microphone.

After we celebrated with yet another bottle of the desert's finest bubbly, I was able to pull Christy away though romance was about the farthest thing from my mind. That shows how serious this was.

"You seem a little upset, Jerry. It's not because Billy offered me that job, is it?"

"Hey, I'm happy for you, it's well deserved," I said. "It's just the collateral damage."

"Dakota."

"I could always put out a contract on her, but with my luck the hitter would miss and get me."

"I could always say no to Billy."

"You had better say no to that old lecher, even if you are working for him."

"I mean say no about the job, silly."

"No, no, don't do that. In this business, it could take years to get a break like this again. I have a better idea."

"Speak."

"Well, it's really the same plan—find the killer and tie up all the loose ends. Then you and I will be the big cheeses and Dakota will just be cheesy."

"I can live with that. But I was also thinking of a Plan B."

"You're beginning to sound like Rondini, but a guy can't have too many plans."

"Well, if it turned out you had to have a female partner, it doesn't necessarily need to be Dakota."

"Wow, you wouldn't mind giving up your own show?"

"Not if it meant being your partner."

"That would be great. But first let's see if we can catch up with Ronnie and figure out who killed Mrs. Edelbaum."

THE Great One was just finishing up his act when we walked into the Silver Cage Saloon. Satyra had already been sawed in half, disappeared from a locked cage and materialized in a cloud of smoke. After that what more was there to do? The saloon was almost full but Christy and I grabbed a table from a couple who were getting out before the encores started. As it was, Rondini and Satyra got a pretty good round of applause, but finally wrestled themselves away from the limelight long enough to join us.

"Nice crowd here tonight," Ronnie was saying while Satyra signaled the waiter. "And nobody in *my* audience got a heart attack."

Satyra added, "Jerry, when you kill, you really kill."

"Sure, pile on," I said. "It gets even better."

"Do tell."

"I'll let Christy break the news along with my heart."

"Don't go overboard, Jerry," she said before turning her baby blues on Ronnie and Satyra. "Here's the deal: I guess Bronco Billy liked the way I handled those doctors tonight and thinks he could use someone like me. He offered me Dakota's afternoon radio show."

"So Dakota becomes a full-time mistress?" Satyra asked.

"Jeez," Ronnie said, "she only works three hours a day now." At this we all paused for thought, seeing as how our own workdays were pretty much like that too. And we didn't even have to sleep with Billy. Well, maybe I lose a little change on the back nine now and again. Anyhow, Ronnie didn't have to sleep with anyone and he works even less than me.

"So what becomes of Dakota?" Ronnie asked.

"Well..." Christy paused for effect.

"Go ahead, Sweetie, I'll just plug my ears."

I'm sure that Christy loves me as much as I love her. Which is a lot. But she seemed to see something very funny in the situation that somehow I was missing. Amid barely repressed giggles she got out the story of how Bronco Billy had decided to team me up with Dakota Holiday. I ordered another round.

After a while my so-called pals calmed down and we began to toss around ideas about the killing. We didn't know what we didn't know, but we did know some things nobody else knew. Like the fact that Deke Rowen had been nosing around the Forbes-Collier spread before trying to kill Christy and me. And that we'd found a hidden studio full of Leibergard knock-offs. And what everybody did know, Bev Edelbaum was tied into the art scene and might have stumble on a few secrets of her own. It could be Deke did her in, but he would have just been the muscle. He didn't have brains enough or the connections to do some kind of art scam. All things being equal, Deke really didn't have brains enough to tie his own shoes. That's why he wore boots.

Around the Circle-K, Deke had hung around with a chubby ranch hand named Slim Bales. Fortunately, Slim seemed to not be wound as tight as Deke was. Still not a lot of smarts, but not a lot of mean either. If we could get him talking, we might learn more about Deke and what kind of games he might have been up to. Of course, by "we" I mean Satyra. Talk about the power to cloud men's minds. Tomorrow Satyra would mosey on down to the corral and see if she could rope and tie old Slim.

The only other key player was Forbes-Collier, but right now he was down for the count. But we had seen a lot of Rex Bowman hanging around with the gallery owner, not to mention his connection to Bev Edelbaum. Christy would try her hand with him. I only hoped he wouldn't wind up in the ICU also. That left Bruce. Bruce Edelbaum, the grieving hubby. He seemed to have recovered enough to complete his stay at the Circle-K without Bev. The bikini action at the swimming pool seemed to be some form of therapy for the guy. Since I'd had him on the show a few times already, it fell to me to see if I could find any cracks in his alibi.

As for Ronnie, he promised to dedicate himself to some heavy thinking in the ayem. He'd also keep an eye on Bronco Billy and Dakota to see if there was anything brewing besides adultery and screwing up my career. On that note we sized up all the accommodations, the girls figured out where they and Mrs. Marshall would bunk, Rondini and I drew each other again, and everybody wished everybody a good night. I did walk Christy back to her bungalow and at least got a hug and a kiss for my effort.

WHAT with Christy not around to snuggle with and with Rondini's snoring aimed in my direction, sleep was hard to come by. I kept tossing, thinking how great it would be if I could get Ronnie and my potential mother-in-law hooked up. Sassie might be a little old for him, but I was sure Ronnie could put some kind of spell on himself. Maybe like a five or six margarita spell. By the time the sun came up, I finally went down. Next thing I knew daylight was leaking around the plywood covering our window and in the distance, the sound of people laughing and playing could be heard. As for me, I had a splitting headache and needed coffee.

I managed to get myself showered and shaved and into some clothes. I searched through Ronnie's stuff until I found some aspirin and swallowed a handful. Now for that coffee.

Since I'd slept through the poolside brunch wagon, I headed up to main building where I suspected Sherm Huntley would be on hand to point me to a latte or something. Along the way I bumped into Christy and Sassie on their way to meet Bowman for lunch at the Mesquite Grille. I tried to drop a hint or two to Sassie about Rondini being at loose ends, but she was all atwitter about meeting up with the famous painter. Not as famous as Leibergard of course, but not bad for Kirby. And from the widow's point of view, at least Bowman was still alive.

After scoring some coffee, I figured it was time to bite the bullet and track down Bruce Edelbaum.

"HOW you holding up?" I asked. Bruce just smiled and shrugged.

"I'm holding up okay, I guess."

He took a long draw from a straw sticking out of the tall, cool one he was working on. I had found him sitting by the pool with the young newlyweds, Dave and Jennifer.

"I'm not interrupting, am I?" I said, pulling up a chair of my own.

"No," Dave said, "please join us. Jen and I are great fans. As a matter of fact, we were just telling Mr. Edelbaum how you brought out that painting yesterday evening."

"Yeah, quite a feather in my *chapeau*, if I do say so myself. Particularly since it was my sponsor's painting, but that's neither here nor there. Did you get a chance to see the Leibergard, Bruce?"

Bruce paused to watch a coed spring off the diving board. "Oh, yes. But not at the public showing. When we first got here, Bev dragged me over to see it. Rex Bowman was showing it to her, or us, I guess, but I don't know all that much about western painting. He was acting like a big deal."

"Was Mr. Forbes-Collier there also?" Jennifer asked, taking the words right out of my mouth.

"No, I don't know where he was, but I didn't even realize it was really his property the way Rex was carrying on for Bev's benefit."

"But was Mr. Bowman showing it to you and you're...ah, to Mrs. Edelbaum, in the Kirby Gallery?" She beat me to the punch again.

"Sure, where else? It was in the back room though, didn't have a frame yet."

She then said, "Mrs. Edelbaum was well informed about western art though, wasn't she? Did she share any of her thoughts about such a special work of art?"

While Bruce Edelbaum hemmed and hawed trying to remember what thoughts Bev might have shared with him, my thoughts were running along the lines of making sure Bronco Billy never gets to see Jennifer Hastings in action. Otherwise the evening show might be Dakota and Jennifer while I wind up back in the Indian suit at the used car lot.

Edelbaum's memory finally clicked in and he described how Bev had studied Colonel Winston and friend for a long time before declaring it a masterpiece. "Well, actually," he corrected himself, "she said it was 'masterful' not a masterpiece, but masterful. I guess it's practically the same thing."

I thought this was a pretty good line of questioning though and Bruce agreed to come on the show that evening to repeat the performance. I invited the newlyweds too. They could watch from the audience if they promised to be quiet. I didn't want to be too obvious, but I did manage to squeeze in a question or two of my own before Jennifer could start up again.

Bruce covered a little of Bev's backstory, how she had been an art major in college and had gone on to manage a gallery in Scottsdale for many years. Somewhere along the line, she met Rex Bowman and became his number one fan. "I know what she saw in him, him being a big shot artist. I never did figure out exactly what he saw in Bev. Maybe she was able to unload some of his work, but who knows. Frankly, the steam kind of left our marriage when he breezed in."

I hoped the Hastings would take this as a hint not to get too close to rich, handsome, creative types. Besides I was already taken. Just kidding.

Turns out neither Bev nor Bruce had met Bryan Forbes-Collier before coming to stay at the Circle-K. "Bowman seemed to know him pretty well though," Bruce was saying. "But he was new to us, at least to me."

I tried to pry something—anything—out of him that I could use on the show, but his attention seemed to be wondering. He'd started focusing on the bikinis lounging around the pool. Not to mention the occasional covert peek at Mrs. Hastings who looked to be in pretty good shape too, though with Mr. Hastings right there, Bruce had better watch his step, speaking of watching things.

Since the air had gone out of the Edelbaum conversation, Mr. And Mrs. H. made their apologies and headed to their bungalow to do whatever newlyweds do in the afternoon. Edelbaum slid his straw fedora down to keep the sun out of his eyes and settled in for a nap. Which left me pretty much up to my own devices.

I saw Sal the Godfather and Gloria playing cards at an umbrella table across the pool. I thought of checking in with Sal to see if he still had an eye for art when Christy wasn't around. Then I thought the better of it.

Maybe the best use of my time would be to follow Bruce's lead and grab a nap in the sun. Dakota's show provided a nice, boring hum to lull me to sleep. As I drifted off, she was mumbling something about how the local law was covering all bases, moving on all fronts, film at eleven—

"...and now, breaking news!"

Breaking fucking news! Dead awake, I quick-stepped on hot flagstones over to a speaker so as not to miss a word because Dakota was practically stuttering. Sal No Last Name and Gloria were hanging over my shoulder listening too. Most of the other guests scattered around the pool just looked at us, wondering why we were freaking out.

"Did she just say..." Sal started to say. "I don't fucking believe it."

"It can't be," said Gloria.

"She just did," I said. "She just said Bronco Billy's new painting was stolen—*again!*"

Chapter 23.

It was like *deja vu* all over again. I gave my spot next to the speaker to Sal and started to the lounge when my cell buzzed with Rondini's ID.

"Jerry, you listening to Dakota?"

"I'm headed her way now. Where are you?"

"I'm here already, so's the cops and Billy Wooten. Somebody robbed that damn' painting again."

"You see Christy or Satyra?"

"Not so far. They may still be with Slim Bales and Rex Bowman, if they ran them to ground."

"Bowman was taking Christy and her mom to lunch a little earlier. I'll swing by the Grille to see if they're still there. You have any details on what happened?"

"Not too much, but it looks like Billy hid the painting at the back of Dakota's closet figuring nobody would look in there."

"So Billy didn't find you or the painting in her closet."

"Not me anyway. I swore off when she threw me over for her career. Apparently, the painting was in the closet when Billy and Dakota left for breakfast. They put the Do Not Disturb sign on thinking nobody would come in the room. I heard that when the deputies arrived they jumped all over Sherman and the housekeeping crew. No painting found but who knows?"

By then I was at the entrance to the Mesquite Grille. Christy and Sassie and Rex Bowman were across the room next to the big window looking out at the ranch's expansive landscaping. I hadn't really thought about it before, but the Circle-K's setting was about a hundred and eighty degrees from the Canyon Golf Club's. The ranch was landscaped to look like a desert even though it was smack in the middle of a real desert. They probably watered their cactus more than Canyon watered their greens. A charming landscape, and from where I was standing, Rex Bowman seemed to be charming the ladies. Everyone was laughing at his banter and having a jolly old time. The bastard.

Anyway, a new thought began rattling around in my head. I decided to let the threesome lunch in peace and take a pass on Dakota's reportage. I got Rondini back on the phone and asked if he could get the Circle-K wheels again. For a change I had mystified him, but he figured he could get the loan of a jeep. I suggested we might not want to give away the secret of our disappearing act either; I didn't know who else might want to play bumper cars with us now that Deke was out of the picture. So we stole away while most everybody else was wondering who wanted an old painting that bad. Besides Billy that is; he had a chunk of dough tied up in it.

"So we're back this evening with a repeat of yesterday's news," I told my radio audience. "No, this isn't a Best of Jerry re-run. Yesterday Bronco Billy Wooten had the great Max Leibergard painting 'Colonel Winston with an Indian Scout' stolen from him while it was still at the Kirby Gallery. Fortunately, yours truly, Jerry Jeremy, was able to return the stolen painting to Bronco Billy, the rightful owner, right here on this very show." At this point Billy kind of harrumphed. I was hoping he hadn't lost patience with the way things were going, despite having twice lost a painting worth two hundred fifty big ones. All told that comes to half a million bucks.

We were about five minutes into the seven o'clock segment of my show, all gathered around a table in the Circle-K lounge, Bronco Billy, The Great Rondini, his beautiful assistant Satyra, Darrell Lee Redhawk, Christy and me. The portable radio station was on the table and we all shared the three mics. A man-sized glass of bourbon sat in front of Billy and it wasn't the first of the day either. The KOW-TV camera crew was filming and I had been clever enough to have my best side toward them. Dakota Holiday was nowhere to be seen, either because her big scoop about Colonel Winston and Friend being snatched again had worn her out or someone else had. Nah, it was the scoop. Or maybe she was protesting Billy's plan to team us up. Anyway, I was guessing the TV coverage would look great in my audition reel.

"Like I always say it takes a lot of gumption to rob a man twice," I wasn't sure that came out right, "but it takes even *more to recover the stolen painting a second time. Christy, if you'll do the honors."*

At this point Christy left the round table and picked up a package from behind the booth. It was about twenty by thirty inches in size and only an inch or so thick, covered in brown wrapping paper. It looked suspiciously like the package that brought on Bryan Forbes-Collier's cardiac distress. *"Thank you, Christy. Is our camera team ready? Perhaps we can ask Bronco Billy to open the mystery package..."*

Billy's eyes bulged out and his face reddened to the point I thought he might be joining Forbes-Collier in the ICU. But all he did was gulp some of the liquid fire in his glass and reach out for the night's surprise.

No surprise to you or me though.

RONDINI and I had dropped in on that little hidden studio I knew about after getting the loan of the Circle-K jeep that afternoon.

"What the fuck..." he said as we looked around the place. Paintings were stacked against the walls, on easels, piled on the table competing with brushes stuck in old coffee cans and a bunch of squeezed out tubes of color. My first visit with Christy had been a bit rushed so I hadn't had time to take it all in. While not every art work there was necessarily a forgery, I showed Ronnie three more finished copies of Colonel Winston and his Trustee Scout and a couple more on their way to being done. They all looked pretty much the same. Side by side, you could see some small differences from one to another, but if you didn't look at them all together you probably wouldn't notice.

Ronnie was saying, "...so unless Max Leibergard churned these out on an assembly line back then, somebody's been helping him out."

"Considering the paint's still wet on these two, I'd say somebody's been helping him out. I'm not sure how this scam worked, but I'd bet Bronco Billy isn't the only owner of Colonel Winston and friend."

"Sure," Ronnie said like he thought of it, "they pop out copies and sell 'em as originals. Only Bronco Billy planned to make a big splash about buying his."

"Anybody who saw his adverts or press releases would know something smelled and I don't mean roses."

Not knowing how many more times Bronco Billy might

have his masterpiece stolen, Ronnie and I figured we'd better take all three of the finished copies.

THE rest of the show was pretty much devoted to rehashing today's burglary, dodging Sheriff Redhawk's direct questioning and the timeline of crimes—a crimeline you might say—from Beverly Edelbaum's killing to my second magical recovery of the Leibergard work. I took some calls from listeners, a few of whom actually knew what we were talking about. Between calls, Darrell Lee as much as admitted the cops were at a standstill. Between campaign plugs, that is.

The Great One and Satyra bowed out to do their act at the Silver Cage while Christy was all smiles, hoping Billy wouldn't forget his promise to give her a show. Oh, yeah, Bronco Billy...mustn't forget whose nickel this was on. Somehow, he didn't seem as happy about getting his picture back as he did the first time.

Anyhow, as I was saying, the rest of the show was pretty much a blur. But after I signed off the air, things took a much sharper focus.

"Arrest that som'bitch!"

I looked around to see who Billy meant, but I realized his finger was pointed at me.

"Arrest him, goddammit, Redhawk, or by God, I'll see to it you never win another term!"

"Me, Bronco Billy?" I said. "Why me? I haven't done anything. Why, I'm the guy got your painting back, aren't I?"

"Sure you did—after ya'll stole it to begin with! Dakota was right about you!"

Darrell Lee looked a little flustered, but was pulling out the cuffs.

"Christy, don't say a word without a lawyer," I said. "Come to think of it, try digging one up for me."

"I'm not arresting her," Darrell Lee said. "You're not saying she's your accomplice, are you?"

"Don't be silly, Sheriff. That's the woman I plan to marry."

"Oh, Jerry!" Christy said, "Is that a proposal?"

THE Great Rondini got as far as a second encore at the Silver Cage before the cops arrested him as my accomplice. The cops must have thought they either had us cold or that we were going to walk anyway because they didn't separate us like they do on *Law & Order*. Anyway we got tossed into a holding cell together down in the Bisbee lockup and it looked like we might be spending the night there.

Redhawk and company hadn't bothered to fingerprint us or take any mug shots yet, but on the other hand they hadn't given us our one phone call either. Not that I knew who to call except Christy and she already knew I was in the hoosegow.

It wasn't the first time for us though. As a matter of fact, Rondini was saying, "Remember that time we got thrown in jail back up in Clear Lake?"

"Sure. You got picked up without a prescription for your medicinal weed. I just went along for moral support."

"Ah, really? Then there was a moral to the story?"

"Yeah, the moral is don't get arrested when your lawyer's out of town."

We'd been on ice for about an hour when they put a drunk in the cell next to us. He must have been a regular because he wished us a goodnight and immediately went to sleep. Still we'd heard enough about jail house informants on TV that we stopped talking about making up an alibi, not that we actually knew what we were accused of. Couldn't be Mrs. Edelbaum's murder or the original theft of Bronco Billy's painting. About all that was left is that we stole it the second time so I could recover it again. While it might make for great radio, Billy Wooten is my sponsor and getting him pissed at me might just get me booted, great radio or not. Come to think of it that's exactly what happened, so why would I do it?

"PUBLICITY, that's why," Sheriff Redhawk said. "Mr. Wooten explained how you were trying to outgun Miss Holiday. On the radio at least. So you kept the pot boiling by taking and returning the picture. 'Course since Mr. Forbes-Collier had a heart attack watching your shenanigans, if he should die the Cochise County prosecutor might have grounds for a charge of manslaughter, maybe second degree murder even."

"Us? Darrell Lee, you gotta be crazy!" I explained. "Sure, I like publicity as much as the next guy—you know, like some guy maybe running for public office—but we didn't do anything illegal."

The cops upgraded our room in the morning from the holding tank where Ronnie and I had spent a sleepless night to a nice tight interrogation chamber. It had a few hard chairs, a small table with an ash tray and a faded sign on the wall declaring the county jail to be by law a smoke-free environment. The only light in the place was shining in our eyes. Somewhere in back of it was a very angry Sheriff Redhawk.

"I've got a witness," he threw in our direction. Strike one.

"You were seen returning together to the Circle-K." High and wide.

"The witness will swear you took a package big enough to hold the painting in question from out of said vehicle." Fastball, right over the plate.

"Next thing I know, the damn' thing shows up on your show." Knuckleball, low and wide.

"I know you don't give a shit how this embarrasses me in front of Bronco Billy after I been working my ass off to get his support."

Well, so far we hadn't struck out even though Redhawk was throwing fast and hard. As a matter of fact Ronnie and I couldn't get a word in edgewise, but at this rate we'd know more about his investigation that he would about ours.

"Come on," Ronnie protested, "you were there, Sheriff, a part of the team. You'll get your share of the credit for recovering the painting. And Jerry and I didn't take the painting away, we brought it back. Twice."

"Then explain to me how you knew where to find it. And don't tell me it was left on the doorstep again or you guys will be officially charged with obstructing justice. That alone will get you five years in this state."

I figured we didn't want to get too specific so I tried to turn it back on Darrell Lee. "Who's the guy who saw us? Bring him on so we can see if he still thinks it was us. I demand a line-up."

"All in due time, but I'll tell you this much—it's a reliable witness who knows you two by sight, not to mention he'd been keeping an eye out for the vehicle. With a little persuasion, he might swear out a complaint you stole it."

"No way," Ronnie said. "I left a note for Sherman Huntley. It told him we borrowed the loaner."

"Well, maybe notes have a way of getting lost," the sheriff replied.

Sherman Huntley. The way I figured it, good ol' Sherm was a perfect fit. Unless I find out I'm wrong, this guy gets no tip.

About then, just as Darrell Lee was limbering up for some serious work with the rubber hose, one of the deputies stuck his head in and crooked a finger at the sheriff. Probably wanted to tell him they were ready to start the water boarding.

Or maybe not.

Like something out of Rondini's bag of tricks, Darrell Lee stepped out and David and Jennifer Hastings stepped in and closed the door. The newlyweds took their time sizing up the room—not a honeymoon suite by any means—and strolled over to our table and took seats facing us. It almost felt like we were ready to pass a little time playing dealer's choice. If we had a dealer or any cards. The Hastings were acting very cool, calm and collected, so I didn't think Billy could've had them pulled in too, but something didn't feel right.

Then David said, "My name is Jack Richards and this is my partner, Virginia Taylor."

Jennifer, uh, Virginia said, "We are special agents from the Federal Bureau of Investigation art fraud squad."

At last, someone to talk to.

"We are prepared," David/Jack said, "to offer you a deal if you agree to cooperate with us."

"Otherwise," Jennifer/Virginia continued, "you will be charged and I'm certain you will be convicted of conspiracy to defraud William Lesley Wooten in connection with the purchase of—"

"—a painting known as 'Colonel Winston with an Indian Scout, Fort Apache, New Mexico' falsely purported to be by the artist Max Leibergard, circa 1874." They finished each other's sentences like they'd been married for years. I was beginning to think the newlywed thing was as phony as the paintings.

Needless to say, Ronnie folded like a cheap suite. What could I do but go along?

Chapter 24.

RONNIE and I gave up everything that happened from the time we first hit Kirby and the Circle-K dude ranch. I covered all the territory from finding Bev Edelbaum's body to Bronco Billy's reality murder concept to finding the forged artworks in the secret studio. Sheriff Redhawk stepped in to the room every now and then, but gave the newlyweds—er, special agents—plenty of space. The sheriff's eyebrows did pop up a bit when I described how Deke Rowen came to be toast in his burning pickup.

"So help me God," I was saying, "I have no idea who clobbered Forbes-Collier and got the original. The second one that was stolen was a fake of course. Christy and I had taken it from that hidden room. I guess the thieves got that too."

"No, they didn't," Virginia, who Smilin' Jack was now calling Ginny instead of Jenny, said.

"If the they didn't, who did?" Ronnie asked.

"Ginny and I stole it," Jack said. "We thought it might stir the pot a little."

"Great. We got stirred right into stir."

"Well, that's not entirely our fault. There is a little matter of telling some untruths to the Cochise County police."

"That could be a felony in and of itself," Jennifer/Virginia/Ginny added.

"Come on, they can't hold that against us. We were trying to help them solve a murder."

"I'm not sure Sheriff Redhawk will see it that way," Ginny said. "But we may be able to help you out on that score."

"As far as we can tell, you've given us the full story. At least you had better have," Jack said. He leaned over the table, his eyes flicking between Ronnie and me, looking for our reactions. Having dealt with plenty of Bronco Billy's used car salesmen, I could tell a pitch was coming. "We might be able to get Sheriff Redhawk to drop the charges if you agree to cooperate."

"And," Ginny said, "when we ask you boys to cooperate, it isn't just to hear about your dude ranch vacation."

BRONCO Billy might have had me arrested, but he hadn't actually gotten around to having Dale Anderson fire me yet and when I powered up our portable broadcast studio, I was still on the air. Ronnie and I had made it back to the Circle-K in time to get an impromptu show together though it was a little light on guests.

"This is Jerry Jeremy coming to you on the Talk of the West, KICK radio. We have a great show tonight featuring my best gal, Christy Marshall, my best friend, The Great Rondini, and the best assistant a magician could want, the, well, the pretty fabulous Satyra. If you've tuned in the past week you know we've been broadcasting from the wonderful Circle-K Ranch where even a dude like me feels at home in chaps.

"Of course, you need to watch your step a little out here in the Wild West. Particularly after they drive a few head of cattle down the road. Or when you accidentally drive your pickup off the highway and it bursts into flames. Or when you wind up holding some hot property. Speaking of which, I really did step in it last night and all I was trying to do was to be the good guy."

"Some nerve they got out here, Jerry," Satyra said.

"Well, look, Satyra, we're just city folk to the locals. Why I'm sure they didn't really mean to arrest me practically as soon as my last commercial for Bronco Billy Wooten's Fine Pre-owned Autos was done. If you were tuned in last night you know that Bronco Billy had bought a famous western painting which was stolen out from under him. However, with a little help from my friends—and I mean the ones on the show tonight—I was able to provide Billy with, if not the same painting, one just as good."

"I couldn't tell the difference," Christy said.

"But then that one mysteriously vanished also," Ronnie added.

"But we replaced that one too."

"I still couldn't tell the difference."

"Tell me, Jerry," Ronnie said, *"what's up with the all these*

paintings? They all look the same. Why is that?"

"Could be somebody really liked that painting."

"I don't think that's the answer, son."

"Then it could be something a little simpler. I think that somebody really liked selling *that painting."*

"They were just rolling off the assembly line," Christy said. *"And maybe we need to tell the listeners that you and I found a warehouse full of them."*

"At least four or five anyway."

"A small warehouse maybe, but I know we've had somebody on your show that had a hand in stocking it."

"Sends chills up and down my spine," I said. *"Particularly when we know that at least two people have died because of these paintings, and speaking from personal experience, two people here tonight came close. That's all we can say about the on-going investigation right now, but those of you listening will hear it as I live it. When the noose tightens...well, let's just say somebody's gonna wish for a longer neck."*

The newlyweds—or rather, the newly feds—had given me and Ronnie instructions on how far to go on the air and I didn't want to overplay our hand. No names spoken on the air was a part of it, at least until an arrest was made. Ginny and Jack hadn't shared any names with us anyway, but a guy would need to be blind not to see who was involved. Forbes-Collier had the inventory and the only one in town who could have done the actual brushing was our old pal, Rex Bowman. I'd hoped that would be enough to jump start The Great Rondini's thought processes, but the high desert must have blown a little sand in his gears.

As for me, I was still trying to figure out why Rex would cosh Bryan Forbes-Collier since they were supposed to be partners. And why would he steal the painting when there were a bunch of replacements already stacked up at Collier's place. Or did Deke Rowen slug Forbes-Collier and take the picture to set a false trail. Rowen was up to something but we hadn't figured out what.

All good stuff. Too bad we couldn't say any of it on the air. Shakespeare may have said the show's the thing, but I don't think Jack and Ginny were fans.

So I took a few calls and chatted with Ronnie and Satyra until they had to run out to do their show. By then Christy had somehow rounded up the merry widower, Bruce Edelbaum. At least we could use Bev's murder to the show's advantage. After

I did a scheduled pitch for Bronco Billy's jalopies, I tried to see if Bruce could fill some air time.

"*Christy, please tell our listening audience who our next guest is tonight.*"

"*Well, Jerry, we have a return appearance by Bruce Edelbaum, who our listeners will remember lost his wife a few days ago. That was Beverly Edelbaum, who—if you'll pardon us for saying so, Bruce—was brutally murdered and whose corpse yours truly, Christy Marshall, along with our host, Jerry Jeremy, found while on an ecological survey.*"

That's my gal—auditioning for my spot since I was sure to be canned any minute. Well, one of us needs to be bringing home the bacon, I just didn't want to get stuck driving Sassie Marshall back and forth to the mall.

"*Thanks, Christy, and thank you Mr. Edelbaum. We know this is a tough time, adjusting to bachelorhood again. How's things out by the pool.?*"

"*Oh, the pool's great. Ya know being able to stay on here at the Circle-K has been a great help in dealing with my grief.*"

"*Sure it is. Been making some new friends?*"

"*Oh yeah, Jer. They've been a great help.*" And if any of his new friends was over twenty-five and didn't like sunning themselves in bikinis, I didn't see them. Brucie added, "*It's been great here. And it's not costing me a cent.*"

"*You too? Er, that is, how is that?*"

"*Your station is footing the bill. I guess Mr. Wooten wants me to stay until Bev's killer is caught. He thinks the sheriff will let me confront him right on Dakota's show. It'll be on TV, too. Though the camera crew seems to have the night off tonight.*"

"*On Dakota's show, huh? I think the TV guys wanted to see if they could get a few shots of Bronco Billy handling Dakota's, uh, career. As fun as it might be to imagine what they're up to, let's get back to me. On my first show from the Circle-K, Beverly was one of my guests, as was Rex Bowman, who she seemed to feel was a talent to be reckoned with. What do you know about that side of your late wife's life?*"

"*Honestly, Jerry, I didn't go so much for the artsy stuff. I know Bev felt it was important, so I went along with it. I suppose I picked up some stuff just from being there.*"

"*Were you close to Rex Bowman like Beverly was?*" Christy asked.

"*Not so much. I mean Bev had him over to dinner and we*

went to his openings and so forth, and yes, I suppose he's a good painter."

"Say, Bruce," I said, "Do you think you could tell one of Rex's pictures from another painter's?"

"Well sure, if the other guy was Picasso."

"So the Indian scout would have three eyes, I suppose."

At this point, Brucie baby stopped and looked like he was thinking something through. Hopefully, it didn't hurt too much.

"I think I see where you're heading, Jer," he said. "I been listening to radio—they play it out by the pool—listening to you and Miss Dakota—I'd sure like to know her better—but there's been a bunch of that Leiber-guy's paintings coming and going, and so there must be a couple of copies of it. Not that I'm saying you did anything funny or anything, but they can't all have been the same canvas."

Christy said, "You know, you might be on to something."

"Like I say, hanging out with Bev I picked up a lot. And who knows if Bowman could make his brush look like somebody else, if we're on the same track." We were, but I couldn't say so.

"So you have any idea why someone would steal Bronco Billy Wooten's painting if there are others just like it?"

"Like I say, I been listening to you like clockwork to see if you got anything on Bev's murder, and I definitely heard you say the Mr. Wooten was going to use the painting to advertise his used car business. Well, as I see it, the only reason for there to be other copies is to sell them as originals, and maybe some other folks already had the same picture already hanging over their mantles. If Mr. Wooten suddenly gets press that shows he has this particular work of art, these other folks maybe might get wise. Ya know Bev was telling me something about copies before she died but I guess I wasn't paying much attention..."

Bruce got a kind of faraway look in his eyes. Maybe he was connecting a few dots. I know I was.

Chapter 25.

"WHAT the hell..." I was shaken out of a dream I didn't want to give up on. You know, that one where I'm Rembrandt and Christy is modeling for me draped in only a handkerchief. My brushes were flying across the canvas painting in acres of skin and then—

Well, that's where some idiot started shaking me by the shoulder. At first I thought it was Ronnie, but the voice didn't seem to match, hollering, "Wake up, sleepyhead," in a falsetto. As my vision cleared I saw it was my new BFF, Ginny What's-her-name from the government.

I saw Ronnie trying to slap away Jack G-man who had him by the ear.

After a few minutes of fighting and swearing, Jack and Ginny had us sitting on the sofa while they towered over us, if a five foot four woman can tower. At any rate, six foot Jack towered over us, while Ginny laid down the law so to speak. I managed to shift an eye over to the clock and saw it was barely nine in the morning. I couldn't stifle a yawn, not having seen that hour in years unless I'd stayed up all night.

"We have data from a confidential source that one Rexford Jonathan Bowman is connected to a ring selling forged masterpieces."

I figured they must have been listening to my show last night and the confidential source was Brucie baby. Anyway, The Great Rondini stepped up, probably using his extrasensory mind-reading powers on the former newlyweds, saying, "I'm guessing you want us to do something? Like buy a couple more Leibergard's? Sorry, but the ones you got from us cleaned out his stock unless there were a few more tucked away someplace."

"You're close, but no," Jack said. "What you will do is go

over to the Kirby Art Gallery, where Bowman is helping out while the owner is recovery, and you will tell him a confidential police source has connected his name to a ring selling forged masterpieces."

"At this point we may have to stand in line," I said. "He's got to know he's under suspicion. We did everything but print up a wanted poster on the show last night."

"We missed it. We don't have any time for entertainment," Ginny said.

"So why us," Ronnie wanted to know, his ESP not being as sharp today as I thought. Still he hadn't had coffee yet so maybe he wasn't banging on all cylinders.

"If we did it, Bowman might wonder why a pair of newlyweds are suddenly in his face," Jack replied. "Since Ginny and I are still under deep cover, you two will be doing some of our more overt legwork."

"Because you've made such a fuss over your reality show investigation, everyone will expect you to be asking questions," Ginny added.

"And no one will think you're smart enough to put it all together anyway."

I wish he'd stop finishing her sentences.

Smart enough or not, we finally got rid of the ex-Hastings. After washing up and getting dressed, Ronnie and I headed over to the buffet where, it being a lot earlier than our normal grazing time, we saw a lot of new people and a lot more food.

"This is the breakfast buffet," Sherman Huntley said like it was some kind of explanation.

"Sure, like we always have," I said.

"No, you always show up for the luncheon buffet. Breakfast buffet is only until 11:30."

"Well, I'll be damned," Ronnie said. "I always wondered why they had so much potato salad."

Anyway once we got our fill of scrambled eggs and such, we headed back to the Paleface Bungalow for a little more shuteye.

"NICE of you to watch the shop, what with the boss man all laid up." Rex Bowman had the open sign on the door of the Kirby Art Gallery and was sitting at the little table where I guessed Bronco Billy had signed over a substantial piece of dough a couple of days ago. He seemed only a little surprised to see Ronnie and Satyra and Christy and yours truly browsing the oils and watercolors and drawings and prints. My opinion was that the inventory was a little heavy on desert canyons and wild horses, but on the other hand, there was nary a picture of Colonel Winston to be found.

After getting our beauty sleep and filling up again, this time at the luncheon buffet, Ronnie and I had rounded up our posse for the gallery visit. The special agents never said we couldn't pull in a few accessories after the fact. And these gals had some accessories and that's a fact. Since everybody at the Circle-K had already tramped through the gallery both before and after the Leibergard theft, the four of us were Bowman's only customers aside from a family of seven passing through on their summer road trip. Rex had to keep jumping up to shoo the kids' away from the artwork, sticky hands and crayons and all. Besides which the art was mostly his so he was being extra protective.

"So, Rex, can you spare us a minute?" I asked as he looked around for any signs of damage once the vacationers moved on to the souvenir shop down the street. I was doing the talking but Christy had the FBI's wire hidden in her bra.

We had figured Rex might not mind Christy poking her chest in his direction. As for me, I was recording it all on the phone in my pocket. Why should the Feds be the only ones to profit from our little adventure?

"What for?" Rex said. "You've practically wrecked my career single-handedly and already dragged me through the press."

"The press? No way, Rex. They don't have a thing to do with it. This is the age of the new media, reality TV and all. I'm even thinking of starting a blog. But enough about me, you hear anything about Forbes-Collier's condition? I'm hoping he doesn't have a relapse when we break this case."

"At least they won't blame that one on me," Christy said.

"You must have sent his temperature soaring," I said. "Can that bring on a stroke?"

"He did not have a stroke," Rex bristled. "It was a coronary. He's had issues with his heart for years."

"Your heart's okay isn't it?" Ronnie asked. "Had a check-up lately?"

"My heart's none of your business. And Bryan is doing as well as expected which is not well at all. He'd be much better if all of you would just leave us alone. What is she doing over there?" We looked where he was looking. Satyra bashfully stepped back from the office doorway.

"Sorry, Rex. Just trying to find the bathroom. There isn't something back there I shouldn't see, is there?"

"I—we—have nothing to hide. Go on, the bathroom's straight ahead."

"Huh, whaddayaknow? I don't have to go all of a sudden." But she continued into the back room like she did.

"Speaking of nothing to hide, Rex, what do you think about all those copies of the Leibergard painting floating around? Where do you suppose they came from?"

"For all I know you had them run off on a copy machine. Bronco Billy wouldn't know a genuine Leibergard from two cent poster."

"You're probably right about Billy, but Forbes-Collier would. And I understand the, uh, cops, great art lovers that they are, think that Billy's wasn't run off on a copy machine. I understand they also think it wasn't run off by Leibergard himself either."

"I assume Bryan had verified the provenance of the work. I understood it was found in the attic of an eccentric oil millionaire who probably bought it from one of Leibergard's heirs."

"Maybe the original was," Ronnie said. "But the copies I saw weren't Xeroxes and who says Bronco Billy actually got the original. That is before it was stolen. We know the replacements were bogus. A kind of sleight of hand. Magicians do all kinds of stuff like that, so I should know."

"Me too," said Satyra having returned from rifling through the office.

"If you are saying Bryan was doing anything illegal, I refuse to believe it. Why would this big ring of art forgers you're describing choose to run it out of a second rate ghost town? Why not New York or LA?"

"Why is a first class artist like you working out of here?" Ronnie asked. "Maybe for the same reasons. Less competition? For the phony masterpieces, it might be easier to forge the provenance from a ghost town. Eccentric oilmen in New York City probably don't have attics."

"I'm here because what I paint is here, just look out the window. I have a condo in Scottsdale, too, for your information."

"Calm down, Rex," Christy said. "No one's accusing anybody of anything. Jerry's just trying to get the record straight for his show. He makes it look easy, but he's under a lot of pressure."

"Of course," Bowman said. "I'm probably just upset that no one seems to care about Beverly's death. She was very close to me and I miss her support."

"She told us on the show how much she admired you and your work," I said. "It would be great to have you back on to tell us a little more about how she fits into the picture, no pun intended."

"Ah well, I don't know, I'll need to think about it. I need a little time consider whether or not to come on. Call me later. I'll be here until six, call me then."

"I'll do that. And you're wrong, you know."

"Wrong about what?"

"I care very much about Mrs. Edelbaum's murder. No one gets away with killing a guest on my show."

"THERE'S a safe in the corner of the office," Satyra said once we'd reconvened at the Mexican place down the block from the gallery. "I took a quick look to see if the combination was on the wall next to it or someplace like that, but didn't see anything that could have been it."

"We need to get into the safe," Christy said. "There may be a clue in it. I bet I could crack it if I got the chance."

"There was also a laptop on the desk."

"We need to get into that laptop," Ronnie said. "Anybody here know how to hack their way in?"

"Well, a guy showed me some tricks back in my computer science class," Christy said.

"Did he get a passing grade?"

"No, but I did."

Sooo... Thanks to Christy's active social life back in school, we had the makings of a first rate felony rap to go with the obstruction of justice beef. We still hoped to corral Rex Bowman for the show, and if he came on, Christy would get her mom to drag him over to Ronnie's late show. That would leave me and the safe cracker free to check out the secrets at the Kirby gallery.

Of course, I had the feeling that Bowman would probably rather talk to the Feds than get another grilling from me, but then people like being on the radio. And with any luck, Bronco Billy might even relent enough to send the camera crew around. But he probably wouldn't relent enough if I didn't pay him a visit and tell him how much I liked his idea of teaming Dakota and me up. Better that than his idea of kicking me off the air.

We had a few rounds of tacos and margaritas to celebrate our plan and while Christy went off to tell Sassie that she might get lucky, I strolled over to Bronco Billy's villa. Billy being Billy had set himself up in the *El Presidente* bungalow which was set off from the rest of us amateur cowpokes. It had a high adobe wall protecting the precious cacti and scrub oak in the front garden. A doorbell with an intercom was set into the wall adjacent to a wrought iron gate that visitors had to be buzzed through. I wondered if a written apology wrapped around a ball peen hammer might not be the best bet, assuming I could get it far enough over the gate to reach one of the big veranda windows. As it turned out when I said it was me over the intercom, Billy not only buzzed me in, but once I had cleared the threshold of the fortress, welcomed me like I was the prodigal son. I just wondered what my new daddy was up to.

"Where in hades, did you get off to?" Billy said slapping me on the back and shoving a Cuban stogy in my mouth. "I been lookin' to say how bad I felt havin' my top cop pull you and your pal in. I was just a little bit peeved about that damn' paintin', ya' know."

"No to worry, Bronco Billy. Ronnie and I had them, er him, eating out of our hands. And we weren't even there long enough to make any new friends in the shower room."

"Hah, you always bounce back, son. I hope The Great Ronzoni feels the same. You can tell him for me that I will make him a deal on any car on the lot."

"That's mighty generous, Bronco Billy."

About that time, Dakota's voice came in from the bedroom, "Okay, Billy, I got us all packed up and ready to go."

"Go? Are you going somewhere, Bronco Billy? Am *I* going somewhere?"

"Now calm the fuck down for a minute, Jerry. I need to get back to Tucson since the lame brain I left in charge of the lot is running the profits into the ground. But you—you don't need to rush. You're our man—that is, KICK's man—in Kirby. Dakota will come back with me and start breakin' in the evening show and you provide her with updates from the field."

"Updates, huh?"

"Sure, two, three times a night."

"Two or three updates on the show Dakota and I co-host, huh?"

"Jus' for the present, Jerry. 'Fore long you're back in

Tucson and the show's fifty-fifty. Don't sweat it. I'll have you do more o' my commercials and pay you off the books. Why you'll be the goddamn' voice of Bronco Billy Wooten's fine used cars."

"Fine, pre-owned cars..."

"Sure, see you got the real stuff, even keeping me straight. I gotta be straight with you too—I'm not sure about finding the killer in all this. Probably was that guy you finished off, the cowboy."

"Deke?"

"Sure, the way I figure it, he bumped off the Edelbaum dame and tried to do you too, since you was gettin' too close. You can prob'ly put that together for the listeners and the TV crew, and be shuck of here in a couple of days. You solved it, Jerry!"

"But it can't be Deke."

"Listen, Jeremy, as my gran'daddy used t'say, don't look a horse in the mouth."

"Gift horse...gift horse in the mouth."

"Sure, it's a gift. You get the credit and come back home so's that gal in there don't get too used to bein' in your time slot without you. You be the hero on this one, Jerry. You bring that Christy gal home too and we can try her out on the radio."

"Yeah, but what about Redhawk," I whined. "He won't think it's over."

"You sure don't know much about real life politics, do ya'." Billy smiled in a kind of pitying way. "That sheriff will think whatever I tell him to think seein' as how he wants to keep his time slot as much as you do yours. I'm his sponsor jus' like I'm yours."

Chapter 26.

I WASN'T sure that Bronco Billy didn't have the right line on Darrell Lee, though I hadn't thought the smoke-free Marlboro man was all that much for sale. But I would have been surprised if Billy had the FBI team in his pocket. Even if I could sell them on Deke Rowen being the murderer, which might even be true, the ex-Hastings were on the trail of the art forgers, Forbes-Collier and Bowman maybe being just the tip of the iceberg forgery-wise. Besides, unless something else turned up in the motive department, Rowen didn't seem to have much incentive to cap Mrs. Edelbaum. Except as a contractor so to speak.

Anyway Dakota and Billy headed back home. Sassie Marshall might be willing to spend a few hours being entertained by Rex Bowman, but I got the impression she was ready to blow town too, which meant Christy would go with her. As for Rondini, he didn't think the Silver Cage would extend his engagement much longer, so my pal and his assistant were checking the airline schedules. And as Bronco Billy made clear, my time at the ranch was rapidly coming to an end.

Truth be told, Beverly Edelbaum hadn't been too good on the show when she was alive, but she had done wonders for me as a corpse. The whole murder mystery thing had gotten us—me—a lot of publicity. For a while it was even trending in a small way on Twitter. And all that video footage could be chopped up and mashed together to make a spiffy reality show for some cable channel. They must have shot a hundred hours of just Christy and Satyra by the pool. There remained only one problem. We were still missing an ending.

Before I headed home, I planned to get one.

Everything was falling right into place though. We had

gotten the portable studio set up in the Circle-K lounge and Rex actually turned up for the show. Maybe he was thinking his date with Sassie Marshall was an opportunity to make friends with a new patron of the arts. Maybe he had another Leibergard to sell. Or maybe the Brooklyn bridge. At any rate, Christy had done the sales job on her mom and Sassie had called Rex with a personal invitation to a late night magic act. I was thinking maybe I could get Rondini to lock him in the Chinese box illusion for a couple of hours. Maybe not.

Anyway, he was on the air with me, and before taking him around the block on the Leibergard forgeries for the second time that day, I portrayed him to the audience as an expert on art who just happened to be in the neighborhood. Christy and I didn't get much more out of him than we had in the afternoon, but he seemed to be a little bit less depressed. Best guess is he'd had a few glasses of Arizona red, that being the color his eyes were shading to. Red eyes aside, the camera guys were all over us, maybe realizing their overtime was coming to an end. I had also been lucky enough to draw a good crowd to the lounge. The cameraman took a number of shots showing the crowd enjoying the show. Of course, I expected the FBI team posing as newlyweds to be there, as well as Sassie waiting for her turn at Bowman, a few new arrivals at the ranch, and surprisingly, Sal No-name and Gloria the Goomah. Maybe I shouldn't have been that surprised about Sal though, Christy having tipped me to the fact that he was more interested in art than I would have suspected. Must be true that you can't tell a book by his thick neck.

"So tell us, Rex, you were close to Mrs. Edelbaum and she was close to the art world, could there be any connection between her death and the phony Leibergard paintings?" If there wasn't, I'd eat Bronco Billy's hat and it's at least a ten-gallon number.

"I cannot say, but I know in my heart that someone will pay for having taken...." Rex's voice broke at this point, his red eyes burning through the audience like laser beams. *"There will be retribution and soon."*

Even Bowman was pushing me to wrap things up. If he knew more than he was telling, I didn't know why he didn't tell me and the listening audience about it. If the gallery caper tonight didn't hit pay dirt, I was thinking Rex might buy in for a couple of points on the reality show. That had to be a better deal than the G-man and -woman could offer. Either way he'd probably have a few months in some country club lock-up for painting like a dead guy. Still, he might wind up with some kind of a one-man show, even if he was pretending to be another man.

"ANYBODY looking?" I asked. Christy and I had just come from the Silver Cage having made sure Sassie had Rex Bowman settled down for the duration. Ronnie planned to milk his encores so we'd have more time to toss the office of the Kirby gallery. Not that he didn't always try to milk his encores.

We had drifted unobtrusively down the main drag from the nightclub to the gallery. Two blocks from the club and we were in the heart of ghost town, nobody but ourselves and maybe a few of the deceased hanging out in front of the place.

"Uh-oh, there's a light on in there."

"That's just a night light, Jerry. There's nothing to be afraid of."

"Afraid? Who's afraid? I just want to make sure we don't walk in on something."

"I know you're not. Let me just check the door."

The last time we checked the door, it was unlocked and Bryan Forbes-Collier was sprawled in a pool of blood inside.

"It's locked," Christy said.

"Maybe that's a good thing. Go ahead and pick it while I stand lookout."

"Uh, darling, you know I can get through most doors, but I'm afraid the guy who taught me how never got far enough to teach me this one."

Hmmm, good news and bad news. I was glad some thug with a UA varsity letter hadn't got far enough with Christy, but it would have been sweet if she could have tickled these tumblers into line.

Christy had wandered over by the side of the gallery and was lighting up a dark walkway along the building with her phone. She said, "Wait here, hon. There may be a back door."

Well, somebody had to keep watch. I didn't want Sheriff Redhawk's crew catching us in another felony.

A minute or two later, the door to Kirby's best art gallery eased open a crack. "Jerry, get in here quick," the door said. So I did.

Another minute or two later, Christy and I were in the back office. I closed the door separating it from the pristine viewing gallery while Christy turned on a small lamp sitting on the desk. The place was a dump. Papers and art magazines in stacks on every surface. A ton of canvases shoved willy-nilly in every corner, but none on the walls. So much for upscale decor. I half expected an old fashioned office safe like you see in the cowboy movies, the kind with one of those big dials full of numbers. I pictured Christy with her shell-like ear pressed against it, listening as her nimble fingers coaxed the tumblers into place. To my chagrin I found that when it came to safes, Kirby, Arizona, was right up to date. At least Forbes-Collier was. It was one of those digital jobs with a keypad and display screen. Unless Christy could hear the electrons jumping, we were out of luck.

"Sort of like the front door, huh?" I said. "You fought off the teacher before you got to this lesson too?"

"Don't say it like that. Let's see what else is here, maybe the combination is jotted down somewhere."

So we gave it the old post-college try. We scoured the desk, the file cabinets, the laptop—"Picasso" was the password—and finally in desperation, old magazines, wastepaper basket and a potted plant past its sell-by date. While I fumbled my way through an unhelpful hard drive, Christy started punching in numbers on the safe, 1-1-1-1-1-1, 1-2-3-4-5-6...well you get the idea. If she found it, I'd let her fill out my next lottery ticket.

"It looks like he didn't pick the easy numbers," Christy said. "You don't happen to know his birthday do you?"

"No, and I don't know his collar size either. But...say, that's kind of funny."

"I could use a good laugh about now," she said, keying in 9-8-7-6-5-4.

"Not ha-ha funny, peculiar funny. Though I never understood why they say those things are funny. I'm not laughing."

"Jerry, it's past my bedtime and the suspense is killing me—spill it."

"It's just that his desk phone only has six digits. The phone number on the label is a number short."

"Jerry, stop! Read me the numbers."

I did and she did and you guessed it, the safe door popped right open. Maybe it was ha-ha funny after all. At least we were laughing now.

The safe had a file drawer and a few compartments. I moved the desk lamp close while Christy started pulling folders out. She said, "These files look kind of old. This one's dated two thousand five. They look like old invoices for rent and frames. Here are receipts for some artworks Bryan sold three years ago and some payments to the artists. Hey—here's a bunch for Rex Bowman's work from afew years ago."

"We already knew they worked together," I said pulling open the compartments. A gold pocket watch that looked to be an antique was in one, two gold double-eagles mounted in plastic were in another. Then I discovered real gold—a USB thumb drive. We had the laptop, we had the password and now we had a few gigabytes that had been locked up in a safe. Christy and I had it hooked up and were running our fingers through its files in a New York minute. Or at least a Kirby one.

It had a lot of invoices and receipts like the paper files only these were more recent. And one folder was marked in red. It contained a series of invoices for the sale of "Colonel Winston with an Indian Scout, Fort Apache, New Mexico" circa 1874, by our boy, Max Leibergard. It was sold at least four times before Bronco Billy bought in. The sales were spread out over eight or nine months and before they started, there were three for "Cowboys Herding Wild Mustangs" circa 1871. Who knew how far back the scam went, it appeared to have been a money maker. Every sale was over a hundred large.

"Look, Jerry. It looks like Bryan split the money three ways. A third to the Kirby Art Gallery, a third to Rex—we already figured he was in on it—and another third to something called the DaVinci Art Storage and Moving Company, headquartered in Las Vegas."

"Who? Where the hell did they come from?"

"Las Vegas it looks like." Christy was mousing and clicking like a maniac now. Going through any file that might lead to a lead. "Ah-ha, gotcha!"

"What, got what?" I said. "Got who?"

"A receipt from the DaVinci thing. Look here, it says the company president is one Salvatore Anastasia—it's got to be our very own Sal No-Last-Name!"

"That's why he's such an art lover, he's making a killing."

"And maybe a real killing," Christy said.

"Don't remind me. Let's get out of here."

I DIDN'T think the authorities would buy my just happening to find that thumb drive outside my door like I'd claimed with the first Leibergard copy, so we left it in the laptop with the file open to the receipt from DaVinci Art etc. Just in case, I wrote the password on a Post-it and stuck it next to the keyboard. The place was such a mess to begin with Christy and I decided it wasn't worth trying to clean up. While she locked the safe, I arranged to have a lamp spill its light into the gallery. Having staged the scene, we slipped out the back way, stopping for a moment to break the glass in the rear window.

Rondini should have finished taking bows by the time we headed back to the Silver Cage Saloon. I couldn't wait to tell him we had a big break in the case and see what he thought we should do next. My plan was to call Sheriff Redhawk to tell him Christy and I had just been out for an evening stroll when we noticed a suspicious light coming from the back room of the art gallery.

"And so the sheriff and crew go in to investigate, find the laptop and put the cuffs on the Godfather," Ronnie was saying.

"That's pretty much how I see it going down," I replied. "I tried to figure out a way to hold on until tomorrow's show, but...."

"Jerry, there's a murderer on the loose," Christy said. "If he figures out we know what we know, there may not be a show tomorrow night. You need to call in the cavalry right now."

We had hooked up with Ronnie and Satyra after their act and we were all huddled around a back booth at the Cage trying to decide on what to do next. I hadn't seen Sassie Marshall around after the show so Rex must be walking her back to her bungalow. He might be a crook, but at least it was a comfort to know he wasn't a murderer.

Meanwhile Ronnie was giving the girls the lowdown on the newlyweds and who they really were. I realized I hadn't seen them since my radio show. I wondered if they were doing what newlyweds usually do. Nah, not them. They probably did their sit-ups, flossed and brushed and were sleeping soundly by nine o'clock.

"...so in the long run calling Darrell Lee instead of the *federales* is our best bet. The local cops can move in, it'll be a win for the sheriff so he'll be back on our side, and he can bring in Taylor and Richards when he's ready. I've seen enough TV to know how the local cops hate the FBI moving in on their cases. Besides the Feds are only interested in art fraud, not the Edelbaum murder. This way everybody gets their own piece of the action."

I knew Ronnie would put it all together. He's not called The Great Rondini for nothing.

I hoped Sheriff Redhawk had gotten over the gag we pulled with the paintings since his main backer in the election had already forgiven me, packed up his mistress and headed for home. Anyway I called the sheriff on his mobile and he picked up.

"Jerry, man, I was thinking of calling you to see how you made out with the Fibbies," Redhawk enthused before I could get out a hello. "And I am a little embarrassed about pulling you in, but you know Mr. Wooten..."

"Hey, Darrell Lee, no sweat, water under the bridge. Anyway Bronco Billy and I are thick as thieves...er, that is we're tight."

"You know, Jerry, old man, I wouldn't mind coming on your show again. We could let the voters hear what we're up against. Let them know we're doing our best and like that, huh?"

"You took the words right out of my mind, Sheriff. We might have something good to sell, er tell, the voters because I didn't call you up just to pass the time of day. I wanted to tell you that while Christy and I were taking our evening constitutional down Main Street, we saw a suspicious light on in Forbes-Collier's shop."

"Well, thanks for the tip, Jerry, but a lot of stores have some kind of a night light on when they're closed. Keeps the burglars out."

"Well, since the owner's still in the ICU, I don't think he could have left it on, Darrell Lee."

"Well, could be on a timer, Jerry. This is the twenty-first century, you know. Even in Kirby."

"Well, Christy thought she saw it moving, like it could have been a flashlight, Darrell Lee."

"Well—you sure, Jerry?"

"Well, sure."

I don't know if Darrell Lee was in the middle of a hot date or something, but it took some prying to get him moving. He finally got the idea after I'd thrown enough hints his way to bury a small Toyota. He said he was on the way, so I rounded up our gang to go meet him. I may have forgotten to tell him that last thing though.

Chapter 27.

THE camera crew had gone the way of Bronco Billy or more likely, the way of Bronco Billy's wallet, but Ronnie and Satyra had smartphones that were more camera than phone. The plan was for them to video me innocently leading the cops to the evidence that would break the case wide open. I was sure my pals at KOW-TV would eat it up, so I wanted to be at the gallery to meet the sheriff and his crew when they arrived. As we were leaving the Silver Cage though, who should we run into but Sassie Marshall coming back in.

"Here you all are," she said. "I was just wondering whether my daughter might want to pick up a little dessert for a midnight snack back at the ranch."

Sure you did, never thinking that Christy might want to hang out with her almost-fiancé instead. And help solve a murder and be on TV. Besides which, I had been planning a special celebration for later after solving the case. I was sure Ronnie wouldn't mind finding someplace else to bed down for the night. Or maybe he'd go for a midnight snack with my future mother-in-law. But I didn't say any of that.

Instead I said, "What happened to Bowman?"

"He had to leave early. Something about his having to get up early for a meeting back in Phoenix."

Phoenix, eh? I'd bet Mexico. Anyway Rex was on the run. Maybe the Feds waited too long to spring the trap, but with Sal Anastasia facing a murder charge, the whole scam would come crashing down. After the sheriff finds the stuff at the gallery, maybe Ronnie and I would pay a late night call on the pseudo-newlyweds. I wondered if we'd catch them sharing the same pillow.

Christy told her mom that she might be available a little later, but right now we were on a mission and why didn't

Sassie come with us. I only had one question about her tagging along, "That cell phone of yours has a built-in camera, right?"

Our little posse reached the gallery way before I figured the sheriff and his deputies would. With a chunk of time to kill, Satyra used her phone to record a reenactment of Christy and me spotting that suspicious moving light in the gallery. While we did that, Ronnie walked around back, documenting the break-in, broken window and all. Mrs. Marshall had instructions to video the squad cars when they pulled up. I hoped they'd have their lights flashing and their sirens on. Too bad they wouldn't arrive on horseback like real deputies. Maybe they'd do a reenactment for the cameras tomorrow. After all, they'd be on TV.

As the minutes stretched into...well, even more minutes, we passed the phones around and took videos of each other outside the gallery. I was tempted to go in and get some shots of us hacking the laptop, but cooler heads prevailed. With my luck, Sheriff Redhawk would catch me red-handed. The whole bunch of us would probably wind up behind bars.

After seemingly ages, the sheriff did show up with his bunch. His pickup had only a blue light on the dash to get him through the nighttime traffic on the road to Kirby and he probably didn't even need that, but the two squad cars following him had their flashers cranking making for a great scene. No sirens, but I was sure that could be edited in later. A few unmarked cars arrived with various crime scene dudes and Darrell Lee gathered everybody around while Christy and I laid out our story. The perky deputy—Lou, as I recall—reminded the crime scene investigators to look for any security cameras that might be in the store. If they found one, she theorized, they might nail the perp or perps in record time.

Gulp.

My mouth was suddenly as dry as the desert out there. I looked at Christy but all I got was a mini-shrug. Either she didn't know if there were any cameras or she was pretending she didn't know me. Must be her college chum didn't give her the advanced course. Not in burglary anyway.

Anyway the cops got busy. In less than a minute the gallery was open and everybody was putting on booties and latex gloves. I geared up too and was following Redhawk in when the lady cop threw a straight-arm my way. "We need to clear and secure the premises. The perps could still be inside. And we don't want to contaminate the crime scene with any extra visitors."

I gave her my best smile hoping she'd realize I could never be a perp. Meanwhile, I tried to think of a way to contaminate any security cameras in there. Christy pulled me aside and reminded me that they didn't find any videos when Bryan Forbes-Collier was robbed, so we might be in the clear.

The crime scene team was vacuuming up the trash and dusting the place all over with black powder hoping to find somebody's fingerprints. One of the deputies was swinging around a video camera with a spotlight on it, apparently filming the crime scene team at work. Maybe they'd switch around in a while and the guys in paper coveralls would video the ones in uniform. I'd probably need the Freedom of Information Act to get a copy of the tape for my show.

Darrell Lee finally waved Christy and me into the gallery to question us on what we'd seen.

"We saw a light moving around," Christy said, "like someone with a flashlight or maybe just the light from a phone."

"You both saw this?" Darrell Lee asked.

"Oh yeah," I answered, triggering the phone in my pocket to record audio of the police in action. "We were right out there and we saw it. We figured maybe with all the crime around town, you'd want to know about it."

Bit by bit, Ronnie and Satyra filtered in and wondered around, casually holding their phones, catching all the action.

"You saw the moving light from outside, even with that lamp flooding the doorway with its light?"

"Well, they could have had a big flashlight. Or a really big cell phone."

"Just from back in the office here, not out in the show room?"

"Oh, yeah," Christy said. "Probably just some kids, Sheriff. You see anything missing?"

"Looks like the safe is still here though real pros would have broke it open or taken it with them. You're probably right, just some kids."

"Sure."

"Though in my experience kids would usually take the laptop, not just leave it here."

"Maybe it's not loaded with the latest games. You take a close look at it?"

"Nah, if it wasn't worth taking, it's not worth spending much time on."

Somehow things were not working out like we planned. I

was thinking of volunteering Christy as a computer expert to help the law check it out. Either that or tape it to Redhawk's nose, when—

"Hey, boss, take a look at this."

A guy in a paper suit was trying to get Darrell Lee's attention, waving at him from the office door.

"What's that, Watkins?"

"This computer. It looks like it has some stuff on those pictures the Feds were all hot to trot about. This lady in the chorus girl outfit showed it to me."

Ah, so that's where Satyra had got to.

GOT it in one. Not.

But at least they finally got it. Forbes-Collier's laptop became the center of attention. Sheriff Redhawk hemmed and hawed for a while, but wound up caving and calling the FBI agents formerly known as David and Jennifer Hastings since the forgeries were firmly in their bailiwick. I hoped the G-people wouldn't take it the wrong way that I called Darrell Lee first. Turns out they didn't pay much attention to me or Ronnie, maybe not wanting to blow our covers. Although everybody there already knew we were working for them.

So the stuff on the laptop tied not only Rex Bowman and Bryan Forbes-Collier to the forged paintings, but also the Italian art lover. The consensus was that while the sunshine boys, Rex and Bryan, may have been holding back information, nobody actually pegged them for Bev's murder, even with Deke Rowen to do the dirty work. Sal Anastasia was another story though.

It looked like our work here was done, at least for now. The sheriff's gang hustled the safe out to his truck, picked up a few more clues they found lying around, Jack and Ginny took possession of the laptop, now sealed in a plastic bag, a sheet of plywood covered the busted window and a deputy was left guarding the now clueless gallery. Maybe they were expecting the neighborhood kids to come back.

The next stop was to be the Anastasia bungalow at the Circle-K ranch. The cops were all checking their pistols, loading shotguns, pulling on bullet-proof vests and visored helmets, except of course, for Sheriff Redhawk who decided to stay with the Marlboro man look. The sheriff aside, it looked like something big was about to come down. What I wouldn't have given for that camera crew about then.

"So, you know, Sheriff, this arrest will pretty much nail the election for you, even without Bronco Billy."

"You think that's what this is all about, Jeremy?"

"Of course not. Absolutely not. Do we, Ronnie?"

"I would hope not, JJ," Rondini backed me up. "It's just...well, let's not get in to that now."

"No, no, not now, not with all the sheriff has on his plate right now."

"What are you two talking about?"

Rondini tried to wave it away. He said, "I'd be the last one to bring this up at this time, but...well, um...."

"Spit it out."

"Better tell him, Ronnie."

"It's just that Jerry and I were thinking—here you are, the hero of all this, breaking the case wide open and all, finding the killer—and you being so modest, probably you won't get the credit you deserve."

"Not that that would keep you from doing your duty, Sheriff. Ronnie's just worried, you know, that in an election year you can't take anything for granted...."

So a little more arm-twisting and Redhawk agreed to let us all come along on the bust with all our smartphone cameras to document him and his brave troops in action. The cop who had the video camera was told to tape everything so I could make sure it was on the KOW-TV newscast. The real deal was to get Ronnie and me in the thick of things for the reality show Billy was going to buy. Not that we wouldn't say something nice about Darrell Lee, too.

After endless preparation, everybody climbed into the cop cars and sped the hundred yards down to the ranch. Apparently Sal's bungalow must have been on the police GPS, because they didn't stop to ask directions and in less time than it takes to tell, the place was bathed in their headlights, not to mention flashing red and blue highlights. Redhawk's team spread out, guns drawn, behind their vehicles while the sheriff busied himself with a bullhorn he pulled out of one of the trunks. I moved in close and got my phone's recorder going while my guys spread out, videoing everything from every angle.

Sheriff Redhawk checked to make sure everyone was in place and seemed a little surprised to find yours truly at his elbow. I told him this would be great for his campaign and he turned back to the bungalow, and bullhorned a warning to Anastasia that he'd better come on out with his hands up.

Everyone held his or her respective breaths. The moment stretched on until we all had to exhale. No sign of the perp although the bungalow seemed to have more than its share of lights on.

"This is the police. Come out of the house with your hands above your head," Darrell Lee shouted through the speaker. "This is your last warning."

Another long pause although nobody was holding their breath this time. The cops seemed to be getting a little restless when suddenly the door opened a crack.

"I think I'm supposed to ask if you gents got a warrant or something," Gloria Palucci said, carefully poking her head around the door jam.

"Please step out, Ma'am," the sheriff said unamplified, skipping the bullhorn.

"Okay, but you know Sal ain't here right now."

After a little back and forth establishing that Sal had left maybe an hour ago for some business meeting—"He didn't pack a suitcase or nothing"—we wound up in the bungalow's little sitting room with Gloria squeezing out some espresso grounds for us.

Aside from the coffee Darrell Lee didn't get much out of her. She only knew Sal left for some kind of appointment some time earlier in the evening. She smiled pleasantly as she insisted the sheriff would need to cough up a search warrant to check around the bungalow. Any more than that she didn't know. She didn't know what time Sal would be back, she didn't know who he was meeting, she didn't know if he knew Forbes-Collier or did business with him. She didn't even know what Sal did for a living or whether she was really his girlfriend.

I guess Sal didn't like to share.

Chapter 28.

BACK in the saddle again. Truth be told, I was more than a little surprised to find myself riding the range once more. My saddle sores were barely healed, but since Darrell Lee apparently didn't have a helicopter or even a four-wheel off-road SUV, the Sheriff and his posse were after Sal Anastasia on horseback.

After Gloria's espresso, everyone had been pretty wired. The cops buzzed around all the usual places trying to locate the fugitive, including pulling Rex Bowman out of bed at three a.m. Good thing Sassie Marshall hadn't gotten lucky or she'd have died of embarrassment. Speaking of which, Christy and I managed to work off our coffee buzz in Dakota and Billy's old bungalow while Rondini and Satyra sat up someplace matching tequila shots. By morning, Darrell Lee had put out an APB, but hadn't found any trace of Sal having taken car, bus or plane out of Kirby. Sure, like there was a bus or a plane.

His next best guess was the desert.

I thought I could have a little fun with that if I could get the sheriff on my show that evening. But then Sherman Huntley reported that some miscreant had taken a couple of horses out during the night. By morning though the animals had already wandered back riderless. For some reason Sherm thought I might have been involved, but I had Christy as my alibi. Maybe not such a good alibi, but I knew it couldn't have been me or her and for once Sheriff Redhawk agreed. He figured Sal, the novice desert rat, was out there someplace dying of thirst.

Besides, a posse on horseback would look great on my reality show. The good news on top of that was that Mrs. Marshall remembered having a real video camera, zoom lens and all, in her luggage. Christy managed to find it someplace in her mom's stuff, so our production values looked to be taking a turn for the better. Horses, deputies, Christy in a halter top—I even skipped shaving for that rugged he-man look.

We had been riding in the hot sun for what seemed like forever, but what Christy told me was maybe an hour or so. All I knew was that we had been passing a lot of cactus and boulders. Not too far in the distance, I saw the tops of some scrubby trees poking out above the sides of an arroyo. It may have been *deja vu*, but I had the feeling I had been here before. The cops had been tracking the horses' footprints or hoof prints or something, and they seemed to be leading us back to where I last saw Beverly Edelbaum. Not alive.

Sure enough, we were back at Christy's and my old swimming hole. The horses all knew the way here and back because it was on the ranch's desert tour. When Sal made his getaway, the stolen ponies might have headed here on their own, and if city boy Sal was anything like me, he'd be ready to take a break by the time he got this far. Riding at night, he could have rested, fallen asleep without tying up the horses and the ponies found their way home. By now Sal could be going walkabout in the desert. Or he could be sitting behind a boulder with a high-powered rifle. Hard to tell. And who was the second horse for?

As we neared the gulch, the sheriff signaled us civilians to hold up while his posse dismounted, and guns drawn, approached on foot. I tried to follow the action, a lot of hand-waving and pointing as the deputies crept to the edge, trying to keep under cover. They must have had that same thought about the high-powered you-know-what. Deputy Lou seemed to have gotten a bead on something or someone as she pointed down into the arroyo. One by one the others joined her, looking down, and then holstering their six-shooters. Christy and I took that as a good sign, so we dismounted—not a moment too soon for me—and went to see what they were looking at. Somebody was snoozing on large flat rock by the pool or maybe he was just catching a few rays. Although we weren't that far away, I couldn't tell what the deal was. For a sunbather, he had a lot of clothes on and there was something odd about his head gear. Still, he did look like he could be a short, stocky Italian.

Meanwhile, Darrell Lee had pulled a pair of binoculars out from somewhere and when he focused on the man by the pool, I heard him give a low whistle. All he said was, "Better get down there," and everybody saddled up. The horses crept their way down the hillside and pretty soon we could see it was Sal. He was quickly surrounded by the lawmen (and woman). Not that Sal had to worry about being surrounded by the law. Sal wouldn't have to worry about anything anymore. Half his head was missing.

"Scalped," Redhawk said. And being Native America, I guess he would know.

"My god," Christy said, turning a pale shade of green. I was feeling like maybe I was matching her shade for shade.

"I see it," Deputy Watkins said, "but I ain't never seen it before."

"Used to be popular around here, a hundred and fifty years ago," Redhawk said. "Though not so much now."

"No offense, chief, er, ah, Sheriff," the deputy was saying, "but you think some of the locals could've got so liquored up they'd go and do this?"

"Listen, Watkins. Why don't you check to see if we thought to bring along a camera."

"Got one right here, Sheriff," Lou piped up, pulling a Nikon out of her backpack.

"Good work, Lou. Let's get some photos from all sides."

The camera handled, Watkins still didn't take the hint. Instead of holding a tripod or something for Lou, he started in on the sheriff again. "Geez, that would of hurt pretty bad, huh?"

"Not so much, Watkins. Take a look over here." The sheriff pushed the body a little more on its side. "I'll be damned if that's not a bullet hole. Course the ME will need to confirm cause of death, but I'd bet he was dead first."

Christy, hoping to get her mind on something besides the body, kept busy working Mom's camera during all this chit-chat, but so far I was just playing the innocent bystander. And innocence is never good in a reality show. While Sheriff Redhawk had his team secure the area with yellow crime scene tape, he himself put in a call to get the medical examiner and the crime scene techs sent out. Hopefully not by horseback.

As for me, still standing by, I put in a wake-up call to Ronnie. Somebody had to figure my next move and The Great Rondini had my vote.

"SCALPED?" Ronnie said to show he was listening while I gave him the 411 on Redhawk's desert dragnet. "Like in the movies? Like cowboys and Indians?"

"I think they prefer Native Americans now."

"Scalped? Not just a close haircut?"

"If it was any closer there'd be nothing left but a smile."

By the time I got through to Ronnie, Christy and I had taken refuge from the sun beneath a cottonwood tree at the far end of the pool. Her color had almost returned to normal, but I suggested she skip the sunburn, so we hunkered down in the shade. Anyway Ronnie was saying he had to get some java before putting his mind on full throttle, so he signed off promising to call back when he'd had time to figure out a few moves ahead.

"I wonder how long before the meat wagon arrives," I wondered aloud.

"Jerry, *meat wagon*? Really? Sal may have been a crook and a killer, but show some respect. Besides, he's not in any hurry now."

"Sorry, I didn't mean any disrespect. I was just wondering if we could get a lift back to the ranch."

"Ride with the corpse?"

"Well..."

"If you really want to leave and they don't need us here, we can ride back. It'll be quicker going back than getting out here."

"That's true. Why is it always quicker going back than coming?"

"Why are you getting so antsy? Do you want to connect with Ronnie to see what he thinks?"

"Not particularly. I'm in no hurry, but no use hanging around here. It's not worth waiting all day just to see them put Sal in the...uh, ambulance, is there?"

We checked in with Darrell Lee to let him know where he could find us, gathered up the ponies, and with my nether regions hardly complaining, we rode off into the sunset. Well, not really the sunset, more like the high noon. Sunset or no sunset, I wondered if anyone had broken the news to Gloria yet.

"OF course you shouldn't mention anything about his being...you know, what was done to him."

"You mean about the killer having mutilated the body?" Sassie Marshall asked.

"Well, scalped. He was just scalped."

"In my book, Jerry, that is mutilation. Maybe it was some kind of a cult thing."

"Mom, the police think that someone was trying to make it look like Native Americans had killed Mr. Anastasia," Christy said. "It was just a feeble attempt to throw off the police, but Jerry and I think we must be considerate of Miss Palucci's feelings."

"Sure, Sal might have been a killer, but Gloria's only a killer's girlfriend."

Christy and I had made the ride back to the Circle-K and somehow I managed to survive although I might have trouble sitting for a while. I hadn't had the chance to get instructions from Ronnie, but I had a plan of my own and was even a little amazed that Christy thought it might be a good idea. My plan was to get Sassie Marshall to gently break the news of Sal's murder to Miss P while Christy videoed it from a discrete distance. Then Christy and I would move in to see if Gloria would be more willing to spill what she didn't tell Sheriff Redhawk last night. But this time, no bullhorn.

We had Sassie rehearse her lines a few times while Christy and I scarfed down a late lunch. Finally, having been fed and watered and with nothing more to do, we walked Sassie over to Gloria Palucci's bungalow and knocked on her door.

And knocked on her door again. And again. By now all three of us were trying to peek in through the curtains. None of the lights were on and we couldn't tell if Gloria's stuff was still there, but she obviously either wasn't in or didn't want visitors, not even the soft-hearted Mrs. Marshall. On the other hand, her main man had tried a runner and wound up dead. Maybe she was supposed to meet him somewhere. Maybe somebody had it in for her also. Maybe...maybe I should get Rondini in on this.

I called Ronnie and got an idea or two from him, and then Christy and I walked Sassie over to the pool and told her to hang out there in case Gloria decided to take a dip. Next we retraced out steps to the Palucci-Anastasia bungalow, aka the Horny Toad Suite, and Christy loided the lock.

The housekeeper had tided things up, but it still looked like somebody had left in a hurry. A few odds and ends of women's clothing and an almost empty make-up jar were about all that remained of Gloria, although Sal's wardrobe seemed to have been left behind. Since we were there anyway, we figured we might as well go through his pockets.

Chapter 29.

"SCALPED! A man's body was sprawled on the rocks next to the spring where Christy and I found the bloodless body of Beverly Edelbaum last week. Mrs. Edelbaum, you may recall, had been on this very show the night she was murdered. That is what triggered my investigation into her death. Now a third body has been found, this one of a man who we believe may have been behind the Edelbaum killing.

"That's right. I did say 'a third body'..." The show was humming right along, broadcasting from the lounge at the Circle-K. As a matter of fact, I was getting pretty comfortable broadcasting from there with a small live audience to keep things...well, lively. The crowd in the lounge had probably come there for food and drink, but the occasional tinkling of glass and silverware added a touch of real-life to the show, and my new BFF, Sherman Huntley had silenced the elevator music they normally use to ease the patrons' digestion.

On this particular evening, a couple of older cowgirls, maybe in their seventies, had caught me on the way in to ask for my autograph. They also got Christy's autograph, and I'm not sure, but maybe they got the busboy's too.

Anyway, Christy and yours truly and The Great Rondini and Satyra were giving the listening audience the rundown on all we knew and maybe some things we didn't quite know. Sassie Marshall passed on the opportunity to be on the air and my suspicion was that it might be because of her involvement with a certain artist. One whose involvement in our little story was another of my suspicions. I had the feeling things were pretty much done with our little dude ranch mystery now that Sal was dead. My next show might be from KICK's studio back in Tucson.

"...three people have died as a result of an art scam being

run right here in Kirby. An innocent woman trying to help out an artist who got himself tangled up in something bad wound up in the bottom of a lonesome watering hole under the desert moon. As you've already heard, a reputed gangster, allegedly running a scam, turns up dead, his hair parted by a tomahawk. But wait—there's more. One more body in fact.

"When Christy and I uncovered the forged paintings at the heart of this scam, artworks supposedly painted by Max Leibergard, we didn't realize we had a killer watching us. An outlaw cowboy driving a muddy pickup truck tried to murder yours truly and hers truly by running us off the highway into giant boulders lining the road just south of Kirby. He found out that it wasn't so easy to get rid of us though. As it was, a fine, pre-owned Jeep Grand Cherokee from Bronco Billy Wooten's Used Cars and Trucks didn't survive, but Christy and I did. Not that it we didn't cut it close, but a bad man named Deke Rowen cut it closer. His pickup found the boulders and went up in smoke, taking him along for the ride."

I played around with the story of Rowen and white-line fever for a while, giving the listeners all the action. Somehow the story always wound up with Rowen trapped in a burning chariot of death. Said chariot needing a wash and maybe a new coat of paint that it would never get now. Christy jumped in with the color commentary and backtracked to where we/she found the hidden studio. We were a little cautious when it came to explaining how we got there or happened to be rummaging around Forbes-Collier's house. As far as we were concerned we were upstanding citizens, brave and true.

When it came time for the station break, I told the audience that they were listening to the radio in case they didn't know, gave the time and the station's call sign, and right on cue, a board op back in Tucson cut to a Bronco Billy commercial. During the break, I floated the suggestion that we connect Bev's death to Sal's using the victims' hairstyles to tie things together.

"Poor lady, she had just been on my show. When her body first floated by, I reached out for her and her hair came off in my hand. I figured she must have been scalped, this being Indian country or Native American country anyway. Pretty unnerving. Turns out it was a wig. She wasn't scalped, but Salvatore Anastasia was. Life imitates art."

I tossed the idea up against the wall, but like a wet noodle, it didn't stick. The team thought it was a little too close to bad taste although that had never stopped me before. But Bev had been a guest on my show, not just some politico caught with his or her pants down so to speak, so after about a dozen or so commercial spots that followed Bronco Billy's, we went back on the air adding Bryan Forbes-Collier to the list of victims, although he hadn't actually died, but at least he'd been mugged and suffered a coronary.

"You know, Jerry," Christy added, "when I spoke with Sheriff Redhawk just before the show, he had placed a deputy outside Mr. Forbes-Collier's hospital room and was planning to ask him about the forgeries as soon as he's recovered enough for questioning."

"He's lucky to have that deputy watching over him. Our third victim, who was found by Christy and me while we were lending Sheriff Redhawk a hand with his manhunt, was a principal player in the scam. It was the man we were hunting and apparently we weren't the only ones. And it was at the very spot where we found Beverly Edelbaum's body just eight days earlier. This time though the victim actually was scalped, but of course, that's neither here nor there. That is h-e-r-e not h-a-i-r; here nor there. You get the point."

We didn't mention Rex Bowman by name, but Ronnie and Satyra and Christy and I spent the rest of the show outlining the way we thought everything went down. Sal Anastasia was the middleman and probably the brains—what a sobering thought that is—of a ring that made forgeries of an alleged masterpiece by the famous artist Max Leibergard who had passed away a hundred years earlier. So at least Max L wasn't around to raise a ruckus. The ring used the Kirby Gallery, not to mention its owner, as a front to sell the bogus art. The buyers were probably all told to keep quiet about their acquisition, maybe because the title wasn't clear or some such nonsense. That way none of them knew about any of the other copies in circulation. The invoices we found in Forbes-Collier's safe indicated that maybe eight or nine had been sold. Before Bronco Billy, the highest price was one hundred twenty big-ones, but all told it was in the neighborhood of three-quarters of a mil. What a great neighborhood, eh?

Anyway, an art patron named Beverly Edelbaum had taken an interest in a talented, but not overly rich artist—Rex Bowman to those in the know—and somehow discovered he was involved in the scam. I think she wanted to blow the lid off it on my show, but didn't want the collateral damage to include Rex so she held off, waiting to see if she could get him to go along with some kind of deal. But she never got an encore, having been murdered and dropped in a desert pool. Bev literally talked herself to death by not talking. It was just my luck I got to see her instead of Christy naked, not that I shared that particular fact with my radio audience. I tried to think the best of Rex Bowman, hoping he didn't tip the rest of the gang to Bev's plan, but somebody did find out and...goodbye Bev. Christy and I voted for Deke Rowen as the actual hands-on guy, probably hired by Anastasia to do the dirty work.

Of course, Bev's murder is what brought Mrs. Wooten's little boy Billy to the party. And he got himself stuck on the idea of purchasing a famous artwork to publicize his used car lot. And if the painting wasn't really famous already, he'd make it famous. And Bronco Billy had enough money to get Forbes-Collier to close the deal, even knowing it wasn't in his best interest. Maybe Bryan staged the hold-up himself to get out of the deal or maybe Sal decided it for him, but as everybody already knew Forbes-Collier wound up in the ICU.

We knew how Deke Rowen died and Sal had cheated the hangman the hard way. I felt the noose was beginning to tighten around...well, I wasn't too sure about who'd wind up in the noose. The only question was who was mean enough and tough enough to do Sal in.

"*This case has had more than its share of twists and turns,*" I was saying, "*and for reasons that will become clear, we have had to keep our audience, not to mention everyone else for that matter, in the dark on certain of our activities. Right, Oh Great One?*"

"*It will be a big surprise to everyone, but Jerry and I have been working on this case as undercover agents for the FBI.*"

"*And you didn't tell me!*" Satyra exploded. "*What if somebody took a shot at you during the show and hit me by mistake?*"

"*Don't forget, I have extrasensory powers. I'd know if an attack was eminent and would take cover.*"

"*Sure,*" I said, "*when Rondini vanishes in a cloud of smoke, you'd know to duck behind the Chinese water torture.*"

"*That's made of glass!*"

"*Even I didn't know,*" Christy said, kind of changing the subject. "*The thing is these two act the same whether they're undercover or junior G-men or just being their normal selves.*"

So as the show wound down, Ronnie and I provided a word picture of our FBI undercover assignment. It was pretty much all fiction, but then Rondini was always an avid reader. About the only part that was true was when we accidentally exposed the newlyweds as our FBI controllers. So I wasn't too surprised when my cell rang right after the show and it turned out to be Ginny Taylor, aka the new bride.

"Oh, Ginny. Did you get a chance to catch my broadcast tonight?"

She did. Damn.

"You should have called when I was on the air."

She felt that might have been inappropriate considering she was supposed to be undercover.

"Ah, yes. I see what you mean."

Of course since her cover was blown now, she said, it might not have mattered.

"About that—"

But that wasn't why she called.

"What's that? Gloria Palucci's gone missing? You don't say..."

She did in fact say. But I decided not to say that I already knew. After all, I hadn't even told my listening audience that much yet.

"What about Forbes-Collier? He's still wired up to a heart monitor in Bisbee, isn't he?"

He was. So far Bryan hadn't disappeared too or even turned up dead. Ginny let it drop that Sheriff Redhawk was trying to get a writ of something or other so he could find out if Forbes-Collier was healthy enough for questioning. And maybe arresting and booking.

Since Gin seemed to be in a gossipy mood, I figured I'd run something else up the flag pole.

"Speaking of the art world," I said, "Ronnie and I were thinking of dropping in on Rex Bowman, you know, just to say hi, see how he's doing and all. Anything you'd like us to ask him while we're there?"

Apparently Ginny had plenty to ask him, but Ronnie and I wouldn't be doing the asking. Redhawk had taken on that chore while the Fibbies were busy finding out Gloria had skipped town. Turns out, Bowman was missing too.

Chapter 30.

THE Great Rondini and Satyra had already headed over to the Silver Cage for their late show while I was on the blower with the FBI. This was to be their finale at the Circle-K so I imagined they wouldn't be able to stretch their free room and board for much longer although Satyra was a pretty good draw at the pool.

Anyway, after Ginny's call, I gathered what was left of my little posse—Christy and her mom—and we went to watch The Great One thrill the tourists one last time.

He was doing a pretty good job of it too. He'd somehow managed to corral a couple of dudettes on horseback and was preparing to make them vanish on stage. I suppose the real magic was that neither pony crapped on his act. But the horses did disappear, leaving their riders, who in turn, went up in a puff of smoke themselves. When the smoke cleared, the horses were back. I could see this going on all night, but Ronnie cut it mercifully short, materializing the girls right back in their saddles and they rode off stage through the audience tables.

The lights dimmed and the act quieted down while Satyra collared a few rubes, er, audience members, who felt it would be okay to have Rondini read their thoughts. "Just a few volunteers to match wits with The Great Rondini, but be careful—he knows what's on your mind..."

Next thing you know he'd be guessing their ages and weights.

While Ronnie read a few minds from the audience, I wondered what he'd do if he could read mine. I was thinking about the call I got from Ginny Taylor, lady G-man. She had said that at that very moment the cops were tearing Bowman's abode apart looking for a clue or two as to his whereabouts. So far all they found of interest were a few more copies of the forged Leibergard paintings. Once our boy got going on something, he just didn't know when to stop. Maybe he should have tried the Mona Lisa.

She was also a little worried about Rex since the last guy to go missing was found dead. If someone that we didn't know about was cleaning house, well, let's just hope the cops find Rex before he, or maybe she, does. Ginny didn't say so, but I suppose the same could be said about the disappearance of Gloria. Of course, it looked like Gloria had packed a bag or two before blowing town. Still, I'd hate to find their bodies down by the ol' swimming hole. For one thing that would leave me with no suspects.

Forbes-Collier's home and art gallery were getting the fine tooth-comb treatment too, as was Gloria and Sal's villa here at the Circle-K. It was tempting to join the on-lookers gathered outside the Horny Toad bungalow watching to see if any more dead bodies were being pulled from the wreckage of the scam. But I had other fish to fry.

After all, I was pretty sure I knew where Rex and Gloria were.

"OUT there?" Christy said. "You think that's where Rex Bowman is?"

"Why sure," I said, looking around at Ronnie and Satyra and Sassie for a little support. "We got a clue. I found this stuck in one of Sal's jacket pockets. And look, it's got the location circled in red. Right there, see?"

"Maybe he was just playing tourist," Ronnie suggested. "Just wanted to get a little of the local..ah, atmosphere."

"I hope it's just not another of Jerry's silly hunches," my potential mother-in-law said. "It may be a long shot, but you haven't much else to go on, so I think you're stuck between a rock and a hard spot." My hunch being the hard spot. Sassie was just full of support.

But she was right about one thing, it was all we had to go on.

"Anybody know how to get there?" Ronnie asked.

"We can get directions off the phone. I'd bet my next contract extension that Sal was headed there to meet Rex Bowman when he bought it."

"Well, it's too late to go running around in the wilderness tonight," Satyra said. "We can think this through while we're having brunch tomorrow. After a couple of Bloody Marys,

Jerry's plan will probably look a lot better."

And so we all tootled off to bed.

Not necessarily the beds we all wanted since Mama Marshall had Christy bunk in with her. Ah well, a big day tomorrow. I probably needed the sleep.

BIG desert. Really big desert. I hoped somebody had remembered to fill the canteens. Maybe pack supplies. Just in case we ran out of gas or got a flat or something. My cell showed no bars at all. Until now the farthest I'd traveled from the Circle-K homestead was a few too frequent trips to the watering hole that had become a drop-off point for the occasional corpse. It wasn't even high noon yet and we had already gone miles past there. The good thing was that we coasting along in a four-wheeler rather than bouncing around on four hoofs.

Satyra had sweet-talked Slim Bales into providing the four wheels and since he didn't want us to make any dents in his dune baby, he offered to drive us. Slim even had a vague idea of where we were going and seemed to be getting us there at speed. Christy had tracked our progress on Google maps while she still had coverage and based on the last reading a couple more hours should do it.

Thank god.

Slim's off-road buggy had open sides and a piece of canvas flapping over our heads, so we were not only boiling hot, we were windblown as well. Quarters being tight I had to hold the studio in a box on my lap too. With all that, I was looking forward to a cold one when we got to the High Cloud Reservation. I felt sure they must have some kind of pop stand there and I hoped the pop was Budweiser. That is, if my stomach was still in one piece from the shaking Slim's pride and joy was giving us as he roared across the desert. On the other hand, we'd be able to skip the Native American sauna after our sunbaked ride out to the foothills nestling the reservation.

The foothills were Bowman country. We had seen his paintings of the foothills, the herds of wild ponies and of the folks who called this home. We'd found a write-up torn out of a travel magazine describing the sweat-lodge ceremony during our search of Sal Anastasia's closet. Someone, presumably Sal, had circled the location and had yesterday's date was written on it. It had to be where he was meeting Bowman. That is until a bullet suddenly cancelled his trip.

Our plan was to place Rex under citizen's arrest while we filmed it all on video. With any luck, we might get a few shots of some NA ceremony to provide a little color for the show. If we missed the Native Americans going into their act, KOW TV probably had plenty of stock footage showing a rain dance or something that we could cut in. I figured that even out on the reservation, the locals would respond to those two magic words I didn't learn from The Great Rondini—*reality television.*

"Hey, Slim," Satyra piped up, trying to be heard over the wind and engine noise. "We need to take a break. I don't know about anybody else, but I'm just about bounced to pieces."

"Ah yup. Ya don' say, gal." Slim let up on the gas and we were jolted all over one another, Ronnie on my lap and Satyra landing on Christy and everyone banging into each other. "Here ya go, folks. Any landing ya can scramble outta, is a good un," Slim chuckled.

The four-wheeler shuttered and came to a stop, the engine wheezing a few times before giving up the ghost. We seemed to be in a bowl of sand and rock, scrubby brush spotted here and there, and no sign of civilization in any direction. A cloudless sky stretched to an empty horizon in every direction, the mountains shimmering in the distance. With the engine turned off, it was eerily quiet. And without the breeze from our forward motion, the heat was merciless. Nonetheless, everybody got out to stretch his or her legs, Slim saying he didn't know if we'd get another chance to stop before reaching High Cloud.

We took big gulps from our water bottles, but in spite of the heat I was dying for a latte. Maybe today, an iced latte.

"'Scuse me, ever'body," Slim broke the quiet. "She's still a bit o' a ride, so if y'all don' mind, Ah'll jus' step behind that boulder there and answer a call o' nature. Ya'll may wanna do the same. Find yore own boulder, o' course."

THOSE mountains looked farther away than ever. We were standing in a huge saucer of sand and barren rock, probably Gila monsters and rattlesnakes hogging the few small spots of shade, the sun beating down. Did I say it was unbearably hot? I was thinking the chance of getting that cold one at the end of the trail was rapidly fading. None of us might get the chance for a cold one.

Except Slim, of course.

He was probably well on his way to getting a cold one. He left us, of course. While we all scattered around looking for our own boulders to answer that call of nature, Slim hopped back in the dune buggy and took off. The only good thing was that none of us had to pee anymore.

I wished I had thought to take the portable studio off the vehicle, but maybe it would come in handy if Slim was planning a career in radio.

"So the tracks show we came from that direction," I said, pondering which way we should head.

Rondini looked and asked, "Are those the tracks we came from or are those the ones Slim left when he bailed on us?"

"I'm not sure. It's only been five minutes and already I'm turned around. I don't know which direction we came from or which way we were going."

"I think my compass app is working though I can't call or text out here," Christy said. "That way should be north according to the phone."

"Mine shows it's that way," Satyra pointed at a different north.

"What about Google maps?" I asked. "Maybe we can get directions."

"I can't get it to open," Christy answered. "What about your phone?"

"I don't want to run down the battery. I need to be able to video our Bowman takedown."

"Well, at least we can document our last hours alive on this planet," Satyra said, panning her phone around to show our situation. Not bad. I could probably work up a complete segment on being abandoned and lost on the desert. I hoped we'd get the chance later to video me pushing Slim Bales under a bus.

So I turned to Ronnie. "What's the plan? How do we get out of here?"

"First, we need to conserve our water. It's still about seven or eight hours before the sun sinks low enough to give us a break in the heat. It should sink in the west so we'll know which north is north if either of them are. Of course, if it gets dark we won't be able to see so we won't know if we're walking in circles. There may be coyotes after dark too."

"Good plan," I said. "Let's walk this way."

We struck out following the tire tracks I thought Slim had

left after dumping us. Or they could have been the tracks that brought us here. Either way, I was pretty sure they either came from or were headed toward civilization of some kind. It didn't really matter which civilization since I was pretty sure we wouldn't make it anyway. Slow and steady that's the key.

"The key to what, Jer?"

"Did I say that out loud?"

"Oh. I thought you had a breakthrough."

"The only breakthrough I had was next time I'll take a horse."

THE mountains in the distance were still in the distance. It seemed like we had been walking for hours, but it didn't seem like we had made any progress. We would have taken a break, but he ground was too hot to sit on and our water bottles were nearing empty. The desert was burning right up through the soles of my jogging shoes so I didn't know how Ronnie was managing since he'd opted for flip-flops, but maybe he knew that Hindu trick about walking barefoot over hot coals.

Christy on the other hand seemed to be holding up better than me. She was marching along like it was a day at the beach. A really big beach. She'd been smart enough to put on extra strength sunscreen while I think I wound up drinking mine. I couldn't quite remember. Anyway, Christy looked really good. I was thinking that if we ever made it back to civilization, I was going to get serious about this engagement thing, maybe buy a big diamond ring, set the date, start calling Sassie Marshall Mom. Well, maybe I'd just call her Mrs. Marshall.

"You okay, Jerry?" Christy asked. "You're mumbling."

"Yeah, I'm okay. I must have been thinking out loud. What did you hear me say?"

"Not much. I thought I heard you say something about calling your mom."

"I'm not getting any reception here, so that's out. But I wasn't really thinking about my mom. I was thinking about yours. I was wondering how she's going to take it when I ask for—"

I stopped in my tracks. I could see something ahead. Something that was not too far away.

"Look!" I croaked. "There! There! It's the Circle-K! It's the pool!"

I could see the cool, blue water of the pool. Girls in bikinis, waiters bringing icy drinks, fun in the sun. I started to run.

"Whoa there, Red!" Ronnie grabbed my arm, Christy and Satyra sat me on the burning ground, they poured the last of the water in my mouth. Just a trickle, but enough to make me choke. "It's a mirage, Jerry. It's not really there. You're just seeing things."

The pool, the drinks, the bikinis all vanished into thin air like one of Rondini's tricks.

"Sure, sure," I said when I stopped coughing. "I don't see them anymore. They're gone."

"It was just a mirage, Junior."

"Sure, I hate it when that happens." I figured my pals were worried enough so I kept my mouth shut about the next mirage. The Circle-K pool may have vanished but it had been replaced by a bunch of Native Americans charging toward us on motorcycles. In spite of the dust cloud half hiding them, they appeared to be all duded out in feathers and buckskins. Maybe war paint too. In my fevered state, I imagined I could even hear their bikes roaring across the desert.

"Look! Who are they?" Christy shouted, pointing in the direction of my bikers.

"How did you get in my mirage?"

"It looks like people," Ronnie said, jumping up and down, waving his arms and shouting.

At that, we all started shouting and jumping and waving, me included.

Some crazy mirage if you'd asked me.

Chapter 31.

So it turns out the desert isn't as lonely a place as you might think. The bikers were a motorcycle-riding branch of the local Yaqui tribe on their way to the mega pow-wow out at the High Cloud Reservation. After hearing we'd been stranded out in the big nowhere, their head guy, David Longfoot, offered to give us a ride.

"You can get all kinds of transportation to pretty much anywhere up at the pow-wow," Longfoot was saying. "Some dance teams got casino sponsors, come in by helicopter."

"Dance teams?" Satyra latched on to the words. "They have entertainment?"

"In a way," Missus Longfoot—Aurora she said to call her—answered. "But this is traditional dancing, like the grass dance or the shawl dance. The dancing ground is considered sacred during the pow-wow."

"Definitely no pole dancing then," I chimed in. "But it sounds like fun, even if it's not exactly the Rockettes. If we can just thumb a ride with you folks to the pow-wow, I think we're gold."

Before we could get Longfoot and his compatriots back on their bikes, Christy got into a deep discussion with her new BFF, Aurora, all about her alma mater throwing a big-time pow-wow each year, it being in Native American country and all. Turns out Aurora had gone to UA also. They were practically sorority sisters. I figured that it was all good and maybe they really would get us to the reservation. Sal's magazine clipping about the gathering of the tribes was burning a hole in my pocket and I was anxious to get there. I'd bet Rex Bowman would be hoping to hitch a ride on one of those whirlybirds to who knows where. If he made it out, he'd be taking the ending of my reality show with him.

The Longfoots—*Longfeet?*—had a half dozen other riders with them plus a papoose or two. They had shed their helmets and jackets in the desert heat and spent a few minutes stretching their legs, wetting their whistles, and I think a few were toking the magic weed. Then, without any visible sign, they picked up their kids' empty juice boxes and put away their water bottles and gathered by their bikes while Chief Dave gave some kind of traditional blessing in their native tongue. Fortunately, Christy had her phone out and caught it on video.

The roar as their engines came to life shattered the silence of the desert not to mention my ear drums, but who's complaining. It was deafening up close, but sounded like salvation to me. So with borrowed helmets and holding on for dear life, we were on our way, bouncing over the terrain at suicidal speeds. If I thought horseback riding was tough on the nether regions, it had nothing on the back seat of a motorcycle pounding over dirt and rocks, and probably a scorpion or two.

We cut across where no man had gone before—or at least no man had lived to tell about it—for the next half hour or thereabouts, finally reaching slightly flatter ground that passed for a road. The ride there wasn't much better, but the bikers seemed encouraged enough to put on even more speed. Fortunately we reached an actual blacktop highway after fifteen or twenty more tooth-jarring minutes and the life-threatening part of the program seemed to be over. From that point on, it was a walk in the park motorcycle-wise.

Unlike the light of my life's alma mater, my college hadn't bothered to throw any pow-wows, so I didn't quite know what to expect. The reservation had a few buildings scattered around the outskirts and a kind of frowzy trailer park, but for the gathering they had gone all out with tents large and small, stands offering a variety of traditional food and drink that turned out to be mostly tacos and soda and beer. A huge, fenced off area with bleachers and a jumbotron was where the activities all took place according to our Indian guides, none of whom looked much like the one in the painting. On the far side of the pow-wow set-up there was a huge parking lot, about a quarter filled. And on the far side of the parking lot, a pretty good-sized casino with enough lights blinking and twitching and flashing to signal somebody on Mars. In spite of the mostly empty parking lot, I'd put money on the casino being more than a quarter filled.

Chief Dave didn't hesitate to pull into the lot though, aiming straight at the casino's door. He told me later that the real good dancing and singing and so on wouldn't start until tomorrow anyway. Just in case I was worried about where his priorities lay, I guess. My other guess was that if Sal was going to meet Rex Bowman here, it would be the casino, not the sacred dancing ground. So with our ears ringing from the roar of the bikes, we stepped into a wall of sound inside the casino. One-armed bandits buzzing and pinging away against a steady background of bells and gamblers cursing, shouting and celebrating.

Dave introduced us to his cousin who was the casino's token Indian—er, Native American—and who in turn, turned us over to a desk clerk who looked a lot like Sherm Huntley. Turned out he was Sherm's cousin; hospitality must run in the family. Anyway, we rented a couple of rooms so we could get cleaned up and have a base of operations. Since the rooms weren't being comped and Ronnie and Satyra wouldn't share, the guys wound up in one room and the gals in the other. At least the rooms shared a wall with a door in it, so I had hopes. If we could get rid of the magicians, we'd put on a show of our own.

"THE question," Ronnie was saying, "is where to find our runaway artist."

"Actually the question is how am I going to do my radio show tonight?"

"Without Bowman you don't have a show. We need to bag this puppy. Besides I'm... well, I'm booked in Austin two nights from now."

"Sal's magazine clipping got us this far," I replied, "but he forgot to write Rex's room number on it."

Assuming he was in the casino hotel and not sitting it out in, say, the trailer park. But then Rex didn't strike me as the starving artist type. Rex aside, Sal's killer was still running around somewhere. I was beginning to lean toward Slim Bales for the perp on that now. After all, he left us to die out in the desert, and anyway, Deke Rowen was his pal. Six of one, half a pound of the other. Slim might have realized the cops were closing in and that Sal might sell him out if in fact Slim was involved in Bev's death at all. Maybe even if he hadn't been.

"You suppose Slim might be here to take out Rex too?" I asked Ronnie.

"My guess is that Rex wasn't a part of the strong arm stuff," Ronnie said. "But then Bryan Forbes-Collier is another story. If Slim isn't here, I'd put money on him being in Bisbee."

"Somebody should call Redhawk and have him double the guard on Forbes-Collier," I suggested. "Who knows, maybe if the sheriff finds Slim and his desert dune buggy, I can get my studio in a box back."

"So without that you're grounded anyway, eh?"

At least the room had AC and a great shower—any shower would have been great at that point—soft beds and a sixty inch flat screen TV. I had Christy rub aloe into my sunburn and we all finished off all the water bottles in the mini-bar.

By now, Rondini and I were feeling better, washed and dried with baggy shorts and logo tee shirts we'd picked up at a shop in the lobby. We figured that gamblers who lost their shirts wound up dressed like us. I made a call to Dale Anderson back at the KICK Radio offices and arranged for the station to play some "best of" in lieu of a live show. Dale did intimate I might be charged for a vacation day though. And might have to pay for the missing equipment. Discretion being the better part of you know what, I didn't ask about expensing my room.

One more call left to make. Darrell Lee picked up on the first ring.

"Where are you guys?" he said instead of one of the more normal hellos.

"I'm right here. So's Ronnie and the ladies."

"Listen, Jeremy, first Anastasia goes missing, then his gal disappears and so does Bowman, and for all I know, maybe their bodies are layin' some place out there in the desert too. Then by all that's holy, you and all your pals disappear."

"Not everybody. Christy's mom should still be at the Circle-K, holding down the fort as it were."

"Okay, maybe she didn't disappear, but she's wondering where her daughter got off to too."

"Not to fear, Sheriff. We're all okay now, but we did have a close call. We have another name to add to the perp list." So I gave him the lowdown on Slim Bales leaving us to die in the desert and how we thought...well, you've already heard all of that, so the only new thing was Redhawk's head exploding when I told him about finding the clipping in Sal's bungalow. Anyway, when he'd settled down, he did say he'd add extra guards at the hospital and put out an all point bulletin to pick up Slim. He also said he'd see me soon, but didn't go into any details and I didn't want to push him.

The ladies had joined us using our connecting door, and since we were starving after our desert outing, we adjourned to find a restaurant. I figured this was something I could put on my expense account since Dale hadn't said not to.

Chapter 32.

THE big gathering was set to kick off in the morning, but it looked like the attendees were planning to whoop it up tonight. Maybe get it out of their systems before the serious dancing began. Me and my tribe had fed both ourselves and the slots before strolling around the gambling hall, just in case Rex Bowman had a thing for the galloping dominoes. Who knows, we could have gotten lucky. Probably better odds for that than most of the Native Americans would get tonight. Of course, Darrell Lee might have hit the jackpot when he said that Rex could be sleeping with the cacti. Slim Bales cleaning house? Maybe, though he didn't look like that tidy a guy.

We trolled the giant casino examining faces at the gaming tables, some happy, some intent, not many sad. None of them Bowman. We spotted *mère et père* Longfoot risking the rent money and being all smiles. At the buffet, folks were lined up half way across the room, their faces anticipating an all you can eat feast for six ninety-nine. Bowman must not have been hungry either. I took a detour through the main doors to the great outdoors. The clanging and whirring of the betting machines was muffled out there and the nighttime temperature had dropped down to the mid-eighties. Right outside the entrance the valet stand was doing a brisk trade in parking and fetching. If he was here, Rex Bowman must have come by cab. By now, I was pretty much on my own, the ladies having decided to upgrade their wardrobes in a shopping mall they had discovered across from the gaming room and Rondini was trying out a card trick or two on an Indian princess. I don't know if she was impressed or not, but a couple of pit bosses were watching very closely.

But if Bowman wasn't planning his own rendezvous here, why did Sal Anastasia have the clipping? I couldn't believe Sal was that much into tribal ways. Anyway I wandered back into the casino and signed a drink up to my room. Standing outside the lounge I pretended to be James Bond, coolly observing the ebb and flow of the crowd, my eyes constantly moving, searching for our AWOL artist. I was also hoping Ronnie was figuring out our next move or maybe what Bowman might be up to. I hoped he was doing more than just showing some babe his cards. Or worse.

Of course, a break from detecting might be just what the doctor ordered. Clear the mind. We could all start fresh in the morning. Mrs. Marshall not being around to mess things up, I might even be able to convince Christy that the shops would still be there then. If we were quick enough, I could still lock Ronnie out of the room for an hour or two. I decided to check out the shopping arcade and see if Christy wanted to play.

I had just reached the big totem pole by the entrance to the mall, when Christy and Satyra came running out to meet me.

"Jerry, thank god you're here," they said talking over each other. "We saw her!"

"Saw who?" I was thinking maybe Beyonce was signing autographs at the video arcade.

"Gloria! Gloria Palucci! She's was just trying on a pair of Jimmy Choo's at the First Step!"

"Gloria? What's she doing here? Maybe we can get that interview."

"No, Jerry," Christy grabbed on to my tee-shirt, "the magazine clipping we found at her bungalow, it must have been hers, not Sal's."

"Hers? But then Bowman's not here?"

"Wake up, Red." Satyra gave me a shot in the ribs. "*Gloria's* meeting Rex here!"

The light bulb over my head began to sputter on. "So Gloria and Rex are teamed up?"

"Sure," Christy said. "And she's right here, checking out the shops. But eventually she's bound to lead us to Rex."

The gals pulled me toward some designer shoe palace they'd seen Gloria picking out high-priced footwear in. Only problem was she wasn't there now. Shoe stores not having fitting rooms, there was no place there we could have missed her.

"Listen, Jerry, you stay out here watching the main drag," Satyra said, "and we'll comb the shops to see where she might have gone."

"Maybe she took off already," I suggested.

"It looked like she just got here. She wasn't carrying anything and no self-respecting shopper leaves without a few bags full."

I prowled around outside the stores, while Christy and Satyra worked opposite sides of the mall, checking inside the shops, the fitting rooms, and whatever other kind of room Gloria might have disappeared into. Basically, the mall was pretty much like any other shopping mall with stores lining the, uh, mall. Only here it was dressed up to look like the main drag of an old western town. Kind of reminded me of Kirby, only with newer old stuff.

I was just about to wander down to a coffee stand called the Happy Hunting Grounds when something poked me hard in the ribs. Same spot as Satyra. I thought it was her at first, like maybe she had snuck up behind me. Imagine my surprise when I heard Gloria Palucci say, "This is a gun so don't turn around. Act like nothing's wrong and walk that toward the door beside the coffee place."

So I was headed towards the Happy Hunting Grounds as planned, but this time not for coffee. She had me push open a steel door marked exit and gun-steered me through. Down a flight of stairs and through another door and we were in the parking lot. I thought I might be able to charm her over to my side, but a compliment on the size of her gun only got me a smack on the back of the head. We finally stopped by a Chevy five or six rows of cars from the door. The car looked like it just rolled off the assembly line, maybe twenty years ago. A guy who wasn't Bowman or even Slim Bales was sitting behind the wheel wearing a cowboy hat with a bunch of eagle feathers stuck in it. Gloria signaled the driver and he popped the trunk lid.

"In you go, Jerry."

"Gloria, come on, it's filthy in there. Why can't I sit up front with you?" I realized I sounded like a spoiled teenager, but whatever works. And maybe it would have worked for a teenager, but not for me. I got the point of the gun in my side again and figured I'd better climb while I still had a few ribs left.

The last thing I saw was Gloria looking down at me like I was a cockroach she wanted to smash. Then she slammed the trunk lid and I was in the dark. In all fairness, it was a roomy trunk, just not very comfortable. And once we got started, I felt her car could use a new set of shocks, and I do mean I *felt* it. While I bounced, I tried to see if there might be a tire iron or good sized wrench left around the trunk compartment, but couldn't lay my hands on anything more lethal than a window scraper. And like they say, never bring a window scraper to a gun fight.

I remembered something from the movies about counting the seconds so you'd be able to figure out where they had taken you. Maybe it worked for James Bond or Sherlock Holmes, but I seemed to lose count every time we hit a pot hole. Maybe I should have counted the bumps instead.

AFTER a while the car rolled to a stop. I hoped I'd get a chance to stand up and work the knots out of my legs before they shot me. I'd hate to be so kinked up from riding in the trunk that I'd have to be buried in an L-shaped coffin. But the trunk lid didn't open. I thought I heard Gloria getting out and slamming the car door, then footsteps heading away from the car. Since we weren't moving and I figured Gloria had stepped out, I worked on finding a way to spring the trunk lock or maybe crash through the rear seat. Rondini does all kinds of escapes in his act, but unfortunately a magician never reveals his secrets which pretty much left me in the dark. The bastard.

I was beginning to think about chewing my way through the gas tank when all of a sudden I heard footsteps again. I could hear them getting closer and though their voices were getting louder, I couldn't make out what was being said. Neither could I tell who was doing the talking. Gloria and Rex? Slim Bales and Gloria? The eagle-feathered driver and who?

Or could it be some passersby who might help me if I called out to them. They were getting closer and if it was the passersby I ought to yell for help, tell them to call 9-1-1 or something. Of course, if it turned out to be the bad guys, what's the worst Gloria could do to me for shouting? Shoot me through her own trunk lid? What if it wasn't even her car? I hadn't quite thought that one through when the trunk popped opened. One guess if it was passersby.

Gloria and Rex peered down at me cowering in the gloom, night having by then fallen. Rex had the gun now and I didn't really want him to poke me with it, so I followed their orders to get out and head up to a rather drab double-wide that I guessed they called home. There weren't any neighbors that I could see, so we definitely weren't in the casino trailer park although maybe that would have been a step up. For Gloria Palucci it was quite a step down from the villa back at the

Circle-K.

I noticed Slim's dune buggy parked next to the trailer, so my guess was the gang was all here. Luckily I couldn't see the vultures circling in the dark.

Indoors, the trailer was just as crummy looking as the outside. I didn't see any paints or canvas in spite of the artist in residence, but I got a clear look at the guy with the eagle feathers. He was a lot older than the rest of the gang and had long, graying braids ala Willie Nelson. He had a lot of silver and turquoise trimmings hanging off him too. Silver arrowheads and all. Rex waved him away and he disappeared into a back room. Then it was my turn.

"Okay, Jeremy, turn around and hands behind your back," Rex said, signaling a pirouette with the revolver. Anyway, I took this as a good thing since who would tie a guy up if he planned to shoot him?

Having spent most of my adult life pitching cars for one Wooten or another, I decided to make my pitch to Rex. I said, "Look, I'm pretty sure Redhawk and the FBI guys have half the cops in the state out looking for me, not to mention the other half are out looking for you."

"I said turn around."

"Sure, glad to. But first let me tell you something I've been thinking about."

"Around, pal. You're not on the air now."

"Sure, but wait a second. We could be on the air right away and the good part is you can tell your side of the story. The radio equipment is right in the dune buggy outside. You could say as how Sal was a bad influence, tell me as how he practically forced you into doing the paint job. How he was the one killed Mrs. Edelbaum and the whole thing. Maybe how Sal got bumped because it was the only way you could get free of him. You'll be influencing the court of public opinion, probably get off practically scot-free. Just gimme a chance. Whaddaya say?"

"I say I'll need to think about it, and while I think, you need to be tied up. Turn around."

So I turned, and as I stuck my hands behind me, I felt a very sharp pain in my neck. My legs turned to rubber and everything went black. Blacker even than the trunk of the old Chevy.

Chapter 33.

I WOKE up with my hands tied.

And my feet tied. And it was very hot.

In spite of the heat and the rope, I nodded in and out of consciousness, not really too sure when I was in from when I was out. I had dreams too horrible to be real and I dreamed I woke up to a much more horrid reality. When I opened my eyes I couldn't see unless I closed them. Giant snakes and bugs circled me while I sat propped against a burning rock in the middle of some kind of wigwam. The place was full of fire and smoke, boiling pools of water, steaming sweat pooled around me and I was already stripped down to just my undershorts.

I thought I saw the eagle feather guy from the trailer, I'd thought he was maybe an out of work Indian chief or medicine man, er, Native American chief, that is, and who knows, maybe a chiropractor. He was naked now and glowing and nine feet tall and the feathers had turned into wings, but somehow that didn't even scare me. I was more scared of melting like a wax doll. My flesh was sagging and dripping before my very eyes. Not far away I thought I could see Slim Bales through clouds of steam and smoke. He wasn't moving except for his becoming a puddle of flesh and bone. I may have nodded off again. Must be the heat.

The pain in my skull woke me. I was being cooked alive but at least the snakes were gone and the Indian driver was just a skinny guy wearing running shorts with a towel around his neck and big barbecue gloves. He glanced my way and noticed I was still among the living. "Hot, eh?" he said, shoveling more red hot stones on the pile.

I sized him up and, figuring he might just be noble and not savage, I said, "You want to untie me now and hand me a

---

towel? I'm ready for a shower."

"No way, paleface. You're in what's called a sweat lodge. It's a very spiritual experience. Your spirit will reach a state of purification. You will become one with the universe. We can smoke the sacred *chanunpa*, the peace pipe. Smoke some very righteous peyote. Very spiritual. 'Course, the only way you're spirit will go out of here today is feet first. Regular sweat lodge ceremony, I get about a C-note from stupid white men. But no charge for friends of Rex. 'Course paying customers all leave still alive. You want the pipe? No charge."

"Thanks, but I'm trying to cut down. How about you just let me out of here now, while I'm still medium rare."

The old man snorted out a laugh and wiped the sweat from his eyes. "You should take the pipe, go out of here on a high. Very spiritual."

He walked away and disappeared behind a blanket that must have been over a doorway. The lodge didn't seem big enough for it to be a second room.

"Hey, pal," I yelled after him, doing the best I could being full of hot, er, heated, air, "where you going?"

"He's gone, Jeremy."

Oh. I had forgotten about Slim. He was here too, tied up too, in his shorts too. I turned as best I could to look him over and he didn't look good. I was kind of worried I might be looking the same myself. I certainly felt as bad as he looked.

"I thought you were on their side," I said.

"Maybe I didn't make the cut. That fuckin' Atokar is gonna cook us in here and say we over did the sweat lodge and the peyote and all that shit. Say it was an accident."

"Who's that did you say?"

"That fuckin' redskin, Atokar. Jake Atokar. He's a pal of Bowman's. Some kind of blood brother or some Indian shit. He's been building up the fire in here to roast us alive. If we can't get out of these fuckin' ropes, we're fucked."

"And if I help you to get loose, then just me will be fucked. You tried it once out in the desert."

"Come on, I'm not like them. They made me do it, otherwise they were going to set me up for the murders. I was going to call the sheriff when I got to the casino and let him know you needed to get rescued. Bowman said it was just a fuckin' diversion so's he could make some kind of getaway."

"Then what are you doing here?"

"Maybe they really didn't want me to call the sheriff."

I was too exhausted to think straight at this point. I felt

the blackness descending again, only this time I knew the trunk wouldn't ever open again.   But somehow Bales had squiggled a little toward me, enough to poke my foot with his foot and bring me back again.

I didn't want to die playing footsie with a fat cowboy. I'd have to throw in with him if I was to get out of this...uh, Native American steam bath. I tried to see if I could squirm a little toward him.

We squirmed, we squiggled, we butt-walked.   I figured Slim probably forgot to hide a switchblade in his shorts, so even when we got close we'd have to somehow untie the knots with our hands tied behind our backs. Each hard-won inch was exhausting in the heat, but while we struggled I decided to take our minds off the boiling hot temp and the pain by interviewing Slim. After all, he wasn't going anywhere.

"So tell me, was Deke involved more than you?"

"Ah, the poor dude. He was the one got me into all this, but he wasn't really bad." Slim grunted and lurched a fraction closer. "They got him somehow, made it look like an accident, but he'd never run off the road on his own, not in his truck."

"Sure," I said, figuring I'd better not follow up on that. "But a lot of folks beside Deke got killed so far."   By now we were twisting our backs together. I was hoping the fat boy might be double jointed. "Bev Edelbaum was the first..."

"That was Sal. Bowman told Forbes-Collier that she had tumbled to the scam," I could feel Slim's fingers trying to work on the knots fastening my wrists, "and then, after they were all on your show, Bryan went to Sal sayin' as how he thought she was gonna spill it to you."

"If she had told it on that first show, she might still be alive," I said, feeling my fingers tingling as the blood starting to return to my hands. "It was not talking that killed her."

"Or you...it coulda been you they killed. To stop any more shows, you know."

"Me?" Forget about being cooked alive, now I was getting nervous. "Why me?"

"Sal thought if you turned up dead, the Edelbaum lady would take the hint and shut-up."

Suddenly my hands were free. I automatically went to work on the ropes around my ankles.

"Um, ah..." Slim was saying, "don't forget we're in this together, right partner?"

"Oh, sorry. No offense." I gave up on my ankles and started getting Slim free. I was hoping when his hands were free, he wouldn't just brain me and leave me here to die. But he didn't. Somehow we got ourselves loose and leaning on each other, managed to hobble out of the dark, steaming sweat lodge—into the white-hot, blazing desert. Nothing like wearing only your underpants in the noonday sun. And me a redhead. Soon I'd be red all over.

When I stumbled out of the sweat lodge, the brightness of the desert firebombed my eyes like a thousand flashbulbs. Slim and I blinked and shaded our eyes and squinted, but still it took several minutes to see where we were. I'd love to say we were still by the big casino parking lot but no such luck. No parking lot, not even any road. We were in the desert again, a particularly deserted part of the desert. Not even a palm tree.

The sweat lodge itself was a far cry from the steam bath back at the Canyon Country Club. The lodge from the outside looked to be a room-sized igloo made out of old blankets somebody picked up at Goodwill held together with rope and a bunch of twigs. Beyond the decrepit wigwam the desert spread out forever while to our backs a few giant boulders looked like they had broken off the face of a steep cliff and rolled down to within a few hundred yards of us. I couldn't help thinking that someday this would all be a housing development or maybe a sister to the Canyon CC, palm trees, swimming pools and all. Must have been the heat.

No sign of intelligent life in any direction. I was including Slim in this dim prospect, when he started poking at me. He was pointing at the rocky plateau, but I still couldn't see straight, my eyes not having adjusted to the light yet. Meanwhile, Bales was getting more excited by the moment, telling me to look at a patch of shade cast by the rocks.

Wait—not the shade—something in the shade. I squinted and willed my eyes to focus, and yes, there it was. I only hoped Slim wasn't seeing a mirage and passing it on to me. I was ninety percent sure it was Bales' four-wheeler. It must have been parked there to flesh out the story that we were just tourists overdoing the sweat ceremony.

Slim and I did our version of a three legged race, holding on and supporting each other as we hopped across the sharp, fiery stones, our feet burning and painful. I hobbled into the shade and collapsed on the back seat, near ready to pass out, while Bales took the front. A bit of good luck—Rex & Co. had left a few of the water bottles from our aborted ride out in the buggy. The water was tea bag hot, but we managed to sip it down. Nothing ever tasted better.

"They must have left the buggy to make it look like we'd drove out here," Slim said. "I wonder where they hid the keys."

"Keys? You don't have the keys?"

"Not unless there's a pocket in my shorts I don't know about."

"What about our clothes? If we're supposed to have come here on our own, we wouldn't have left our clothes behind."

"I dunno. Maybe they put 'em in the lodge. You wanna go check it out?"

"I'd rather die here. At least they left us the water. And that's not all—look!"

"What's that?"

"It may be our way out of here. It's a radio studio in a box. And it has a mobile connection if there's any signal out here. Ouch—this case is hot!"

"You can call for help on that thing?"

"Not exactly. As I understand it, it's only one way—we can broadcast and the station can pick up the signal okay, but we can't call 9-1-1 or anybody. Usually I have a second phone connection to the station. But if I can broadcast we might get somebody's attention."

"Sweet!"

"Too bad I left the instructions back at the ranch."

"Jesus! You telling me you don't know how to make it work?"

"Sure, I can make it work. I'm almost positive I can. I just need to try a few of these switches here."

I got the power lamp to light up on my third try. Some kind of dial showed some kind of numbers, maybe something to do with frequencies you see on the radio dial, but I didn't need to know that now. I flipped a switch or two more hoping they were the right ones and a green light on the microphone came on. I was sure that was progress.

"Mayday. Mayday. This is Jerry Jeremy and I need help. If you hear me call 9-1-1. My life is in danger, somebody is trying to kill me. Mayday. Mayday..."

"What the hell are you doin'?"

"Trying to get some attention. Whacha think—should I tease my regular show. You could be my guest if we get rescued by air time."

"Dude, I think I'm gonna' be all jailed up when or if we get out of here. I'm hoping you'll tell the cops how I helped save your ass."

"I'll be glad to, Slim, but I just had a thought. Maybe you can do something for me while we wait to be rescued."

Chapter 34.

MY idea was to just broadcast my show now, somewhere around seven hours early. With any luck the engineers back at KICK would pick up my signal and record it for play back at a later time. That way if I did wind up dead, either from thirst or from Slim changing sides or if Rex's trusty Indian scout returned, my show would still go on as scheduled. Of course, they'd have to use the pre-recorded commercials for Bronco Billy's jalopies, but I didn't think he'd mind since his painting would have paid off in free publicity after all.

That aside, I also harbored the somewhat slim hope the station's engineer would pick up the signal and get me a ride home. Preferably in a cop car. Since Slim was here and had been on the inside of the local crime wave, I figured he was the perfect guest on possibly my last show. For my opening monologue I decided to start by setting the scene:

"Good evening to everyone out there listening to me, Jerry Jeremy, on KICK radio, the Talk of the West. I don't know when you'll hear this, but I'm broadcasting from deep in the desert and it's around high noon. At a guess, the temp is pushing a hundred and twenty, so before I melt, let me introduce my guest for this afternoon.

"Cecil Bales, better known as Slim, is a ranch hand at the Circle-K where we have been broadcasting from this week..."
I led off with how Rex Bowman tried to murder me and Bales, and how I was able to break loose and rescue Slim in the bargain. After all, if this was my last show, a little poetic license was called for. I wanted my audience to miss me. Anyway, we spent a whole segment—about twenty minutes air time—telling the world how I was a hero and that Slim was an almost innocent bystander who fell in with a bad crowd. While we talked I got Slim to try hot-wiring the ignition although

Slim was a little insulted that I thought he'd know how. Turns out he didn't actually have the foggiest. Who knew?

By this time we needed to bring it back to the art scam which, to hear Slim tell it, he'd only heard about second hand from Deke who was an almost innocent bystander who just fell in with a bad crowd. I passed on discussing or dissing Deke's fatal driving skills, not being sure how Slim would take it. If I got out of this alive, the truth about Deke's accident would be fresh meat for the reality show, which by now I took to be a reality itself.

Slim and I recapped our pow-wow in the sweat lodge, Slim putting Bev's murder on Sal Anastasia so she wouldn't give away the scam. I played up the part about how it could have been me who bought the big one instead of Bev, my life in danger and all. Eventually I got to the part about how Bronco Billy bought another copy of the forged painting and planned to publicize it as a newly discovered masterpiece of western art. *"So,"* I continued, *"I'm guessing Sal stole the painting from the Kirby Gallery to keep Bronco Billy Wooten from publicizing it. But why did he cold-cock Bryan Forbes-Collier who was in on the scam with him?"*

"Well, to be honest, I think my buddy Deke just got hisself pulled into the robbery. I'm sure he didn't plan to steal the picture or pound Forbes-Collier senseless. I won't say I was there, but I know what happened."

"So your friend told you what happened?"

"No, uh, not exactly. I saw it with my own eyes, but I didn't know it was, uh, gonna go down."

"So you weren't involved. Nothing for you to worry about then. Anybody else there besides you and Deke Rowen?"

"Uh, well Forbes-Collier was there too."

"Uh, yeah. Just the three of you?"

"Well, Miz Palucci was there too. Forbes-Collier might not have opened up for just Deke and me."

"Let me get this straight, Sal Anastasia sent his significant other with you and Deke instead of going himself?"

"Sure. Well, uh, I can't say how significant she was."

"Weren't they sharing a bungalow at the Circle-K? Always together?"

"Heh, I can't say that they were always together. I mean this guy, Anastasia, might have thought so, but I know Gloria had other ideas."

"Whadda you mean?"

"Well, uh, Deke, he started disappearing some nights.

We'd be having a brew or three and he'd get a text message and he'd say something'd come up and he had to go. So, then after a few times this happened, I put it to him, what was happenin'. He finally told me he was gettin' lucky, you know what I mean? One night I snuke out and followed him and damned if he wasn't meetin' Miz Palucci down by the stables. They went in and I took a look in the tack room window and old Deke was doin' her."

"So Deke and Gloria Palucci were having an affair?"

"Well, yeah, I guess so. He was doin' her anyway. She was a lot older than us, but from what I could see from the window, she was in pretty good shape."

"But Deke couldn't have been the one to kill Sal, since he'd already had that fatal accident. Forget Sal for now, what was the deal with the gallery robbery?"

"Well, uh, like I said, I was just a there by accident. Deke said I should come to help carry something. We met Miz Palucci up in Kirby and I was a bit surprised, I mean I knew by then Deke was bangin' her, but I thought it was supposed to be a secret. Anyway I figure she's the one got Deke to go along with the deal. I guess it was way before the gallery would open 'cause everything was all locked up yet. But she banged in the door and Forbes-Collier opened it and we all pushed in."

"Then what happened? Didn't Bryan Forbes-Collier know you were there to take the painting?"

"Lookin' back on it, it's kind funny. I mean I don't think he did know why we there."

"So he put up a struggle?"

"No, he got socked before we grabbed the picture."

"Deke just walked in a clobbered him?"

"Well, sorta. I mean Gloria just said somethin' like, 'do it now,' and Deke did it. He had a short piece of pipe he'd been holding down by the side of his leg, so's the guy couldn't see it, I guess."

"It sounds like maybe they'd planned it in advance. It couldn't just be Gloria's idea to smack down Bryan Forbes-Collier, could it? Bryan wasn't another lover interest, was he?"

"Well, could be since she seems to get around. I always wondered though if Sal had set it up to scare Deke. What I kinda thought it might be, see, is that Sal somehow knew about Deke bangin' his old lady and told her and Deke to put Forbes-Collier in the hospital for sellin' the picture, so Deke

212 Donald J. McGill

might think next time it might be him taking the ambulance ride. Who knows, it could happen like—" Slim took a big pull on the water bottle *"—that."*

"Let me have a go at that bad boy." I reached for the bottle.

Slim pulled back, holding it away from me. *"Hey,"* he said, *"it's almost gone. I'm savin' the rest."*

"What are you, the water bank?"

I reached around his fat gut and he pushed me back.

The heat, the water, the grim reaper, we were about to settle things permanently. My listeners would know one of us was about to sign off for good.

"You hear that?" Slim held up his hand as a truce sign. I grabbed the bottle and drank, practically drowning.

"Yeah," I choked out, finishing off the water.

The sound of a car or truck or something else made by man was slowly getting louder, coming closer.

I started to cut the mic, but stopped. If we were being rescued, I wanted to get it on the air, assuming our little broadcast was the reason we were being rescued. On the other hand, if it wasn't the good guys, if it was fuckin' Atokar, or maybe Rex himself, or even Gloria and her Glock, well, it couldn't hurt to have a record of my final moments. I hoped not anyway.

I realized Bales was still talking. *"...doesn't sound like a four-wheeler, but...wait, look over there. A lot of dust for just a truck."*

"I see what you mean. And if I'm right, it's the second time in two days I've seen those dust trails." I was suddenly feeling very good. The sound of motorcycles could be clearly heard, and unless it was a contingent from the Arizona highway patrol, the only bikers who would be tearing up the desert would be David Longfoot's mob—looking for me I hoped.

The bikers surrounded the sweat lodge in ever-tightening circles, raising enough dust to choke to death any villains still lurking there. Bales and I were gagging on dirt and sand as David Longfoot brought the parade to a halt. *"Jeezus, Jeremy, you're redder than I am,"* went out on the airwaves before I had a chance to stop coughing and switch the studio in a box off, although sweeter words were never heard by me.

The Native You-know-what's managed to contribute enough clothing to cover both Slim and me to some extent. While Slim got a tee-shirt to go with his underwear, Aspen

Longfoot rummaged around in her saddlebags and came up with a flowered muumuu-like dress that I could use to protect my modesty. At this point it felt like a tuxedo. Her mothering streak even extended to pouring Gatorade down our throats. A couple of the boys poured water over our heads like it grew on trees. Wet and burping, I introduced Slim as the guy who'd left me stranded in the desert yesterday which got him a few odd looks like maybe they'd leave him today. But after a little grumbling and warpath talk the guys settled down when I claimed Bales was my prisoner under citizen's arrest. We finally doubled up behind a couple of riders and headed for the big pow-wow.

Although the Bales broadcast was great, I knew his next interview would be behind bars. Maybe it really was a citizen's arrest.

Chapter 35.

I HAD thought to salvage the studio in a box when the tribe came to my rescue. I didn't want Dale Anderson to get mad about losing it, particularly since I had already trashed one of my sponsor's cars. So I managed to hang onto David Longfoot's coattails with one hand and the studio with the other while we bounced across the rocks and sand. By now I was getting used to the ride.

We eventually made it to the High Cloud reservation and casino. While my Native American pals took Slim to the local *gendarmes* for booking on littering in the desert or something, I tried to be as inconspicuous as possible crossing the gaming floor in a flowered dress. Strangely, no one seemed to notice so maybe it was a regular thing around here.

Thank god, I made it to the elevator and from the elevator to my room where Christy took a few shots of my outfit. If there had been a hospital handy I'd have checked right in, but instead Aspen Longfoot and Christy managed to get me in a nice cold bubble bath. While I cooled, Satyra and Ronnie whipped up a couple of margaritas to restore my electrolytes. After a while I began to think I might actually live. And everybody was saying I looked a few pounds thinner too. Not bad for a day's work.

"Hey, babe," I said to Christy, "let me have your cell phone for a minute. I need to call the station."

It was great. We were in the middle of nowhere and I could dial up the station, just like that. Besides I didn't want my main squeeze taking any more snaps of me in the tub since the bubbles were evaporating.

"Hi there, this is Jerry...yeah, Jerry...Jerry Jeremy." Must be a bad connection. "Let me speak with Dale Anderson."

This led to a long pause, but Dale finally picked up and

wanted to know how I was doing.

"Well, I'm doing great now, but as you heard, this morning was a bitch." I hoped it was okay to say that to a born-again dude.

"You know," I had to repeat myself, "this morning. Didn't you listen to my broadcast?

"My broadcast earlier today. I only made one.

"It was from that studio in a box thing you gave me. I nearly was murdered.

"Not on the air. Murdered before the broadcast. Didn't you hear the story? Big scoop, really big scoop."

Dale put me on hold to call the engineer in charge this morning. I couldn't wait for him to come back, but when he did I practically had a relapse—"Whadda you mean you never got it?!"

I couldn't believe it.

Me, Jeremy "Jerry" Jeremy, KICK's top of the line radio talk show host, almost got killed, but I still managed to get a major scoop anyway and the station says they never got the call!

I might just as well drown myself in the bubble bath. Instead I had everybody scram out of the bathroom while I got out and dried myself off. While throwing on a pair of fresh jeans and a tee shirt that Christy had picked up for me, I wondered if I could get a jail house interview with Slim Bales. Probably by now he'd be lawyered up, if only with the public defender. Fat chance for a do-over.

"I don't understand it," I said joining the party. "The station says they never got my interview with Bales."

Nobody in the room seemed particularly thunderstruck. Christy and Ronnie and Satyra looked to be hosting the Longfoot family and a few of their buddies from the motorcycle club. Drinks, food, TV games for the kids... I hoped Dale wouldn't mind the room service charges. Small price to pay for their saving my bacon. "Say, how could you guys know where to find me if my show didn't get on the air? I figured that it was my SOS. Not to mention maybe a Peabody."

"Actually," David Longfoot said, "it was Aspen. She saw you get kidnapped."

"The kids were getting kind of cranky," Mrs. L said, "so I thought I'd take them to the mall so they could get a toy or some ice cream. That's when I saw you hanging around outside the store. My guess was that you'd got dragged shopping and was just killing time, so I was going to go over and say 'hi'."

David handed her a fresh brew, probably sensing it would be a long story.

"Before I could get to you though, I saw that blonde lady come up and take out a pistol. She just marched you right off, but I decided to follow you. But first I sent Dave Junior and Packy to get their dad. When I caught up with you outside I saw her get you in the trunk of her car—"

"Well, I would have put up a fight but there were too many bystanders."

"Maybe. Anyway, I saw the make of car and the license. She took off, but not before I got to my Harley and followed her."

"We could have got the whole gang last night," David was saying, "but Aspen's phone was out of juice so she couldn't call."

"The battery's not very good. I need a new phone, honey. Suppose it was something important?"

I suggested that it was pretty important to me, but maybe I could get the station to spring for a new charger at least.

"So that being the situation, I had to ride all the way back to the casino to get David and the guys. But when we got back to the place they took you to, nobody was home. The guys jimmied the door just to make sure. I hope nobody's going to get in trouble for that."

"Don't worry. The sheriff and I are best buds. Besides Ronnie and me, we've been working for the FBI. I can get you in the burglar protection program. But that aside, if we were already gone, how did you find me?"

David looked surprised. "Haven't you ever heard how Indians can track anything that moves? Even across the desert?"

"I thought that was just in the movies."

"Well, probably. We tried to think where these guys could have taken you. As it turns out, the house they took you to is owned by this guy Jake Atokar. We found that out 'cause one of my guys—Jimmy over there—" Jimmy raised his beer bottle in recognition "—is a cousin of Jake's. Well, Jimmy remembered that Jake had this sweat lodge scam he pulled every now and then, you know, charging white eyes a couple of bills to get high while sweating."

"You mean people pay for that? Lucky me, I got comp'd. Wait 'til the casino hears."

"Hey, it can kill you if not done right," David said. Like I didn't know.

Aspen added, "That's why the cops shut him down. A couple of close calls, people wanted their money back."

"So this Jake," I said, "he said something about being blood-brothers with Rex Bowman. Any idea where they might hang if the cops haven't found them at the house?"

"How would the cops know about Jake's house?"

THE good thing was that Rondini was able to work his magic at Cactus Mike's Rent-a-Car down off the casino lobby. Instead of holding on for dear life behind one of Longfoot's biker buddies and bouncing across the desert, Ronnie had managed to rent a jeep using his long-suffering Discover card. Of course we were still bouncing, but doing it in style. David's motorcycle pack was leading us back to Atokar's place to make a citizen's arrest on the Bowman mob. Or maybe it was the Palucci gang or ex-Anastasia family. Well, you get the idea.

When we had made it back from the sweat lodge, David and company had turned Slim over to the local cops who were waiting on Sheriff Redhawk's imminent arrival. The locals wanted to put me in a cell too, but I guaranteed I wouldn't step foot out of my casino hotel room and that pacified them since they couldn't think of a crime to pin on me. But in all that confusion, nobody actually told them about the mob's hideout. Sure, the bad guys had a bunch of guns and who knows what else, but in my hotel room, the Native Americans made it sound like they'd handle that with no problems. I kinda wondered how long they'd been partying.

"There's a place up there, Jerry," Christy said pointing in the middle distance.

"What a dump," Satyra added. "No wonder they say crime doesn't pay."

The bikers slowed as they approached the doublewide and circled around on the dirt where real people would have a lawn. Ronnie parked in the driveway where Gloria's car had been last night. In spite of the noise and dust announcing they had visitors, no one seemed to be peeking out the windows or coming to the door. As the bikers killed their engines and the dust began to settle, the little house on the desert was ghostly silent. No lights peeking through the blinds, no radio or TV playing. Everyone remaining in place, looking around, waiting for me to go first. So Ronnie and Christy and Satyra and I quietly got out of the jeep and staying close together, holding on to each other even, we started slowly walking toward the house. I was hoping the drawn blinds didn't conceal Gloria standing behind them, taking aim with an AK-47.

Nobody home.

We had tried looking through the not quite closed blinds and through the windows around back. We finally knocked on the door and rang the cow bell hanging beside it in lieu of a doorbell. Longfoot's guys found an unlocked window and one of them shimmied in, an unlocked window being an invitation in these parts, I guess. The door opened and we all tramped in. My past experience as an uninvited guest made me a little ticklish about tripping on a body in the dark, but Aspen Longfoot found the light switch and a bare bulb in the middle of the ceiling lit up the room. No body. And no one in the place.

If Gloria or Rex had any luggage, they had taken it with them, although it looked like Jake Atokar had not packed, a couple of beat-up suitcases still stuck under the bed and a few old jeans and flannel shirts hanging in the closet. David Longfoot pointed to an eagle feathered headdress wrapped in tissue paper was still on the closet shelf. Cousin Jimmy said Jake would never leave without that headdress. Tradition aside, it was worth a few hundred bucks cold cash.

No other clues jumped out at us except maybe a small bag of marijuana which didn't seem to work into the art scam particularly. Anyway my Native American friends confiscated it so it shouldn't fall into the wrong hands. We were all using our phones to video the goings on just in case, but basically the bust was a bust.

"They probably went back to the lodge," Ronnie suggested, "planning to make it look like you sweat to death, but when they found you missing, they took it on the lam."

"Speaking of taking it on the lam," Satyra said, "maybe we should blow this pop stand before the party gets out of hand."

"And I'm thinking that we better loop in your pal, Darrell Lee," Christy added. "We've been holding back a lot that he would have liked to have known first."

David got the drift and started herding up his guys while my team headed for the jeep. We'd have to eat dirt following the bikes back so we wouldn't get lost, but our ride was air conditioned and had roll-up windows to keep out the elements. On the way we decided to stick kind of close to the truth in our confession to the law. I'd say that we had all heard about the big pow-wow here at the High Cloud Reservation and thought it would be a cool way to wrap up our visit. That Gloria was here and mistakenly thought we were on her trail, it being just a weird coincidence. No one was more surprise than me when I found a gun in my ribs and later was face to face with Rex Bowman. We'd skip the part about our return trip to the hideout just now. I'd just give Darrell Lee enough of a description to find the place and have it watched in case the eagle scout returned.

We kicked the plot around, stretching and shrinking it a bit, though I couldn't be sure what I might have told Slim in the privacy of the sweat lodge when I thought I was going to be dead. Since Slim seemed to be in a singing mood, I tried to think through the places in my story that might take on water. We all rehearsed our parts a few times to make sure everything held together.

Deep down we all knew Redhawk wouldn't buy a single word of it.

Chapter 36.

AT least we still had our rooms at the casino. Darrell Lee and the FBI newlyweds, arriving late to the pow-wow, were turned away from the inn and the closest thing to a stable was the four hundred car parking lot. I wasn't sure if the cops could commandeer your hotel room like they do your motor when they're in a hot pursuit. Maybe that's just something they do in the movies, but since The Great Ronnie turned the jeep back to Indian Mike, we didn't have to worry about them taking our wheels.

The sheriff and the Fibbies finally wound up finding minimal accommodation at the local hoosegow. I wondered if they planned on sharing a cell with Slim Bales. On the other hand, probably neither they nor Slim would get much sleep, since there'd be a really big concert with Slim as the main soloist. Anyway we'd found Redhawk and Special Agents Richards and Taylor (aka the Hastings) waiting for us when we got back to the casino. I filled them in on Slim's interview and all, but did neglect to mention my return trip to Atokar's place. They all seemed a little dubious of my story, but I wasn't pressed on it since I dropped the dime on Gloria and Rex's little love nest, not to mention the general direction to the sweat lodge. The local cops seemed to know the way already.

After getting the download, Darrell Lee told us to hang loose at the casino and not to get in any trouble. I'm not sure why he felt it was necessary to add that last part. He did say we could go watch the Native American's whooping it up at the shindig when it started. So Ronnie and I and the girls drifted across the gaming room finally coming to rest at a quiet table in one of the lounges.

"I wonder if they have entertainment here," The Great One said, maybe figuring a way to pay for his trip back to San Fran.

"Hey, we're going to be on TV," Satyra piped up. "The reality show Jerry's making. We'll take a limo home when our contracts come through."

She's a glass is half-full type, I guess. Or maybe a credit card is half-full type. Maybe Bronco Billy would loan them one of his jalopies if this worked out.

"So what's our next move?" Satyra said.

"Find Rex and Gloria," Ronnie suggested. "Everybody else is either dead or in custody."

"Jake Atokar's floating around someplace too," Christy reminded us. "If Rex and Gloria aren't already with him, he can probably lead us to them. All we need to do is find him."

Ronnie countered that by saying Atokar must be on the lam by now, what with the cops all over his place. While Ronnie figured that Rex and Gloria would be together, Jake might have lit out on his own. The question was where any one of them might have gone.

"Good question, where's that old ESP when we need it?"

"I can't waste my special powers—I'm saving those for a hot date—but I would bet that when the cops get Slim's confession, they'll want to put the screws to Bryan Forbes-Collier. See if they can use Slim as a wedge to get Forbes-Collier to spill *his* guts.

"And since Slim already spilled to me, there's no reason we can't give Bryan a wedgie, er wedge, too."

Ronnie patted me on my sunburn. "That's my boy," he crowed.

We were smart enough not to check out of the hotel, since we'd need to return the rental to Indian Mike and might need to sleep over. By keeping the rooms, we might also keep Darrell Lee from realizing we'd broke the only two rules he'd laid down for us. Anyway, after we cracked the case there's no way he would hold a grudge. So there we were, on our way to Bisbee, on the road inside of maybe two or three hours after promising Darrell Lee we wouldn't be. I admit it had taken Ronnie and me almost twenty minutes to rent a car at that hour, so the only other hold up was waiting while the ladies bought new outfits for the trip, did their nails and hair, and for all I know, had a massage. I guess they wanted to look their best knowing we'd be shooting video for the reality show. After all, don't we all have priorities?

At least the road to Bisbee was paved which was an

improvement. While Slim had provided some inside gossip, we felt sure Bryan Forbes-Collier knew the whole story inside and out.

BY the time we got to Bisbee, it was well past visiting hours which we'd kind of expected, it being two a.m. The front door was locked and the emergency room looked a little too exposed, so we circled the place, keeping to the shadows as much as possible. Around back, away from the public eye, we found dumpsters which from their smell must have been used for kitchen refuse or maybe the odd body part. It was next to a loading dock that had a roll-up door, now rolled all the way down of course. It had a big padlock for security, but on closer inspection—Christy was just reaching for a bobby pin or something—we saw it wasn't locked at all. The shackle of the lock was just stuck through the hasp on the door. A wonder it kept anybody out.

Next to the door were buttons marked open and close. Open sesame. Surprisingly the door made almost no sound as it rolled up although even the quiet rattle seemed loud in the early morning stillness. We stopped the door after only a couple of feet, leaving just enough room to scooch under, but hopefully not drawing any attention to its being open. Dim night lights showed us we were in a room with boxes of paper towels and latex gloves, and on some shelves stacks of the kind of scrubs nurses and doctors wear.

"Well, we need to blend in, right?" Satyra said.

We pulled the green scrubs over our street clothes and found some long, white lab coats to put on over everything. Ronnie discovered a box with stethoscopes which we slung around our necks like we'd seen on TV. "I may not be a doctor, but I play one on..." Aw, shaddup!

About the only thing we didn't find was a map telling us where to find Bryan Forbes-Collier. We actually didn't know if he was still in the ICU or back in a room or where either of those might be, but having come this far we weren't about to turn around. Using our best stealth mode—I'm not sure that anyone seeing us sneak along the hallway would take us for medical staffers—we crept silently toward the core of the building. Until we reached a bank of elevators. At this juncture, we stopped to argue in urgent whispers whether to take the elevator or the stairs.

Rondini finally carried the day by pointing out that the fire stairs are probably locked from the inside. I couldn't argue with that—the security once you're in the building is probably a lot better than the security to keep you out of the place to begin with. Anyway Christy wasn't too sure she could pick the lock if we got trapped in the stairwell.

So the plan was that Christy and I would stay where we were while Ronnie and Satyra would ride the elevators trying to find the ICU or the cardiac ward or whatever. Once the elevator whisked them to parts unknown, Christy and I began to poke around the floor we were on which seemed to be a basement level filled with administrative offices rather than hospital beds. While we didn't want to be too far from the lifts in case the others came back, we scouted out some of the cubes and private offices. I had my hopes up that somebody might have left a snack or the remains of a brown bag lunch since I hadn't had solid food for quite a while. As I looked around for a refrigerator or lunch room, I heard the clickety-click of fingers dancing across a keyboard.

Not some admin on OT though. Christy had discovered a PC that someone had forgotten to log out on. Bisbee General's most intimate secrets were ours. At least one secret, called the patient directory, was and Christy was busy using same to locate our boy.

"Hmmm, it has the floor and room—and look—it has maps! That might be just what we need."

Inside of five minute we not only had Forbes-Collier's location, but how to get there, as well as his weight, blood pressure and a blow-by-blow description of his heart condition. At least now we knew for sure he wasn't faking. So our next question was how to find out where Ronnie and Satyra had run off to. They weren't in the database, so I needed to revert to the old methods. And I had my fingers crossed that Ronnie's phone was on vibrate when I called him. Luckily he was on my speed dial since pressing the right numbers with my fingers crossed would have been tough.

We all met on the fifth floor where the computer said Bryan Forbes-Collier could be found. This time of night there didn't seem to be many caregivers on duty, so by ducking into handy patient rooms when we heard anyone coming, we managed to slip through the hospital unnoticed. The sick and dying didn't seem to mind us popping in and out, probably figuring we were part of the medical staff, there to keep them from having a good night's sleep. I was a little worried that Darrell Lee might have left one of his deputies guarding Bryan.

Our basic plan was that Satyra would play doctor with him so the rest of us could sneak in.

I said it was basic, didn't I.

Anyway we didn't need it. No guards, no nurses, no candy stripers, just a guy with a bum ticker in a hospital bed sound asleep.

We all took turns nudging him awake until he finally screwed his eyelids up and realized he wasn't alone. "What time is it? You the ...?" He seemed a little at a loss for words. "You're the woman from the radio. You were there when I had my coronary."

"That's right," Christy said. "We all just wanted to see how you were doing. I hope you feeling better."

"We would have brought some flowers or a plant," I added, "but the gift shop isn't open this early."

"Wha...what time is it? Is it morning?"

"It is someplace, but we're not here for that. We came to help you take a miss on the next heart attack."

Satyra asked if she could turn on a light or two, it being too dark for good video recording. Ronnie told her sure and aimed one lamp in the patient's eyes.

"Look," I said, "You know and I know you're in big trouble. I don't know if you've been keeping up with the news, but Sal Anastasia has been knocked off and Gloria and Rex tried to kill Slim Bates and me. The whole scam is falling apart and the cops are looking for your partners right now."

"What partners? I know nothing about what you are saying."

"Maybe you can get your hearing tested while your here. Didn't I just say they tried to kill Slim and me, both of us, at the same time? Slim and I got to know a lot about each other, our being in the soup together. We dodged that bullet, but we spent a couple of hours chatting about art and life while we ducked. As a matter of fact, I interviewed Bates and he spilled his guts. The interview hasn't, er, aired yet, but when it does you are going to be the man in the barrel."

"What do you want? If Bates already told you everything, why are you buggering me?"

"I want your angle on it. Bates knew a lot about people getting hurt—including you—but I need a little more of the back story. How did this all come about? Who really ran it? Did you know Deke Rowan was bedding Sal's wife? Who were you bedding?"

"Why are you doing this?"

"For my show of course. Why else?"

"Your show?"

"Look, my pal here, The Great Rondini, and his lovely assistant, Satyra, are going to video this on their phones. I'll use a little of it on the radio but the big reveal will be on TV, a reality show all about how I uncovered the art scam and solved a couple of murders. Bates gave me the scoop and made things look pretty bad for you, but here's your chance to turn the tables—er, that is, tell your side of the story. Bates is with the cops right now, probably turning state's evidence or joining the witness protection program. You spill to me and you'll enjoy the power of the media and all that.   Everybody loves television. C'mon, get it off your chest and maybe you won't need all those electrodes."

Christy took his hand and gave him the baby blues. She cooed, "We know you weren't behind Mrs. Edelbaum's murder. You probably just got in over your head with a bad crowd."

"How long before the cops get here?" Forbes-Collier asked.

"Hard to say. They were giving Bates the third degree back at the High Cloud Reservation, but they could be on their way here by now. Maybe they've got a chopper going. Let's wrap this up or the next time you tell your story, it might be to the judge."

Forbes-Collier was a hard sell, but we had painted him into a corner. He caved and Rondini and Satyra got their iPhones ready while Christy and I ditched the doctor's garb and took positions on either side of the bed. Ronnie would shoot of all three of us while Satyra would focus on Bryan Forbes-Collier. I figured we could take some reaction shots of Christy and me later and have them edited in. I even had the phone in my pocket recording the audio as a backup.

Chapter 37.

"*TAKE it from the beginning, Bryan,*" I said. "*How did you get involved in this whole thing? Whose idea was it anyhow?*"

At the start Bryan had gagged a little and had to clear his throat enough to get the words out, but once he got rolling he covered a lot of ground. He told how Sal had already brokered a few legitimate purchases through the Kirby Gallery, scouting western art for mid-level collectors. Although that brought some business Bryan's way, selling art in the middle of a desert had been tailing off for a while. At the same time, Rex Bowman, his number one artist, was looking for a bigger audience thanks largely to Beverly Edelbaum's encouragement. Then Anastasia came to Bryan with a proposition that would make them both rich.

He said he'd happened across a letter from Max Leibergard in the Phoenix museum telling about a painting of his that depicted some cavalry officer and his Indian scout. Only nobody had ever laid eyes on the daub. To this day, it might still be tucked away in somebody's attic or hanging over some rube's fireplace. But even if it wasn't, they could say it was and that they rescued it. Bryan could fake the provenance and Sal would sell the painting to one of his collectors.

As they thought the scheme through, it would be even better if they sold the painting to several of Sal's pals. They could fake it over and over again, telling each purchaser that it was maybe Nazi loot or something and to keep it under wraps for their own private enjoyment. That way no one would be any the wiser.

The plan was practically foolproof according to the man on the heart monitor. All they really needed at that point of course was the painting. And Sal realized that even his clients were high enough on the food chain to know a quick knock-off from the real deal, so the forgery had to be good. At least half-good anyway.

"*So why did Rex get involved?*" Christy asked. "*If he was planning on big things with Mrs. Edelbaum's support, how did you talk him into creating the forgeries?*"

"*Talk him into it? Are you joking? Once he heard about it, he cut himself in. I couldn't get rid of him. Of course, he did a great job of it, he's a fabulous painter. But he is ambitious and the money made his eyes absolutely spin.*"

I asked Bryan to tell our viewers how things went south.

"*I said it was practically foolproof. We never envisioned an idiot of your caliber getting involved.*"

"*I'll take that as a compliment. So Beverly Edelbaum was trying to push Bowman's career. On my radio show, she practically nominated him for Pope.*"

"*Sure, she wanted to promote his career. I think maybe she had other hopes as well, probably just Rex leading her on though. He wanted her to support him financially. I believe he told her he was tied in to the forgery business and needed a large sum of money to buy his way out. I'm not positive, but that may actually be true. I know Sal did not want him to quit. When you showed up and we all wound up on the radio, Sal and Gloria and I were scared shitless—*" we'd beep that out in editing "*—that she was going to expose us on your program. She hinted around a little trying to throw a scare into us.*"

By now, Satyra and Ronnie were leaning in, not wanting to miss a word. I hoped they were still getting it all on video because in my mind's eye I saw this all playing out on my TV show, maybe inter-cutting Bryan's song with footage reenacting the radio show where it all started. I pushed on, "*So was Bev killed to keep her from talking about the scam on my show?*"

"*Well, maybe, but it could be because she might just pay Rex to come over to her side and leave us without our painter. I knew both Gloria and Sal were worried both of being exposed and about losing Rex's abundant skills. Of course, I was not aware of any plan to kill Mrs. Edelbaum. I hoped we could get Rex to continue with the paintings, even if he did so on the sly. Knowing Rex that seemed a likely happenstance, getting the Edelbaum woman to bankroll him while still collecting his share from us. He might even have sold a few of his own works in the bargain.*"

"*Who was it who actually killed Beverly Edelbaum then?*

Your story seems to point to Sal Anastasia."

"Who else would it be—not Mr. Edelbaum surely? I don't know if Anastasia actually did it with his own hands, but if not, he must have been behind the murder. That cowboy, Rowen, was a nasty enough piece of work to have actually been the killer if he was paid enough. Afterward Anastasia had him beat me up to make sure I wouldn't go to the police and tell them about the whole thing. I told Anastasia that I hadn't signed on for any murders."

"Then stealing the painting you sold to Bronco Billy wasn't the reason you were attacked?" Christy asked.

"Not the entire reason, no. Sal and Gloria didn't like the fact that Wooten was going public with the painting and wanted to get it out of sight, but the beating was really to warn me not to break ranks."

"Wow!" I said. "That shows how the wrong move can really mess things up. My listeners love it when politicians pass a new law that winds up making things worse than they were before. Unintended consequences they call it, right?"

"No, I don't know. I have no idea what you're talking about."

"If Deke Rowen hadn't put you in the hospital, Christy and I wouldn't have found the stash of forged paintings in your barn."

"What? You were in my barn?"

"Well, yeah. Where did you think we got all the copies we used to replace the paintings stolen from Bronco Billy? It was great. Right there on my show."

Forbes-Collier looked a little dumbfounded at this. Maybe he hadn't really thought about where all those copies came from, having had a heart attack and all. I thought about trying to break it to him that he might be short a couple of bottles of *Chateau Sidewinder* also. And that he'd probably want to change the sheets too. But maybe not now.

Tell him, that is. There'd be plenty of time to tell him later. I was sure he'd get a good laugh out of it.

Anyway it was time to give him a breather. While Bryan collected himself, Christy rubbed his temples and prayed he wouldn't flat line in the middle of our video. Meanwhile I checked with the camera crew who told me they were doing great. But I had Satyra and Ronnie play back a little of their work just to make sure. They still had battery enough to get through about another thirty minutes or so. For the big finale I'd place Forbes-Collier under citizen's arrest, so I wanted to make sure to get that on tape or whatever it is that it gets recorded on in those phones. After finishing off Bryan's orange juice which he hadn't actually touched, and after Satyra and Ronnie found their marks, I joined Christy next to our guest and we began where we'd stopped.

"*Just to fill in the gaps in your memory,*" I said. "*You were in the hospital right here in Bisbee. Matter of fact, you still are. Anyway, I was a little suspicious of how somebody could get into your gallery and smack you in the head without you having seen anything. Christy too.*

"*So we decided to take a quick look around your place to see if we saw any clues. You know, peek though the curtains and all.*"

"*And try your hand at breaking and entering. You're lucky I don't press charges.*"

"*Let's not start throwing charges around quite yet, Bryan.*"

"*Actually,*" Christy added, "*the door was open. We thought maybe someone was injured inside or maybe a burglar...*"

"*Don't worry. I'm not pressing charges. You didn't break anything did you?*"

"*No—break anything?—no way.*"

"*Absolutely not,*" I agreed.

"*Not finding anything, you then went to the barn?*" I was beginning to wonder who was interviewing who, but anyway the plot was thickening.

"*To tell the truth, we didn't really think about the barn, but the next morning...*"

"*You spent the night in my home!*"

"*Ah, well, it was late anyway, but I was saying that we spotted Deke Rowen's truck in your drive. We went out the back as he came in the front...*"

"*What I wouldn't give to get my hands on that bastard.*"

Christy and I looked at each other. Forbes-Collier certainly wasn't keeping up with the news. I gave Christy the nod, figuring Bryan might take it better from her.

"*Sure,*" she said, "*he really was a bastard, maybe killing Mrs. Edelbaum...*"

"*He gave you a concussion,*" I added. Meanwhile Ronnie crouched in for a close up knowing what was coming.

"*And that morning, you know, uh, Bryan,*" Christy snuck up on it, "*he really did try to run Jerry and me off the road into some huge boulders.*"

Forbes-Collier gave looked from Christy to me and back again. *"Was a bastard' you said? Was a bastard?"*

"Well," I said, *"he's a bastard no longer."*

"He tried to kill us," Christy said, *"but he lost control of his truck and smashed into the boulders himself. And, well, he was pretty burned up."*

"Yep, crashed and burned."

Forbes-Collier nodded once and said, *"Good riddance to bad rubbish. I'd have preferred to kill him myself, but I'm glad he died a horrible death."*

So we'd reached a certain point in the story beyond which Bryan Forbes-Collier had been laid up in various ICUs and medical wards. There wasn't anything more he could tell us, so the time had come to put the 'cuffs on him. That is if I had any 'cuffs. Instead I'd have to wing it.

"Put your hands up!" echoed through the room.

Hmmm, that wasn't me.

Chapter 38.

THE words were still hanging in the air when they were joined by their brothers coming from the doorway. "I said to raise your hands!"

While our hands reached for the fluorescents, our eyes all turned to that doorway and the mystery of where Rex and Gloria had run off to was solved.

And any question of whether they were armed and dangerous was answered also.

Rex waved his gun to mime us putting our hands up. And I hate mimes.

"Mr. Bowman—may I call you Rex?—Rex," Rondini called him, "we were just hearing Forbes-Collier's—Bryan's— side of the story. Capturing it on video. But wouldn't you like to tell us your side too." Ronnie pointed his iPhone at Bowman.

"Sure," I said. "So far it looks like Sal Anastasia was the real bad guy. Uh, no offense, Ms. Palucci. I know you were close."

"Not that close," she replied. "I was glad when the rat beat it."

"Ah, well good. See, no problem then. You know Sal didn't get very far?"

"I was glad about that too."

From his hospital bed, Bryan piped up, "You've come to help me get out of here? Mexico is looking awfully good about now."

Rex looked mildly surprised, as though he had forgotten about the guest of honor. Rex said, "You're too sick to travel, Bryan. We're not stealing an ambulance, that's for sure."

"Then why are you here?"

"Tying up a loose end. Now we need to worry about couple more loose ends. We didn't expect to find your new best friends here."

"Why me? I understand the police have Slim Bales. He'll spill the goods on all of us. You can get away, but I'm stuck to an IV drip."

Rex waved the pistol at Ronnie and Satyra. "Turn off those phone and hand them over." After collecting what could have been the best part of my reality show, he said, "Sorry, Bryan, but you know too much about me."

"But Bales…"

"No! Bales doesn't give you a way out. I don't give a damn if he tells the cops about the paintings or that I'm traveling with Gloria here. They may even think I had my friends kill Sal because of Gloria, but it wouldn't hold water. Sal had already run out on Gloria, she was mine for the taking, so they don't even have a solid motive. Besides I know my brother Jake was careful not to leave any evidence behind. Admittedly the scalping was a bit much, but they can't tie it to him just because he's Indian. Our Native American sheriff is probably convinced it was a white man trying to make it look Indian. But when it comes right down to it, you know too much about me."

"I don't know anything, I swear. I would never say anything."

Gloria looked at Forbes-Collier and said, "It doesn't matter at this point. My sweet Rex has just told everybody here he was behind Sal's death."

"But that's just hearsay," I said. "I'm sure your lawyer could get it all thrown out."

"Not that we'd actually repeat any of this," Ronnie said. "My god, no."

"We let you go and it would be all over radio and TV before we got out of the parking lot," Gloria argued. Persuasive, and probably true.

"Enough of this," Forbes-Collier said. "Just because *they'd* talk, doesn't mean I would."

"Ha!" Satyra said. "You'll make a deal with the cops. Get a lighter sentence or maybe witness protection. You even agreed to talk to us so the public would think it wasn't your fault at all."

"That's not the same. I swear I wouldn't incriminate you, Rex."

"So what have you been telling this pack of news hounds? I wonder what's on these phones." Rex tossed one on Rex's bed and told Christy to pick it up. "Play it. Let's just see what you all have been discussing."

So we got to hear the unedited playback. I still had the phone in my pocket going so it recorded the interview for the second time. I would have liked to save the battery for whatever was going to come later, but didn't want to get caught playing with something in my pocket. It might be misinterpreted.

The last thing on the video was when Rex and Gloria asked us to stretch for the ceiling. But everyone was feeling a lot more relaxed now, hands down and all. Just to prove he was listening, Rex said, "So you thought my eyes were spinning, eh Bryan?"

"I said you were a fabulous painter, Rex."

"Whatever." Rex looked from the gun in his hand to Bryan. "I figured a pillow over you face would settle things, but now, with all these people to care for, I need to think about it."

Gloria spoke up at this point, "That can still work. He's found dead here, everybody thinks it's his heart again. Before that though, we call Jake to come take the witnesses off our hands."

So much for being relaxed.

"Jake would love to get his hands on Mr. Jeremy here, wouldn't he?" Bowman turned his head and his pistol my way. "When you turned the police on to his home and his sweat lodge, Jerry, my friend Jake vowed to make your death long and painful if he ever got the chance..." I gulped. "...and here's his chance."

"Aren't you overreacting a little?" Christy asked. "You're not in that deep, even with the Sal thing. I'm sure the court will take into account that Sal had your friend and patron gruesomely murdered. You simply got even with him by, well, you got even with him anyway."

Rex had that surprised look again. So did Gloria and Bryan this time. I myself tried *not* to look surprised at their being surprised.

"That's certainly no reason for a massacre, is it?" Rondini piled on, but I began to think maybe Rex had something else he was worried about. Anyway, something seemed to have made up Bowman's mind for him. Probably Gloria. Maybe she was the real brains behind it all.

Rex used the other iPhone, the one he didn't give to Christy, to make a call. He talked without saying anything very explicit, like he thought Ronnie's phone might be tapped, but we all got the idea anyway. Jake Atokar would be appearing soon in our little neck of the woods. And we wouldn't like it when he got here.

"In case anyone is wondering," Bowman said, "Jake is not far away, so let's just settle down until he gets here and nobody will get hurt...yet."

"You paint a great word picture too," I said. "But before the heavy artillery gets here, why don't you tell us what's really going on."

"Don't fret about it," Gloria said.

"Maybe they should know why you're planning to kill them," Forbes-Collier suggested.

"If you're so anxious to share," Bowman said, "why don't you tell them, Bryan? It'll be just one more reason to finish you off."

"All right, I will. It appears now that none of us have much to lose by letting the cat out of the bag. The reason Miss Palucci teamed up with Rex here, wasn't because Sal ran out on her. Gloria thought Sal Anastasia was a wimp. She hooked up with Deke Rowen first, then with Rex. Sal was practically a peacenik compared to these guys. Sal didn't have Beverly Edelbaum killed, Rex did."

"No way!" Satyra...er, exclaimed.

"What!" Christy said. "I can't believe that. She was his number one fan."

"She was and he did. I told you Rex was after the almighty dollar. His hope was that that fine lady would help promote his career, maybe even funding it, all the while he would be getting the dough, which was getting to be considerable, from the forgeries."

"She was a rotten bitch," Bowman said. "She wanted to own me. Me! She thought the art was all about her. Her and the other rich pricks who deigned to give us poor workers a few pennies for which we should be ever so grateful."

Forbes-Collier added, "Rex killed her because she was going to expose him as a fraud. She discovered he was making forgeries and was going to expose him for his own good."

"My own good, hell! She was going to ruin me. I even offered to stop, but she still threatened to expose me if I didn't do what she wanted. She wanted me to be her pet lapdog."

"She got what she deserved." This from Gloria Palucci.

Christy asked Rex how it came to be that Beverly Edelbaum discovered he was making the fakes.

"How indeed. Another score for me to settle with my bed-ridden friend here."

"Surely, Rex, you don't think I told her?" Bryan Forbes-Collier said.

"You're the only one who knew that had any dealings with her. Maybe you thought you could use her as a lever to cut my share down, I don't know. But it had to be you, not that it matters now."

"And you plan to kill us because we know it was you?" Christy said, more of a statement than a question if anyone was keeping score.

"I plan to have Jake take you someplace very lonely, I don't care where, and he will take very good care of you all. I don't care what he does to you first as long as you wind up buried somewhere in the desert where you'll never be found."

"We may not be found, but you will be," Ronnie said. Great time to pick an argument with an armed lunatic. "The cops are looking for you, don't you know, and they know you killed Anastasia. Bales is singing his head off too, so it won't take them long to put the rest of the story together. If you even make it out of Bisbee, they'll be right behind you every step of the way."

I picked up the pitch and said, "That brings us back to why not let us go and we'll tell the cops how you deserve a break for, well, for letting us go. You know it would be even better if you gave me the gun and we put you under citizen's arrest. No handcuffs or anything, but I could interview you for my show. You know, tell your side of—"

"Shut it! I have, as they say in the movies, got nothing to lose."

"But Gloria—so far she's just a bystander," Christy said. "If you have any feelings at all for Gloria, do as Jerry says or at least let us go. Don't make Gloria an accomplice to murder."

"What, this piece of fluff? Her options are to stick with me until I'm tired of her or else join you in the desert."

"But, Rex, you can't possibly mean what you're saying." Gloria looked a little shaken now that she might wind up on our team.

"You think I didn't know you were screwing Deke Rowen? You wanted him as your protector after you saw what happened to the Edelbaum woman. You latched on to me after Rowen managed to kill himself with his poor driving."

"But, Rex, baby..."

"Please give it a rest. Get a pillow from the other bed and hand it to Jeremy."

"What do I need with a pillow?" I said, fearing the worst.

"I'm going to make a deal with you," Bowman said. "You're going to put it over Bryan here's face and hold it down until he stops breathing for good. You do that for me and I won't shoot your girlfriend in the kneecap."

"But there's no need for that. Can't we just wait until your pal Jake gets here? Smothering Bryan would let him warm up a little before the main event."

"First one kneecap, then the other. Then I'll work my way up to her elbows and shoulders. You can save her excruciating pain before she dies. Now take that pillow and snuff out that piece of shit!"

I was holding the pillow now. Could I knock the gun out of Bowman's hand with it? Or would his first shot take the pillow fight out of me? I faked a move toward Forbes-Collier, getting ready to swing the pillow at the .45 in Rex's hand, tensing up for the most important swing in my life, when a deafening blast from the pistol—well, deafened me.

I jumped over to catch Christy, but suddenly realized she wasn't hurt. It was Bowman who crumpled to the ground. Satyra kicked the gun from his hand and Ronnie picked it up. But Bowman wasn't going to use that gun—or anything else— now. He wouldn't need anything, not any more, not with a neat round bullet hole in his forehead.

Rex Bowman, as you may have guessed by now, didn't have the only gun in the room. Forbes-Collier must have been expecting visitors. He nailed Bowman with a single shot right through his hospital sheets. Forbes-Collier's sheets, not Bowman's—although if Bowman had a sheet, we could have pulled it up over his head at this point. When I looked back from Bowman's newly-minted corpse, Bryan had surrendered his *pistola* to Christy and Satyra was videoing her reading him his rights.

Then all hell broke loose.

Chapter 39.

JAKE Atokar tiptoed silently along the hallway. He had moved stealthily up the hospital's stairways and through its dimly-lit halls, pulled by his sharpened instincts ever nearer to his target. His sixth sense never failed, a special hunter's telepathy, always guiding him to his prey whether deep in the wilderness or across the barren desert. Or, as in this particular case, through a deserted hospital during the graveyard shift. Good thing about that sixth sense too since Jake could neither read nor understand the signs posted to guide hospital visitors around.

He slipped quietly along the hallway, sensing that his quarry was not far away. Rex—his blood brother—must be nearby too. That he was sure of. He would find his brother and take care of the enemies blocking his brother's escape to Mexico.

The thought of torturing and killing the palefaces excited and aroused him. He would add their scalps to the one he had already collected, only this time his victims would be alive. He would bring them to a holy place in the desert, one that Rex had once shown him, and there he would skin them alive. It would appease the spirits and the world would be once more in harmony.

That was his story and he was sticking to it.

Jake Atokar had entered the building through the loading dock, the only unlocked, unguarded entrance. He now wore a white lab coat he'd found in the boxes behind the dock. Doctors on TV wore coats like these, he had seen them do so. This way Jake would blend in, the coat would camouflage the hunter. Unlike the TV doctors, in his hand was a warrior's tomahawk, a weapon already used to scalp one enemy. His other hand carried a Glock semi-automatic pistol with a fifteen round magazine. Jake could feel the battle to come in his blood, he could practically smell the enemy. He tightened his grip on the pistol and moved quietly toward the battleground.

WHILE Atokar roamed the lower halls of Bisbee General, Sheriff Darrell Lee Redhawk was deploying his deputies like an Army commander on maneuvers. He had his troops spread out, sealing off the exits to hospital. His squad cars had blocked off the streets, their lights burning into the ground floor windows. Anyone fleeing the building would be easily spotted. Anyone hoping for a good night's sleep on the first floor would be sorely disappointed. Already faces were showing up, peering through blinds, pale in the brilliant lights. Or maybe just pale in fact, hospitals being where the sick hang out. Night nurses were dispatched to quiet the patients, to let them know it was only a murderer, not the doctors' striking against Obamacare, so nobody need fear for their safety. As long as they stayed in bed and didn't get caught in any crossfire that is.

The sheriff and his men were familiar with the hospital and its routine, having brought in the assorted accident victims and ailing prisoners over the years. Redhawk located the night administrator, a middle aged gent named Barney Melendez, who provided keys to control the elevators and was in turn recruited to take the sheriff and his SWAT team up in one. The law didn't know if any of the villains had beaten them to the hospital, but they didn't plan on taking any chances.

The sheriff, his deputies, the SWAT team and the Fibbies, all using the maximum number of hand signals and head points, their radios silenced, their whispers whispered, fanned out from the elevators on the hospitals fifth floor. In spite of the shuffling of their boots and the jostling of holsters, handcuffs, radios, cell phones, ammo pouches and ticket books hanging off their belts, the SWAT team crept through the hallway with little more noise than, say, your average high school football team wearing their cleats.

Along for the ride were special agents Richards and Taylor, not wanting to be left out and having avoided doing anything much to crack the case so far. All this I found out later while taping a few interviews for my show.

Of course, each of the many long arms of the law saw things in a slightly different light, like who was actually leading the charge—was it Redhawk, our Marlboro man of the West, or was it the cute and cuddly , not-really-newlyweds. Since it was my show though...well, do I really need to say who got the starring role?

Barney, the hospital's nighttime guy, pointed out the Forbes-Collier room and was sent back to mind the elevators while the cops took up tactical positions on either side of the doorway. A couple of brave volunteers edged up carrying a massive battering ram and at a signal from Redhawk started the ah-one, ah-two, ah—

BAM!

The sound of Bryan Forbes-Collier's peacemaker echoed throughout the hospital.

The cops—having planned a surprise attack—were surprised themselves, and not in a good way. Not sure what was happening, they first froze in place, then looked to the sheriff for more head bobs and hand signals. Darrell Lee, taken aback himself, had thoughts of somebody's innocent blood being spilled all over his re-election campaign.

Not more than thirty or forty seconds later, with no more shots coming through, say, the door, Redhawk waved the battering team onward and they splintered the door. SWAT team, cops and special agents poured into Bryan's room like a flood of gun-toting humanity.

Satyra being even quicker on the draw got most of the charge of the slight brigade on video. I made a mental note to remember to tell Rondini to give her a raise when this was over.

IF the cops were surprised to hear a gun shot from Forbes-Collier's room, Jake Atokar was positively frantic. The fact that it was from a higher floor was as much of a surprise as was the shot itself—the battle had started and he was far from the field of glory.

Who had fired the shot? His blood brother? The skanky white squaw his brother had taken up with? An enemy white eye? The cops? Jake hoped the cops weren't here already; it would be a fight to the death if that were the case. He stood very still, not even breathing, listening for more shots, but heard nothing.

Jake stripped off the doctor's lab coat and tearing off his Kanye West tee-shirt, he let out a blood-curdling scream. Bare chested, armed and dangerous, he ran to the elevator bay and pounded the button to go up.

Meanwhile on five, Barney Melendez cowered in the elevator. In spite of the police lockdown, he noticed that someone on two had called for the elevator. Probably a night nurse or someone from housekeeping hadn't got the word and was now stranded on the second floor. Whatever, Barney was glad to have an excuse to slip away from the police action. There might be more gun play yet, and what with ricochets and wild shots, Barney would feel safer running the elevator for stranded hospital staffers. He turned the key and headed down.

Jake was getting more wound up and frantic waiting for the elevator. Why was the white man's magic so slow it being the middle of the night? Then, like a promise fulfilled, the green arrow above the first set of doors lit and a bell chimed to announce an elevator had decided to stop for him. As the doors began to open, Jake plunged into the car and halfway in, he froze. The car was not empty. A little guy in a white lab coat was there, plastering himself against the elevator wall as surprised to see Jake as Jake was to see him.

Barney immediately hit the up button and since he had the car under manual control, it immediately caught Jake Atokar in the closing doors and started up with Jake half in and half out.

Ordinarily, Barney, realizing he had someone trapped in the doors, would have reversed the controls to let the person out. But the half of Jake Atokar that made it inside the elevator was the half that was wildly swinging a huge tomahawk. Barney couldn't get close to the controls without being clubbed and wasn't sure he wanted to risk it. Fortunately for Barney, the shock of getting caught in the doors and being jammed into, well, the door jamb, as the elevator rose, also caused Jake to drop his Glock semi-automatic in the hallway.

THE Forbes-Collier hospital room had filled with men and women in uniform. Even the FBI agents wore jackets with FBI printed on the backs. Baseball caps, too. Everybody except us civilians had badges of some kind hanging around their necks. Somehow, in spite of having been undercover for the G-people and having given Darrell Lee all his good leads, Ronnie and I and the girls wound up face down next to Gloria Palucci, hands cuffed behind our backs. Of course Rex Bowman was down on the floor too, but him they didn't bother handcuffing. Bryan

Forbes-Collier, our latest informant-interviewee, on the other hand was being treated like a guest of honor. Wait'll the cops get the lowdown watching my reality show.

It took a while to get everything sorted out. Forbes-Collier admitted that the pistol with Christy's fingerprints on it was his and he was the sharp-shooter that put the hole in Rex Bowman's head.

Just to be safe Sheriff Redhawk said we'd all be given paraffin tests to see who actually pulled the trigger. After taking a vote or something, Darrell Lee also agreed to take off our handcuffs—not Gloria's—if we played him the videos and recordings we'd made on our phones. I had to argue that it was copyrighted material and we wouldn't let the phones out of our hands, cuffed or not. Finally we agreed he could take the phones and recordings as evidence if he agreed to send us copies.

So we pieced all the pieces together. Sal Anastasia, maybe with Gloria's encouragement, convinced Bryan Forbes-Collier that he could avoid bankruptcy by fronting phony paintings as real. Sal had been dealing with a number of medium range collectors who didn't have a lot of scruples when it came to artwork that was bound to increase in value. Their greed made them vulnerable shoppers for off-market goods.

Bryan was already handling Rex Bowman's legit paintings and suspected correctly that Rex might want a slice of the pie. So Rex studied up on Leibergard and worked out a painting that could pass muster. Since it was simpler to just keep making the same thing, that's what he did. The buyers were told to keep a low profile for a couple of years since there might repercussions otherwise.

Things were going along just fine, until Beverly Edelbaum got close enough to Bowman to figure out what was going on. When she decided a couple of years in the jug would do wonders for the boy, Rex headed her off at the pass and had Injun Jake do her in. They thought that should have put an end to it, except I didn't like the idea of a guest on my show floating face down in the ol' swimmin' hole.

I started investigating and that brought my sponsor, Bronco Billy, personally out to the Circle-K. Some might say he was looking for an excuse to spend his evenings with our daytime blabber, Dakota Holiday, but I think it was to make sure the murder was getting the proper amount of air time. When Forbes-Collier tried to show off by displaying the forged Leibergard, it gave Billy the chance to buy it and announce he would be using it for a big-time publicity barrage. Since that wouldn't sit well with Sal's other clients—obviously being swindled—Sal had Deke, Gloria and Slim Bales drop by the gallery before opening and smack Bryan right into the hospital while stealing the painting.

However, Bryan being in the hospital gave Christy and me a chance to search his place and find copies of the Leibergard with the paint still wet. When Deke tried to run us off the road, karma caught up with him big time. Having discovered the forgery set-up, we started pulling on a few of the other loose strings and the gang began to unravel.

Rex decided to downsize by having Atokar kill Sal before he and Gloria could take a powder. If things had gone his way, Christy, Satyra and Ronnie would have dehydrated out in the desert and I, after dodging that bullet, would have wound up as a puddle in the sweat lodge. Slim Bales was tossed in the melting pot too, so as to cut down on potential witnesses.

Speaking of potential witnesses, Rex and Gloria stretched hospital visiting hours to drop in on their bed-ridden buddy. Turns out he had more life in him than they thought. Plenty of life as well as a Magnum .357. Exit Rex Bowman.

We had pretty much captured all of that with our phones and Ronnie got some great footage of the SWAT team prying Jake out of the elevator doors to finish up. We would need some serious beeping of Jake's last words, of course. His last words before meeting with the public defender, that is. As for Barney Night-guy I snagged an interview where he re-enacted his side of things for the camera.

He handled the Indian warrior pretty good to hear him tell it.

Chapter 40.

THE Great Rondini gripped the bars across our window, one on either side of his head, and stared at the buzzards hovering in the thermals outside of the Cochise County jail house. The sky was a brilliant clear blue and the shadows cast by the occasional passing car were crisp and...well, shadowy. "...somewhere the sun is shining bright, the band is playing somewhere and somewhere hearts are light..."

"But we're stuck here in Mudville, Casey, old chum. Our lawyer done struck out."

"Not to mention we could use a bit more of the AC. It's pretty warm in here."

I told Ronnie I'd complain to the guards.

We had been cooped up in here for almost three weeks, serving a stretch for imitating federal agents. The obstruction of justice charge and interfering with a policeman in the performance of his duties having been dropped. Apparently you can't say you're a fed even when the feds put you up to it.

Fortunately they never tumbled to Christy having picked a few locks along the way.

And I heard that Satyra managed to throw herself on the mercy of some judge she met at a local biker bar. He was either a member of the bar or maybe he just hung out there. Anyway Satyra had scooted for San Francisco and home for the duration. She's making ends meet assisting one of Ronnie's frenemies, the Incredible Irving in his act. Ronnie's hoping she'll pick up a few new tricks.

As for the reality show, thanks to Ben and Ollie, my pals from KOW-TV, I got some help from their staff pasting together my reality show during visiting hours. In spite of all the recording, the experts said the show was too static and cut my twelve part series down to an hour including commercials.

Still it was pretty good, if I do say so myself.

I would have liked to have had some jail house interviews with those participants still alive, but Bryan Forbes-Collier got a doctor's note to keep him out of the hoosegow and Slim Bales managed to give his jailers the slip. He's probably down in Mexico by now. Jake Atokar was still in custody, in solitary, thank god, so as to protect the other criminals. But I passed on the chance for another interview with him since I didn't want to give him another chance at me.

As for Gloria, well she turned state's evidence and was already out on the street. Every now and then Ronnie or I thought we saw her sitting on one of the benches in the plaza, maybe waiting to testify against us. But it probably wasn't her. After all, why would she be laughing?

The reality show seemed to have boosted Darrell Lee Redhawk's TVQ and he now looks to have a lock on the upcoming election. We're hoping for a pardon if he wins. After all, without me, he wouldn't have had even one murder to put him in the spotlight.

And speaking of spotlights, Bronco Billy decided to sponsor an hour show on TV for Dakota Holiday. I think he must have stolen the idea from one of the Spanish-language channels. So he has Dakota, dressed in something low-cut and tight around the hips, pitching his used cars and trucks to a camera right there on the lot. English speaking though. Maybe it'll catch on with the locals; after all it's quite a break from having a guy dressed in buckskins doing a rain dance.

As for the love of my life—

"Hey, Jerry, it's about that time."

That's Rusty, one of the deputy marshals who pick up after us here in the county clink.

"Hey, I didn't realize it was time already," I replied, not realizing how time flies when you're all jailed up. "Can you turn up the volume a little?"

"Well, Jerry, for you, okay. Normally I don't like to disturb the other prisoners, but maybe they might like it."

"Hey, no sweat," Ronnie said. "We'll come out there to listen. I could use an espresso too."

So I pushed open the cell door and we moseyed over to the coffee room. The county staff had one of those neat espresso machines that used little pods to make the Joe. Suitably caffeinated, we pulled up a couple of lounge chairs and joined Rusty and the on-duty team around the speakers streaming the KICK broadcast. Dulcet, pear-shaped tones flooded the room.

Mine, of course. A commercial I had recorded some time ago for the Wooten car lot, pressed into service while I was out of service.

I sounded great. That's where radio has it all over TV. You don't have to watch Bronco Billy's office wife pushing the clunkers. The commercial was just a plug for Billy's used cars, but it nearly brought tears to my eyes. I couldn't wait to get back behind the mic. Unless, of course, some kind of TV gig popped up. Who knows? I had already had the reality show on my bio.

As the commercial faded, I settled in for the main attraction. Not me, of course. Not even old "best of" shows of mine, though I thought maybe I should call Dale Anderson about that. After all, Bronco Billy had agreed to have him keep me on half pay while I was incarcerated. Anyway, I was settling in to hear—we all were—the hottest new Talker of the West—Christy Marshall, my best gal.

Who knew? All that college learning was paying off with a new talk show. Every day she was on in Dakota's old spot. Pretty good for a new kid. When I got out, she'd have the afternoon show, I'd have evenings, and we'd have the mornings to ourselves. Not counting Mrs. Marshall, of course.

Too bad that thing with Bowman didn't work out.

More Jerry Jeremy adventures

After you've finished *Talked to Death,* keep reading for a preview of

But Wait—There's Murder

Chapter 1.

WHAT could top this? Knock-out cuisine, snappy service, a pretty lady saying how great I am, and a table right in the front window. That last item is so any fans scurrying along the rainswept San Francisco sidewalk could spot yours truly. And of course, they wouldn't want to miss the other beautiful lady sitting with us, and I do mean the one that can lay claim to a special soft-spot in my heart. Not to mention she shares the mic with me on our morning drive show.

After all, getting a glimpse of San Francisco's new radio sensations ought to brighten up somebody's otherwise gloomy day.

Of course, you probably know me already if you spend much time driving to work. Jeremy Jeremy—that's right, Mom and Dad must have wanted twins—better known to our listeners as Jerry Jeremy, talk show host. Sure, I bet you remember when I was here before.

I don't mean here at the Le Bistro restaurant. I mean you may remember when I was here at KPMT, Big Talk Radio, my old station. Well, I'm back, and oddly enough, I'm even back on KPMT. And this time I'm actually doing the morning drive slot, the slot with radio's biggest listening audience.

That is, I and my aforementioned dream girl, Christy Marshall, are doing it. She's not only my partner on the new show, she's my soon to be partner in life, my number one fiancée. If you spend much time playing in traffic, you've probably heard us on the air already.

Anyway, by the time you tuned in—at Le Bistro, that is—we were all working our way through luncheon salads, meat and potatoes having gone out of style. But there was nothing to complain about, the grub being on KPMT's dime. After all, we were wooing a new sponsor.

In fact, most of the serious wooing was being done by Rita Silvano, Big Time Radio's shapely new VP of sales. She's the babe you see putting the dent in her KPMT expense account. As a matter of fact, Rita snared the top job in the KPMT sales department not that long ago, having fought her way to the near-top selling beaucoup airtime to a bunch of lecherous sponsors. Talk about having to fight your way up.

Anyway, the wooing wasn't being lost on Big Jack Harris, he being *the* hot new Bay Area car dealer. I wasn't sure how lecherous he was, but Rita had stacked the deck by bringing Christy along also. And where Christy goes—particularly if there is anything lecherous to be done—I go too.

Big Jack Harris was not only prime sponsor material, he was a major sponsor on one of our competitors, KDAB Radio, so reeling him in would be a big-time catch. I could just picture him stuffed and mounted on the wall next to Rita's desk. He'd look good mounted there, being forty-ish, athletic and square-jawed.

Rounding out our party was Charlie Wooten, way past forty-ish and way past athletic, but another well-known car dealer and big time sponsor that Rita had brought along. More about Charlie in a minute.

Like I said though, lunch seemed to be going well enough, particularly since Rita seemed to have Smilin' Jack eating out of her hand, no pun intended. Roping him in would be doubly sweet for Rita since it would be a zero-sum slap in the face for KDAB's station manager, Dwight Billingsly—our gain, his loss. Dirty Dwight had lured KPMT's morning team, Freddy and Betty, over to his station a little while ago. Let's get even.

Not that I wanted Freddy and Betty back, Christy and I having taken over their slot. But more about that later. Meanwhile, we were biding our time, chewing our kale, and waiting for an opening to tell Jack how good we were.

Jack for his part couldn't hear enough about how good *he* was, and how good *his* cars were, and how *he* was a veritable tidal wave in Auto Sales Two-Dot-Oh.

"The internet of cars, that's the future," Jack was saying. "Sure, there'll be self-driving at some point, fully autonomous vehicles, but the millennial buyers, that's where today's market is happening. These kids still drive themselves, but maybe they'd leave parallel parking to the auto-pilot, nobody being really good at that."

Being a talk show host, I know a straight line when I hear it. "You know, Jack," I said, "Christy and I have a huge demographic in eighteen to thirty-four-year-olds." I hoped that was the age group he meant. With any kind of luck Jack wouldn't know what a millennial was either. Meanwhile Rita Silvano was busy spouting a bunch of statistics, so I guessed I wasn't too far off.

I would have loved to see this guy take the plunge and maybe unplug Freddy and Betty on KDAB in the process. If you've been following my rise and fall and rise again, you'd have heard of them—you might remember that once upon a time Pamela Kay Paulson thought they went with her breakfast corn flakes like, well, like whatever people eat with their cereal. Oh yeah, in case you've forgotten, Mrs. Paulson owns KPMT and the five-hundred-thousand watts that brings me to you every day. More about her later, too, but for now just remember Freddy and Betty are lower than pond scum.

Anyway, the new guy wasn't quite eating up the stats the same way he'd finished off his quinoa-stuffed artichoke. Or the way he even ate up Rita's apple polishing, not to carry the food metaphors too far. "Social media—that's where the millennials spend their time. I keep thinking that is where I should be spending my advertising budget. Facebook ads, you know. Carpet bombing tweets on Twitter. That'll get a real return on my investment."

To her credit, Rita kept up the attack, Christy added a little schmoozing, I used my best smile, and Jack finally seemed to be teetering on the edge. Well, anyway he was until our fifth wheel began to wobble.

Said wheel being the new boss at KPMT. Like I said before, we'd get to Charlie Wooten and probably now's the time. Not so very long ago, Charlie himself was *the* red-hot car dealership hereabouts, but for reasons unknown, he decided to make the jump from sponsor to station owner. Instead of just buying in like a normal guy might do, he did it the hard way. He married Pamela Kay Paulson, KPMT's owner. His new duties nowadays, aside from servicing Pamela Kay, pretty much kept him away from the showroom. Maybe that was why Smilin' Jack was rubbing him the wrong way.

"The problem with the youngster market," Charlie rumbled, sticking his oar in, "is that they don't have the earning power to take on a real premium automotive brand. What with the interest on loans, on-going servicing and such, the premium brands are always gonna give you the best return. What the hell, I made a fortune doin' it that way."

That and having me read his commercials about five times an hour.

"Listen, Wooten," Jack Harris fired back, waving his finger in Charlie's direction, "that was fine in *your* day,"—Charlie having been around the block a few times— "but the millennials have turned Silicon Valley on its head. And I'll have you know that I have no problem getting these nerds out of their Mini-Coopers and hybrids, and into a Beamer or a Porsche. Show me an IPO and I'll show you a bump in sales you could only dream about. To speak candidly, I'm in business to put dealerships like yours out of business."

The talk was getting hotter by the minute, bubbling up to an argument temperature. Jumpin' Jack was...well, kind of jumping in place, while Charlie's face was now about the shade of the tomato soufflé Rita had left on her plate, her appetite apparently having deserted her. Charlie shoved a twenty into a passing busboy's hand and told him to bring back a double bourbon "toot sweet," whatever that meant.

I felt maybe I'd better jump back in and let this guy know that if he signed on with Big Talk Radio, he wasn't just getting a good-looking sales VP, he'd be getting a good-looking morning team too.

I said, "Jack, you may not realize it, but I've had more than a little experience on four wheels. Why once upon a time, I was doing PR for Charlie's cousin. His lot is the biggest in Tucson. And you can't count the number of ad-reads I've done for Charlie. His dealership kept KPMT afloat through some rough times, and now, well look, now he's the boss. I don't want to toot my own horn, all car talk aside, but I like to think my ad reads helped put him there. What could be better—a radio station run by a car guy?"

In spite of the pitch and all the compliments, Charlie still looked more than a little put out. Not by me, I hoped. No, it had to be Jack Harris driving him to drink, no pun intended. After all, it was Charlie who made his fortune selling the finest cars on the freeway and he was proud of it. I know his jalopies were the best because I said so in all the commercial reads.

Anyway, back to Jumping' Jack Flash. "...Nobody, but nobody, is better at selling cars to the up and coming techno crowd," he was telling us. "I'm one guy who can get them off their skateboards and into an upscale ride." So, he's a gas, gas, gas. "I know the market," he kept on, "I know the value proposition, I don't even know everything I know. I forgot more than Charlie here ever knew; that's why he made the jump to a second-rate media outlet. Not that looking for an out is anything to be ashamed of, old man."

"You know, Jack," this from Rita, "Charlie has really brought new life to the station and we are trending to a younger audience, millennials, gen X's..."

"Sure, Rita, I understand, that's where you work right now. But you don't need to keep defending Charlie. Why don't you and I spend a little time together working out a media strategy—I need somebody to work full-time with me on this. You know, smartphones, Facebook, the new media. You could work very close with me, be my *personal* VP. Who knows where that could lead?"

Charlie Wooten looked like he knew where it could lead, and he didn't look like he liked it. After all, if anybody was going to fool with the help, Charlie probably thought it ought to be him. What was left of his hair was standing out like he'd stuck his finger in an electrical outlet. I was hoping his head wouldn't explode all over Rita's sales pitch.

About this time Christy figured it was time to stick her oar in. "All kidding aside, Jack," she said, "Jerry and I are quite a team. Just check our Arbitron ratings. We've got the morning drive demographics you want, plus we're streaming on the internet, smart phones, wi-fi, whatever. We can do everything for you, but the test drive. Charlie's had real success with Jerry. He'll vouch for that."

"Hah!" Snarlin' Jack said. "And all this time I thought you dragged Charlie along, so he could beg me for a job, not to give me a snow job."

Charlie gave him a look that I didn't like and Rita looked like her mascara was about to run. Charlie said, "I'm beginning to think maybe KPMT is too small to be pitching ads for two car dealerships."

"Now you're getting the message, old boy, emphasis on 'old'. I'm gonna' drive your car lot out of town. No pun intended. Before you know what hit you, you'll be selling Hyundai's out of a strip mall in Bakersfield."

"C'mon, guys," Christy said, having broken up more than a few frat brawls back in her college days, "this is supposed to be a win-win deal. We can handle both dealerships—"

"I got something you can handle all right, but my business is strictly hands-off while Wooten's sitting here."

"Please, Jack," I said, "lighten up. Charlie owns most of the station and pretty much all of me. You can't throw him out of his own meeting."

"Never you mind, Jerry," Charlie snarled, "you people can work out all the details you want for this deal, but he will never hear a word about *his* damn' lot over *my* airwaves."

By the time he'd gotten that out, Charlie himself was already half-way to the door, the tab for lunch being left for Rita to handle. After all, that is what sales VPs are for, right?

Half of the restaurant watched Charlie storm out while the other half had their eyes on Rita who looked like she was doing the pee-pee dance sitting down.

My only thought at this point was whether I could get these two guys on the show together. Why waste all this steam with no audience. Like I'd been telling Christy, on talk radio what's a little bloodshed if the ratings are good?

Anyway, about this time, Christy suggested that she and Rita take a trip to the restroom so they could repair one thing and another. Like all the king's horses and all the king's men, I was left to put the pieces together again with a steaming Pirate Jack.

"So, Jack, how about those 'Niners? Who they going to trade in the off-season? Whaddaya think? New head coach? New announcers?"

SOMEHOW the sports talk got me through until the ladies returned. After all, I am a talk show host. The recomposed Rita pulled a few reams of figures and projections out of her purse, we all gulped some espresso and the rain outside let up. I won't say it was exactly sunny when Jack begged off another round of java and made his goodbyes, but the rain had stopped and inside things seemed a little brighter too. Maybe the Rita would be able to make another run at Big Jack Harris. Or maybe he would make a run at her.

Either way, it was getting close to nap time, Christy and I having gotten up way before dawn to do the morning drive show.

Chapter 2.

SOME lunch, eh? No wonder Rita Silvano was popping Tums by the handful.

The three of us—Rita, Christy and I—were just stepping through the restaurant's double glass doors, all eyes on Jack Harris, departing prospect. A break in the traffic gave Jaywalkin' Jack an opening to cross Bush Street between the greens. He was reaching the halfway mark when an engine's roar got our attention. We looked in time to see a king-sized— maybe even a colossal-sized—pickup truck charge down the block, freezing Jack Harris, deer-like, in its high-beams. Our shouts died in our throats as the monster truck nailed him dead-on. Jack landed in a crosswalk about thirty feet away and was pretty much roadkill when we got to him. When we did, we wished we hadn't. I've scraped better-looking stuff off my shoe. All the king's horses and all the king's men—well, you know the rest. He was Flat Jack Harris now.

The afternoon was winding down now, the rainclouds draining away any color left from the day. Shadows were crisscrossing their way up the street. And, well, the accident did happen awfully fast. So, it may have been just a trick of the light, but I would swear the truck was a certain silver colored model. I was just as sure Fast Jackie must have had any number of pissed-off customers who got stuck with one of his lemons, and God knows how many disgruntled ex-employees seeking justice without bothering with a lawsuit.

On the other hand, just a couple of days ago I got a ride up to Napa from Charlie Wooten. We'd driven up to get a few samples from a sponsor pushing the local wine. At the time I thought that Charlie had a pretty sweet ride. That is, if you're into trucks. He had a big, shiny, new double-cab number. I'd pretty much swear it was silver too. I was hoping that silver was a popular color this year.

YOU may be wondering how two rivals for top dog in San Francisco's little world of car dealers wound up breaking bread together. If you've been paying attention, you'll remember that Christy and I were riding the airwaves in Arizona since I had been blackballed from Bay Area radio, Pamela Kay Paulson, KPMT's owner, being the chief baller. Strange how *karma* works though—sometimes you get the tiger and sometimes the tiger gets you. In my case, I didn't even know who the tiger was.

Anyway, before I was run out of town, Charlie Wooten Fine Imported Autos had taken a shine to me and had been a Big Ad Buyer on Big Talk Radio. I'd been doing Charlie's commercial reads on my evening drive show—this all before I met Christy. Somehow, I got crosswise with Pamela Kay and wound up on a Tucson radio station.

I'm not sure exactly what happened while I was cooling my heels in the hinterlands, but somehow Charlie wound up wooing and wedding the widowed Pamela Kay. I'm guessing though that I must have come up in their pillow talk and just like that (imagine my fingers snapping), Christy and I were apartment hunting in San Francisco. Rent being what it is out here, I hoped the Wooten-Paulson honeymoon would last a very looong time. One divorce among the bosses and we'd be out on the street.

The point being that my allegiance is to Charlie, not some tromped-up Jackie-come-lately car dealer. Maybe I really *didn't* quite see what that speeding truck looked like. What with all the excitement, I never did get the chance to ask Christy and Rita what they thought *they* saw, not to mention what the half dozen or so bystanders recording everything on their iPhones might have gotten.

AFTER elbowing our way close enough to see Harris' poor cold body, I stepped away to speed-dial my producer so he could get the media machine in gear. Meanwhile, somebody in the crowd must have called 911. It seemed like only minutes before the EMT guys had the lifeless body of Jack Harris loaded into an ambulance and the cops had shown their sorrow by closing down the street. That sounded pretty good. I thought I might use it on the next day's show. Just to pay my respects, of course. I also hoped I'd track down Charlie before the cops did. I wanted to get a few sound bites for the news team.

My producer, Kinta White, was still at the station, so he got the details including that I would be guesting on the evening news with a full report. Kinta had been my producer back when I had the evening drive show and he was now getting up at four a.m. just to produce me again. Lucky guy.

Now, where's Charlie? I was running through some of the spots I knew in my mind that he favored when a grim young woman in a blue uniform tapped me on the shoulder. I gave her the good smile I use for fans, but it turned out she wanted a little more than that, like my name, address, phone, driver's license, where was I when the hit and run—well, the hit and ran by now—happened.

Another cop was apparently getting the same from Rita and Christy, only they all looked to be a lot more chummy. I didn't know why, but for some reason they seemed to be taking turns looking my way. And every now and then one of them would point in my direction. I hoped there wasn't any confusion about whether I had been driving or just standing here on the sidewalk.

I spent a minute or two telling my lady cop that I was someplace else and didn't see a thing. After telling me not to go anywhere, she headed over to the cop practicing his stand-up routine for the ladies. I hoped she wasn't annoyed, but by the time they looked my way again, I was gone. Next time they pointed, it would be at thin air.

Chapter 3.

I WASN'T actually sure where Charlie might have run off to, but I did know a place where they served up Red Rover Bourbon.

The Sinking Son on Pier 3 was about the only watering hole anywhere near the financial district that carried Charlie's preferred libation. A shot of Red Rover might make most guys' eyes water and their stomachs do a churn or two, but I was guessing from the way lunch went—forget about the aftermath—that Charlie might have a craving and, well, old habits die hard. And Red Rover was just the stuff to do the killing. Uh-oh, I didn't mean to use the k-word considering all the post-luncheon events.

It was only about a hop, skip and a jump to get from where we were to the "Son," but about then a raindrop or two or three started to fall. Having lost my umbrella back in Tucson, where it seldom rains, I ducked across Jackson Street into MacNally's, past the bar and tables, past the rest rooms and kitchen, and on out the back door into the little alley.

I skirted around a few more raindrops, and more than a few garbage cans, into the back of a travel agency where I had once booked a trip to Hawaii. I went out the front this time, jaywalked across Washington and down a driveway into the parking garage under the Alcoa Building. I came out the other side and crossed over to the Embarcadero Center which connects four big towers together, keeping me dry right into the Hyatt Regency.

By the time I crossed through the Hyatt's lobby, only slightly dampened by spray from the hotel's indoor fountains, the rain had pretty much let up and I was able to saunter across Embarcadero Plaza to the waterfront saloon.

I'D BARELY gotten a drop of rain on me by the time I reached the entrance to the bar, and I didn't even need to worry about what to do with a wet umbrella. Not that it would matter much in this joint. It was tucked between what had once been working docks, but now mostly served the steady comings and goings of commuter ferries to the 'burbs across the Bay. And by serving the commuters, I mean both the ferry piers and the bar.

Aside from the glow of a giant TV screen and a little bit of gloom coming off the water, the saloon was a pretty hard up for lighting so it was taking some time for my eyes to adjust. I carefully felt my way along the long mahogany bar that had come by sailing ship around the horn with the forty-niners, or so I had been told. When I got close enough, I could make out a guy standing beneath the carving of a half-naked wooden lady on the back bar. Jake something I remembered—the guy, not the half-naked lady. He was the presiding mixologist, or at least as close as this dive had to having one. As dark as it was, I figure I'd let Jake be my eyes for a while. He had better be—during my bachelor days my tips had probably put his kids through college.

Meanwhile, the TV over the bar was cutting back and forth between cell phone footage from the scene of the crime—uh, the accident, that is—and a few on-the-spot stories.

At the moment it was a woman-on-the-street interview with an eye-witness. Actually, with my eye-witness—my partner in crime-busting, Christy Marshall. Probably singled out from the out-of-towners because she was beautiful, photogenic, and was there.

"*Excuse me, I'm Will Huang from KCTY-TV On-the-Dot News. Were you here when the accident took place?*"

Christy said, "Absolutely. I was just coming out of Le Bistro with a colleague from work and my fiancée. We saw it happen right before our eyes."

"You actually saw it happen?"

Christy pulled his mic hand in close while shouldering him out of the picture, saying, "Yes, of course I did. I'm Christy Marshall, KPMT—Big Talk Radio, and this is my colleague, Rita Silvano, also from KPMT."

At this point TV guy Will Huang and Christy seemed to be arm wrestling for the mic. Good thing Christy spent her college years fighting off the Arizona backfield. "Rita and I had just finished—"

Will twist tried a backward twist.

"—lunch with the—"

Rita kicked his foot out from under him.

"—victim and possibly his—"

Willie H. had one knee on the ground and his shirt collar half torn off by now.

"—killer!"

At this Will Huang, On-the-Dot News, froze, open mouthed.

While Christy panted from the Willy workout, Rita held up the mic in victory. "Tune in to Big Talk Radio tomorrow morning," Christy puffed, "for a triple eye-witness account," puff, "of this tragic accident with Rita, me, and of course, my co-host and... hey, where did he go?"

After shaking our heads over the accident, I told Jake to draw a cold one for me and another for himself. And bartenders being good listeners, I said, "You know, it's great to be back in the Bay Area. Good ol' Charlie Wooten. He gave me a shot at the morning show—that was my co-host just being interviewed—and our ratings are through the roof. I can't wait to see what tomorrow's are with that tease. Say, you haven't by any chance seen—"

A heavy clap on the back broke my train of thought.

"Howdy, Red, I see you needed drink too, after putting up with that idiot motor mouth."

Charlie Wooten. Who would've guessed he'd be here? Besides me, that is.

"Hey, Charlie. That's no way to speak of the dead, even a dead motor mouth."

"Well, son, he's dead to me that's for damn' sure."

Jake said, "Whaddaya know, Charlie, it was just up here on the news." He pointed at the sixty-inch screen over his shoulder.

Charley acted a little confused and he's not a great actor. "You didn't see it?" I asked, amazed anyone in such a small saloon could miss such a huge TV.

"Well, whatever the hell you boys are talkin' about, I musta missed it. I was catchin' a few rays out on the back porch, even if it is only January. A man can't even fire up a cigar in here anymore."

The "back porch" being three lonely umbrella tables in the alley behind the restrooms.

"Maybe you'd better sit down, Charlie," I said. "That is, if you don't already know what I'm going to say."

"What the fuck am I, a mind reader?" But mind reader or not, he situated himself on a convenient barstool.

"Well, Charlie," I tried to broach it slowly, "what would you think if a lot of people on TV were describing a truck that looked just like yours?"

"Ha, I'll bet it didn't have the Wooten Fine Imports logo on the doors."

"Gee, did anybody say anything about the logo, Jerry?" Jake asked.

"I not sure I remember that, but I think I think more than a few people may be checking some of the videos for it soon. You didn't loan your truck out to anybody did you, Charlie?"

"What the fuck are you talkin' about, son? I left my truck back in the KPMT parking lot."

"Well, some folks on the TV were describing the truck, that is, a truck—might be any old truck—that looked just like your truck. What a coincidence it looked like yours, this truck. Well, no point in sugar-coating it, Charlie. That truck we're talking about, the one that looked like yours, well, it ran down Jack Harris."

"He hurt? Is he dead?"

"None deader."

Charlie leaned back and let out a roar heard halfway down the block. He was laughing so hard that if he hadn't been sitting, he'd have been rolling on the floor. Tears came to the old boy's eyes he was laughing so hard.

It was just then that the boys in blue showed up and took Charlie away. My best guess is that they didn't get the joke.

If You Enjoyed This Preview...

Get the full **But Wait—There's Murder** and other terrific Jerry Jeremy adventures in the Talk Radio Mystery series on Amazon.com.

I hope you liked **Talked to Death**, and if you did, I'd appreciate any kind words or ratings you might care to leave in a Goodreads or Amazon review.

And to see any forthcoming mysteries or just to tune in, please visit www.DonaldJMcGill.com.

Author's Note

AS YOU know by now, I write and publish the Talk Radio Mystery series featuring Jerry Jeremy and his pals. I make my home in Marin County, California just across the Golden Gate Bridge. I have lived in the Bay Area long enough to be a native San Franciscan, which out here is just about long enough to start getting junk mail.

WHEN NOT plotting the occasional murder, I work in high-tech and my resume even has a few companies with radio and internet TV stations. As for the real talk radio, I got hooked driving back and forth to Silicon Valley. Those shows made the commuter trip fly—even when traffic didn't. My guy, Jerry Jeremy, is a light-hearted take on what one of those great talk show hosts might be like—if they landed in the middle of a murder case or two.

www.ingramcontent.com/pod-product-compliance
Lightning Source LLC
Chambersburg PA
CBHW030242200626
46816CB00002BA/469